# Against All Odds

## Book 6 of the Lone Star Reloaded Series

A tale of alternative history

By Drew McGunn

This book is a work of fiction. Names, characters, places and incidents are the product of the author's overactive imagination or are used fictitiously. Any resemblance to actual events, or locales is coincidental. Fictional characters are entirely fictional and any resemblance among the fictional characters to any person living or dead is coincidental. Historical figures in the book are portrayed on a fictional basis and any actions or inactions on their part that diverge from actual history are for story purposes only.



Newsletter Sign Up/Website address:
https://drewmcgunn.wixsite.com/website

V1

ISBN: 9781089225966

# ACKNOWLEDGEMENT

As the Lone Star Reloaded series draws to a close, I'm thankful for the support my wife has given me over the past couple of years. There were many nights she fell asleep waiting for me to finish each chapter.

Despite publishing this book through Amazon Direct Publishing, this effort was hardly a one-man show. I'd like to thank Graham for schooling me in becoming a better self-editor and for all of the help cleaning up each of the manuscripts. And to Jackie, who designed some awesome covers that did a great job melding historical and speculative fiction together.

And to the guys and gals at Alternatehistory.com for keeping me motivated to post each new chapter. Your feedback helped the story stay grounded and kept the worst excesses of alien space bats at bey.

# Table of Contents

## The Story So Far

Our intrepid hero, Will Travers, veteran of the Second Gulf War, finds his mind and soul cast back through time to 1836 into the body of William Barret Travis. With only weeks to avoid a martyr's death at the Alamo, Will contemplates fleeing from San Antonio de Bexar but realizes he can't abandon men like James Bowie and David Crockett to die at the old Spanish mission. Instead, he crafts a plan that is both daring and a little bit crazy to defeat Santa Anna long before the Mexican dictator can consolidate his army. Will manages to scrape together nearly every Texian soldier west of the Brazos River and meets Santa Anna on the Rio Grande River where Texian arms bleeds Santa Anna's vaunted Vanguard Brigade, before strategically retreating to the Nueces River, where the Texians destroy much of the Mexican army and capture the hapless dictator.

Once independence is secured by treaty with Santa Anna, Will joins with other famous Texians like Sam Houston and David Crockett to form a constitution for the nascent republic. He helps the constitutional convention craft a document avoiding the worst of the Southern slave codes, and which allows a path to citizenship for the Cherokee.

After narrowly surviving an assassin's bullet, Will takes command of the entire army of Texas. But he has barely begun to transform the army when the frontier erupts into violence as the Comanche ride out from the Comancheria and attack Fort Parker, on the edge of the Texas frontier.

Despite an early defeat at the hands of the lords of the Great Plains, Will eventually drives the Comanche to the peace table. In the ensuing years, he refines both the tactics his army uses as well as its weapons.

Despite a fragile peace between Texas and Mexico, the treaty signed by Santa Anna has never been enforced until President Crockett orders Will to take the army to secure Santa Fe and Albuquerque for the Republic, in accordance with the treaty from six years before. The army is more than eight hundred miles away when Santa Anna sends a force under Adrian Woll to capture the Alamo.

Total annihilation at the Alamo is only stopped by A. Sidney Johnston's arrival with every army reservist he can scrape together, while Will is still hundreds of miles away with the regular army. After burying the dead, Texas prepares for total war with Mexico.

Total war is expensive, and a long campaign will destroy the fragile republic. Will has every expectation of a quick war. The Mexican commander is rash and headstrong, but before the campaign can begin, he is killed in a freak accident and his cautious second-in-command, Juan Almonte takes charge and changes the Mexican strategy to one of defense.

Almonte forces Will into several pitched battles, where the Texian army's skill, tactics and superior weaponry are pitted against Almonte's defense in depth and tactical retreats. Months drag by, and inflation and debt eat away on the Homefront as Will's Texian army grinds down Mexico's Army of the North.

Santa Anna, exasperated by the glacial speed of the campaign, sacks Almonte for failure to produce a victory and takes command, as he brings north another twenty thousand men. In a battle that dwarfs every previous conflict between the two nations, Santa Anna tries to overwhelm Texian defenses only to come up short. In the ensuing retreat, the dictator once again falls into Will's hands.

Meanwhile, back in Austin, President Crockett resigns his office and turns over command of the Republic to his vice president, Lorenzo de Zavala and heads into the west with a column of Texians, which includes Will's son, Charlie, who runs away from home to have an adventure. Crockett easily defeats the lightly defended garrisons of Mexican California, but before he can enjoy the fruits of his labor, he is gunned down, and Will's son is kidnapped.

After learning of the kidnapping of Charlie Travis, Will resigns his commission, placing family above country. In a race against time, Will follows the kidnappers' trail across the continent, following them from California, across the isthmus of Panama to South Carolina, where he and a few intrepid Texas Rangers rescue his son and kill the kidnappers.

After Will brings his son back to Texas, he focuses on his business interests until the annexation faction, in the person of Richard Ellis, inherits the presidency upon Lorenzo de Zavala's untimely death and begins to roll back the advances made over the past decade. Fearing for a future in which Texas becomes entwined with the peculiar institution of the American South, Will comes to realize if he wants to stop the rush to annexation, he had no choice but to run against Ellis for the presidency.

Banking on his own popularity, Will wins on an anti-annexation platform and charts a path designed to slowly kill slavery in Texas by championing a bill that requires all children born on or after January 1, 1852 to be born free. This enrages the plantation owners in East Texas and they rebel against Will's administration, plunging Texas into civil war.

# Chapter 1

24 October 1851

G.T. Beauregard listened in silence to the officer in butternut who sat beside him during the carriage ride from Beaumont. General Peyton Wyatt's golden hair was streaked with silver. The forty-seven-year-old former quartermaster general of the Republic of Texas was the highest-ranking member of the army to recognize his loyalty lay with his family and friends from the South.

"Your Louisiana boys are a sight to behold, G.T. Such colorful uniforms and their flair for drill are a credit to your state."

Beauregard wasn't sure if he was more irritated by the casual familiarity the Texian general took or the unspoken 'but.' Beauregard set aside the feeling, "I detect a 'but,' Peyton." Two could play at being overly familiar.

Wyatt said, "Say what you will about President Travis, but his idea about uniforms that blend better into the background makes a lot of sense. When he and I led the campaign against the Comanche, our boys fared better because of our butternut uniforms."

As the carriage dipped into a chuckhole, Beauregard repressed a smile as Wyatt's broadbrimmed black hat slid over his eyes. "Perhaps. But the only enemy we've been faced with is the occasional stray slave. The pageantry of our uniforms scares the hell out of a few runaways."

He found it galled him less than he expected. The fact was the Texian battalions in their butternut brown were harder to see, especially when they were deployed in their open formation.

The carriage topped a low rise, and from his seat, Beauregard could see the army encampment. More than four thousand men were camped on the coastal plain west of town. He had no idea what kind of a general Wyatt would be when forced to face President Travis' army, but he was apparently a skilled Quartermaster. The rebel camp was orderly, and rows of tents were neatly spread across the plain. Several companies were at drill in a field. The rhythm of the training felt wrong. The men were deployed in a thin line, spaced further apart than even a skirmish line. It seemed profane; infantry should be massed together to make their musket fire more devastating.

When he said as much to Wyatt, the Texian responded, "Massing men with the Sabine rifle is overkill, G.T. Most of your men are armed with muskets, accurate to a hundred yards if you're lucky.

Your average man will fire three aimed shots in a minute. One of my riflemen can fire six or more aimed shots in a minute, at targets as far away as four hundred yards. The open order tactics let us cover more terrain with a single battalion while putting out the same rate of fire as a couple of your regiments."

Beauregard frowned. Even from a half-mile away, watching the Texian reservists go through their drill, it was clear Wyatt had a point. "I wish you'd been able to secure more of your Sabine rifles, Peyton. Quite a few of my men are armed with rifled muskets, but many of these volunteer companies carry the old model eighteen-twelve from the Springfield Armory and the like. I'd like to get my hands on more of your breechloaders."

As the carriage rolled to a stop before a large canvas pavilion, Wyatt climbed down and said, "Then the instructions from the provisional government should please you, G.T."

Later, the two officers stared at the map of eastern Texas. Their conversation was broken by the sharp blast of a train whistle nearby. Over the din, Wyatt said, "More supplies?"

"You've got friends across the south, Peyton. More volunteer companies are being mobilized in Mississippi and Alabama. Those who can't physically come to your aid are contributing supplies."

"Keeping us in food and clothing's important. I can't imagine how difficult it'd be without the rail," Wyatt said.

Beauregard dipped his head in agreement, "All the more reason for us to finish Fort Jackson and Fort

Austin at the mouth of the Sabine River. Ships trying to run those forts, chock full of heavy artillery, will get blown to bits."

Wyatt said, "We can import the guns, but a quicker way to acquire them is to take the weapons foundry at Trinity Park. Most of the army is spread out between San Antonio and the Pacific coast."

Beauregard had heard of Trinity Park. Along with Houston, the town was the industrial heart of the Republic. Capturing either of these towns would put a dent in President Travis' ability to wage war, once he realized John Wharton, Texas' Secretary of State, was never going to be able to force a peaceful resolution. He studied the map and traced a line from Beaumont to the Trinity River. It was only forty miles. From the Trinity River, less than two hundred miles separated his army from their target in Austin.

"Damned shame the militia still loyal to Travis has torn up as much of the track as they have. We could be there in a few hours were it not the case. Now, it'll take a couple of days to reach them. Peyton, what do we know about the defenses in and around Trinity Park?"

Wyatt turned away from the map and let his eyes drift to the west. "Precious little. There are a couple of companies of reservists between West Liberty and Trinity Park. Maybe two hundred men. Right after Travis was sworn in, we formed a battery of artillerists there, but never received the funding for any field artillery."

Wyatt's eyes hardened as he stared into the distance. "A few folks who arrived from the Trinity River the other day said Ben McCulloch is there. On paper, he's responsible for all of Texas' reserve battalions.

Damn him. He's just as much a Virginian as me. He knows Travis' Free-birth bill is insanity. He should have joined us, but he seems to have misplaced his loyalty." He turned back to Beauregard, "When it's time to advance, I want to be there with my men."

Beauregard traced his finger along the map. As a West Point graduate, the provisional government had elevated him to command the joint Texas-Louisiana army. While Wyatt had commanded troops, it had been years ago. He'd spent the last decade as a paper-pusher in the Republic's army. It would be impolite to decline the request, but as Beauregard studied the map, he decided the Texian rebels could be best used on the flanks. His men would capture the town. When newspapers reported on the victory, it would be his name in the headline.

Captain Jesse Running Creek felt his breath escape when he stepped onto solid ground on the east side of the Trinity River. The iron and wooden bridge behind him was solid but raised high above the river to allow steamships to pass below. The township of Liberty, once the seat of government of its namesake county, boasted a dilapidated riverfront, where boats could be loaded with cotton or other goods and hauled down to Galveston for shipment to the world's markets. Nowadays railroads carried the loads once transported by steamships. The docks were empty. Any boat plying the Trinity had been commandeered by his men over the past few hours.

Jesse waited until his riding companion joined him before remounting. As General Ben McCulloch climbed into the saddle, he said, "Compared to West Liberty, Liberty Township looks like a one-horse-town, where the horse has died."

Jesse chuckled. "The mills and factories are either in West Liberty or farther up the river at Trinity Park. Progress left this town to fend for itself."

The two officers guided their mounts around scattered burned railroad ties as they left the elevated railroad bed and entered the town. A wide street separated a few buildings along either side. The railroad ran alongside Main Street all the way through town, straight as an arrow. Jesse amended the thought. The railroad bed still ran through town. Every railroad tie had been burned between the river and a few miles east of town. Every iron rail had been collected and taken to Trinity Gun Works where they were being melted down and turned into small arms and field pieces for the army.

While most of the homes in town appeared to be occupied, a few were clearly abandoned. Those men had evacuated their families, deciding that being on the road between two rival armies was bad for their health.

When Jesse said as much, McCulloch replied, "I hoped and prayed those fools in Beaumont would see some reason. John Wharton wasted too much time trying to talk sense into them. And what kind of thanks do we get for not crushing them under our bootheel?"

Jesse felt his lips curl into a frown. "Who'd imagine the governor of Louisiana would allow so many of their men to filibuster with our rebels?"

One of Jesse's special Rangers, Corporal Ellington, emerged from the shadows of one of the abandoned houses, rifle carried at the ready. "Hey, Chief," the nickname grated on Jesse. Since the revolution more than fifteen years earlier, thousands of Cherokee, Choctaw, Chickasaw, and Creek had made their way to Texas. He was hardly the only Cherokee in the regular army, but as captain for one of the army's special Ranger companies, formed initially and trained by Jack Hays, he had risen further than most. Still, he mused, chief was a better nickname than some he'd heard.

The Ranger continued, "Sadler and Allen are past the edge of town. Beyond that, we got no perimeter this side of the river."

As hope faded for a peaceful resolution to the constitutional crisis created by the rebel government in Beaumont, Jesse had been ordered to take one of his platoons from the Alamo and move it to West Liberty. Once there, he'd taken one of the platoon's three squads and placed it at the bridge over the Trinity River between Liberty Township and West Liberty. The squad consisted of three 4-man rifle-teams, one of which was on the east side of the river.

As they rode past the sentry, McCulloch said, "Those brown and green patches your men are wearing on their jackets makes seeing them in the trees difficult, Captain."

Jesse turned to his companion whose butternut jacket was unadorned with the camouflaged patches his Army Rangers wore. "Imagine what it'll be like for the rebels when they run into my Rangers."

McCulloch turned grim. “There’s only forty miles between here and Beaumont. This peace is just the calm before the storm. If the rebels move against us, we’ll have just days to react. Dammit, but I wish the president had given me permission to mobilize more of our reserves.”

Jesse offered, “The last time we mobilized all the men for war, it nearly destroyed the country. Maybe President Travis is just trying to avoid tipping over the apple cart.”

“Perhaps, Captain. But it’s worth remembering that we’re the poor sods in the apple cart. If it tips over, we’re the ones who’ll fall out. I don’t need to tell you neither General Johnston nor President Travis have seen fit to support us with more men. I’ve got four companies of reserve infantry, you and your platoon, a platoon of Marine reserves, a battery of militia artillery from Trinity Park and a few more odds and ends. Your Rangers have confirmed the rebels and their allies could move against us with six battalions. A bit more than four hundred men against thousands.”

In the distance, to the east, a faint blast from a railroad engine confirmed they had even less time than McCulloch had foretold.

A bit later, two Rangers jogged into town, their mottled uniforms challenging to see against the brown of the dusty road. One, a Ranger named Saddler, said, “Chief, we saw a train disembarking soldiers. Must have been a whole battalion, maybe more. Not sure, but there may have been a second train behind the first. Their soldiers were spreading out, and we decided not to stay and ask how many were coming to supper.”

Jesse turned to McCulloch, "We've got a couple of rifle pits dug on the other side of the river. I suspect our neighbors from Beaumont will arrive shortly. Let's get back across and prepare the table for company."

Once on the western side of the Trinity River, McCulloch took Jesse aside, "Captain, there's nothing but four miles between this bridge and West Liberty. I need you to hold the rebels back for as long as possible. When I get back into town, I'll send the rest of your platoon forward."

Jesse climbed up onto the rifle pit's lip, scanning Liberty Township. On the other side of town, dust rose into the sky, no doubt kicked up by the boots of hundreds, perhaps thousands of soldiers. Until the rest of his platoon arrived, he had, including himself, a baker's dozen to hold the bridge. He had supreme confidence in his men and their training, but the odds were too long. As he slid back into the narrow trench, he thought about how he found himself in his current predicament.

It had been his last furlough, shortly after President Travis had signed the Free Birth bill. He'd gone home. Jesse had been caught by surprise to find the town in which he'd grown to adulthood split down the middle between those who agreed with the president and those who favored slavery. His father, a merchant with trade ties stretching from the Atlantic to the Pacific, relied heavily on slaves for the labor in his warehouses. He had voted for Richard Ellis in the last election.

In a moment of Déjà vu, when Jesse had dismounted in the wagon yard in front of the warehouse, he'd heard his father's voice shouting, "Co-lo-neh, don't piss on my boot and tell me it's raining. Travis' plans will drive me to bankruptcy."

When he walked through the warehouse's wide doors, Jesse saw his father standing toe to toe with Sam Houston. They were an incongruent sight. Simon Running Creek wore brown woolen trousers, a white silk shirt, and a brown vest. While unadorned in design, the material was expensive. Houston wore buckskin trousers, a homespun gray shirt, and a jacket cut from a colorful woolen blanket.

Houston used his height to look down on Jesse's father. "I'm shooting straight with you, Simon. Throwing in with men like Collinsworth is like climbing into a bag with a rattlesnake. Our people's only hope is to support the legitimate government in Austin."

"Our people? That's rich, Co-lo-neh. You show up here with your tail between your legs every time you face a reversal among the whites."

Houston seemed to flinch at the insult. The fact it held enough truth made it sting all the worse. He stepped back, "I've only always done my best for the People. We've been given a birthright here in Texas. Going against the government will only breed resentment and undo the gains we've made."

Jesse's father clenched his fist as he stared daggers at the man his people called the Raven. "Why the change, Sam? You've been beating the drum for annexation since we defeated the Mexicans back in thirty-six. Now you're saying no to annexation. I wish you'd make up your mind."

Houston's brown locks shook about his head, "Means and methods matter, Simon. If we throw in with men calling for rebellion while calling it annexation, we're no better than rebels. Rebels against a government we've supported and who've supported us. You know I disagree with Travis. Given we're an agricultural people, slavery makes sense. But not when measured against rebelling against the government."

The two men glowered at each other as Jesse cleared his throat. When they turned, the anger in their eyes burned away. The young Cherokee officer found himself enveloped in a bear hug from his father as Houston pounded him on the back.

Later, after Houston had left, Jesse told his father he didn't want to fight against any Cherokee, but that he wouldn't fight against his fellow soldiers, even if most of the tribe decided to back the rebels.

The memory fled as he saw something across the river move between two houses. "Chief, there's men moving through town. They're in range."

Jesse shifted his eyes to the long, straight road running alongside the railroad bed, and to the east, outside of town, the dust cloud he'd seen earlier now materialized into a column of infantry. Looking at it through his binoculars, at the head of the column, he saw a flag with a single white star on a blue field. It was the men from Louisiana.

"Fire when you've got a target," Jesse said. At least he wasn't facing any Cherokee this day.

Jesse had lost track of time as he looked over the lip of rifle pit and tried to see through the thick haze hanging over the riverbank. As he slid another brass cartridge into the gun's breech, he couldn't help thinking of one downside of the M46 Sabine rifle; the rate of fire was so fast that smoke from the gunpowder built up more quickly than other rifles, obscuring the field of fire.

A gust of wind lifted the smoke, giving him a clear view of the railroad bridge. A few forms lay still where they'd fallen. But behind the nearest row of houses, Jesse could see a large force assembling. He snapped the rifle to his shoulder, aimed, and fired, levering the breech open before chambering another round. Two of his men were already down, hit by lucky or well-aimed shots from the opposite bank. He gauged enough men were preparing to charge the bridge that his small squad would be swept aside. He was about to give the order to withdraw when he heard the pounding of running feet behind him.

Turning, he saw the rest of the platoon racing toward the rifle pits. The platoon's commander, Lieutenant Tremaine, was in the lead with more than twenty men following close behind. Faster than Jesse could have imagined, they crowded into the pits.

It was none too soon. A standard bearer, waving a blue flag, sprinted around one of the buildings onto the railroad bed. Surging behind him was a wall of soldiers. Sunlight glinted off their bayonets as they dashed for the bridge.

Jesse chose the most practical way he could imagine to give the order to fire. He raised his rifle, sighted down the barrel and squeezed the trigger. Every man who could crowd along the front of the rifle pit opened fire on the advancing horde.

Jesse stepped away, letting one of his men slither by, replacing him on the firing line. To get a better view, he climbed up, knelt next to the pit, and watched the flag bearer reach the bridge before he tumbled, hitting a rail before falling onto the steep riverbank below. Men were toppling over. Some landed on the bridge, joining those who had died there earlier, more still spilled into the river.

Jesse slouched low when he felt the hot breath of a round zip past his ear. More soldiers had come forward than could readily funnel across the bridge, and they lined up on the top of the riverbank and returned fire at the Rangers. Bullets dug into the dirt embankments in front of the rifle pits. Overhead twigs and leaves that hadn't already lost the battle to Autumn rained down on his men.

No binoculars were needed to tell Jesse that an entire battalion was lined up on the edge of Liberty Township in addition to several hundred more men funneling onto the bridge. Despite the reinforcements, holding the railroad bridge wasn't possible.

McCulloch had been gone for less than two hours. The four miles back to West Liberty could be walked in as little as an hour. He wasn't sure how he'd do it, but Jesse was determined to make the enemy bleed for every foot between the river and town.

# Chapter 2

Rifle fire crackled in the distance. G.T. Beauregard ignored it as his eyes scanned the bodies laid out alongside the railroad bed. A score of men dead. Far closer than the rifle fire were the screams coming from the Baptist church which now housed most of the wounded. While his army may have captured the railroad bridge over the Trinity, it had come at a high cost.

Behind him rode General Wyatt. Tamping down any uncertainty he felt, Beauregard said, "I thought you said there were only a few militia in West Liberty. Those were regulars, by God."

Wyatt shook his head, "I said that McCulloch could draw on a couple of reserve companies. Our reserves are better equipped than your volunteers, G.T. But those weren't reservist. I'll stake my rank that those were Rangers."

Nonplused, Beauregard said, "You mean those ranging companies Texas keeps on the border with the Comancheria?"

"I wish. No, Texas has a few companies of special riflemen whose training and skill go beyond regular infantry. They're called special Rangers. It can get a bit confusing, but President Travis liked the name, so it stuck."

A bit later, Wyatt's estimation was proved correct when they saw two dead men in butternut uniforms. Irregular patches of browns, greens and grays were sewn on the jackets. In death, the men seemed small, but their jackets blended into the ground on which they lay far more than Beauregard liked. Only in his wildest dreams had he thought leading an army toward the Texas capital would be easy. He was too much of a pragmatist to let flights of fancy dictate his moves.

As if he needed more of a warning, near the abandoned rifle pits rested C company of the 2nd Louisiana Volunteer Infantry. They had crossed the bridge first. More than eighty men from the company had gone into battle. Now there were less than fifty resting under the live oak trees. Some of the men stared into space, as though their minds were a thousand miles away. Others wore haunted looks. Beauregard pursed his lips. If this is what victory looked like, he didn't want to see defeat.

To the west, he heard the sharp crack of the Rangers' rifles measured against the booming musketry from his command. He turned and waved an orderly over, "Tell Colonel De Russy to deploy half his regiment as skirmishers. The rest should form up well behind."

He glanced at the sky. Even if they were not able to get through as fast as he'd like, the army would still reach West Liberty by mid-afternoon. Assuming there were no other surprises.

The road to West Liberty ran through a dense forest, broken here and there with farms carved from the Texas wilderness. The homes were abandoned. As Beauregard rode by them, he couldn't tell if the owners had fled weeks ago, or whether they had retreated one step ahead of the Rangers. As the forest thinned, he could see a vast stretch of farmland separating the forest from the town. Scanning through his binoculars, the town looked like a disturbed anthill, with folks running back and forth.

Smoke curled from the locomotive that was pulling out of town, heading west, toward Houston. Beauregard swung the glasses toward the edge of town. Although their butternut uniforms made the Texian soldiers harder to see, it didn't make them invisible. A thin line of riflemen was deployed along a split-rail fence east of town. There were more than two companies.

"Wyatt! You said there were only a couple of companies between these two towns. There's got to be more than three hundred men deployed over there. And why in the hell are there US infantry in the town?"

Wyatt scanned the line, growing grim as he did so. "At eight hundred yards, I can see how those uniforms could be mistaken for American. But those are Marines, probably from one of the reserve companies around the bay. Maybe a platoon. It looks like McCulloch has scraped together three or four hundred men from the surrounding area."

Beauregard handed his binoculars to an orderly before turning to Wyatt. "Peyton, I want you to send your Tenth Infantry around the flank. Your men will cut the line between Trinity Park and West Liberty. I'll send Second and Third Louisiana forward. Fourteen hundred men should be able to push into town. I'll hold the First Louisiana as a reserve force as well as your Seventh Infantry. Your fifteenth Infantry will hold the southern flank."

Wyatt looked Southward. More cotton fields spread out in that direction. "We could send them around and cut off McCulloch's men. Capture the entire command, that'd be quite a victory."

"Tempting. But I want McCulloch and his men to not feel entrapped," Beauregard said as he scribbled orders on a notepad. "If they feel they have a way out, maybe they'll take it rather than putting up too hard a fight. As it is, I'm sending most of our cavalry wide around their southern flank to cut the railroad a few miles back. I don't mind giving McCulloch a way out, but I don't want reinforcements coming in by train."

Later, a blue-jacketed officer from the New Orleans' Washington Artillery waited for his gunnery sergeant to set the friction primer on the 6-pounder's touch hole. Then he took the slack out of the lanyard. Beauregard nodded to him and said, "You may commence, Captain."

The ground shook beneath their feet as the gun fired, recoiling back a half dozen feet. Its projectile screamed downrange, exploding behind the Texian line nearly a thousand yards away. The other four guns in the battery opened up, adding the weight of their iron to the barrage. Beauregard looked at the thin line on the opposite side of the cotton fields, as shells detonated around them. It was easy to see the open order tactics used by the rebel Texians made them harder to hit than the solid block of infantry, where the men stood shoulder to shoulder to fire their muskets or rifles in mass volleys.

When it was time to send the infantry forward, he ordered them to advance in a skirmish line.

A horse neighed as a whip cracked overhead. Andy Berry grimaced at the need. But the sound of battle washed over the artillery column, as the gunners urged their teams of horses to a gallop. He touched his spurs to his mount's flanks and dashed ahead of his battery. Part of the 3rd Battalion of Artillery, one of two reservist artillery battalions, his battery was the most recently formed company-sized unit in the reserves. The day had started normally, but when a rider arrived a couple of hours earlier, raising a ruckus about the rebels on the march, he'd mobilized the men from the Gun Works and Trinity College who served in his battery, and they had raced toward West Liberty.

As far as Austin and the nation's budget was concerned, his battery was without equipment. But as he glanced behind, he knew nothing could be further from the truth. Six teams of horses pulled their gun carriages and caissons. Three of the carriages held experimental rifled guns. Like their small arms counterparts, they were breechloaders. Unlike their small-arm counterparts, a screw on the breech created the seal, keeping gas from escaping. It was no less experimental than the propellent Berry had fashioned from the nitrogenated processed cotton.

As his battery rode to the sound of the fighting, Berry allowed the worry he felt show. NPC was still notoriously unstable. He'd managed to fire several dozen rounds successfully over the past few days. But that came after a series of failures, with blown breeches. Before, the tests had been in a controlled setting, the friction primer triggered by a lanyard hidden behind a thick blast barrier. If the barrel burst, no one was hurt. But now, if something went wrong, the lives of the men in his battery were at stake.

The other three carriages carried Dick Gatling's contraption with its rotating rifled barrels. It had been several years since Gatling had invented his gun, but it had remained hidden at Trinity Park during President Richard Ellis' pro-annexation administration. Even after William Travis won the Presidency, funding for the weapon had been anemic, given the poor state in which Ellis had left the military. Still, Berry felt better about the three Gatlings. He knew they worked.

Riding at the head of the column, he saw smoke drifting over West Liberty as he came to the first empty field. One of the town's churches was ablaze, likely struck by a shell. Fire licked into the sky. But most of the smoke rolled into town from the attacking riflemen coming from the east. Men were crossing an open field, toward town. Steady rifle fire from the reserve companies defending West Liberty kept the advance against them at bay, for the moment.

From where Berry sat astride his horse, the range to the rebels was extreme, the three cannons had an effective range of more than fifteen hundred yards. He wasn't sure if they could reach the advancing rebels.

He turned to order his men forward when something tugged at his sleeve and pinched at his arm. Glancing at it, he saw a rip in the fabric. He slid off his horse and gripped it. He pulled his hand away, and blood smeared his palm. Less than half a mile away coming from the east, a line of men poured through the trees in open order. At the center were two flags. The Texas flag flew beside a blue flag with a single white star.

"Enemy to our left!" Berry yelled. "Hurry up. Form a line along the road. The first crew to unlimber their piece and fire on those bastards gets ten dollars each."

The untried breechloading cannons were in the lead. A gunnery sergeant slid off the seat atop the caisson and shouted orders to the other men serving the gun. Several of them dismounted from the six-horse team and unlimbered the caisson and gun carriage. Other men disconnected the caisson from the gun carriage and rolled the ammunition cart back well to the rear of the gun. Once they had done that, men grabbed their equipment and raced back to the gun while two of their number carried the shot and powder charge forward.

A gunner twisted the screw open, and another rammed the shell into the breech. Then a canvas bag full of black powder was shoved into the breech. One of the men grabbed at his leg as a bullet knocked him from his feet. A thin screen of rebels had advanced more than a hundred yards, and although they were still more than six hundred yards away, a marksman could get lucky and hit his target.

The breech was slammed shut, and the screw turned until it locked. Another gunner set the friction primer over the vent and attached a lanyard to it. The gunnery sergeant took a moment to sight down the barrel before running back. "Ready!"

The men assigned to the gun stayed clear of the recoil as the gunnery sergeant pulled the lanyard taut. "Fire!"

The gun recoiled several feet as the shell raced across the empty field, exploding in the space between the advancing riflemen and the rest of the battalion, held in reserve.

The second gun fired as Berry tied off a rag around his lower arm. He fumbled for his binoculars and scanned the enemy. The Texas flag flew in the center of the advancing soldiers. He spat and swore, "God damned rebels."

He adjusted the focus and made out the letters stitched across the flag. It was the Tenth Infantry Battalion, a reserve unit recruited among the farms and towns along the Neches River in East Texas.

By the time the third cannon was fired, the first gun crew was preparing to shoot again. The crew moved clear of the recoil, waiting for the gunner to pull the lanyard when Berry was thrown to the ground. His ears were ringing as he climbed back to his feet. The first gun hung from one of its wheels, a large hole blown in the reinforced iron breech. The gunnery sergeant, who commanded the ten-man gun crew was down, blood pooling around his head. Several other men were injured. Berry shook his head as tears stung his eyes. It was his decision to use propellant made from NPC. It was too unstable, and his men had paid with their lives.

As the survivors of the first gun dragged their compatriots away from the wreck, Berry's second-in-command hurried over, "Andy, er, Captain Berry, the Gatlings are ready. Permission to engage the skirmish line?"

As the noise in his ear dissipated, Berry nodded and watched the young officer, a younger cousin who usually ran one of the gun works' furnaces, run back to the section of Gatlings.

Even though Berry'd heard the Gatling gun fire before, as first one, then another and finally the third opened fire, the horrible noise was like a giant piece of cloth being ripped apart. Back on his feet, the young captain watched the guns find the range and toppled the riflemen who had been advancing.

Even though the enemy riflemen used the same open order tactics, and were spread apart, the Gatlings sprayed their bullets by the hundreds. Despite an effort to move their line forward, eventually, the colonel commanding the Tenth Infantry recalled his troops. Berry saw more than a score of bodies lying prone on the field before him as the remainder collected their wounded and retreated.

Resisting the urge to cheer, Berry looked back on the broken gun and quietly ordered his men to cease fire. "Let's reposition the battery and open fire on the enemy's main line."

G.T. Beauregard watched the men of the 2nd and 3rd Louisiana stream back onto the road to the Trinity River. Both regiments had been fully committed, assaulting the enemy line. The rate of fire from McCulloch's riflemen had been terrible to behold. Even though his men had advanced as skirmishers, the aimed fire had inflicted heavy casualties. He had been on the cusp of ordering the 1st Louisiana Infantry forward when death had hammered his right flank.

*That battery that didn't have any guns, apparently has them.* Beauregard silently cursed General Wyatt's inadequate information. He wasn't sure what was worse, watching cannons that could fire with scarcely any smoke of gunpowder or the hideous shredding sound of the guns that spit bullets by the hundreds farther than rifled muskets.

He didn't have the numbers yet, but he suspected he'd lost more than a hundred men against McCulloch's riflemen. Casualties at that level weren't sustainable. Not with a mere two thousand Louisianans and about the same number of rebel Texians.

His teeth hurt from grinding them, and as he opened his mouth to relieve the pressure, Wyatt rode over, "They turned back the Tenth with those fiendish guns before they turned them on the main line."

Beauregard wondered about Wyatt's provenance as he struggled with his temper. "Payton," he ground out, "I thought you said the battery in Trinity Park didn't have any guns. Your information was woefully lacking."

Wyatt's face colored as he coughed. "I swear, the army had not assigned any guns to them."

Beauregard let his temper slip. "Did it ever dawn on you that a town that manufactures arms and weapons might have their own guns and didn't need any damned help from Austin?"

Chagrined, Wyatt said, "What now?"

"There'll be more men arriving from Alabama and Mississippi soon. We'll leave a force at Liberty Township, and when we advance, we'll find another way across the Trinity River. If we can't get to Austin this way, we'll go around them."

He watched his Louisiana boys carrying their wounded comrades in handmade stretchers. Getting at the Travis government in Austin wasn't going to be as simple as taking each point along the railway. They were going to need more time and would have to travel overland. While he had severe reservations about Wyatt's worth as a tactical officer, the fact that the soldiers under his command were well armed, uniformed, and supplied was proof that Wyatt was a gifted quartermaster.

The rebel Texian officer seemed reticent. "Going far enough around the enemy may prove more of a challenge than it's worth. We get more than five or ten miles away from the railroad and any advance we can manage will be slow as molasses. If they have even an inkling of what we're doing, any movement has a fair risk of being countered."

Beauregard pursed his lips. It wasn't what he wanted to hear, but a single glance in the direction of the old growth forest gave him the impression that Wyatt was likely right. Changing the subject, he said, "I want you to take charge of all the supplies coming in on the railroad. We're going to need wagons, and lots of them. We're going to need more doctors and orderlies. When we take the fight to Travis' soldiers, I want to make sure our injured don't have to walk five or ten miles to get to a doctor."

Jesse Running Creek wiped his grimy face. A cut over his brow stung as sweat ran into it. He stood and slung his rifle over his shoulder as he watched his men stand from their hiding places behind a split-rail fence. As he stepped away from the railing, his feet kicked a pile of spent cartridges. He'd fired more than a hundred rounds throughout the afternoon.

The platoon of Marines who had anchored his Rangers' left flank was also rising from their defensive position. They'd taken more casualties than his men. Two more of his Army Rangers had been killed, and another seven were injured. Still, he had two-thirds of his platoon ready. He knew what he wanted to do, and that was to pursue the rebel army. He'd happily lead his men back to the Trinity River sniping at the retreating command. He needed to consult with General McCulloch and see what forces were available.

He sent his ordinance sergeant to find more ammunition, and he headed toward the center of the defensive line. He'd only gone a little way when he saw the captain of one of the reserve companies standing over a line of the dead. Jesse came to a stop when he saw the distinctive figure of Ben McCulloch in the line.

One of the men standing near, wearing captain's bars, said, "Captain Running Creek, they was already retreating. Hell, the battle was done won when General McCulloch stood. It must've been a lucky shot. But he was hit in the breast and fell dead where he stood."

The hodgepodge force in West Liberty had been under McCulloch's direct command. There were no regimental officers present in town. Jesse shook his head, *What a shitty situation. A general and a handful of captains and four hundred men.* Jesse didn't like it, but until someone higher ranked showed up, as the only regular army captain, he was in charge.

The smell of burning wood cut through the acrid smell of gunpowder. The first thing was to deal with the fire in town. An unlucky shell had detonated inside the Methodist Church, but if the fire didn't spread, it was a small price to save the town. He detailed a company from West Liberty to see to the security of the town. He was about to send another company's ordinance sergeant to find more ammunition when the sergeant he'd sent out earlier trudged over to him, a worried look on his face.

"Chief, there are boxes of paper cartridges in the armory, paper cartridges by the thousands. But not a single brass cartridge remains."

Thoughts of following the defeated enemy died. *Oh, I'd chase after them if all I had was a shoe to throw at them*, but he knew that was folly. He sat down on a bale of cotton used as shelter in the battle and pulled a small notebook from a pocket. He jotted something down and handed it to the sergeant. "Get over to the telegraph office and send this to Austin."

# Chapter 3

1 November 1851

Will Travers drew in a lungful of air as he stepped off the walkway leading back to the hacienda-style presidential mansion. Turning left, he strode north on Colorado Avenue. The crisp November air filled his lungs as he lengthened his stride. Part of him wished he'd given in to Davy's plaintive begging to come along. But his youngest, at eight years, wouldn't be able to keep up with him for long. He needed time to think, and while the mansion's library and his own office in the Capitol Building were available, he didn't want the interruptions common to either place.

Part of his reason for the walk was it was the only exercise he managed to squeeze into his crowded schedule. He wasn't the twenty-seven-year-old man whose mind and soul had been transported through time and space into the body of William Barret Travis anymore. He chuckled ruefully as he considered the thought. He was very much that man, but he had left twenty-seven behind more than fifteen years before. At forty-two, he found it hard to keep off the weight that came with middle years.

With each passing year, it grew harder to recall the details of his life before the transference. Oh, he still remembered the day he passed through time and space like it was yesterday. He'd never forget the roar of explosions and the rat-tat-tat of machine-gun fire in the minutes leading up to his Humvee rolling over a roadside bomb before he lost consciousness. Nor would he forget the frozen terror that filled his veins when he realized he'd woke up in the body of William "Buck" Travis a few weeks before the Alamo.

No, it was the faces of his parents that were almost impossible to recall. It was books he'd read when he was a youth whose passages and ideas became harder to remember. It was forgetting what it felt like to have the cold breath of an air conditioner on his bare skin that reminded him, more than anything else, the world before the transference was gone forever.

His other reason for the walk was he needed to be alone with his thoughts. The telegram he'd received the previous day consumed him. The young captain who remained in command in West Liberty had packed more ill news into the short message than Will could have imagined. Ben McCulloch's death was a blow that would reverberate through the army. He wasn't just the commander of Texas' reserves; apart from Sidney Johnston, he was the only other officer in the military with experience commanding brigade-sized forces. If anything could have been worse, it was the fact that the rebels' attack was the final proof John Wharton had failed to bring the insurgents back into the Republic's fold.

War was now inevitable. Will realized he was grinding his teeth as he reached the last street before Austin ended and the prairie started. He turned the corner and resumed his fast pace. *Why did I think sending John Wharton would bring peace?* As Secretary of State for the Republic, he had been Will's best shot at defusing the conflict between the pro-slavery faction and Will's government. He shook his head in frustration. The idea seemed foolish, in retrospect.

Since his arrival in Buck Travis' body, Will's conflict with slavery's supporters had been inevitable. Only blind luck had kept him from dying at the hand of an assassin's blade in the days when he and other prominent Texians had been writing the constitution. He should have expected that between his election as president and the free-birth law, war was a sure bet.

In his heart, he knew he'd sent John to talk to the rebels because Will was sick of war. Setting aside the seven years he'd spent in the army before the transference, he had spent eight more fighting one war after another for Texas. More than a third of his life had been spent wearing his country's uniform, and he'd hoped against hope Wharton could have stopped the coming conflict.

Thinking about the rebels in Beaumont made Will angry. The free-birth law had hardly been the only thing he'd done as president. He had expanded military funding by a quarter in the past three years. He had opened a dialogue with the southern bands of Comanche. The warlike tribe was a long way from settling down like the Cherokee, but it was a start. He'd even paid off the last of the foreign bondholders. For the first time since the founding of the Republic, nearly all public debt was held by Texas' citizens.

Before the rebellion to the east had reared its ugly head, Will had been planning on several new enterprises. The population in Austin had grown so much he was ready to introduce legislation establishing a flagship university in the capital. No doubt, he was very proud of Trinity College, but it was a private institution, mostly concerned with mechanical engineering, medicine, and monetizing inventions created by its faculty and students.

He'd also been planning on laying the keel on a new warship. He'd hoped to skip the trials and errors of the ironclads of the US Civil War that barely floated and launch the first of the steel naval cruisers. He'd planned to transform Corpus Christi into a port capable of building the large warship. Texas needed more than a single port at Galveston to protect and expand trade. The planned facilities would have triggered a rapid economic expansion on Texas' southern coast. Now though, an experimental ship that would have cost more than the entire naval budget was a non-starter.

Will cursed under his breath. He cursed the rebels in East Texas for starting a conflict they'd not win. He cursed the governor of Louisiana for encouraging the filibuster. Lastly, he cursed his country's precarious financial situation. During the last war with Mexico, many of the bonds had been bought by Southern bankers and businessmen. Will couldn't see the same men putting down gold and silver for Texas bonds when those same men were funneling money and supplies to the volunteer regiments being raised to dislodge him from the presidency.

"Good thing no one else can hear you. They might mistake you for a sailor the way you cuss, instead of an old army man."

Will jumped in surprise as Sid Johnston joined him as he came to the northeast corner of the town and turned onto East Avenue. "What the hell, Sid. Spying on your president these days?"

"It's not spying when some folks want you dead. I've got a couple of Rangers who keep an eye on you when you take your morning constitutional." Johnston said.

"I ought to order you to stop that nonsense."

Johnston laughed as he patted Will on the back. "I'd hate to have to ignore you. I take my orders from your boss."

Will chuckled as he settled back into his long gait. "Becky can be a mite protective."

"And persuasive."

Will said, "What's got you up from San Antonio?"

"That damned telegram from Captain Running Creek," Johnston chewed at the words as he spat them out. "My God, the first move on the chess board and those damned rebels have castled us. I don't know what I'm going to do without Ben."

He paused, sucking in air. "How in the blazes do you manage to walk so fast? Ben knew all our reserve battalions like the back of his hand. He knew which could be mobilized fastest and which were the best trained. I'm going to miss that bastard."

As he waited for Johnston to catch his breath, Will nodded. "I'm already missing him. I should have listened to you when you begged me to send you and the army to crush those assholes in Beaumont. At least Ben would still be alive now."

Johnston chuckled, "You do have a way with words, Buck. What would you have me do about these, ah, assholes in Beaumont?"

"I've made a hash of things, Sid. If I'd told you a few months ago to go crush these rebels, the problem might have gone away. Now, we've got Southern militias coming across the Sabine. Anything we do is going to resound across the Southern states."

Will started walking, and a moment later, he heard Johnston's steady tread keeping pace with him. "We're at war now, Sid. How many men can you move against the rebels, and how quickly?"

"I've managed to collect two battalions of riflemen at the Alamo. The other three are spread pretty thin, but I can order them to begin shifting toward the east. I'm awfully short on cavalry. I've got less than a hundred horsemen available. But I've got half the army's field artillery sitting at the fort."

Will shook his head, "Numbers, Sid. How many men and how soon?"

"Around two thousand men. I can have them rolling east within a week."

Will said, "I don't want to strip the cupboard bare. Let's mobilize a few battalions of reservists while leaving the rest to run their farms and work the factories."

Sid's smile was predatory. "Give me another three or four battalions, and I can move more than four thousand men against them."

"Then do it."

Johnston stopped again to catch his breath. "What about those Southern militias?"

"If they're on our side of the Sabine River, they're enemy combatants. Our minister to the US will raise holy Hell with President Cass about them. But I don't want any of our boys getting confused and finding themselves in Louisiana or Arkansas. The last thing we want is this thing blowing up and bringing in the US."

When Johnston leaned up, his face red with exertion, he said, "How do you manage to walk so fast? I'm drilling men every day, and I can't keep up with you."

Smiling conspiratorially, Will lifted one of his feet and showed Johnston the rubber soled shoes. "Vulcanized rubber."

Wind rattled the small windowpane set high in the wall of the tiny room. A stove was squeezed into one corner, and a table was in another. Brevet Major Charlie Travis looked down at his wife who nursed a cup of hot tea as she sat at the table. Tears streaked her cheeks as she returned his gaze.

"I wish you didn't have to go, *maya lyubov,"* Her Russian accent was thick as she hiccupped from crying.

Charlie knelt by her side and ran his hand over her swollen belly. He didn't want to go either. She was eight months pregnant, and for the first time since he'd run away to join his Uncle Davy in an expedition to California, he was fearful. It wasn't for himself, but the idea that his wife would likely give birth to their first child while he was away left a hole in his heart. But he forced a warm smile onto his face, "Tanya, it's going to be alright. The doctor in the fort has experience delivering children."

Tatiana Rostovna Travis cut in, "But he's so young. How can Dr. Allsup be a good doctor?"

"He's trained under my father's friend, Dr. Ashbel Smith. He's a graduate from Trinity College." Charlie took his young wife by the hand and drew her into an embrace. He wiped away a tear and continued, "When the baby's born, if I haven't returned, I want you to go stay with my family in Austin. Becky would love to have you there. Liza also loves you, too."

Tatyana looked doubtful, "But your father is the president. He can't possibly want some foreign-born daughter-in-law underfoot. It would look bad."

Charlie swept a strand of her hair from her face and leaned in, kissing her. "Mrs. Travis, if you haven't noticed, almost everyone in Texas is foreign-born. My pa wasn't angry that I married a gold prospector's daughter. He just wished he'd been able to attend the wedding."

She melted into his arms. "Alright, Charlie." Playfully, she placed her hand on his uniformed chest. "I think you don't want all these single soldiers to stare at your wife."

Charlie threw back his head and laughed, "Cut to the quick, I am." In truth, he hated the idea of his wife being alone, even in a fort as large as the Alamo. Most of the officers' wives were born in the United States, and Tanya didn't fit in as well with them as Charlie would have liked. But with only weeks to go before the baby was due, it seemed best to wait until after the pregnancy for her to travel to Austin to be with his family until he returned.

He took her by the hand and guided her out of the small kitchen, "I'll show you how jealous I am, my dear."

Later, he buckled the gun-belt around his waist, grabbed his boots from the foot of the bed and slipped from the tiny room that served as their bedroom. It was better this way, that Tanya remain asleep. It wasn't like there would be a parade to send him off to war. His train would leave within an hour, taking him to the camp outside Houston, where the 9th Infantry battalion was assembling. The 9th was a reserve unit recruited from the stevedores and gutter-rats from Galveston and Houston, and they were mostly foreign-born. He still couldn't believe the battalion's second-in-command had betrayed the Republic and joined the rebels in Beaumont. But for that surprising betrayal, Charlie would likely have remained a company commander in the 1st Infantry. But now sporting the gold oak clusters of a major, he was heading east to serve as the reserve battalion's executive officer.

Andy Berry ducked instinctively when two panels of sheet metal clanged together, like a gunshot.

"Son, you're as nervous as a cat beside a rocking chair. You alright?"

"Yeah, Pa. Just sounded like something out of Revelation," the younger Berry said.

John Berry, Sr. looked thoughtful. "If anything can come close to the damnation of hell, a battle would be it. All the same, don't let your ma hear you talk like that."

Berry tipped his head in acknowledgment. His parents were devout Baptists. *Hell, I'm devout, I just wish Pa would give it a rest.* He changed the subject. "Did the government confirm payment for the last of the cartridges?"

The elder Berry nodded. “Ten thousand dollars for nearly four hundred thousand rounds.”

Andy whistled appreciatively. “Nice. Have you looked at the new schematics for another rolling press? If we can produce more sheets of brass, we can make more ammunition.”

His father took Andy by the arm and led him over to where two women measured gunpowder into a machine that fed the propellant into brass cartridges. “I’m scraping the bottom of the barrel to find men who can work in the gun works. I’ve had to hire women to work in some of the lighter jobs. If I went along with your proposal to add another production facility for more ammunition, I don’t know where I’d get the workers to run it.”

Berry shook his head, discouraged. “I guess it’s only going to get worse, with the mobilization.”

His pa shrugged. “Maybe. But President Travis has extended a waiver for the men working in the gun works. What we’re doing here is too important. Without more guns, Travis will have a harder time putting down those philistines in Beaumont.”

Berry changed tack, “What about putting a factory in Houston, or even Galveston? There’s workers there for hire.”

“Maybe. But Andy, I don’t want to spread our resources too thin. If we open an ammunition factory, who’d run it? We need our people here.”

The discussion over, John Berry left his son standing on the floor, watching two men wrestle with a brass sheet, and feed it into a machine that would cut it into hundreds of blanks. Those blanks would be taken to another device that would machine them into cylindric rounds.

Five thousand rounds daily were not enough to supply the army. The gun works had manufactured more than twenty-four hundred rifles that used the cartridges. Until the battle less than a week ago, more than half the weapons had remained crated and stored in a warehouse in Trinity Park. When he'd built the ammunition plant a few years earlier the idea that they could make more than two and a half million rounds of ammunition sounded far-fetched. Now that he'd done it, it was discouraging to know it was a drop in the bucket to what the army would need to carry the war to the rebels.

An idea began to form. Berry knew his pa was right. Labor *was* a problem. Putting a factory in Houston or Galveston might work or not. If the government had to dip into the poorer trained militias in the towns around Galveston Bay, any factory he put in those towns could be shuttered for lack of skilled workers. But what about...

Berry raced out of the manufactory, hurrying home. He had a letter to write and no time to waste.

Ignoring the slave holding the polished silver tray, Jason Lamont took a glass of lemonade from it. The refreshing drink felt sweet as he tipped the glass up and drained it. The crash of musketry sounded across a fallow field. He'd grown used to it, having watched the men of the Palmetto Guard drill over the past month.

He scrutinized them as the company shouldered arms and quickstepped across the field. They looked splendid in their matching gray uniforms and kepis. The kepis had caught on in Louisiana, with its heavy French influence and had spread across the South. Lamont had even heard rumors that a volunteer Zouave regiment in New York was now wearing the round, flat-topped hat with a narrow leather visor.

Two more companies were at drill on the plantation. More than two hundred South Carolinians ready to answer their kith and kin in Texas, who were embroiled in a life and death struggle with the illegitimate Travis administration. He set the glass down and dismissed the slave, giving no thought to the fact William Travis had won a democratic election.

"Uncle Jason, a coach is coming up the road." A young man bolted around the corner, nearly running into him. It was his sister's youngest son, Elliott.

"Slow down, Lieutenant Brown," Lamont drawled. "Did you recognize the carriage?"

The young man said, "No, Uncle. It's a jim dandy carriage. Must be someone important."

"Jim Dandy?" Lamont didn't care much for the slang his nephew used. But that was only a minor irritant in comparison to the other sin committed. The slave had left, and he was alone with Elliott. He leaned in and growled, "You may be my sister's son, Lieutenant. But that doesn't give you permission to be familiar with me around the boys or even the slaves. We're military now, and you of all people, I expect to act like it."

The young man gave his best impression of standing at attention. Lamont had seen better, but he let it slide. The boy was family, after all. Satisfied his warning had been taken to heart, he said, "Let's go see who's calling upon us."

When they rounded the plantation house, Lamont saw an ornate coach pulling up the drive. The black driver was dressed in colonial style livery, complete with knee britches and a tricorn hat. Before the coach rolled to a stop, another slave leapt from the back and dashed to the door, where he opened the door and unfolded a set of steps. A man of middle years stepped from the carriage.

Lamont's eyes grew large. He knew Joshua Ward, Lieutenant Governor of South Carolina, well. Ward owned a sugar plantation on the coast.

Lamont brushed imagined dust from his gray jacket and hurried over. "Colonel Ward, a pleasure to see you here at Saluda Groves." He acknowledged Ward's honorary rank in the state's militia.

Ward turned to the carriage driver, "I'll not be too long. Check the horses and be ready to go shortly."

He smiled at Lamont and shook his hand. "I've heard good things about you, Jason. What you're doing is likely going to be very important," he waved toward one of the companies of volunteers drilling in a nearby field.

Ward took him by the elbow, "Let's go see our brave boys at drill."

With that, Lamont left his nephew staring at the regal carriage and let Ward lead him away.

"A telegram arrived a few days ago from Texas. There was a battle outside of a town called West Liberty," Ward said. "General Beauregard was defeated."

Lamont felt conflicted. A victory against Travis' abolitionist army would be one step closer to seeing the upstart Travis get his. On the other hand, there was a reason he was raising a regiment of volunteers. He wanted to be there when the sons of the South dealt the mortal and final blow to Travis' army. "How bad was it?"

Ward shrugged, "It could have been worse. He led a combined army of Louisianans and Texans into battle, less than four thousand men."

Lamont barely registered Ward's truncation, dropping the *i.* "How large was the enemy's force?"

"Less than a thousand, we think. They were behind barricades, defending the town. You've seen their Sabine Rifle?"

"Yeah," Lamont said, remembering back to when Travis had stormed his slave quarters to rescue his son. Seven years it had been, but his leg was quick to remind him of his wound whenever he put too much weight on it. "Breechloading, like John Hall's rifles."

"Better. They're able to shoot eight or more rounds in a minute." Ward paused as he watched the company of infantry practice wheeling into line-of-battle. "How fast can your men shoot?"

Lamont gulped. "It's hardly a fair comparison. I've managed to arm my entire regiment with rifled muskets. Hell, some are even from the gun works in Texas. But we're doing well to fire three rounds in a minute."

"The good news, Colonel Lamont, is that Travis won't be able to muster up more than ten or fifteen thousand men. Against that, we're prepared to overwhelm him with our volunteers. We'll send as many as seventy thousand if we have to." He paused, looking at Lamont through the corner of his eye. "That's where you come in. Governor Means and I have been in discussion with other like-minded leaders, and we've decided that three regiments of South Carolinians will join their fellow Southerners in Texas, expanding the existing filibuster. You're to send out an order to the other companies in your regiment to assemble in Columbia in a fortnight."

Lamont felt a thrill run up his spine. He'd soon taste the smell of gunpowder for real as he led his men into battle. His leg twinged and he leaned heavily on the cane he was forced to use. Soon he'd pay back Travis for the misery the abolitionist had visited on him.

"How do you think President Cass will react?"

"I wish I could tell you that he'd do as he's told," Ward said, "But he's railing against the filibusters, saying they're illegal. But there's damn-all he can do about it. Senator Butler chairs the judiciary committee, and he's convened a hearing on servile insurrection in the South because of Texas' abominable Free-Birth law. In the meantime, our Southern Congressmen are doing their utmost to legitimize Beauregard's filibuster."

As Lamont nodded, a thought came unbidden, sending an icy chill into his gut. "If we've managed, at least for the time being, to block any federal response to our actions in Texas, what's to keep Yankee abolitionists from sending their own volunteers to swell Travis' army?"

# Chapter 4

16 November 1851

He sat in the corner of the room, listening to the other men talk. In one way, he felt honored to be invited to attend the meeting, but in another, he felt like a silent conspirator. Horace Greeley slipped his pencil back into a pocket and closed the notebook. He'd remember anything worth remembering. He resisted shaking his head—no, he'd never forget anything said during this meeting.

The current speaker's voice rose as he said, "They're damn near practicing treason and that fool, Lewis Cass will merrily let them get away with it."

Cravat untied and hanging around his neck, Solomon Foot said, "What do you expect from a Democrat, even one from Michigan, eh, Senator Seward?"

William Seward glared at his fellow Senator from Vermont. "I'd expect him to not let a bunch of yahoos from Louisiana play at filibustering in Texas, that's what."

Greeley scanned the room, and his eyes fell on a Representative from Pennsylvania, who had not run for reelection a few weeks earlier, David Wilmot. "Were I not disgusted with my own party, I'm sure I'd disagree with both of you, but unfortunately, in the Senate, my party has been taken hostage by the fire eaters from the deep South."

With a look of warmth surprising from one of the Whig party to a Democrat, Seward said, "You've certainly fought the good fight, David. Your efforts to restrict slavery to the fourteen Southern states is appreciated. But all of that is for naught. I fear that a wave of filibusterers will overwhelm the legitimate government in Texas and then insist we kiss their ring and annex the conquered republic."

Wilmot blanched at the comment. "Surely, it won't come to that. The newspapers have been talking up the victory the Texans won over a bunch of filibusters from Louisiana. It sounds like their professional army should be able to put paid to a few thousand Southern adventurers."

"And if that's all they were to face I'd agree," Seward moved across the room and stared at a map on the wall of the United States. He jabbed his finger at the map, "But I've learned that thousands more from four or five states are preparing to join the Louisianans in supporting the Texas rebels. By the time spring planting comes around, there could be as many as seventy thousand Southern filibusters in Texas. Against that, I don't give the Texas regulars much of a chance."

Wilmot sagged in his chair, "Surely not that many, William?"

Seward ran his finger along the top of a near-empty glass of whiskey before replying, "Today it's the deep south letting their young men galivant off to play at soldiers in Texas, but by the springtime don't be surprised if a few Virginians, Kentuckians, and hell, maybe even a few Marylanders are taking the mail packet boats to New Orleans to join in this Southern folly."

Foot interjected, "And that's why we're here this evening, gentleman." He focused his gaze on Seward, "Is there any chance that we can force the issue in Congress? A bill ordering those interlopers back to their home states? Sending the army to seal the border between Louisiana and Texas?"

Seward's harsh laughter sounded like the braying of a donkey. "Senator King has tied up several committees, discussing how servile insurrection is imminent because of Texas' new abolition law."

Wilmot shook his head. "That's hard to fathom. It'll be years before Texas' law will have an impact on slavery in Texas, let alone in the South."

Greeley's eyes narrowed; *how could he be so naïve? Say what you will about Southerners, but they're taking the long view on their peculiar institution.*

"From your lips to God's ears, David," Foot said, "But I wouldn't count on that. Already parishes across Louisiana have reported an increase in runaways. One reason Louisiana was able to come to the aid of the Texas rebels so quickly is the number of volunteer units has swelled in the last year or two to satisfy the needs of the slave patrols."

Standing in the shadow of the room was a fifth man. Greeley had taken his measure when he'd arrived. He was tall, black hair streaked with gray. He wore a permanent scowl. When he spoke, the other men turned to him. "Talk seems to be the national institution of our nation, but it won't relieve the misery of the slave."

Seward met his frown with one of his own, "And what would you have of us, Mr. Brown?

John Brown said, "Act on your convictions, Senator. If you won't send in the army, and you say that these slavers will overrun Texas, what then is to happen?"

Seward pursed his lips before turning to Greeley, "So, Horace, is this why you brought your fellow New Yorker with you? To be our conscience?"

Greeley played at the edge of the notebook as he weighed his response. "The balance of power in Congress is such that men like Senator King can stymie progress. I thought you called this meeting because, like Mr. Brown and myself, you are tired of nothing being done to end the injustice against the abolitionist government in Texas."

"But you want what I can't give. President Cass alone can order the army to Louisiana to seal the border. He won't do it, and Congress can't pass a bill supporting it."

Stepping up to the fireplace, Brown stuck his hands forward, warming them. "A fire burns in the heart of the South that burns against civilization, Senator. If you can't act, then have the decency to stand aside while those of us with conviction to act do so."

"What are you proposing, Mr. Brown?" Seward's features were aglow with light from the fire.

Brown rubbed his hands together before the fire in the hearth. "Two can play at filibustering, gentlemen. I intend to raise a regiment of men in New York who love liberty and freedom for every man, woman, and child in our nation, and take them to Texas to fight alongside Travis' legitimate government."

Light from the fire gave his eyes a red hue as the other men in the room stared at him, stunned by his proposal.

19 November 1851

The sun should have still been in the western sky, as Captain Jesse Running Creek looked upward. He was rewarded by a solitary drop of rain landing on his nose. The sun was still there but hidden behind threatening clouds.

Still, rain would be welcome, it would extinguish the few fires that lingered on the eastern bank of the Trinity River. It had been a few days now, and most of the fires were extinguished from when the rebels and their Louisiana allies had destroyed the railroad bridge.

*Really, it's a shame they didn't stay to fight*, Jesse thought as he turned away from the sky and looked through the woods. Three companies of the army's Rangers were dug into rifle pits in the woods on the western side of the river. More than two hundred men armed with the Republic's best rifles hunkered down. Most prayed the rain would hold off.

Not Jesse. Scattered between rifle pits, hidden under branches cut from the surrounding trees, were dozens of boats, hauled from the railhead in West Liberty. He prayed for rain. The rebels on the other side of the river were content to stay in their own rifle pits, occasionally firing across the river, as a reminder, Beauregard's little army may have retreated, but they were still a going concern.

Behind the tree line hugging the river, Jesse heard the army. Johnston had arrived a couple of days earlier with elements of the 1st and 6th Infantry battalions and several field artillery batteries from the Alamo, all regulars. Additionally, the 9th Infantry battalion and 2nd Cavalry squadron from the reserves had also arrived. In all, more than two thousand men. And more men were on the way. From Galveston, the 1st Marine battalion was expected by rail soon. Units from across the vast expanse of the nation were being recalled. Before the end of the year, Jesse knew the army would be larger than the one President Travis had taken into Mexico eight years before.

But until then, Johnston's small brigade was it, unless the president mobilized more reserve units.

Jesse's prayers were answered later as the heavens opened and the rain poured down, quenching the remaining fires on the river's eastern shore. He tightened his poncho around his neck as icy water trickled down his back. Better soaked than an easy target for the riflemen on the other side of the Trinity. He resisted the urge to look at his pocket watch. The signal to begin would come soon enough; worrying about the time wouldn't hasten it.

As though thinking about it would make it happen, the ground beneath him rumbled as thirty field pieces opened fire. “Up, men!” he shouted as he grabbed the nearest boat’s wooden gunwale and raced toward the river.

The bow bit into the water, splashing water into the bottom of the boat, as Jesse scrambled aboard while his Rangers grabbed the oars and paddled as though their lives depended on it. Shutters on lanterns were flung open, spilling weak light onto the river’s eastern shore. If a sentry over there could see anything through the pouring rain, Jesse would have been surprised. Flashes of brief light cut through the storm as riflemen opened fire.

The sergeant beside him chuckled. “Fools just burning powder now. I can’t see my feet in this damnable soup, what the hell do they think they’ll hit?”

As if the comment required an answer, Jesse heard a scream on the river as one of his Rangers was hit. “Faster!” he screamed as flashes of light showed more men opening fire on targets the defenders couldn’t see.

He was thrown into the brackish water sloshing in the boat’s bottom when it crunched into the shore. But no orders were necessary as his men swarmed from the boat, bayonet-tipped rifles leading the way. Far closer than before, the sound of gunfire filled his ears as Jesse scrambled after his men. He could see several more watercraft grounded into the muddy earth as Rangers swarmed forward.

From atop the riverbank, a steady stream of rifle-fire poured down on his men, despite the torrent of rain and darkness. From above, a voice drawled, "Get your asses into the trench, boys. Kill 'em all."

Jesse swore as rebels with breechloaders fired down on his men. Despite the antediluvian deluge, the weapons fired, as soldiers levered open breechblocks, inserted paper cartridges, and forced tin percussion caps on smoldering nipples.

He tripped over one of his men who lay sprawled on the slope. Like his men, Jesse carried a rifle, and he snapped it to his shoulder and fired at a muzzle flash above. He slid a brass cartridge into the breech and cocked the gun before firing at another flash.

More flashes appeared as more rebel soldiers filled the trench at the top of the slope. Jesse heard a wet splat and felt something warm hit his face as a ranger tumbled into him, knocking him into the mud. *We've got to get off this slope, or we'll all die.* He climbed back to his feet and reloaded his rifle. "Come on, boys! I'll see you in hell in the morning!"

He scurried over the body in front of him and climbed halfway up the hill before he slammed his rifle into his shoulder and fired at another flash. Now though, he could see faces behind the flashes above. Then the world turned upside down as a shell detonated over the trench. Like a deadly rain, broken pieces of iron sizzled as they dug into the soft ground.

His feet digging into the mud, Jesse clambered over the lip of the trench. It was as though the devil himself had paid a visit to the men, who moments before had been sending death down on him and his Rangers, and they lay broken and bloody in the bottom of the pit.

Rangers jumped into the pit and bayonets flashed as lightning split the sky overhead.

A misty drizzle made the gray dawn feel even colder than it was, Charlie Travis thought as he watched the hated blue flag with its single star flutter to the ground, replaced by the familiar lone star flag rising into the sky through his binoculars.

Wagons creaked as they rolled by, and Charlie moved away from the muddy road as black teamsters coaxed their tired teams of horses down the road to the river. The wagons were oddly shaped, like small boats on wheels. Yelling at the teamsters were men from the Alamo's engineering company.

When the wagons reached the slope down to the river, the teamsters grabbed their teams and held them steady as engineers took over, untied the pontoons, and lifted them from the frame then slid them on their flat bottoms into the river below. More engineers grabbed the pontoons and tied them to ones already floating in the water. Planking was laid down on top of the floating pontoons.

Charlie watched for a few minutes as the ersatz bridge took shape in the Trinity. A few more hours would see it reach the other side.

"Major," a voice from behind startled Charlie, and he turned and saw General Johnston. A warm smile replaced his shocked expression. "For a moment, you reminded me of your father, standing there, red hair dripping with rain."

Charlie saluted, trying to keep the smile that pulled at his lips from stealing the martial air he attempted to convey. "General, sir. We'll have the Ninth ready to cross once the Engineers finish the bridge."

Johnston patted him on the back, "No doubt, Major. Now that our Rangers have finally cleared the last of Beauregard's rebs out of Liberty township, I'm going to take a boat across and take a gander. Why don't you join me?"

Once on the other side of the Trinity, Charlie found himself climbing the steep riverbank with the aid of a rope, looking up at the backside of the army's commander. The rope was slick from the rain, but the use of a pair of gloves made short work of the climb. The first rifle pit he saw had a dead man dressed in a butternut uniform. A breechloading rifle, identical to the one issued to the men of the 9th lay beside the fallen soldier.

Beyond the trench, several more bodies were laid in a neat line. Sewn on their butternut jackets were irregular patches of brown, green and gray. The Rangers had pulled their own dead away from where the fighting had been the thickest throughout the night but left the rebels where they'd died.

"Ugly business war is," Johnston said from his side.

"I reckon so." At that moment, Charlie's mind had gone back to the horrific final minutes at the battle of the Alamo, nearly a decade before. He could taste the acrid smell of gunpowder mixed with flour as he had stood in line, as a thirteen-year-old, gripping his father's rifle as he and the other survivors waited for the final charge that never came. When they realized a relief column had arrived, he and the other men streamed from the battered chapel where they saw Sidney Johnston marching into the fort with his soldiers.

His thoughts retreated from the past, and he repeated, “Yes, I reckon so.”

Johnston turned from the line of dead Rangers, and said quietly, “When the bridge is finished, Major, detail enough men to bury all of these men.”

As he walked with Johnston through town, Charlie couldn’t help noticing the hamlet was finished. What hadn’t been damaged a few weeks earlier when Beauregard’s army had crossed going west, had been wrecked in the previous night’s fight.

When he’d said as much, Johnston replied, “Probably so. Liberty was the town progress forgot after West Liberty became the largest town in the county.”

Johnston paused, staring at the charred remains of a building. A blackened hand stuck out from beneath a long, charred board not entirely claimed by the flames which had destroyed the building.

Johnston shuddered, “I hope so, Charlie. Better to let the ghosts of this place reclaim it.”

Hastily constructed rifle pits had been dug on the edge of town. Most of the Rangers were dug in there. One of the Rangers, muddier than most, sat behind the remains of a wooden wall. Through the grime, Charlie recognized the dirty man.

Forgetting decorum, he blurted, “Jesse, my God, man, what happened to you?”

The young Cherokee officer looked up and said, “I fell getting out of the boat.”

# Chapter 5

Becky Travis rolled over, her hand searching for the warmth of her husband's body, but her fingers gripped the tangled blankets covering their bed. She cracked open an eye as the gentle light of dawn seeped through the curtains. Will was gone already. Her sigh was so loud she couldn't help laughing at herself. But she enjoyed those rare moments before the day began when she could snuggle next to her husband, especially on a cold winter morning.

She closed her eyes; perhaps she could sleep a bit longer before Liza or Davy stirred. Before she could doze off, she heard the plaintive cry of a newborn. She grabbed her pillow and pulled it over her head. It did no good as the baby's cry pierced through the pillow's feathers. A moment later, she heard the soothing voice of Tatyana, calming the infant.

Charlie's young wife had arrived a few days earlier, only a week after giving birth. Becky had scolded the young mother for traveling with the newborn, but only after welcoming them with hugs and kisses. Now, though, she wished little Leo had remained sleeping for a bit longer. Once she was awake, Becky grabbed a heavy, woolen gown from the back of a chair and put it on as she left the bedroom.

She found Tanya nursing Leo in the kitchen. As the baby suckled, the mother cooed softly in her native Russian. The smile Becky gave her first grandchild, if only by marriage, was genuine. After feeding the baby, Tanya, dark circles under her eyes from lack of sleep, happily handed Leo to Becky, who placed him on her shoulder and patted his little back. She ran her fingers through his silky red hair. *No doubt your father's son*, Becky thought. Charlie's features were clearly imprinted on his firstborn.

Tanya slumped into a chair, murmuring in Russian. Becky gave her a quizzical look.

"You did this twice, Mrs. Travis, when did you manage to sleep?" Tanya's accent was strong.

Becky smiled. "That's nothing. My ma had five children. Now, how about calling me Becky? This Mrs. Travis stuff makes me feel old. Land's sake, I'm only thirty-three."

As Leo drifted off to sleep, Becky turned when she heard someone clear his throat. Diego, the mansion's majordomo stood in the doorway. The mestizo butler held a note in his hand, "Señora Travis, a telegram just arrived for you."

She accepted the folded note, stamped on the outside with the Across-Texas Telegraph company's logo. Unfolding it, she read the neat script from the telegraph office clerk, *Mrs. Travis, Joe did something foolish. I need help. Hattie.*

Seeing Henrietta's name on the bottom of the telegram brought a lump to her throat, as Becky realized how many years it had been since the freedwoman had cooked and cleaned for her household. The war with Mexico had ended in 1843, but its destructive effects had left the Republic's economy in shambles at the same time Will was chasing down Charlie's kidnappers. Forced to leave San Antonio, Becky and her family had no choice but to part ways with Hattie, whose home was with Will's former slave, Joe.

That was how Becky found herself stepping down from the passenger car in San Antonio a few days later. Eight years had passed since she and her family had made the town their home, and the city was barely recognizable. While the central square still existed, businesses crowded the streets that radiated from the square. The wooden bridge she and her family had crossed nearly a decade before on their way to hide in the safety of the Alamo was now made of iron and brick.

Despite the years, her feet knew the way to her old house, and without realizing it, she let them guide her. It was a short walk. When she came to where the house once stood, it was gone. In its place stood a red brick building. A bright yellow sign was fixed above the building; it read *Maverick's Mercantile*.

Becky blinked back a tear. She had so many memories of their home there. Both her children were born in the house. Now it was gone, swept away by progress.

She willed her feet onward; there were nothing but memories at her old home. Hattie still lived in the same modest house she and Joe had built more than a dozen years before. A simple garden covered the front yard, and as Becky made her way through it, the front door swung open, and Henrietta stood there. The freedwoman was only a few years older than Becky, but her hair was already losing the battle to gray.

"Miss Becky, you're a sight for sore eyes. Bless you for coming." Henrietta met her halfway, and the two women, one the wife of the president of the Republic and the other a freedwoman of color hugged in the middle of a garden full of mustard greens and chili peppers.

Later, as Becky sipped a cup of coffee, Henrietta explained, "Joe and Cuffee been doing big business with the army. They've been carrying supplies up the military road to Ysleta and Santa Fe, too. Joe, he's been promising me a new home. Said he was going to hire me my own Irish maid, the silly fool of a man."

She brought over a platter of tortillas from the stove and a plate of butter and sat in the chair next to Becky. "Lordy, what'd I do with an Irish maid. Maria, she lives next door, helps me if I need it. She showed me how to make these corn tortillas that Joe loves so much."

Becky looked around the room. A couple of doors along one side led to the small bedrooms, and another led to the backyard, where another garden covered nearly every square foot. “When’s Joe due back?”

Tears spilled from Henrietta’s eyes. “He’s ‘sposed to be home a month ago, Miss Becky, but him and that damned fool Cuffee done joined the militia in Santa Fe. They’s going to be called to duty against the rebels.”

Becky lowered the tortilla she’d been about to bite into, stunned. “They did what?”

She’d heard every word Henrietta uttered, but the words were too outlandish to believe. “That’s not possible,” she managed to say.

“You know it, and I’s know it, but those fools don’t.” She stood and went into one of the bedrooms and returned a moment later with a letter and gave it to Becky.

The flowing script was in Spanish. “I took it to my neighbor, Maria, and we went over to San Fernando where one of the priests translated it. Joe had a clerk write it.”

Although it was changing, many folks in San Antonio were fluent in Spanish. Joe had picked it up over the years, carrying supplies for the army to the outposts to the west. Unfortunately, Becky couldn’t read it. “Hattie, what’d Joe say?”

Clenching the letter, Henrietta said, “The local colonel, some fool of a man named Montoya decided to recruit a company from the drovers, freight haulers, and muleskinners who travel between San Antonio and Santa Fe. He done found enough fools to fill up a company’s worth of colored men. The letter says Joe and the rest of the battalion are going to march this way after the beginning of the year. You've got to tell Marse Will and have this stopped. It's too dangerous."

Becky had never imagined anyone would arm a company of Negro soldiers. Although she believed that if someone like General Beauregard knew a militia company contained freedmen, he'd use it to stir up more hatred against her husband. The last thing Will needed was more enemies.

But as she saw the raw pain on Henrietta's face, she recalled Will telling her about how it had been Hattie who had talked Joe into sheltering Cuffee after slavers had come looking for him in Trinity Park. She had willingly laid her and her husband's lives on the line to save Cuffee from being taken back to South Carolina in chains.

"I'll talk to Will and let him know about Joe," she offered. She knew the anguish Hattie felt. Every time Will had ridden off to war, part of her died inside until he returned safely. How many women had waited in vain for their husbands, who never returned? Yes, she would talk to Will.

The boy rubbed his hands together as he tried to keep warm, watching the train roll to a stop. Steam vented from the locomotive as hundreds of men swarmed from the dozen or more passenger cars. They looked splendid in their dark blue jackets, as they began setting up camp in the fields south of Chicago.

Jimmy cast a nervous glance about. Nobody had time to worry about a stray runaway. He refused to let the jitters he felt get in the way of seeing the men from the 1st Provisional New York Cavalry Regiment as they erected tents. In all his fourteen years nothing rose to the same level as watching the soldiers, and that was saying something, he thought. Before his father's murder, William Alonzo Hickok had run a station on the Underground Railroad. Watching the gratitude on the faces of the escaped slaves had filled Jimmy with a sense of purpose, but that died on the night slave catchers had burned down the family farm and killed his pa.

There was no denying that over the past few months, more slaves were escaping and making their way north to freedom. Some folks blamed more runaways on some new law down in the Republic of Texas while others said the slavers who killed his pa wanted to make an example him and close that escape route. All that Jimmy knew was the men setting up camp were going to fight the slavers, like the men who'd killed his pa. He wasn't sure how he was going to do it, but when they broke camp on the morrow, he was going to be on the train heading to St. Louis.

His hands went to his stomach which growled in protest. Jimmy's last meal had been in Joliet yesterday. It wasn't long before cooking fires were burning on company streets as the soldiers from New York settled in for the evening. Jimmy meandered toward the camp, drawn by the smells.

A crowd of well-dressed men was following a tall, bearded officer across the railroad tracks into the camp. The eagles on the officer's shoulder boards declared he was someone important. Jimmy, forgetting his hunger, fell in behind the last of the well-heeled men, curious.

"Colonel Brown," one of the men shouted, "Joe Allen of the Chicago Tribune. What do you hope to accomplish with your regiment? The Federal army refuses to recognize your command."

Jimmy stood on his toes to see over the shoulders of the newspaper reporters, to see the tall, gangly Colonel Brown. "Gentlemen, when the men of New York realized the great injustice being committed by the men of the South against our kindred in Texas, they answered the clarion call of liberty and freedom. We ride in opposition to the filibustering of Southern fire eaters. If President Cass doesn't see fit to respond to that which is right in front of him, that's on him, not us."

Another reporters' hand shot up, "David Bradly of the *Democrat*. Seems to me you've gone the wrong direction. Galveston's a lot easier to get to from New York by way of the Atlantic. Why come to Chicago?"

Jimmy liked the unpleasant way Brown smirked at the reporter. "President Cass, as we've already mentioned can't see the problems these southern filibusters are creating, and he's only making it worse to deny us the freedom to sail from the eastern ports. Thankfully, the railroads, so new to our beautiful country, are not regulated by the president, lest we have to ride the entire way on our horses. We'll cross the Mississippi and take the new rail from St Lewis to St. Joseph. From there, we'll travel through the Western territory and from there on to Texas."

"Colonel Brown! Josiah Elliott of the *Chicago's American*. What with the South's intransigence, the Western Territory is closed to settlement. The army has banned travel through the region. What will you do if the army tries to stop you?"

Brown frowned at the reporter, "As the Lord said, wist ye not that I must be about my Father's business?"

Jimmy sensed the confusion on the reporters' faces as Brown stared down the group. When one turned to go, Brown continued, "We are on a crusade, one that is destined to bring freedom to the colored man. His chains must be sundered, and that is our Lord's commandment. I believe the order to which you refer prevents settlement of the region. We are free to travel through it. But if lukewarm Lewis Cass orders the army to stand in the way of the First New York, the outcome will be on the President's head, not mine."

The reporters furiously scribbled on their note pads as they hurried back into Chicago. Uncertain about the furious expression on Brown's face, Jimmy fell in at the back of the pack until they left the camp. The idea of sending slavers to perdition sounded good. There was nothing he'd enjoy more than putting paid to men like those who'd killed his pa. But the fearsome colonel made Jimmy's knees weak.

Walking along the edge of the camp, hunger overcame his good sense, and Jimmy eventually begged enough food from the soldiers to satisfy his hunger. As the men of the 1st New York settled down for the night, Jimmy heard the soft refrain of carols drifting over the camp. He hadn't thought about it since leaving home, but it was almost Christmas. It would be the first Christmas since his pa had been murdered. The thought brought an unwelcome tear to his fourteen-year-old eye. He rubbed it away, determined to be brave. Men don't cry, he reminded himself as he walked by the cold, silent railroad cars.

*It's cold*, Jimmy thought as his teeth started chattering. When he walked by a boxcar with its bay door slid open, he stopped and peered inside. While it was dark, he could smell the strong odor of horses and hay. The wind picked up, cutting through his jacket. Crinkling his nose at the smell, he clambered into the car and found piles of hay against the wall. He collapsed and burrowed under the straw until his bottom bumped against the floor. As the hay's insulation warmed him, Jimmy Hickok drifted off to sleep to the sound of distant Christmas carols.

Becky closed the door softly. A candle still burned on the nightstand. Her eyes grew wide when she saw her husband. Will was propped up on a pillow, an open newspaper lay on his chest. His quiet snore brought a smile to her face.

She slipped off her shoes, exhausted. The trip to San Antonio to meet with Henrietta had taken the entire day. She marveled how the railroad could take her from Austin to San Antonio in only a couple of hours and back again all inside a single day. In the years before the train arrived, it would have taken the better part of a week to go to San Antonio and back.

"Your ma said you'd gone out," Will's voice broke the silence.

The tension Becky had felt since meeting with Henrietta broke when she heard her husband. She took the newspaper from him and leaned in until their lips met. When she broke the kiss, she said, "Hattie sent a telegram. You won't believe what foolishness Joe has been up to."

Will propped himself up on his elbow, "It must have been important for you to leave the children with your mother."

Becky's worried expression softened, there was no hint of criticism in Will's voice, only curiosity.

"Hattie received a letter from Joe, well, Joe dictated a letter to her. Some dandy of a militia colonel in Santa Fe formed up a company of colored soldiers, and both Joe and Cuffee joined up. The letter said they were to be mobilized. Will, how can he do that?"

Her husband's eyebrows arched upwards. "Damned if that fool Montoya hasn't gone and done it. That's one genie we're going to be hard-pressed to put back in the bottle."

"What did this Montoya fellow do?"

Will climbed out of bed and helped her untie the back of her dress as he said, "Hiram Montoya runs supplies along the Santa Fe trail. He's not a big dog, but he commands one of our reserve infantry battalions. He wrote a letter to Sid and George Fisher, telling them he was going to raise a company of freedmen."

Becky shook her head as he helped her remove the uncomfortable corset. "Poor Sid. He must have thrown a conniption fit at the idea. What about Mr. Fisher, as Secretary of War, surely he backed Sid."

As he helped her into a nightgown, Will chuckled. "That crazy Hungarian asked how many battalions could we field if we actively recruited freedmen. No, love, George Fisher is probably the most liberal man I know when it comes to the question of giving black men a fair shake."

"Who won?" she asked.

Will grimaced, "If I could wave a magic wand, I'd do it and make sure that every man who loves Texas could serve in the army without restriction. But for the time being, Sid's convinced George to allow the company to be used for engineering projects, like digging trenches and the like."

Becky felt the tightness in her chest loosen. "That doesn't sound too dangerous."

"Montoya's going to be drilling those freedmen with rifles. By the time the battalion reaches the front, those men aren't going to take kindly to being told they're second class soldiers, fit only for unskilled labor. No, Becky. The first time they get the chance to fight, Montoya's freedmen are going to put paid to a very long list of grievances against those damned rebels."

Will turned away from the map on his desk, ignoring the looks from the other men in the room. He fumed in frustration. The opportunity to quickly nip the slavers' open rebellion was gone, and there was only one person to blame. Finally, he said, "The curse of governance is that too often we fight the last war. I have obsessed over the fact that we damn near destroyed the Republic fighting against Mexico. We mobilized every man that could carry a rifle. While it's true we won, we nearly caused the wheels to come off the wagon of state. I've been guilty of worrying so much about the risk to the economy of mobilizing one more soldier than necessary, that I've not given you the tools you need to succeed."

A. Sidney Johnston, commander of the Texian army, flushed at Will's admission. "I'm not sure I'd go that far, Buck." Except for the Secretary of War, the men in the room had served together for years. Despite the formal setting of Will's office in the Capitol building, there was a familiarity between the men. He continued, "But I'll not deny, if we'd had more men, I could have defeated Beauregard in the Piney Woods."

Juan Seguin leaned over the map of East Texas. "Those *cabrónes* who betrayed us gave Beauregard his victory. If you'd been facing two thousand men from Louisiana, your army would have celebrated Christmas in Beaumont."

Johnston sent a sheepish smile in the direction of the vice president. "Thanks, Juan. But if it had just been the rebel soldiers, I'm convinced we'd have swept them aside, even if they were all armed with breechloaders. It was the damned piney woods. Outside of towns and farms, East Texas is a wilderness. We had enough field artillery that if we could have deployed them, they could have turned the tide. Hell, we couldn't even use our cavalry effectively. There's a reason we've spent the last fifteen years developing a doctrine in which our infantry, cavalry, and artillery work so closely together. Combined arms defeated Santa Anna in Mexico, and if we can deploy our army effectively, they'll defeat Beauregard, too."

He realized he'd raised his voice, and he smiled apologetically before adding, "But we need more men, too."

Will gave a short nod and turned to the rotund Secretary of War, George Fisher. "George, what have we got and how much of it can be deployed?"

Fisher spoke with a heavy Eastern European accent, "It pains me to say it, but the rebels managed to cobble together eight infantry battalions and a cavalry squadron from the reservists and the militia in East Texas. That's five to six thousand men we can't call upon. Before the rebellion, we could have mobilized an army of more than fifty thousand, assuming we totally mobilized every man of military age."

The Hungarian immigrant, whom Will had appointed his Secretary of War rummaged in the pocket of his rumpled coat until he pulled a sheet of paper from it. He unfolded it and said, "On paper, we still have the ability to mobilize almost forty battalions of infantry, twelve of cavalry, and six of artillery." He smiled apologetically, "But that's on paper. Realistically, Mr. President, I'd not expand the army to any more than twenty thousand men, maybe a bit more if Congress will authorize the recruitment of some of those Irish and German laborers who've washed up on our shores over the past few years. That still leaves around half our manpower in factories, mills, stores, and on their farms. While it will have serious repercussions for our economy, it shouldn't cripple it."

"George, I'll leave it to you and Sid to determine which battalions should be mobilized," Will said. "Can we arm a force that size?"

Fisher grew thoughtful before slowly responding, "I believe so. When East Texas rebelled, we lost more than three thousand of the M1842 rifles and about the same number of the older Halls rifles. Some of our militia units will have to use the Halls rifles until we produce more of our modern rifles at the Trinity Gun Works."

Will turned to Johnston, "You've talked to Andy Berry more recently than the rest of us, how much can we rely upon their production numbers?"

Johnston stroked his salt-and-pepper mustache, "It could be worse, but it could be a hell of a lot better. We're facing a serious bottleneck in the production of metal cartridges. We used up nearly half of all our reserves for the new model breechloaders and Gatling guns. Berry's not going to be able to increase production on his brass cartridges above five-thousand rounds per day."

"He's going to have to if you're going to have the resources to carry forward the war against the rebels," Will said. "He's going to have to find a workaround."

Johnston nodded. "He knows. He's signed an agreement with Colt Manufacturing for them to supply us with one hundred thousand brass cartridges each month. He's close to arranging a similar deal with the Harpers Ferry Armory, once the US War Department gives its blessing. If he can get both contracts, he said he'd increase production on the M1846. Right now, only twenty-five hundred of these rifles have been issued. He can produce another five thousand this year."

Will groaned, "God help us if we're still fighting this war by the end of this year. The reason I'm authorizing such a large mobilization is that I want to knock the rebels and their allies out of Texas before the spring planting."

His thoughts turned to John Wharton. The long-suffering Secretary of State had done everything in his power to heal the rift between the rebels and Will's government, spending several months cajoling the slavers in Beaumont to lay down their arms. But by the time the rebels had invited Beauregard's filibusterers into Texas, it had been too late. Now Wharton was sailing to Washington to lodge a protest with President Cass against the South's illegal filibustering. "If John can get President Cass to come down on the state governments in the South that are aiding the filibustering, the flow of volunteers to Beauregard's army will dry up, and you'll be able to force the rebels to surrender."

Seguin's audible sigh caught Will's attention. The vice president said, "But what if Cass is as ineffectual as we fear? States like Alabama and Mississippi seem hell-bent on sending even more men to join Beauregard. The *Picayune* from New Orleans had an article that as many as seventy-thousand volunteers could filibuster against us. How do we stop that?"

# Chapter 6

Late January 1852

The cold air retreated from the heat of the blast furnace and sweat beaded on Andy Berry's forehead as he led his guest into the foundry. Bundled in the heavy greatcoat issued by the army, his guest quickly unfastened the buttons. "Damned if you don't feel like you're stepping into hell, Captain Berry. How do you manage it?"

Andy shrugged. "You get used to it, Colonel Sherman. To be honest, I'd rather face the heat of the furnace than feel the hot breath of a jagged piece of metal sailing by my face."

Sherman nodded, "An unfortunate hazard of war, Captain."

Berry shuddered at a memory. "Not when it's from one of your own guns, Colonel. I'll be damned if I want any of the guns we're making here to blow up when our boys are firing them."

"You make a salient point. What are you doing to avoid that happening again?

Andy guided the artillery commander through the foundry to where several barrels rested on a platform. The guns' breeches were open. The breechblock assemblies were on another platform. The young industrialist knelt by the open breech and patted the thick metal. "The problem is that despite the thickness of the iron, it's still just iron. The processed nitrogenated gun cotton exerts too much pressure for the iron to withstand."

Sherman dipped his head in agreement. "That NPC you and Mr. Borden created is some of the most potent stuff I've ever seen. But what's the solution to blowing the breech open?

"In the short term, we'll use black powder. It's messy and corrosive, but it doesn't put the same pressure on the iron as NPC."

The artillery colonel picked up the breechblock assembly. Berry hid his smile as the other man struggled under the heavy weight. As the colonel returned the assembly to the platform, he asked, "Do you think you can tame NPC? Make it less volatile?"

"I'm not the expert on it, that'd be Gail," Andy admitted. "But he tells me that so far, he's found dozens of ways that don't work to tame the instability of our gun cotton."

Sherman chuckled. "I trust Mr. Borden still has all his fingers?"

"He's more careful than I am. But all I'm dealing with is molten metal over here. I'll take that over gun cotton any day." Andy said.

Sherman beckoned him to follow as the colonel fled the foundry's oppressive heat. When they exited the building, he asked, "We've been using black powder in our guns for longer than Englishmen have walked this continent. I think we can continue to rely upon it a while longer. The reason for my visit has more to do with those iron tubes back in the foundry."

Andy shivered. He wore only a jacket and woolen trousers. "Wasn't it enough that you transferred our guns to the regulars?" He had felt no anger after Sherman had ordered his own breechloaders and Gatling guns transferred to the army's 1st Artillery. After the battle of the Trinity, Andy had decided he'd rather serve his country by providing the sinews of war rather than using them.

A ghost of a smile crossed Sherman's face. "I needed them more. Actually, I need even more now."

"Let's get out of this cold," Andy said. He led Sherman across an artillery park next to the foundry. The park was nearly empty. A few of the new breechloading field pieces sat at one end. As they entered his office, he offered his guest a chair before sitting on the edge of his desk.

"How many more?"

Sherman took off his hat and set it on the desk next to Andy before replying, "Did you know, there are more than three thousand men assigned to our artillery, between our regulars, reservists and militia?"

Andy whistled appreciatively at the number. "That's a lot of men. How many guns do we have?"

"We have ten batteries of artillery in the regular army. About half are assigned to coastal defenses or heavy artillery at the Alamo. The other half are field artillery. It goes downhill from there, fast. On paper, we have twenty batteries of reservists, fifteen of which are supposed to be armed with field artillery. That's ninety guns. We have thirty. There's a similar number of field pieces for our militia, and there's twice as many men assigned to those batteries. And, honestly, I don't want to tell you how old some of those guns are. We bought surplus stocks from the US. They were left over from the War of 1812."

Andy grimaced at the prospect of his own reservists drilling on forty or fifty-year-old guns. Not for the first time was he grateful the president was prioritizing manufacturing. It kept the men he cared for employed in Trinity Park instead of mobilizing with the army.

He ventured, "How many guns do you want, Colonel?"

He felt Sherman's eyes bore into him as the artillery officer said, "Three hundred."

Andy nearly fell off his perch on the desk. He sputtered, "Three hundred! You might as well ask for three thousand. If I worked my men night and day for the next year, I might be able to produce three hundred, but I doubt it."

Sherman laughed as he returned to his perch. "You asked how many I wanted. I need enough to arm the regular army and about half the reserves. How many can you make between now and the end of March?"

Berry pulled on his goatee as he thought about the production schedule. "If I can find a few more workers I could add a second shift in the foundry. If I do that, I might be able to deliver forty, if everything goes well."

Late March 1852

Charlie glanced at the wooden scaffolding crossing the Trinity River. The railroad bridge was far from being finished, but the latticework was proof the owners of the railroad were committed to putting it back in operation. Rumbling from below drew his attention to the pontoon bridge spanning the Trinity at water level. Another battery of artillery was joining the army.

And what an army it was, he thought. The last of the reservist infantry battalions had arrived yesterday, all the way from Santa Fe. A warm breeze blowing in from the Gulf brought the battalion's flag snapping to attention. The unit's motto, *"Victoria o Muerte!"* was emblazoned in red across the white bar at the top of the flag. Below, in golden thread was embroidered, "21st Texas Infantry." The entire battalion, seven hundred men, stood shoulder-to-shoulder at attention, waiting for an inspection from the army's commander.

"Nine hundred miles by foot, Major Travis. Your father managed that a decade ago with the whole army in forty days, in his effort to reach the Alamo when Adrian Woll's army attacked. Montoya managed it in fifty."

Charlie turned and smiled at General Johnston. "As I recall, had you not arrived with the army's reserve before him, sir, I'd likely not be here today."

He took the general's reins as Johnston climbed down from his mount. The general said, "I'm glad Colonel Garibaldi could spare you for a bit. I thought you'd enjoy reviewing the twenty-first with me."

As Johnston was speaking, the battalion commander, Hiram Montoya, approached. "My men are ready for your inspection, sir."

Charlie fell in behind the other officers as they slowly started down the long double line of men. The soldiers' butternut uniforms were soiled after so many days marching. There were patches where wear-and-tear had taken their toll. But the soldiers' rifles were clean and freshly oiled. Charlie stopped in front of a young, Hispanic soldier and took the gun to inspect it. Like the rest of the men in the 21st, he had been issued the M1833 Halls Breechloader. Charlie couldn't help but wonder what circular route the rifle had taken to end up in the Santa Fe armory. Briefly, he speculated if Joe, his father's former slave, had been one of the freight haulers who might have delivered the rifles.

He handed the weapon back, and the young soldier held the rifle at attention for a moment before gently setting the butt on the ground. Charlie hurried to catch up to the other officers.

A few feet ahead, Johnston came to a sudden stop. "What the hell?"

Charlie followed his gaze and saw something he'd never imagined seeing. Before him in butternut brown was an entire company of colored riflemen. Johnston recovered his surprise and said, "A moment, Colonel." He took the Hispanic officer by the elbow, and they walked away from the long line of soldiers.

Although he was standing well away from Johnston and Montoya, Charlie could hear every word. "So, it's true? The president told me that you'd recruited a company of Negros, but I didn't believe it."

Montoya's voice carried a note of defensiveness. "Every one of these men is free. Many of them you trusted to carry supplies from the east to the garrisons in the west. Seems to me if you can trust them to carry supplies along some godforsaken road across the Chihuahuan desert, they deserve your trust now."

Johnston turned a skeptical eye on the men, who were standing at attention. *They must realize they're being talked about,* Charlie thought. If it were possible for the ebony-skinned soldiers to stand any straighter, they did so as the army's commander and their own colonel stood just outside of earshot.

"I don't like it, Colonel. It's a distraction and runs the risk of creating divisions within our army." Johnston's voice was low, Charlie had to strain to hear it.

Montoya growled, "Are you ordering me to send them home? I won't do it."

Johnston shifted from one foot to the other. "If you refuse a direct order, I'll sack you and put someone else in command of the twenty-first, *Colonel* Montoya. Don't be too quick to tell me what you won't do." He paused, stroking his graying mustache. "But, no. I'm not ordering it. While President Travis has given me wide latitude how I conduct this campaign, he insisted I find a place for your men."

Montoya's sigh of relief brought a smile to Charlie's lips. He was glad his father was willing to take a chance on the colored soldiers. Johnston continued, "Right now, the engineers with the railroad have asked for some more men. They've got the wood for scaffolding but not enough men. I'm assigning your colored company to help."

Charlie saw the stormy expression of Montoya's face and waited for the explosion. Johnston raised his voice, "Major Travis. I want you to detail a company from the Ninth to help with the bridge, too. I'm sure some of Colonel Garibaldi's gutter-rats can be put to good use."

Charlie couldn't hide the smile on his face. His opinion for Johnston's tact went up a step. He'd known the General since he was a young boy, and he'd known Johnston's views on negros matched most Southerners. But the years of working with his pa had taken the edge off those views. Ordering another company from the Ninth to assist would soften the blow to the colored soldiers under Montoya's command. As he thought about it, Charlie quickly realized, the irascible men from Company E would be volunteered. The company was a melting pot of Europeans—mostly Irish with a leavening of Germans and Italians. But there were also some men there who'd worked on railroads before washing up on Galveston's wharves.

Montoya seemed mollified by Johnston's willingness to not completely single out his soldiers, and they continued the inspection. Charlie was nearing the end of the line when he stopped in front of one soldier. The soldier was older than most of his compatriots, strands of curly gray were showing at his temples.

"Joe, my God, what the hell are you doing here?"

The frozen expression on the soldier's face cracked into a smile, as his pa's former slave said, "Just doing my duty, Master Charlie."

Another voice from the second line of soldiers piped up, "You old coot, you ain't supposed to call an officer by his Christian name, that's *Major Travis!*"

Charlie's eyes grew wide as he saw Cuffee standing behind Joe. He'd not seen the runaway since shortly after he'd been rescued by his pa eight years earlier. Cuffee wore a full, bushy beard and he'd put on a few pounds over the intervening years. *Decorum be damned*, he thought as he reached through the line of soldiers and pulled Cuffee forward.

"You're a sight to behold. It looks like Hattie's been feeding you well."

Cuffee mumbled, "She's been good to me. Joe's been like my pa."

Sensing someone standing behind, Charlie turned and saw Johnston and Montoya. "Major, is there a problem with this particular rifleman?" Johnston said, as his lips twitched.

Charlie reddened, as he realized every eye in the company was on him. "No, sir," he managed. "This is the man who helped rescue me when I was kidnapped."

At that moment, he recalled hunting along the Trinity River with the runaway and before that, when Cuffee had labored beside him when he had been held captive in South Carolina. He alone, among the slaves, had taken the time to befriend a scared fifteen-year-old.

Charlie raised his voice, "There's not another man here, who I'd rather have by my side when we take the fight to those goddamned rebels in Beaumont."

It was the right thing to say, he thought, as the men on the field broke into cheers.

The youth tied the reins to the saddle horn as his horse drank in the cool water of the muddy river. Trooper Jimmy Hickok's blue jacket was sized too large for his growing frame, but the cold north wind that turned his cheeks red barely touched his hands because the sleeves were too long.

He turned at another horse nickering and saw his friend, Watson Brown, nudging his mount into the river. Even now, two months after stowing away on one of the regiment's box cars, Jimmy was amazed at how his life had changed since then.

After he'd fallen asleep in the hay, he found himself woken up by a lanky New Yorker with sergeant's stripes on his jacket. The sergeant had cussed and cuffed him about the head, and he had been convinced if the train hadn't been rocking along at more than thirty miles an hour, he'd have been thrown off the train on his ass.

Instead, after the train rolled into East St. Louis he'd been hauled before the regiment's colonel, John Brown. The stern officer, grim-faced with a flowing black beard spilling onto his uniform, had asked him, "Boy, do your parents know where you are?"

Jimmy had fired back, "My pa is dead, and my ma's got more mouths to feed than President Cass has got sense."

Brown's smile had been the only time Jimmy had seen mirth on the deeply religious but very dour Colonel's face.

The next question was, "What happened to your pa?"

"Slavers killed him; said they was making examples of men who helped runaways flee."

In a whirlwind of activity after that, Jimmy found himself sworn into the regiment and wearing a uniform two sizes too large. The regiment was ferried across the river where another train took them all the way to St. Joseph on the Missouri River.

From there, the regiment had moved through the Western Territory, drilling as they moved along. A few squatters had settled in the region, but apart from them and some Indians, Jimmy saw nothing that reminded him of his home in Illinois. He'd sat around the campfire at night and listened to the Colonel's thundering voice, sometimes Brown would read from the Bible and other times he'd rail against the slavers in the South.

Brown had said, as they started across the Western Territory that it would have already been open for settlement by God-fearing men were it not for the stench of slavery on the nation. Despite the Compromise of 1820, the Senators from the slave states had refused to allow the Western Territory to organize unless the people who settled could vote to allow slavery. Brown had spat, "Popular sovereignty they say, I say squatter sovereignty!"

And now that the 1st New York had arrived on the Red River, the border between the Western Territory and Texas, maybe things would change. So far, Jimmy wasn't very impressed with army life. It was hurry up and wait and then sitting in the saddle all day, listening to the squeaking of leather.

A voice penetrated through his thoughts, "Father says we're to cross into the promised land, Duckbill."

The men of the 1st New York had taken to calling him "Duckbill" on account of his long nose. Coming from most of the troopers it bothered him, but from the sixteen-year-old Watson, there was no heat in it, and it had become a mark of their friendship.

Watson continued, “He says there’s a town about fifteen miles that away,” he waved across the river. “It’s full of slavers and their get. We’re going to cross this poor excuse for a river and liberate those downtrodden slaves.”

Jimmy found the river crossing uneventful. Wagons were floated, and the horses swam the river, as there were neither fords nor ferries nearby. As the regiment rode through the dense pine and oak forest, Jimmy stayed near Colonel Brown. As one of his runners, if the colonel needed anything, Jimmy was handy to run the errand.

The trail the regiment followed was nothing more than a narrow wagon road. A cavalry trooper raced his horse along the wagon track until he pulled up in front of Brown. With a hasty salute, he said, “Colonel, There’s plantation up ahead. It ain’t much, but they’ve got slaves.”

The thousand men in the regiment were strung out along the wagon road, and when Brown stood in his stirrups, he called out, “Pass the word, we ride to liberate Lord Jehovah’s children. Unless we’re fired on, keep your fingers away from your triggers.”

A bit later, Jimmy followed Brown into the expansive clearing where the plantation house stood. *Calling that a plantation house is a bit like calling Homer a city,* Jimmy thought, allowing his thoughts to return to the place of his birth. The plantation building was a log cabin, bigger than most. Near the edge of the clearing were a half dozen smaller cabins. Also, along the tree line, were stacks of logs. Apparently, as the land was cleared, excess lumber was stacked for future use. Most of the clearing was set aside for farming.

In front of the big cabin stood a middle-aged man and woman standing in front of eight or ten younger people. Troopers from the 1st New York separated them from an equal number of colored men and women.

Jimmy studied the slaves. They were hardly the first negros he'd seen. From time to time, fleeing slaves had hidden on his pa's farm on their way north on the Underground Railroad. These were the first he'd seen who were still trapped on their master's plantation.

From his saddle, Brown frowned as he looked down on the plantation owner and his family. "You have waged war on these poorest of the poor. What have you to say for yourself?"

The planter eyed the armed troopers standing on either side of his family before looking up at Brown. "War? That's rich coming from the man holding a gun on my family. My entire life, I have poured my own blood into the land. I brought my family here to carve a place out of the Texas wilderness." He looked across the clearing at the slaves for a moment before continuing. "I scraped and saved and borrowed enough to buy the means to build a legacy for my children."

Brown's frown turned into a sneer. "The blood you pour is that of the slave. They deserve our compassion, and you bind them in chains."

The planter glared back, "These poor and downtrodden you're so all-fired to protect, receive more from me than the meanest factory worker in your filthy northern factories."

Brown spat at the planter's feet. "Tell that to the man whose skin is flayed away by the inhuman whipping or the woman whose virtue you steal as master."

He raised his voice, turning to the slaves, "Your chains are gone. This is your day of Jubilee." He turned back to the planter, and like Samuel from the Old Testament, passing judgment on Saul, said, "Mene, mene, tekel, upharsin."

He gestured to the soldiers surrounding the man and his family, and they grabbed him by the arms and hauled him away from his distraught wife, who screamed. The man's sons who stepped forward, found themselves staring down pistol barrels.

Troopers forced the planter against the wall of his home. The man refused to look at the men who pointed their weapons at him. Instead, he glared daggers at Brown, who sat, unflinching in the saddle, returning the glare. After what seemed an eternity to Jimmy, Brown raised his hand and in a single, violent gesture, dropped it suddenly.

A single shot echoed across the clearing. One of the troopers standing guard over the planter held a smoking pistol. The planter collapsed against the wall, where blood pooled beneath him.

# Chapter 7

18 March 1852

Will untied the restricting cravat that time and history demanded he wear and threw the black silk cloth down on the floor of his library in the presidential mansion. "What the..." he knew what he wanted to say, but his children were down the hall with their mother and grandmother. He bit back the profanity as he struggled to control his temper. "Why is it that this news took more than two weeks to get here?"

He addressed the question to John Wharton, his Secretary of State, and Juan Seguin, his vice president. They had arrived after church with news of the murder outside of Clarksville. Will left his jacket on as the room was chilled because the weather outside was still biting, even though Spring was only days away.

Seguin shrugged. "It happened up by the border with Arkansas. Most of the militia in Clarksville sided with the rebels, Buck. They've arrested our customs agents on the border, and they've cut the telegraph line."

Will collapsed into the well-worn chair at his desk and swore. “I’m not going to have rabble streaming into Texas and turning this into a broader war, Juan.”

Wharton interjected, “I fear what’ll come if this isn’t brought under control. But technically, the area *is* under martial law, after all, it’s in rebellion.”

“John,” Will swore, “Brown.”

He seethed as he thought about the history he knew from his own memories of a world gone forever. In that history, Brown had been an ardent abolitionist, who had taken the war to the pro-slavery faction in Kansas before attacking a federal arsenal in Virginia in the years leading up the civil war. He’d been charged with treason for the attempt to incite rebellion among the slaves. In a history that would never be that lived only in his memories, the South had used fear and intimidation to maintain control over the slave population. It was no different than the world he now inhabited. In that other world, when abolitionists like Brown threatened that order, Southerners had reacted predictably.

Slowly, he sighed and chuckled. “Is it really paranoia if someone really is out to get you?” he mused.

Juan gave him a curious expression. Wharton frowned at Will for a moment before his lips gradually curved into a smile. “Not really. We Southerners have lived with the threat of insurrection for a couple of hundred years. This John Brown fellow sees all of us as devils complete with pitchforks and tails. Well, maybe not all. After all, word is, he’s asking for us to take his regiment and enroll it as volunteer cavalry in our army.”

He continued, “Part of me finds it appealing. We’re land rich and people poor. If this war grows and draws in even more southern volunteers, we could be facing ten times as many men as we are now. What can we mobilize? Maybe twenty-five or thirty thousand men?"

Will said, "Maybe less if we don't want our economy to collapse. Turning every able-bodied man into a soldier is a good way to destroy our economy. But I take your meaning. On the one hand, Brown's men represent a source of manpower, which we may badly need. But on the other, Brown's brand of abolitionism is bound to stir even more Southerners to fight against us. He's a dagger poised at the heart of the Southland."

Wharton nodded. "Exactly. The question is, can we afford to hold it?"

Seguin went over to Will's desk and opened a drawer. He pulled a decanter out and a few glasses. "I swear, Buck, I don't know if you're trying to hide the good stuff from your children or us. God in heaven, John, but this is complicated."

He poured a drink. "If we ignore what Brown did and welcome him into our army, the reaction from the South could be apocalyptic. If we condemn Brown's action and send him back north, the South is likely to be just an incensed, because Brown is a genie that once unleashed, you can't put back in the bottle."

Will took a drink from Juan. "To hear the two of you talking, it doesn't sound like there's much of a downside to welcoming Brown. Either way, now that he's killing slaveholders, I'm damned if I do and equally damned if I don't."

Seguin took a sip of the fiery drink. "There's a third option. What if we arrest him for the planter's murder? A trial might act as a salve."

Wharton took the third drink and said, "That was my first thought. There's a bit of perverse pleasure this Virginia boy would feel in seeing that damned Yankee swinging from gallows. But I left Virginia behind a long time ago. The question isn't what's good for Virginia, or South Carolina, but what's in Texas' best interest. We're getting a lot of positive press in Northern and European newspapers. Hell, Giuseppe Garibaldi commands the Ninth Infantry largely based upon Texas' willingness to confront the question of slavery."

He took a long pull on the drink before continuing. "If we try Brown for the murder, we risk undoing a lot of the goodwill we're accruing with foreign powers. Hell, that assumes we could even arrest him without starting a fight with his own men."

He drained the glass and set it down. "He's a dagger, no doubt about it. The best place for that dagger is in your hand."

28 March 1852

He bit the end of his pen as he re-read the article.

> *Word, at last, has reached the newspaper of record of Colonel Brown's 1st Provisional New York Cavalry's exploits since leaving civilization behind at St. Joseph, Missouri. The report arrives from opposite the twenty-fifth state, in the Texas Republic, in the desolate frontier town of Clarksville.*
>
> *Upon discovering a large family of enslaved negros, the gallant Colonel Brown and his brave troopers found they had suffered under the*

*overseer's harsh whip. Further, the wealthy slaveowner had sworn allegiance to the traitors against civilization in Beaumont, where the rebels defy the legitimate government of Texas.*

*In the struggle to break the chains of oppression and slavery, the planter, Cornelius Perry was killed. We are pleased to report all of the negros were exculpated and are on their way north.*

Was it too much? Horace Greeley weighed changing some of the wording. After all, the only thing known for sure was the planter's name and that Colonel Brown's men *had* liberated the slaves from said planter. After a final read-through, he set the pen down. It would do. Facts were less important than the truth. Truth was why people paid two cents to read his paper. His readers needed to understand the plight of the slaves down South. They needed to be motivated to do something to end the travesty, and if he needed to gloss over the details, well, that's just what a newspaperman did.

He stood and walked over to the window. From there he could see City Hall. His thoughts traveled far beyond the machine politics of Gotham. He knew Brown's attack on the plantation in East Texas had practically burned up the telegraph lines across the country when word had leaked out. Southern Congressmen like William King claimed the murder of Perry was proof positive servile insurrection was a growing threat.

Greeley worried that King was using the crisis in Texas to further his own political ambition. He turned away from the window and picked up an article written by one of his reporters reporting from Washington City.

*'Tis said the time to make hay is when the sun shines. Senator King from Alabama has taken this to heart. In the aftermath of the Attack on slaveholders' interest in North Eastern Texas, in an area under control of the Junta in Beaumont, Senator King has held court in the Upper Chamber, holding hearing upon hearing over the slanderous allegation that Colonel Brown executed Mr. Perry in cold blood. King has put forth a bill demanding President Travis of Texas arrest Brown for the alleged murder of the slaver. As of yet, there has been no response from Austin.*

Greeley picked his pen up and after inking it, made a few adjustments before putting the article to the side. A typesetter would be by shortly to collect it. The next piece was from the same reporter but picked up the narrative from the perspective of Northern Whigs.

A smile flickered across his face as he read the acerbic words of William Seward.

*Senator Wm. Seward, when asked about Colonel Brown's incursion into Rebel-held Texas, was quoted as saying, "The fire-eaters should have reconsidered their ill-advised Texas adventures. Now that the boot is on the other foot, may they find it pinches mercilessly."*

*When asked if the worthy senator favors additional aid to Texas, Seward replied, "The United States are neutral in our neighbor's domestic disturbances. To that end, it behooves President Cass to relocate the army to the Louisiana border with Texas to stop further filibustering. As the President is content to dither while Texas burns, if men of valor in the North wish to aid men of like mind in Texas, who am I to stop them, for that matter, who is President Cass to stop them? That ship has long sailed from its harbor."*

Greeley set the article down. His pen hovered over the text as he gave it one more perusal. He liked it just fine, he decided, and he added it to the articles ready for the typesetters.

Seward's words, while matching the convictions of most abolitionists in the North, gave him pause. The presidential election was less than ten months away. Both the Whigs and Democrats would be hosting their conventions in the summer, and he couldn't help but admit, at least to himself, Seward's views could lead to conflict within the Whigs' ranks. As popular as Seward was in New England, among Southern Whigs, all loyal unionists, they would as soon hang Seward as look at him.

In the North, the faction within the Whig party that favored abolition was large. In the South, the Whigs viewed slavery as a necessary evil in some cases and in others, a societal good. Greeley feared the two wings might deadlock over the issue of slavery. With Southern adventurers filibustering in Texas, there was no fig leaf behind which the Southern Whigs could hope to hide. Even if it tore his party asunder, Greeley decided, abolition must become a central plank in the Whig platform and whomever the Whigs nominated for president would be a Northern man of convictions.

It would be better than the battle royal the Democrats would face, Greeley decided. In the North, some Democrats favored the Southern view on slavery, there were also Democrats who supported abolition. In the South, you had Democrats who clambered for Secession at the drop of a hat, while others were firm unionists. If they couldn't figure out their political allegiances, they could come out of their convention in a three- or four-way race.

No, Greeley decided. While the Whig party might be heading for a splintering into two factions. The Democrats were fracturing into three. With the thought of what might befall the Democratic party in the summer, Greeley picked up his pen and began to write.

29 March 1852

"That was a waste of time, Payton." G.T. Beauregard said, slapping his gloves on his trousers in frustration.

The army's Quartermaster General nodded as he tugged at his own gloves. "I believe we could have put that damned loudmouth Robert Potter in his place if your own governor hadn't shown up."

Beauregard swore, his voice laced with acid. "God help military men. Politicians demand that we kowtow to their demands, and then when those demands bring ruin, they blame us. I wasn't expecting Joe Walker to show up and tell us how the cow's going to eat the cud."

His voice shifted into a falsetto that sounded remarkably like Potter's. "If you don't chase down that Yankee rabble, the whole of civilization will come undone."

Wyatt chuckled. "I didn't realize you had a flair for the theatrics, G.T. For a moment, I was sure I had been transported back in time, like some specter of Dickens'

Christmas past, to repeat the last hour of my life. Heaven forbid."

The two officers reached the street, content to keep their backs to the modest courthouse that served as the provisional government's capitol building. "You know, Payton, I don't want to appear unsympathetic about that fellow who was gunned down by that Brown fellow or ignore the possible threat a regiment of cavalry crossing the Red River, but they're nearly two-hundred-fifty miles away through some of the most inhospitable country a bunch of abolitionists will ever find."

Wyatt said, "I don't like giving credit to Bob Potter, but even a broken pocket watch is right twice a day, and he's right about the need to send a message, both to the folks living up near the Arkansas border and to Southerners alike."

Beauregard shook his head, "I'll not deny that. But once the reinforcements arrive from Mississippi, Georgia, and the Carolinas, I intend to attack Johnston's army. From a military standpoint, Brown's a minor distraction, too far away to quickly connect with the enemy. Unfortunately, Governor Walker agrees with Potter. How many men do you reckon would mobilize in that corner of the country if we ordered them to take on Brown and his men?"

The sound of a train whistle nearly drowned Wyatt as he said, "On the muster rolls, we've got five or six hundred men up near the Red River, but on a good day you'd be lucky to turn out three hundred."

Beauregard grimaced. "If the rumors are true that Brown brought down upwards of a thousand men, I'm not sure how effective three hundred would be. I'm not looking for Leonidas and his Spartans, we know how that turned out."

The jingling of bridles and squeaking leather came from the direction of the train depot, interrupting their conversation. A column of gray jacketed cavalry was riding two abreast. At the head, one of the troopers carried the blue flag with a single star adopted by the Southern volunteers.

"Expecting more men today, Payton?"

Wyatt nodded. "A few hundred cavalry from Alabama."

Beauregard studied the men riding by. Every one of them wore a pistol at his hip. Like as not, they carried Samuel Colt's newer model revolvers. Rifle scabbards were attached to each trooper's saddle. He liked what he saw. They carried themselves with the air of men who'd give worse than they'd take.

He leaned over to Wyatt, "Perhaps we've found a solution to our problem." With that, he waved to an officer, riding alongside the column. The bearded officer wheeled away from troopers and guided his mount over. Beauregard felt the cavalry officer's intense gaze as he casually saluted.

"A fine cavalry squadron you've got there, Major."

"Yes, sir," the officer drawled. "Just point me and my boys in the direction of the enemy, and we'll kill a chance of 'em."

Feeling buoyed by the enthusiastic reply, Beauregard said, "By God, I like your spirit. General Wyatt and I were just talking about an itch that needs scratching. Why don't you find my headquarters once your men are bivouacked, Major..."

"Forrest, sir. Bedford Forrest."

# Chapter 8

11 April 1852

*This is a hell of a way to spend Easter*, Charlie Travis thought as he gripped the wicker basket. He chanced a look up. The airbag was tied closed with a silk rope, to keep any hydrogen from escaping, and stealing the airship's lift.

Then he looked down and felt his stomach trying to climb its way out of his mouth. He leaned back and swallowed hard. "You might not want to look directly down. Can get a mite dizzy doing that."

Charlie resisted the urge to snap at his companion. The young student from the mechanical and technical school that was part of Trinity College, was busy connecting a wire into the portable telegraph box pushed up against one side of the basket on a tiny table. Swallowing his own bile, Charlie managed to choke out,

"How many times have y'all tested this damned thing, Sam?"

"Plenty of times, Charlie. We even took Mr. Borden up in the balloon before hauling it to the front. *This* is the third balloon we've made," Sam Williams said defensively. "So, the odds of this crashing and killing us isn't near as high as if we were still using the first balloon."

"What happened to the first balloon?"

"It crashed. But the man in the basket only broke his arm and leg."

Charlie's stomach lurched as the long rope connecting the balloon to the ground was let out further. He had to focus on something else before he lost his breakfast. "How'd your pa let you do something like this? I can't imagine Sam Williams, banking impresario that he is, would let his son ride in this, let alone on a battlefield."

Sam grinned. "Once Austin decided to follow Pa into business, nobody really complained about me attending the mechanical engineering program at Trinity. I guess Pa's happy I've found something that challenges me."

Charlie frowned as the wind buffeted the basket, making it sway back and forth. "I've met your pa, and he doesn't seem the kind of man who'd let even his second son climb into a balloon on a battlefield."

Chuckling, Sam said, "He doesn't know about this. I'd like to keep it that way." He leaned over the telegraph box and pressed his finger against a metal key. "Plus, as of yet, I'm the only student crazy enough to volunteer who knows Mr. Morse's code. What about you? I heard you were second in command of an infantry battalion."

Charlie closed his eyes as the wind made the basket sway more than before. “Colonel Garibaldi volunteered me. Said having eyes overhead like an eagle would be worth more than having me as his number two.”

With one hand, Charlie gripped one of the ropes connecting the basket to the balloon. With the other, he clasped the binoculars around his neck. “Alright, how much further do we have to go?”

“The ground crew will tether us at a thousand feet. From there, we’ll be able to see seven or even eight miles away.”

Charlie wrenched his eyes away from the basket’s bottom and blinked away tears at the yellow orb of the sun rising in the sky. He looked through the binoculars, scanning Johnston’s defensive line. For the past couple of months, the army had been preparing to advance against the rebels and their Southern allies. Supplies had turned West Liberty into a sizable depot. A steady stream of rifles, cartridges, and field pieces had flowed out of the gun works and iron foundry in Trinity Park. The ink on the order to march, to come to grips with the rebels, was still drying when General Johnston hastily countermanded his own order when he learned Beauregard was bringing his army west.

“Why’re the rebels attacking? They’ve sat on their asses all winter long. Why now?” Sam Williams looked at him with passing confusion.

Charlie shrugged. “Probably for the same reason General Johnston had been about to attack. For the rebels to win, they have to either destroy Johnston’s army or force the army back to Austin and demand my pa surrender the capital.”

Sam offered, "And for us, it's the opposite, we've got to destroy their army or capture their leaders in Beaumont?"

Still scanning the ground below, Charlie said, "That's right. Personally, I'd rather take the fight to the rebels. Sitting here waiting for Beauregard's army to attack seems like a lost opportunity."

Sam snickered, "General-in-chief Charles Travis, master, and commander. Why doesn't Johnston listen to you?"

Charlie gave the seventeen-year-old Williams a rude gesture before continuing. "We've got a bit more than seven thousand men here. The recent volunteers from the South have swollen the rebel army to twenty thousand. The general may have decided it's better to have the enemy bleed on our defensive positions instead of the other way around."

A flash of something caught Charlie's attention. In the distance, he saw several more flickers, followed by roiling white smoke. Several seconds elapsed before he heard the thunder of enemy field guns firing on the defenders.

Any thought of being an armchair general fled Charlie's mind as he tallied the number of flashes. He swung the binoculars toward the Texian army's hastily dug field works. Geysers of dirt flew into the sky when shells burrowed into the trench works before detonating. The blue jackets of the provisional Marine battalion stood out in an army uniformly adorned in butternut. Those Marines sheltered behind dirt walls.

"A battery of guns, about nine hundred yards east of our right flank."

He heard the rhythmic clacking of the key striking the metal plate and knew his words would arrive below as fast as the teenager could transmit the message.

At the other end of the defensive works, several miles away, more rebel guns opened fire. More hastily erected trenches sheltered the men protecting the army's left flank. He saw the flag of the 9th infantry flying defiantly over the earthen ramparts.

After giving the details to Sam, he turned and edged around the teen, who tapped out the last bit of information, and looked to the west. The Trinity River was in the distance. Even from a thousand feet in the sky, it was but a ribbon of blue. Despite the rebels' destruction of the railroad bridge over the river, it was still the most direct line between Beaumont and Austin, as far as settlements, farms, and infrastructure were concerned. Had Beauregard decided to flank the army, Johnston could just as easily put the river between the two armies, thwarting the rebel army's advance.

The sound of more artillery brought Charlie back to the other side of the basket. Several dozen flashes revealed where the enemy's grand battery was located. As the news was telegraphed to the waiting men below, Charlie wondered how the men in the center of the Texian line were handling the bombardment. Jesse Running Creek's Ranger company was there, holding the center of the front along with the rest of the army's Rangers.

The problem with East Texas, G.T. Beauregard thought, was there were too few roads. With much of the railroad destroyed between the Trinity River and Beaumont, there had been no choice but to use the road that ran alongside the railroad bed. While it was well-maintained by the standards to which he was accustomed, the solitary road was insufficient to handle an army of twenty thousand as they marched into battle.

Even though only forty miles separated Beaumont from the Trinity River, those forty miles were through one of the densest forests which he'd had the misfortune to traverse. Even so, farms and plantations had pushed the forest back from Beaumont a few miles. He was grateful for the cavalry under his command, but the near-impenetrable wood through which the army pushed made him glad he'd dispatched the Alabamans under Major Forrest to the north. Until he could break out of the Piney Woods, his cavalry was of limited use.

Breaking out of the Piney Woods really was what today was about. Since encountering General Johnston's scouts yesterday, he had deployed his own cavalry and skirmishers to screen his moves. Not that it mattered much. Without the benefit of other well-maintained roads, flanking Johnston's army was impractical. He'd have to use his men to carve a path through the woods, carry boats along to ferry his force over the Trinity. There was scant hope he could cross the river without confronting the enemy.

He raised his binoculars to his eyes. Instead of meeting his command in the dense forest, like they had a few months before, Johnston chose to fortify his army along a shallow creek running parallel to the river a few miles away.

Now that most of his army were volunteers from the South, there had been rumblings through unofficial channels that if he didn't use his formidable army to destroy the enemy, he'd find himself replaced by someone who would take the fight to Johnston.

If he failed, who would they replace him with? It wasn't as though he was the only West Point graduate who could command the army, but *Dammit, I'm the best one to command* it, he thought.

So, he'd been up since the previous night deploying his artillery in whatever groves and pastures that were available. His remaining cavalry had been dismounted and put on the flanks. He didn't think Johnston would attempt to flank him, not when he had far more men under arms than the Texians, but best to not take chances.

He had deployed his infantry behind his artillery. He'd been planning for this moment for several months. So, too had his army. There was no getting around the compelling reasons for massing musket fire. To force an enemy from the field, you had to kill or maim enough to break their morale. Volley fire had been an effective tactic a hundred years before anyone heard of Napoleonic tactics.

Now though, Beauregard refused to send his men against the Texians' guns standing shoulder to shoulder. He's spent the last few months begging rifled muskets from state armories across the South. The net effect was his army would still advance through the thicket with too many muskets and too few rifles. It was also the reason he was sending in his Texas Brigade against the enemy's center. Most of them were armed with breechloading rifles and were, for now, better trained than much of his army.

The strategy was simple. His artillery would open fire first and soften up the enemy's defenses. Then the infantry would advance, under cover of both the artillery and the forest. With a three-to-one advantage, Beauregard intended for his men to swarm over the enemy. Because of the heavily wooded terrain, the defenders would be deprived of clear fields of fire. The thought his men could approach undetected to within fifty yards of the enemy line in some cases brought a smile to his face.

"Sir," a voice broke through his reverie. "It's time."

Beauregard turned and nodded at his orderly. "Pass along the order."

Riders raced away with his orders, and a few minutes later, the southernmost battery opened fire, followed a few minutes later by the northern batteries.

Several officers waited nearby for orders. As the thunder of the guns rolled across the wilderness, he let a moment of optimism through. "Gentlemen, I do believe we've caught the enemy napping. With any luck, our artillery will pound the enemy to pieces. It'll be the devil's own problem returning fire with any accuracy. You've got to see something to hit it."

One of the men pointed into the western sky, "What in the name of Jehovah is that?"

Beauregard turned and looked up. Floating over the enemy line was an observation balloon.

Captain Jesse Running Creek leaned back against the wicker gabion, and fished a handkerchief from his pocket, running it across his grimy face. He looked at the cloth, it was smeared with dirt. But the gabions were in place and sandbags filled in the gaps. Now all there was to do was wait.

"Chief," his first sergeant collapsed beside him, "Hell of a way to spend Easter Sunday. Preparing defenses so we can send a lot of bastards to Hell."

He took the handkerchief Jesse offered and wiped his own dirt-stained face. As he handed it back, he wore a half smile, "I hear tell, Indians have fertility celebrations instead of Easter, what do the Cherokee do?"

Jesse glowered at his first sergeant. "Dunno. My pa dragged my ass to the Baptist church, probably the same as yours. And if I squirmed around too much, I'd get a hiding the likes of which I'd not soon forget."

His sergeant pulled a plug of tobacco from his haversack and bit a chunk from it. "Not me, I hid in the woods. But, Lordy, the whipping I got afterward made me wish for the second coming."

The ground shook and from the east came the thunder of artillery. In the narrow strip of no-man's-land between their hastily fortified position and the thicket of trees, a geyser of dirt sprayed into the sky when a shell plowed into the ground as it exploded.

Jesse grimaced as he climbed back to his feet and picked up his rifle. "No rest for the wicked, Sergeant. Before long, second coming or no, there's a lot of men that'll find themselves in Hell tonight." He raised his voice, "Stand to, men. Stay low, but let's keep an eye on where those trees start. Not much time to react if they come a-running."

Time dragged on as shell after shell churned the dirt in front of their position. Occasionally a shell would strike a gabion or pulverize a sandbag or explode over the crudely built fortification. Before long, the guns behind their lines replied.

It seemed that for every shell falling in front of them, the artillery under Colonel Sherman threw back three rounds in response. As a shell exploded nearby, and the gabion he sheltered behind shook as shrapnel peppered it, Jesse didn't care if their own artillery were better, faster, or more accurate than the rebels. He just wanted to barrage to end.

Just like it had started, the barrage from the Southerners stopped nearly as suddenly. Jesse shifted a sandbag squeezed in between two wicker gabions and looked past the no-man's-land. He swore when he saw men wearing butternut filtering through the trees.

"We've got rebels to our front. Fire as you will," Jesse shouted. He slid the barrel of his own rifle through the wedge, resting it on a burlap sandbag, and drew a bead on a solitary soldier who was running between two trees. He fired and watched the soldier tumble to the ground as he grabbed at his leg.

Jesse levered open the breech and inserted a brass cartridge. He snapped the breech closed and fired at another living target.

Men, wearing the same butternut uniforms as the regular army, were firing back at Jesse and his Ranger company. And there were a lot of them. Bullets thudded into the opposite side of the gabion.

"Chief, take a gander," Jesse's first sergeant said.

Looking toward the tree line, there were hundreds of men, crouching behind trees or seeking shelter near the ground. Jesse cursed and said, "Pass the word to the other companies we're about to get visitors."

Before the rebels declared their intent to overthrow the government, the small professional army had six specialized Ranger companies; they were four-hundred and fifty of the most hardened and best-trained soldiers in Texas. While many infantry companies and cavalry troops were stationed across the Republic's far-flung borders, those six companies continually drilled for war. Every week, they spent hours on the firing line, practicing. Or marching. Jesse's legs tingled as he thought about how much marching his men had done. When they hadn't been shooting or marching, they had held wargames, pitting one company against another.

The army had more than doubled since the rebellion, but those six companies were all the Rangers in it. And they held the position at the center of the Texian fortifications, a few hundred yards in front of the army's grand artillery battery. If they cracked, the whole line could unravel. *And there are a hell of a lot more of them than there are of us,* Jesse thought as he looked through the gap between gabions.

From the woods, he heard a shrill yelping sound as thousands of men raised their voices, steeling themselves for what was to come. A glance confirmed they were running between the trees, some stumbling on the undergrowth. Jesse raised his rifle and fired. Along the entire line, thousands of rifles barked out, responding to the attacking rebels.

In Jesse's narrow view, he saw dozens topple to the ground. But even more leapt over their fallen comrades, racing to reach the barricade between them and the defenders. Jesse reloaded and fired again.

Centered in the middle of the Ranger's defense was a battery of four Gatling guns. The shrieking ripping sound of their fire could be heard over the roar of the Rangers' raging fire, as more than a thousand rounds per minute were sprayed like a fire hose dousing a fire. But the fire they extinguished were the lives of men racing across the field of battle.

Jesse watched in horror as men tumbled to the ground, torn apart by the heavy slugs from the Gatlings. Despite the constant fire from the guns, many enemy soldiers reached the barricade, stepping over their fallen comrades.

Jesse dropped his rifle and yanked the revolver he wore at his side. He raised the pistol and fired at a rifleman, clambering over the wicker obstacle. No sooner had his victim fallen away than he was replaced by another man, whose scream of rage was turned into a cry of pain when Jesse fired again.

Six rounds, six shots. Six men who tried to kill him were heaped on the opposite side of the gabion and sandbag fortifications. The hammer snapped onto an empty chamber, and Jesse's mind registered his weapon was empty. He was ready to throw it in the face of the next man who tried to claw his way over the barricade.

It dawned on him the Gatlings had fallen silent, and the gunfire nearby was slacking. Gunsmoke swirled around where he and his Rangers had made their stand,

and the no-man's-land was cloaked in low lying smoke. As the ringing in his ears faded, he became aware of voices screaming out in pain. One plaintive cry, higher pitched than the others, called for his mother.

"Lord have mercy," Jesse turned and saw his first sergeant. A rag had been wrapped around his wrist, but blood seeped through the cotton, streaking his hand red. "The only thing worse than a battle won is one that is lost."

The smoke between their barricade and the nearby trees cleared enough so that Jesse could see. The ground was carpeted with dead and wounded. Close by the trees, he saw enemy soldiers going among the fallen. When they found an injured comrade, a couple of more men hurried forward, carrying a stretcher.

Colonel Jason Lamont put more pressure on his left leg, and although it twinged with pain, he could put his weight on it.

"Colonel, I think you twisted your ankle when your horse fell on you. It'll hurt for a week or two, but you'll be fine. At least as much as the leg will ever be. Now, if you'll excuse me. There are a lot more boys that I'm not going to be able to say that about, who need me."

Lamont waved the regimental surgeon away. What remained of the day promised grim work for the doctor, who had a few months before been running a thriving medical practice along the Saluda River. He gripped the cane he'd used since Travis shot him in the knee years before.

The steady crackle of gunfire in the distance was a constant reminder the battle was not yet over. Despite two attempts earlier in the day to knock General Johnston's Texians from behind their makeshift fortifications, the army had failed in its task. Now, elements of Johnston's army were in pursuit. The idea of the smaller Texian army pursuing the much larger provisional army reminded him of a little dog nipping at the hoofs of a horse.

If the dog were too aggressive, he'd find the horse could still kick and do a lot of damage. As if to bring that home, a battery of horse-drawn artillery rolled by. A small troop of cavalry rode ahead, clearing the road of retreating foot soldiers. The army still had a lot of fight left in it. There were thousands of men who had yet to be fed into the meat grinder of battle. The challenge that previously hobbled Beauregard's army, along the narrow lane, now posed the same problem to Johnston's Texians as they hounded the Southern army.

"Uncle, I mean, Colonel, thank God you're alright. I heard about your horse and thought you'd been hurt."

Lamont turned. His nephew, Elliott Brown, rode toward him, winding his way between clumps of soldiers from the regiment, who, like Lamont, were waiting for orders.

Young Elliott Brown's neatly pressed and clean gray uniform was now streaked with dirt and torn where sharp thorns had tugged at it when the regiment had advanced through thick undergrowth. But he wore his kepi at a jaunty angle, reflecting the resilience of youth.

He slipped a hand into his jacket and retrieved a folded note, "Major Moultrie's compliments, he's bulled back his battalion wing. They've been replaced by those Georgia boys who arrived last week."

Lamont took the note and read the hastily scrawled script. "How many men did he lose, Lieutenant?"

Brown scratched at the weeks' worth of scruff on his face. "Adding it to what we lost when we attacked the enemy earlier today, I've confirmed thirty-five dead and a bit more than a hundred wounded. But some of them won't survive the retreat to Beaumont, Uncle."

Lamont was tempted to correct the familial familiarity, but he bit his lip when he saw the haunted look on his nephew's face. Instead, as he stood on his bad leg, he managed to bite back the pain he felt. In the young officer's battle-worn face, Lamont saw his sister, the boy's mother. He wanted to tell him how proud he was of the young man. Every time he'd turn around, looking for a runner, Elliott had been there. The words hung in his throat. He gripped the young man's arm and nodded. Then he said, "Before I beg that horse from you, go find General Hampton. Tell him the Third is assembled and ready for whatever is to come."

He watched his nephew ride off, in search of the brigadier commanding the small South Carolinian brigade before settling himself on a log to wait. War wasn't what he'd expected. As a teenager, his copy of *Ivanhoe* had fallen apart from his reading and rereading it. The image of Ivanhoe's nobility played no small part in how Lamont saw himself and other members of the planter aristocracy. Soldiers nobly riding or marching off to war, with the promises of their wives and sweethearts in their hearts met their match in the Piney Woods of Texas. Guns that could tear a line of soldiers to ribbons held no glory. Idealized images from the Revolutionary War couldn't hold a candle to the death and destruction the Texians had visited on him and his men.

A bit later, his nephew cantered back to him, a look of relief on his face. He dismounted and handed the reins to Lamont, "We've been ordered eastward. General Hampton's been instructed to prepare a defensive line near our encampment outside Beaumont."

# Chapter 9

Late April 1852

Jimmy bit back a sob. Tears spilled down his powder-caked cheeks as he stood over the open pit. The body sliding down the side, wrapped in a blanket was small. Too small to be Watson Brown's torn and bleeding body. The regiment had fought a running battle starting the day before, continuing until just after dawn. The rebels and their slaver allies had finally dispatched cavalry to challenge the 1st New York's primacy in Northeast Texas.

Jimmy shuddered, closing his eyes as for a moment he relived the hell of the past twenty-four hours. They had just finished burning another slaver's house and were preparing to head south, Colonel Brown had decided to accept President Travis' offer to join the freedom-loving Texian army when word arrived of rebel cavalry approaching. Colonel Brown had deployed his little army on one end of the clearing in which the farm was burning. He sent forward a platoon to see what was coming, and they waited.

To Jimmy, time crawled by, as he waited, his nose stinging with the smell of burning wood. Thirty minutes or an hour passed, he couldn't say for sure when he heard gunfire coming from where the troopers had gone. Moments later, a horseman streaked across the field, riding at a horse-killing speed. Before he could bring his mount to stop, he had yelled, "There must be a hundred rebels behind us, Colonel!"

Brown stood in his saddle, his thundering voice could be heard across the field, "Up, men! We'll send those sons of perdition to judgment!"

At first, it seemed a jaunt to Jimmy as he galloped after the colonel. He and Watson were determined to keep up with Brown, ready to carry any order. They had gone less than a mile when they joined the platoon that had gone ahead. Sure enough, they were being pushed back by men dressed in brownish uniforms. Most were dismounted, sheltering behind trees, firing on Brown's men with what seemed impossible speed.

Watson said, "Hellfire, Jimmy. They're armed with breechloaders."

The colonel must have heard his son. He bellowed, "At them, boys! Get in close and let's end this."

Some of the men tried racing through the woods, but there were too many trees, and a rider and his horse made for a big target. Brown dismounted and led several hundred men forward. Most carried muzzle-loading carbines and they fired as they advanced. Jimmy stayed close to the colonel. They had closed to within a hundred feet when he became aware of a burst of gunfire on the regiment's left flank.

Almost instantly, the advancing line ground to a halt. An officer's voice rose about the din of battle. "Wheel to the left, men, we're flanked."

To Jimmy, it seemed every slaver in creation had landed on the regiment's flank. Colonel Brown flung himself into the saddle and rode into the milling mass of men to the regiment's left. Following hard on the colonel's heels, Jimmy pulled up when he saw gray jacketed men forcing blue-jacketed troopers back, rolling up the dismounted line.

In the confusion of the battle, Jimmy had emptied his pistol as he and Watson stayed close to the colonel. Chaos reigned. Before long, the regiment was retracing their route, retreating the way they had come, past the still burning farmhouse. The rest of the day had been a painful blur.

At some point, during the night he'd found himself surrounded by men in gray jackets, firing and swearing as they descended on Brown's headquarter command, the Southerners were gone nearly as fast as they had appeared. Jimmy ran his finger through a hole in his sleeve as he realized how close he'd come to becoming a casualty.

Slowly he became aware of a voice raging. "No, no. Not Watson."

A drop of rain splashed on Jimmy's forehead, bringing him back to the present of the gray morning. Another drop followed. He looked into the leaden sky as a few more drops fell. They mixed in with the tears cascading down his cheeks.

He turned to the colonel. Brown stood back, his left arm in a sling, his right, holding a Bible. The expression on the colonel's face mirrored the cumulus clouds overhead. Like the thunder in the distance, Brown rumbled, "Like Job I am. Tested by the Almighty. Like the Israelites of old, by day, we will follow the cloud of the Lord and by night his burning presence. Our blood that has been shed is the price to redeem God's children, enslaved though they may be. We will take the fight to the heathen, to Esau's children. They have sown the wind, let them reap the whirlwind."

Drops of rain became a steady patter, and Jimmy donned his vulcanized rubber poncho as he waited for the pit to be filled in. By the time the troopers finished burying their comrades, the rain had turned into a downpour, as though the Almighty attempted to scour the stain of battle from the face of the earth. He couldn't help rolling his red-rimmed eyes heavenward and wonder why he'd ever left home. His best friend lay in the pit, dead, and for what purpose? As the bugler sounded Boots and Saddles and the rest of the regiment mounted up, Jimmy felt more alone than ever.

"Papa, tell Davy to leave me alone," a young voice piped up at the dinner table.

Will turned his attention away from his conversation with Juan Seguin and eyed nine-year-old David Stern Travis gravely. The boy wore an impish smile, knowing he'd done something to upset his eleven-year-old sister and enjoyed every minute of it.

The boy's auburn locks fell to just above his eyes, which twinkled when they stared at Will. Will's lips twitched. His son's irrepressible smile had won over many adults who'd dined with Will and his family over the years, and Will found himself ready to return the smile until Becky elbowed him in the ribs.

Wincing, Will said, "That'll be enough, David. Leave your sister be."

The boy settled down. Over the years, Will's children had learned when their father was calling them out. Usually, David was "Davy," and Elizabeth was 'Liza.' But when they were being called to muster, it was David or Elizabeth, followed by their middle names. Far more often, he had to put his incorrigible son on notice.

As though that were the signal, the door from the kitchen opened, and a couple of servants employed in the presidential mansion brought lunch to the table.

In between bites, Will turned to Becky, "Funny how they always go to the parent they think will be the most sympathetic."

Becky took a sip from her glass before saying, "Liza knows her papa will keep her devil-may-care little brother in line."

Will chuckled. "And Liza knows she can't pull anything past her mother."

Juan Seguin's wife leaned over and said, "See, Juanito, the president and Senora Travis have the right of it. With only two children at home, they're no longer outnumbered."

As if to underscore her words, she waved toward the end of the table where three of their own children sat.

Seguin allowed a small smile. "I'd wish for all of them to be still at home. Like Buck and Becky worry over Charlie, you and I worry about Jose and Juan. I wish all our children were with us, sitting around the table, eating dinner. Knowing they're risking their lives on the front keeps me up at night."

Later, following the after-church dinner, Becky and Maria shooed the children out of the dining room and left Will and Seguin alone. After watching Becky go, Will turned to his vice president, "We try not to worry the children, but Becky and I were worried sick after news of our victory over the rebels a few weeks ago until we received a telegram from Charlie telling us he had come through unscathed."

Seguin nodded. "I know the feeling. It breaks my heart to see Maria reading the newspaper, scanning the names of soldiers killed or wounded in battle. The only relief is seeing her sad smile afterward. Sad for all the mothers and wives who've lost a husband or father, but glad we're not in their number."

The door to the kitchen opened, and an older Tejano came through, carrying a pitcher. He spoke with a heavy accent, "More lemonade, your excellency?"

Will smiled and held up his glass. Ice clinked in the glass as it filled up. Briefly, he was grateful to the faculty and inventors at Trinity College, who had invented a commercial ice making machine the previous year. For a modest price, any family in Austin could have blocks of ice delivered.

He took a sip of the cold sweet drink before continuing, "I was disappointed to receive word from Colonel West. Our best chance at cutting off the rebels from Louisiana was our attempt to destroy Fort Austin at Sabine Roads."

"More names in the newspaper, Buck. Although, had West succeeded, he could have blown up the bridge's support pylons on our side of the river." Seguin said. "I wish we could just sail the Gulf Squadron up the Sabine river and blow up the damned bridge. Cut Beauregard and his army off, and we can end this rebellion once and for all."

Will found himself nodding in agreement. "You and me both, Juan. President Cass tells us he's ordered the Southern volunteers to return home and then tells us that blowing up the bridge over the Sabine would be poorly received."

He swore before he continued, "Poorly received? An act of war is what he meant. That fool is doing nothing to stamp out the Southern volunteers spilling across the Sabine. And he has the gall to threaten us if we damage any part of the bridge in Louisiana. All he'd have to do is order General Scott to send in the army, and they could close the border. But Scott sits in New York drinking fine wine and hobnobbing with high society while the army is encamped in Missouri and in the Indian territory, doing nothing."

Seguin said, "The Whigs and Democrats will have their national conventions in the next couple of months. That could change things. Do you think the Democrats will stay with Cass?"

"Not likely." Will reflected on the question before elaborating. In the world he'd come from, both the Democrats and Republicans of the 20th century had been durable united national parties. In the world in which he'd lived for the last sixteen years, he worried things had diverged so much that the Republicans might not emerge at all. In their place, the Whigs and Democrats were a motley collection of regional alliances. He added, "The Northern Democrats have had as much of their Southern counterparts as they can stomach. They may share the same views about tariffs and the overall role of government as their Southern neighbors, but by and large, they favor the national union over their Southern neighbors. Cass is loathed by both wings of his party. If he escapes from the convention with his nomination intact, I'll be surprised."

"What about the Whigs?"

Will shrugged. "Couldn't say. Most of them in the North are applauding our Free-Birth law, well, except those who say it doesn't go far enough. I suspect that they won't be able to help themselves but to nominate someone who's sufficiently abolitionist enough for New England. But that'll be too much for the Southern Whigs to tolerate. I hope the Whigs don't fracture, but it's a possibility. If the Whigs win in November, they'll crack down on these damned Southern Volunteers who are adding their own numbers to the rebels."

"For our sake, I hope the Whigs win," Seguin said, "but every time the winds blow against Southern Democrats, the worst of that lot scream secession. What'll we do if they lose in November and decide to secede?"

The lemonade in Will's mouth seemed to turn to ash, as he considered Seguin's question. After swallowing, he said, "We'll blow that bridge over the Sabine to hell and gone."

Major Charlie Travis cussed the wind that swung the wicker basket back and forth beneath the giant, silk balloon.

"Who'd I piss off again to get stuck here with you, Sam?" Charlie's stomach lurched as the wind shifted direction and yanked at the basket.

Seventeen-year-old Sam Williams laughed as he checked the wires to the telegraph. "That's easy. Go up in something like this once, and you're the expert. Since its first deployment, this fat bitch has had a perfect record. General Johnston thinks it's safer for you up here than charging into battle beside Colonel Garibaldi. I guess he didn't read the report about the first one catching fire when the firebox failed."

"Remind me again, why you volunteered, Sam?"

"The height doesn't bother me, I'm not afraid of falling."

Charlie closed his eyes, wishing the basket would stop swinging, "I'm not really afraid of falling. No, I'm just afraid of what will happen when I hit the ground."

Sam laughed, "You won't hit terminal velocity until fifteen hundred feet. There's always the chance you'd survive. We're ready to start transmitting."

The balloon hung over the Texian line, just outside of Beaumont. Across from the army's trenches were the rebels' defensive works. He'd heard General Beauregard had studied engineering at West Point, and it was evident some thought had gone into the defenses ringing the town.

If Beaumont had held more than a thousand souls before the war, Charlie would have been surprised. But as the largest town in the part of Texas in rebellion, it had multiplied over the past half-year. The oldest part of the town was a haphazard maze of roads, barely more than cattle trails. The newer sections radiating from the railroad were platted with grid-like precision. All of it, old and new, nestled against a bend in the Neches River.

"There are a few boats on the river, Sam. I thought the navy had bottled up the mouth of the Sabine River. Damned shame they haven't been able to get past those forts down at Sabine Pass."

After Sam finished sending a message down the wire wrapped around a strand of the thick rope tethering the balloon, he turned, "I've heard that several coastal forts that had been closed over the past few years were emptied of their heavy coastal guns by the Southern volunteers and shipped west. We know what they've got at Forts Austin and Washington, but I wonder if they've fortified the Neches north of where it runs into the Sabine?

Charlie lifted his binoculars to his eyes and followed the river toward where it emptied into Sabine Lake. Farms largely replaced the dense forest along the riverbank up and down the Neches. Several large plantations nestled against the river. It was cotton planting season, yet the fields were empty. As he swept his binoculars one way and then the other, he idly wondered if the slaves had run off or if they had been forced to build the embankments and bastions protecting Beaumont from Johnston's army.

After a final pass, he said, "If the rebels have fortified the river, they've done so closer to where it feeds into Sabine Lake."

He let the glasses fall onto his chest, suspended by a leather strap, and looked at the two armies scattered across the landscape below. The rebels and their allies formed a bubble around the town with both left and right flanks anchored on the Neches, north and south of town. He estimated their fortifications stretched close to three miles. More than twenty thousand men sheltered behind those walls. Worse, trains continued to come and go, bringing in fresh supplies and replenishing Beauregard's losses from the 2nd Battle of the Piney Woods a few weeks before.

General Johnston had pursued Beauregard's retreating army in the aftermath of the Texian victory, but the rebel general had been content to sacrifice hundreds, if not thousands of men to shield his retreat. Charlie thought Johnston could have forced another battle before the rebels had reached the safety of Beaumont except the pursuing army was only a third the size of the force they pursued, and he shuddered to think about the number of men killed or wounded to gain their victory in the Piney Woods.

Now, Johnston husbanded his forces in redoubts surrounding the rebel bulwarks. While he had been a student in the cadet program at the Alamo, Charlie had studied his father's victory at the Battle of Saltillo now a decade past. Travis had defended a narrow valley with steep walls leading to the town of Saltillo with fortified redoubts. They were diamond shaped forts with a few field pieces and a couple of battalions defending the earthen walls. But they had been close enough to provide overlapping artillery fire.

Johnston now adapted the design to his own needs. Encircling the enemy's entrenched position, Johnston's small army had built ten diamond shaped redoubts. Less than four miles separated one end of the army from the other, and the redoubts were set six or seven hundred yards apart. If the rebels attempted to attack any of the forts, they could be supported by the troops on either side.

Charlie eyed the no-man's-land between two of the redoubts. Two thousand feet was a long way to shoot for a rifleman, but the soldiers armed with the M1846 had a rifle that could hit a target at that distance, even if the men carrying it were not yet skilled enough to be effective at that range.

"Sam, could you hit someone six hundred yards away?"

His telegraph operator shook his head. "Not likely. You know that if your father decides to mobilize the students at Trinity College, the war's as good as over, right?"

"God help us if that happens," Charlie laughed and pointed below. "If those bastards in Beaumont attempt to attack one of our redoubts, it's not really the riflemen in the next one over that they have to worry about, but the artillery. Berry's new three-inch breechloaders have a range of nearly five thousand yards. If the enemy were to attack our centermost redoubt, it would be inside the range of every cannon on the line."

Sam peered over the edge of the basket, "I doubt General Beauregard would be so accommodating as to do that, Major. I'd have thought the Gatlings would be enough to stop those bastards from attacking."

"We've managed to put one in each of the redoubts, but we're short of ammunition for them," Charlie said, "We were supposed to get a shipment from Colt Manufacturing in Connecticut, but it's running late. General Johnston fears the shipment was intercepted by some Southern privateers along the Atlantic coast."

# Chapter 10

4 May 1852

Becky Travis tucked the receipt into her purse as she waited for the armed guard to open the door at the Commerce Bank's Austin branch. As she stepped out of the stone and brick building, she turned and looked at its façade. White stone blocks faced the street, and several windows were cut into the two-story structure. The preacher was fond of saying how pride was a sin, but when she thought about how her husband and Samuel Williams had established a banking system in the Republic years earlier, she felt pride. And she wasn't ashamed of it. A source of ready credit in the Republic, the bank had helped to launch many businesses over the past decade.

Her pride hadn't brought her to the bank on that Tuesday morning. Since the war began, hundreds had been widowed and orphaned, and several of the churches in town had established a fund to help some of the women who had lost husbands since the rebellion had begun. She had transferred money into the charity, comforted by the knowledge her modest contribution would put food on a woman and her children's table or help to keep a roof over their heads.

She waited on the corner of the street for a carriage to roll by and couldn't shake the idea of how many women and children had been left destitute by the death of their husbands and fathers, and how blessed she was that her own family remained intact. She shuddered at the thought of her own children being alone.

As she stepped into the street, she felt a sharp tug on her purse and turned. A young girl in a dirty calico dress held onto one end of the bag. Her eyes were round in terror as she realized Becky's grip was stronger than her own.

The waif let go and started to run away, when Becky instinctively grabbed her arm, yanking her off her feet.

"Let go of me!"

The girl was thin. Too thin. Becky's hand nearly encircled the girl's arm. Dark circles ringed the girl's eyes above gaunt cheeks and a dirty face. *How long has it been since she's eaten?*

"I don't think so." Becky fired back.

"I'll scream."

Aside from a few vehicles on the streets, they were alone. "Go ahead. Scream all you want," Becky paused, weighing her options. "Or, you can come along with me—"

Wide with fear already, the girl's eyes grew larger yet. "Don't turn me over to the Rangers."

"—and we'll get you fed," Becky finished.

The girl stopped pulling against Becky and considered the offer. Hesitantly, she said, "Alright, Miss."

As she guided the girl to the Stagecoach Inn, Becky never let go of her arm until they were seated in the restaurant. It was between breakfast and lunch and the dining area was nearly empty when a waiter came over to take their order.

"Mrs. Travis, a pleasure. What can I get for you?"

Becky nodded toward a slate board where the breakfast special had been written. "Good morning, Micah. Two specials, please."

The girl's expression turned from sullen hostility to a mixture of curiosity and awe. She stammered, "He called you *Mrs. Travis.* Are you the president's wife?"

Becky offered a warm smile and nodded. "Now that you know my name, what's yours?"

The girl looked down at the white starched tablecloth, her cheeks colored bright red. "I'm so sorry about earlier. I had no idea it was you I was trying to steal from." A tear trickled down her dirty face. "I'm Johanna."

Becky reached across the table and took the girl's fragile hand in hers. "Where's your family, Johanna?"

Her tears ducts opened, and a sob escaped from the girl's lips. Becky fished a handkerchief from her purse and handed it over to Johanna. "Take your time, sweetie. There's no hurry."

The waiter returned and set several plates on the table piled with flapjacks, grits, and bacon. First, one pancake disappeared and then another as Johanna grabbed them from the platter and stuffed them into her mouth, barely chewing before swallowing.

"Slow down there. You'll make yourself sick," Becky said as she intercepted a small hand reaching for a third. "How long has it been since you've eaten?"

"A few days. I was picked up by the Rangers and the captain, he made me shine his boots and then clean out the stables before he would let me eat anything. It was disgusting."

"Why'd the Rangers pick you up?"

More slowly, the girl picked up a fork and cut up another flapjack. "I, uh, tried to take another lady's purse. She caught me and took me to the Rangers."

Becky forced a smile. "You're really not a very good thief, Johanna."

The girl giggled. "Horrible." The smile faded, and she continued, "But I've got to eat, and both of my parents are gone."

"What happened?"

"My ma and pa had a farm a few miles outside of town. It wasn't much, but they were proud of it. But when the war started, Pa had to become a soldier. He sent his pay to us, and we got along okay until someone came from the government and told Ma that my pa had been killed."

Johanna bit into a piece of bacon before continuing. "The money stopped coming, and one day after I came home from the school on the Seguin town road, I found my ma in the barn. She hanged herself."

By now, Johanna's tears had stopped. She looked embarrassed after eating all the food on the plates. The matter-of-fact way the girl had described her mother's death left Becky sick to her stomach, and her plate untouched. "Did you let folks know that lived nearby?"

Johanna nodded, "I told the Jacksons. Their pa is in the same company as mine was. But I didn't stay with them. One of the boys, he's older, I didn't like the way he looked at me."

The disgust in the girl's voice left Becky with a strong idea about those looks. Becky had been lucky. Before she and her mother had joined her father in Texas, what few boys who'd come calling on her had been as innocent as she had been. In Texas, a few men who had looked to advance their careers by calling on the President's daughter had always been polite when they had called on her. But when she met Will, she knew she'd met the one she was meant to be with. He'd been both courteous and familiar. Sooner than she'd have imagined possible, he filled the role of both suitor and friend.

Even so, she felt compelled to protect the young girl sitting across the table. She deserved better than to be fostered onto another local family who may or may not protect her. She deserved to be with people who loved her. "What other family do you have, Johanna?"

The girl shrugged. "We moved from Cincinnati when I was a little girl. My only family was Ma and Pa."

When the waiter returned, Becky signed the bill and told Johanna, "Come on. I've got a place you can stay while you and I figure out the best thing for you."

Johanna frowned, "Whatever you do, please don't take me back to the Rangers."

"I suppose it's a stalemate, Payton. If we launch an attack on any of Johnston's redoubts, they'll chew us to ribbons," G.T. Beauregard said as the two officers stared at the nearest enemy fortification nearly a thousand yards away.

Payton Wyatt, the army's chief quartermaster, added, "And if they attack us, we can do more damage to them than they can to us."

They stepped down from the wooden parapet and headed down the ramp. As the officers climbed into the saddle, Beauregard looked up into the sky. The lone balloon hung over the enemy position. "Damn that thing. They can look down at us and see everything we're doing. Every time I shift a regiment from the line and let them rest, they see it. If they ever decide to risk an attack, they'll see our every response."

Wyatt shook his head. "We've tried using howitzers and mortars to hit the thing, but it's simply too high up and too far away."

In the distance, the whistle from an arriving train pierced the air. "More men and supplies from New Orleans, I'll wager. What's the latest from Major Forrest?"

Beauregard shook his head, "Hardly anything. He sent word that he defeated Brown and his abolitionists in a battle a few weeks ago, but since then, Northeast Texas has been silent as the grave. If we could open a second front, come in from Arkansas, that would force Johnston to split his army. Despite his repeating rifles and those infernal 'Gatlings,' we could sweep him aside."

As they reached the two-story courthouse, they found several horses tied to hitching posts.

"I thought Jim and Robert would be gone by now," Wyatt said, referring to Robert Potter and James Collinsworth.

Beauregard noted the drab military style saddle blanket on the horses, "I don't think those belong to our confederates."

From the door to the courthouse, another unfamiliar voice said, "Confederates? What an interesting expression."

William Hardee used the handrail to swing down onto the station platform from the passenger car. The station had a new, almost unfinished look to it. In fact, most of the buildings near the station were also of recent construction.

"Looks like a boomtown, Captain Whittier. Hard to believe there's a siege when you arrive by train," Hardee said.

His adjutant, Captain Henry Whittier ordered a couple of slaves to have their horses unloaded from one of the boxcars before he looked around. "Yes, sir. But to read about it in the newspapers, that's the only way in or out of town."

Hardee ran his fingers through his brown hair. "Seven thousand holding in more than twenty. My God, things have not gone the way the Committee envisioned. G.T. was supposed to be in Austin by now. Instead, Austin's surrounding him."

A few minutes later, their mounts were brought over, saddled, and ready to ride. Despite the new construction around the railroad, the town was on the small side, and it took but a few minutes to reach the courthouse. They walked through the four rooms, but it was late in the afternoon and whatever passed for the provisional government had left for the day.

Hardee was returning to his horse when he heard voices outside. From the deep shadows, he could see two officers dismounting. One said, "I don't think those belong to our confederates."

*What an interesting choice of words.* Hardee stepped into the doorway. "Confederates? That's an interesting expression, General Beauregard."

Later, in the courthouse's largest room, which until recently had been reserved for jury trials, Hardee watched Beauregard's expression as he read correspondence from the Southern Cross Committee. The committee, made up of many of the South's most prominent fire-eaters, was coordinating the efforts of all the states from the deep South, unofficially, of course. Hardee knew the contents of the correspondence. He'd have not been present were it otherwise.

Beauregard set the papers down and pinched the bridge of his nose, as though willing a headache to let him be. "A training camp, General? The committee wants me to oversee turning our volunteers into soldiers? The largest part of me hates to leave something incomplete, General Hardee, but an order's an order, even if the committee doesn't really grasp what we're dealing with here."

"What doesn't the committee understand, General?" Hardee eyed his counterpart quizzically.

Beauregard folded the correspondence and slid it back across the prosecutor's table. "We may have numeric superiority, but Sidney Johnston's entire army is armed with breechloading rifles. And I don't know how they've pulled it off, but their artillery also uses a breech-locking mechanism that lets them fire twice as fast as our muzzleloading guns."

Hardee hid his distaste at the news. It was easy enough. He'd been reading Beauregard's reports for weeks, by now.

Beauregard said, "What will do you do with this command, Bill? A headlong attack will needlessly kill hundreds of these men."

Hardee let the familiarity of using his Christian name pass. He and Beauregard shared the same rank, and the circumstances were informal. "I'd not do anything to needlessly spill our soldiers' blood, G.T. If I can open a second front against Johnston, I'll do so. But I think I can play for time until after the national conventions in Baltimore are over. Once we know who'll be replacing President Cass at the head of our party's ticket, we'll be better able to plan for the upcoming campaign."

Beauregard mused, "It seems only natural for me to think we'll keep the presidency, even if we must dispose of Cass during the convention. But I fear the odds."

Hardee could hardly disagree, although he spun it the best he could. "If we can stay united between Northern and Southern factions, we can defeat anybody the Whigs nominate."

The bitterness of Beauregard's laughter grated against his ears. "Then we're doomed. The Whigs are sure to win. What then?"

Hardee liked his next word even less than Beauregard's braying laughter. "Secession."

25 May 1852

Black smoke billowed into the morning sky, obscuring the dim yellow orb which seemed to be a tiny pinprick of light poking through. Captain Jesse Running Creek raced across the open ground and threw himself into one of the wood-reinforced trenches. His feet sank deep into black mud as other Rangers tumbled into the trench to either side. Turning one way then the other, the fortified position was empty. His feet made a sucking noise as he picked them up, one at a time until he stood on wooden planking.

A few odds and ends littered the ground. As he stepped over a pile of trash, Jesse peered over the lip at the back of the trench. A gentle slope ended at a second row of trenches a few hundred feet back from the defensive works he and his men now held. No flags fluttered above the trenchworks. It seemed devoid of life.

"Sergeant," Jesse said to a nearby NCO, "take a couple of rifle teams forward, through the communication trench and see if that line is as empty as it appears."

Moments passed before one of the Rangers came racing back. Breathlessly, he said, "It's empty, the whole damned line, Chief. Not a rebel between here and Beaumont, itself."

Throwing caution away, Jesse climbed over the trench's wooden planked back wall and stood, staring to the east. Beaumont was less than half a mile away. All that stood between him and the town that had housed the rebels was another empty trench. Despite the distance, he could hear the crackle of fire as the train depot's wooden timber was consumed by a growing blaze. Even as he watched in the distance, the fire's embers leapt between buildings as a nearby roof began to smolder.

Thirty minutes later, Jesse stood upwind of the burning husk of the modest two-story courthouse, which had served as the rebel's capitol building until that morning. Heat radiated from the inferno, stopping his men from getting any closer.

A voice startled him out of the hypnotic effects of staring at the fire. "Couldn't see anything swinging up in that godforsaken balloon this morning. All that smoke has made it impossible to see very far."

Jesse turned and saw Charlie Travis. The youthful major climbed from his mount and tied it to a tree before continuing, "Any idea why they gave up a perfectly good fortified position? Had General Johnston ordered an attack, I'm damned if I think we could have cracked this nut."

Shrugging, Jesse said, "I heard that General Beauregard was recalled. Some Georgian name of Hardee commands the rebels and their allies. I don't suppose there's much chance this Hardee fellow's going to keep right on going east, right across the Sabine?"

"That'd be too easy. There's still forty miles between Beaumont and the Sabine River. There's plenty of places for him to put up a fight. My money is on him digging in on the Texas side of the river."

Jesse shuddered. "Unless we can destroy those rebel batteries at the mouth of the Sabine River, I don't much care for the idea of leading my men against those odds."

The courthouse's burning frame groaned and collapsed, sending embers eddying into the sky, interrupting Charlie's response. They stared into the building's glowing remains until a noise from behind startled them out of their reverie. Jesse turned and saw a couple of files of men moving along each side of the road. They stood out in their dark blue jackets.

Charlie offered, "When it's time to go at the rebels, we won't be doing it alone. Those boys are from the First Massachusetts Volunteer infantry. They arrived a couple of weeks ago from Boston."

Jesse studied the men passing by. Their uniforms were new, and their rifled muskets still carried the bluing on their barrels. "Can they fight?"

The young officer glanced to the east, toward the Sabine River. "They traveled more than two thousand miles, Jesse, just to get here. Every one of them is a volunteer. While we may not be able to take their measure until they're thrown into the crucible of battle, what we've seen looks promising."

Jesse allowed a smile to slip onto his face. "Another thousand men. A few more battalions from our friends in the North and we can knock Hardee back into Louisiana."

Charlie untied his mount's reins from the tree and swung into the saddle. "Not just from the North. We've recruited another battalion from the gutter rats in Galveston and Houston. Not one in five of them speaks English properly. Most are straight off the boat from Ireland, Germany, and Italy. When General Johnston is ready to attack, he'll do it with at least two thousand more men than we started this campaign with."

The young major wheeled his horse and cantered back toward the Texian army's lines. Jesse watched him go, feeling buoyed at the news.

# Chapter 11

6 June 1852

The chair legs scraped across the worn floor. A moment later, wood squealed against wood as the room's occupant forced the window of the small hotel room open. Only a ghost of a breeze stirred the faded curtains.

As Horace Greeley returned to the chair and picked up his pen, he decided any breeze was better than none. He flipped open the inkwell's lid and dipped his pen. As his hand rested above the paper, he considered the chaos that had been the National Convention of the Democratic Party.

Lewis Cass had shown up, expecting an easy path to re-nomination. Greeley chuckled. Cass must have been the only person in attendance who thought he'd receive his party's nomination. Under other circumstances, it would have been a reasonable assumption; after all, he was the sitting president.

When the southern fire eaters, who dominated the Southern delegations, nominated the former Senator from South Carolina, Robert Rhett as their presidential candidate, it was clear Cass's odds of winning the nomination were diminished.

No sooner had the fire eaters nominated the radical Rhett than a northern faction that had grown weary of the Southern Democrats' filibustering expedition into Texas, chose their own candidate, Stephen Douglas. Different factions nominated several other men. The most notable, Jefferson Davis, was prominent among the moderate wing of Southern Democrats.

Greeley shook his wispy mane of hair and set his pen on the paper.

*Those whom the gods would destroy they first make mad. Such was the state of the Democratic National Convention this year. President Cass arrived in Baltimore on the first of this month, confident in his ability to unite his fractured party, ignorant or ill-informed of the passions arising from the ill-advised filibuster by our Southern cousins.*

*When the radicals aligned with the Southern Cross faction nominated Robert Rhett, it must have caused President Cass great consternation. Rhett's nomination was a repudiation of the President's attempt to keep the federal government above the conflict west of Louisiana.*

*The forlorn president, now beset by factions within his own party, was soon accosted by Northern Democrats, who for the exact opposite reasons provided by the Southern Cross faction, were upset by his refusal to maintain the status quo. They nominated the highly regarded Senator from Illinois, Stephen Douglas.*

*Twenty ballots and five candidates later, the convention was hopelessly deadlocked. Enough men favored someone whose name wasn't Douglas or Rhett to deny either faction a majority.*

*Although dear reader, it may seem unlikely that anyone in the sultry climes of the South isn't hot-tempered, those who by contrast to the fire eaters, are moderates, nominated the former Senator from Mississippi, Jefferson Davis. Over the next few ballots, enough men gave up their allegiances to President Cass and the honorable Senator Rhett to give Senator Davis the slimmest of majorities.*

*Alas, you may think this the end of the tale, but the gods struck the Democrats after Senator Davis' nomination. That night, the Northern Democrats reconvened a rump convention at Marsh Market and nominated Senator Douglas as their candidate.*

*It would indeed take a monumental failing for either Democratic faction to clinch the golden prize of the presidency against a united Whig Party.*

Greeley replaced the candle, burned to the nub, with a fresh one, and read his words. He corrected a word here and added punctuation there. With a nod, he took a shaker full of sand and scattered a bit across the page.

20 June 1852

The flimsy wooden door slammed behind him as Horace Greeley entered his hotel room. The cheap chair creaked dangerously as he threw himself into it as he glared daggers at the blank sheet of paper on the desk before him.

*Count on the Whigs snatching defeat from the jaws of victory.* His thoughts were dark as he worked to order them into some semblance of order. *How hard could it be to find a little bit of unity in the face of the Democrats' chaos?*

In the very hall the Democrats had used a couple of weeks earlier, the Whigs had convened their own national convention. The goal was simple. Unite behind a candidate that could defeat the Democrats in November. Not an insurmountable goal, given how the electoral college favored the Whigs.

*I should have known things were not going according to plan when that fool, Millard Fillmore was the first to be nominated. William should have been the first name to have been nominated.* Northern liberals had arrived in Baltimore with plans to rally behind William Seward from the outset.

In a moment of charity, Greeley conceded, *either could have been acceptable to the vast majority of Whigs. A conservative or a liberal, at least both were good Northern men. Why in God's name did regional sectionalism have to plague our party as well?*

It wasn't really a surprise that Southern Whigs had offered forth their favorite son, John Tyler. It was expected. There was a long if informal, tradition that if the presidential nominee came from one section, then the vice president would come from the other. Tyler's nomination could have been seen as an audition for the vice presidency.

Only it wasn't. Greeley shook his head as he recalled his surprise when the convention was suspended after more than fifty ballots. Fillmore's supporters refused to give way to Seward's, and after four tense days, nobody had a majority. Grimacing, Greeley dipped his pen and began to write.

*Lest our readers come to the conclusion that the Democrats are alone in their insanity, rest assured the disease has thoroughly infected the Whigs as well. As of the twentieth of June, little clarity has been gained after the completion of our National Convention. Not to be outdone by their Democratic neighbors, the Whig's southern faction nominated John Tyler. This newspaper had long seen Mr. Tyler as the perineal bridesmaid. Since 1840, this is the third time he has been nominated to head our Whig ticket. Yet it is the first time his support wasn't diluted by each successive ballot.*

*Our own esteemed Senator from the Empire State, William Seward, was the second nominee for the presidency, following the nomination of Millard Fillmore. One expects during the balloting for votes to fall away from one faction, as a clear consensus candidate arises. While Senator Seward built a small lead in the early balloting, neither Fillmore nor his supporters wavered.*

*As it seems to be in vogue, the reason for the lack of comity, like everything else, is Texas. Seward's views, which align with the newspaper of record, require the Federal Government to act to place a wet blanket on the fire eaters in the South and their ill-fated filibustering expedition against another sovereign country. The army exists to carry out the national policy of the federal government, and if it needs to be used to interdict supplies to the filibusterers in Texas, then Seward is the man to make that happen.*

*Millard Fillmore has tipped his hat to those who favor the rights of the several states over the authority of the federal government, although he condemns the actions of the fire eaters. His plea of states' rights falls on deaf ears when southern volunteers are attempting to subvert another nation's legitimate government.*

*Virginian John Tyler saw no reason to give up his quixotic quest so long as no one approached the necessary one-hundred-forty-nine votes.*

*On the fourth and final day of the convention, with the party hopelessly deadlocked, Tyler's supporters withdrew from the convention. They will settle on his vice-presidential running mate within the next day or two as they prepare to mount a Southern Whig campaign. Their plank demands an end to the filibustering but also seeks a plebiscite in Texas regarding annexation. Lest the reader thinks they indeed favor the rights of all Texans, the plebiscite they support is regional, encompassing only the portion of Texas in rebellion against their legitimate government. Only against the insanity of Southern Democrats do the Southern Whigs appear reasonable.*

*It may be some time before the smoke-filled rooms in Baltimore hotels reveal who shall carry the banner of Whiggish ideals in the November election. As of yet, the supporters of Fillmore and Seward are meeting in said rooms. Should they be unable to find a compromise, the nation may find itself in a five-way race for the presidency.*

Greeley chewed on the end of his pen as he read the words on the page. It summed up the desolation he felt. Only the Whigs would manage to field three candidates against the Democrats' two.

3 July 1852

Jimmy Hickok gripped the saddle horn as his horse reared onto his hind legs. The boy barely managed to hold onto his seat before his mount's hooves crashed back to the ground. A massive pine tree rose up before him. Had he not been racing the horse hell-bent-for-leather, he'd have veered to one side or the other. But focused on his mission, Jimmy had only seen the tree with moments to spare.

The youth would have cussed except the orders he carried from Colonel Brown were clenched in his teeth. Instead, he used his knees and reins to canter around the pine tree. The sound of gunfire had never completely gone away as he had charged forward, to where the regiment's forwardmost element was engaged with rebel cavalry.

He urged his mount to a quick canter when a bullet struck a tree he was passing by. Bits of splinters missed him and his mount, and he urged the horse back to a gallop. The hot wind was blowing through his hair when he felt a tug at his arm. A hurried glance showed where another bullet had ripped open the blue kersey cloth revealing a filthy lining made from linen beneath.

Through the forest, Jimmy spotted the scouting company. They were dismounted, firing at targets he couldn't see. He spied the company's white and red banner fluttering, carried by an NCO. Mixed in with them were other blue-jacketed men. Jimmy recognized the regimental flag of the 2nd Missouri Volunteer Cavalry Regiment. The newcomers, many of whom were recent German immigrants, had crossed the Red River a week before.

Despite his fourteen summers, Jimmy wasn't blind to the fact that without the arrival of the 2nd Missouri the previous week, it would have been the 1st New York in retreat instead of Forrest's rebels.

As he drew up next to the first officer he found, Jimmy slid off the saddle. *No point in being a bigger target than I have to be,* he thought. He took the letter from Colonel Brown from between his teeth and handed the soggy missive to the officer.

As the officer unfolded the letter, he eyed Jimmy warily. "You could have tucked this into your jacket, you know. I swear, if the ink is smeared, I'll cuff you one you'll not soon forget."

As the officer read, Jimmy noticed the gunfire had died away. His reverie was interrupted when the Captain burst out, "I'll be damned if I'll take one more step."

He gestured to a three-foot-tall granite obelisk standing next to the trail that passed for a road. Tilting his head to read something carved on the pillar, Jimmy repeated, "RT?"

The captain pointed to the other side of the marker, "Says this here is the meridian Boundary, established in A.D. eighteen-forty. That may not mean anything to you, boy. But on the other side of the marker is

Arkansas. We cross that line, and we'll kick up more shit than we can shovel away."

Jimmy was startled by a voice from behind, "You'll watch your tongue, Captain."

Turning, the boy saw Colonel Brown riding up, his perpetual frown carved on his always serious face. "The only manure I see is retreating into the distance. Why haven't you followed?"

"If we follow them, we'd be crossing into Arkansas, Colonel. Illegally." The captain's expression was worn and painful, as though disagreeing with Brown was the last thing he wanted to do. "If we do that, God alone knows how badly that's going to be taken back east."

Brown's dark, bushy beard shook as he swung his eyes to the east, as though he could still see the retreating enemy. "The men who invaded to roll back the little bit of freedom and liberty Texas is willing to grant to the Negro race are evil, Captain. They are renegades and rebels. If the people hereabouts aid them, then they are outlaws, too."

The jingle of iron and the squeaking of leather announced the arrival of the rest of the regiment and the 2nd Missouri. Brown wheeled around, taking his place at the head of the column. "Captain, fall in. I want your company to keep an eye on our rear."

The colonel's burning eyes searched out someone else until they fell on Jimmy. "Boy, send my compliments to Captain Ashford. I want D Troop to scout out our advance. If Forrest decides to turn and fight, I don't want a surprise."

As Jimmy climbed back into the saddle, Brown stood in his stirrups and raised his voice like a preacher at a tent revival meeting. "We advance men. We'll not rest until we've destroyed our enemies and brought the year of Jubilee to the oppressed."

Jimmy's jaw hung open as he watched the colonel canter by the boundary marker.

The column of more than a thousand men had ridden by when the youth dug his heels into his mount and raced alongside the column. He wasn't sure what would come of invading another state, but he trusted Brown to lead them to victory.

# Chapter 12

12 July 1852

The bridge over the Trinity River was still under repair, and the railroad bed between the Trinity and Beaumont was bare of iron rails and wooden ties. Under better circumstances, Will would have been able to travel from Austin to Texas' easternmost town in as little as six or seven hours. Instead it had taken him and George Fisher two days to reach Beaumont and another full day to reach the trenchworks surrounding the rebel stronghold on the Sabine River.

As the two men rode ahead of their Ranger escort, the Secretary of War, whose voice was heavily accented, said, "If you'd told me the rebels would abandon Beaumont for even stronger fortifications, I'd have called you a liar."

Will let a small smile surface. "Dangerous thing, George, calling your boss a liar."

The corpulent Hungarian laughed, "True. But then I'd seek my fortune in California, like so many others have done. What word have you heard from Major Hays?"

Will's smile turned wistful. "He and the men that traveled with him into the American valley in Jefferson have done rather well. The last letter I received said that he's turned into a rather shrewd merchant in San Francisco. I wish we'd held onto more of California than we did. While some gold has been discovered in Texian California, the lion's share has been to the north, in Jefferson."

Fisher slapped his hand on his saddle horn, "It could have been worse. To hear Michel Menard talk, the bonds we're floating to defeat the rebels are backed by the gold on our side of the border."

As they pulled up before a large log cabin, over which flew the lone star flag, Will said, "I know, but when I think about how much gold we negotiated away when we sold the US most of the land we won from Mexico, I wonder if we did the right thing."

Once Fisher rolled himself off his mount, he said, "The past is the past. Let's go talk with General Johnston about the future."

Will repressed a chuckle. If the past truly belonged to the past, he'd have not found himself trapped there. No, the past was more malleable than he'd have ever imagined when he was forced to find a solution to letting the past kill him and one-hundred-eight-seven other men at the Alamo. Sixteen years later, the world was a far different place than the one he'd studied before the transition.

He could hear Sidney Johnston's voice from within the cabin, "I don't care how many wagons it's going to take; I want you to bring every bullet you can from Trinity Park. I can't mount an attack or defend against one without more ammunition."

As Will stepped into the dimness of the cabin, the maps strewn about a large table made him reconsider. *Maybe in some ways, it'll always be the same.*

"Howdy, Sid. Problem with supplies?" Will asked.

Johnston's face lit up at the sight of Will. "Resign the presidency. You can have the army again. I quit."

Will returned the smile. "Not happening. When my term's over, I'm going to sit on my porch in my rocking chair, scaring cats, and telling children to stay off my grass." He grew more solemn. "Are there problems with supplies?"

"Except for ammunition, the only supply problems we have is being eighty miles from the railroad. We're running wagons back and forth pretty much all the time. But we're short on the brass cartridges our M1846 rifles use. Doesn't help that the Gatling guns use the same ammunition."

Will wasn't surprised. He'd read the reports from Andy Berry, who'd expanded production in Trinity Park, and signed several contracts with manufactories in Hartford, Connecticut, and New York City to provide more brass cartridges. But with more than three thousand rifles using the brass ammunition, and several full batteries of Gatling guns, the nation was struggling to keep the army supplied.

Fisher interjected, "Do you have enough to fend off an attack, General?"

Johnston nodded. “Probably. But not enough to take the fight to the enemy. Not yet."

He straightened a map and opened a window, letting the hot summer sun chase away the cabin’s shadows. Will recognized the fortified bend in the river, behind which the rebels and their Southern allies sheltered. Johnston pointed to the map. “They must have been preparing these while they were still holding Beaumont. Their trench line is anchored along a bend in the river. Only about a mile or so of trenches, and behind that, they’re protecting the railhead into Texas. No shortages of trains pulling in supplies, or men.”

Will stared at the map. “Why do you think they pulled out of Beaumont? We’d have paid a terrible price to capture the town.”

“I’m not sure, but I’ve heard that men like James Collinsworth thought that by inviting in the filibusters that they’d be able to win a quick war against us. When that proved wrong, the more men who flow in from states like Louisiana or Alabama, the smaller the influence the rebels have.”

Fisher added, “I’m sure Collinsworth and Potter thought that when they decided to overthrow your administration, they believed every Texian from the deep South would rally to their cause. They probably expected widespread support. At best, perhaps sixty or seventy thousand people have joined their rebellion.”

Johnston said, “Their failure to push us past the Trinity didn’t help their cause. When it became evident that they weren’t going to push further to the west, their ambitions were forced to become smaller.”

Will shook his head. “I understand that. But why retreat all the way to the Sabine? They’ve surrendered nearly all the territory they held and threw the people who supported them into the wind. I don’t understand that.”

“Do you mind if I sit?” Fisher asked as his large frame collapsed into a chair at the table. “I have a theory. Men like Collinsworth aren’t calling any shots anymore. They’re entirely dependent upon the filibusters to support them. The problem is that these Southern soldiers answer to the various state governments. The men running those governments are focused on the November election. I think they’re conserving their position here on the Sabine River because they expect to win the presidency. If they win, not only will they be able to muster all of their state militias, but they’ll also be able to direct the US army to support the rebels.”

Will snorted derisively. “In what world will those fire eaters in the Southern Cross manage to win the White House? The Democrats fractured. Their northern faction picked Stephen Douglas. The Southern, Jeff Davis. Despite the Whigs fracturing, they still hold the upper hand.”

Fisher dipped his head in acknowledgment. “I was telling you what I think their plans are, not whether those plans hold water. I agree with you. Even if Davis managed to win, he’d be stuck with too few members of the House of Representatives. That, and the same tactics the fire eaters have used to hobble any effective response from Lewis Cass, were he inclined to get off his ass, would be used by the Northern Whigs to clip Davis’ wings.”

"And that brings us back around to why we're here today, Sid," Will said as he took the seat next to Fisher. "If we could defeat the enemy and knock them back into Louisiana, what kind of impact would that have on the US elections?"

The Secretary of War said, "It could take the wind out of the Fire Eaters' sails."

Johnston countered, "Or unite the lower South firmly behind them."

Will shrugged, "For the sake of the discussion, let's go with the first option. How many men do we have currently under arms?"

Johnston said, "Around twelve thousand men in the army. About twenty-six hundred men in the navy."

Fisher joined in, "I know we can't mobilize every loyal man in Texas, but *if* we could, we have access to another thirty-five thousand men."

"God help us, we've got enough trouble arming and supplying the men we have mobilized now, George, how could we manage more?" Johnston said.

Fisher replied, "We're not going to mobilize them all, Sid. But we already have a model for this. We're supporting the two regiments of volunteers recently arrived from New Jersey and Massachusetts. Nearly two thousand men."

Hearing about the recent volunteers triggered Will's thoughts. "What about that cavalry regiment that came down through the unorganized territory? Brown's First New York? I thought they should have arrived by now."

Johnston grimaced. "I sent a report about that. Turns out the rebels dispatched some cavalry under some fellow name of Forrest. I received word a couple of days ago that this Colonel Brown has been tangling with this Forrest fellow somewhere up by the Red River. It's possible the rebels forced Brown to turn back."

Fisher added, "Or it's possible that John Brown and this Forrest fellow have taken the fight back into the western territory or Arkansas."

Late July 1852

The white stone building stood on the corner of Brazos and Ninth Street. Becky stood on the street, watching as a man dismounted and tied his horse to a hitching post before striding into the building. A crucifix perched atop the building and a wooden sign stood next to it. It declared to passersby that all were welcome to enter Saint Patrick's Church, the lone Catholic congregation in the Republic's capital city.

Raised a Presbyterian by her mother, and now sharing the Methodist faith of her husband, Becky had grown up listening to anti-papist teachings. With friends like Maria Seguin, Juan Seguin's wife, her dislike of Catholicism had largely fallen by the wayside. Even so, her feet seemed reluctant to carry her the thirty feet necessary to enter the church.

A hand hooked around her arm, and a soft voice said, "Becky, thanks for waiting for me. With all these men, I'd feel like Daniel cast into the lion's den without you today."

Becky's eyes radiated joy when she heard Maria Seguin's voice and felt the feisty woman's presence by her side. "I don't think we'll be alone. I invited several women from the Episcopal congregation. They said they'd be here, too."

With Maria by her side, Becky crossed over the grassy lawn, and entered the small sanctuary. The pews were pressed against the walls, and several tables were in the center of the building. Chairs ringed the tables, and about half of them were occupied. As Becky found a seat next to Maria, she scanned the room. She recognized David Ayres in one of the seats. He was a lay Methodist minister from near Harrisburg. Many years earlier, he and his wife had taken care of Charlie when Will had been fighting Santa Anna.

When Ayres saw Becky, he stopped talking to the man next to him and stood, "Madame Travis, a pleasure to see you."

Becky dipped her head. "Mr. Ayres, a pleasure."

"Allow me to introduce to you, Reverend Baines." Ayres indicated the man beside him, who stood and nodded to Becky. "To Mrs. William Travis." She recognized the name. Baines was prominent in Baptist life in the eastern part of the Republic.

On the other side of Ayres was a middle-aged man wearing a Catholic cassock. A small crucifix hung from his neck. His full cheeks stood in contrast to the dark circles under his eyes. Becky heard Maria give a slight gasp. "It's Bishop Odin," she whispered. Becky had heard the name before. As the Republic's population had burgeoned, the Pope in Rome had recognized the fast-growing Catholic community in Texas with first a prefecture and then later with a diocese. Odin was, as Becky recalled, the priest who had heard Santa Anna's last confession, before the former dictator had been executed after the Mexican War, nearly a decade earlier.

A few minutes passed as others joined those around the tables, then Bishop Odin cleared his throat. He spoke with a distinct French accent, "I want to thank President Travis and Vice President Seguin for extending an invitation to discuss the growing problem of widow and orphans in Texas. Their wives, Rebecca Travis and Maria Seguin, have graciously agreed to attend this meeting, representing the administration. As Saint James said, religion that is undefiled before God visits the fatherless and the widow in their tribulation."

Becky scanned the room, noting the nods of agreement he received from men and women not generally inclined to heed his words. The bishop continued, "We are faced with a crisis today. Hundreds of women have become widowed, and hundreds more children have been left orphans. As I took a carriage to the railroad station in Galveston to come here, I looked out the window and saw boys standing outside the station, begging for alms. Nearby, women who only months ago prayed for their husbands return, sold themselves for a loaf of bread. Our Christian duty is clear. We must do something to provide shelter for the orphans and sustenance for the widows."

Moved by Odin's plea, Becky said, "My family has been affected by this crisis. We have taken in a child whose father and mother both died. How many other children are without shelter or food?"

Reverend G.W. Baines' voice was rich and sonorous as he said, "My own congregation has provided meals and is checking on the women in Huntsville whose husbands will never return. We've been blessed to find homes for orphaned children. It has placed a strain, however small, upon our church. If more is needed, I can talk with families and see if we can take in more children."

David Ayres nodded in agreement. "Our own congregation has done the same. I'll talk to my wife. I'm certain my family can take in a few children in need of a home."

Becky smiled at their personal generosity. From the stories Charlie and Will had told her, Ayres would give the shirt from his back to take care of those in need.

She said, "Reverend Ayres, you're a light in the darkness. My husband swears that he knows of no one more generous than you. If it were possible for a few generous men or even congregations to meet the needs of all widows and orphans in Texas, we'd likely not be here. We need to find a solution bigger than any of us that will provide for all of our orphans and widows."

The bishop, from his seat near the head of the table, clapped his hands when Becky finished. She flushed as he said, "Bravo, Mrs. Travis. I couldn't have said it better. As a matter of fact, I would like to offer a proposal."

He had the attention of everyone in the room. "I'm aware that both the Baptists and Methodists in Texas have associations. The Episcopalians have a diocese in the Republic. Of course, we Catholics have our own diocese, too. What I'm proposing is that we pool our resources to establish something larger than what any of us can do by ourselves."

Reverent Baines said, "What have you in mind?"

"A commission," Odin replied. "As Christ issued his commission to his disciples, so we, too, should go forth through the Republic and gather those children who can't be readily placed with nearby family or friends. We should move heaven and earth to provide for those widows unable to meet their needs and those of their children. If each association and diocese provide what support they can, and we pool our resources, we will be able to provide food and shelter for everyone displaced by this horrible war."

Baines wore a thoughtful expression. "I can't promise anything. We Baptists have a penchant for doing things our own way. However, the war has left us deeply divided. And that has left us unable to do all that we'd like. I'll have to talk to several others. If I can convince them that by partnering with Methodists, Episcopalians, and Catholics, that we'd do far better than just by ourselves, I might be able to get approval."

The Bishop said, "A committee overseeing this commission would seem prudent. If you can talk your association into helping, it would only make sense that one of your number would need to be on the committee."

Ayres stood, his chair scraping the floor. "I feel as though I want to race away now and get permission from our own mission board. But I notice that there are four denominations present. That would put four men on the board." He nodded to Baines, "Assuming you can convince your fellow Baptists. I'd like to propose a fifth member. Someone whose interests should be above our own."

Odin tilted his head, in a question, "Do you have someone in mind, Reverend Ayres?"

Ayres, smiling from ear to ear, nodded at Becky, "Yes, sir. As our mission is to help alleviate the suffering of all widows and orphans in the Republic, I propose that the president of this commission be our own First Lady, Mrs. Travis."

Early September 1852

"It's funny how a body can get used to swinging under one of these big balloons, Major."

"Speak for yourself, Sam," Charlie Travis said as his knuckles turned white, gripping the edge of the wicker basket.

As the nominal second in command of the 9th Infantry, Charlie should have been on the ground, preparing the battalion for the day's operation. Instead, from where the balloon hung in the sky, he had a clear view of both the Texian fortifications and those of the rebels and their Southern allies. Colonel Garibaldi had no shortage of officers who could act in Charlie's capacity as executive officer. It still galled him that the Italian had been the officer to suggest him for his current assignment, a detached observer, reporting on the enemy's every move. The 9th had been reinforced with several new companies, men who'd recently arrived from the Italian peninsula, inspired by news reports in Italian newspapers of Colonel Garibaldi's exploits in what was becoming known as the Texas Civil War.

Charlie realized he'd spoken aloud when Sam said, "Never understood why it's called a civil war. There ain't nothing civil about it." He checked one of the connections to the telegraph machines before continuing. "It's clear today, Major. Can see for miles. I wish to God we could see north a couple of hundred miles. I'd like to believe our Yankee volunteers along the Red River have knocked Forrest's rebels all the way back to Little Rock."

Charlie ignored the ground below and looked to the north. Farms dotted the landscape along the Sabine River, but interspersed between the farms were the thick Piney Woods of East Texas. Far north of where the last farm hugged the riverbank, the dense forest continued. Beyond that was the Red River, nearly two hundred fifty miles away. The news in the Northeast was grim. Reports of bushwhacking between Brown's little army and the Southern cavalry under a Major Bedford Forrest continued to trickle in throughout the summer.

His father was worried the situation between Brown and Forrest was spinning out of control. There were reports of John Brown being burned in effigy in cities and towns across the South. Word was, thousands of men were signing up to serve in volunteer regiments across the region in response.

Horror stories of farms burned to the ground and the menfolk executed were detailed in the New Orleans Picayune newspaper almost daily. Countering that were reports from Colonel Brown complaining that Forrest was disregarding the rules of war when he executed prisoners in retaliation.

Charlie closed his eyes and shook his head as he recalled reading a newspaper calling his father a hypocrite for endorsing the execution of Santa Anna under the Zavala administration while tolerating John Brown's war crimes. Most of what was coming out of Southern newspapers about the war in Texas was nothing more than propaganda, and usually, his father was quick to rebut the propaganda through Texas' newspapers. But about their accusation against Brown, the president was silent.

However, his father was taking the deteriorating situation in the northeast seriously and had recently dispatched eight of the twelve mounted Ranger companies serving in the Frontier battalion near the Comancheria in hopes of bringing order out of the chaos created by Brown and Forrest.

As though Sam Williams could read his mind, the youth said, "You reckon the Texas Rangers your pa dispatched are going to stop the killing?"

Charlie thought about the rough and ready Rangers who served in the Frontier Battalion. Unlike the Rangers assigned to the army, who were highly trained specialists, the men serving in the frontier battalion served more as mounted police on the border with the Comancheria. They wore no uniform but had over the past decade adopted a badge made from Mexican silver pesos, cut in the shape of a star. When Charlie had once asked his father about the confusion of fielding two very different types of Rangers, Will had said, "There's some things you just don't mess with, and Texas Rangers are one of those things."

Charlie considered Sam's question. "Another three or four hundred men will likely let us close the door for Southern filibusters coming down by way of Arkansas. Maybe that'll tamp down the killing."

The youth said, "Do you think they've been ordered to arrest John Brown?"

"For what?"

From his seat next to the telegraph, Sam expertly rolled his eyes, like only a teenager can. "You know, for killing those farmers."

Charlie shrugged. "Not sure if the Rangers could get away with it. There's a lot more Yankee boys up there than ours, you know."

"I hope so. I don't cotton to most of the articles coming out of New Orleans, but if you put Santa Anna and John Brown on the same saddle, you'd not find any light between either one's backside and the leather."

Charlie chuckled at the image, "I suppose you're right. But right now, Brown's our murderer, and that's worth something."

Sam shook his head, "Maybe. But he's like shooting one of those old-style revolvers with the cap and ball. If you don't have the powder packed just right or one of those percussion caps misfires, you could have all the rounds blow up in your hand."

"You do have a way with bringing things into focus," Charlie allowed. "Why do you want him brought to justice?"

"He's killing civilians. They're just farmers. They ain't broken any laws. Once we've whipped the rebels, those farmers he hasn't killed are going to be our neighbors. If he's allowed to get away with murder, he's going create a division that won't be healed until I've got gray whiskers."

With that, Sam stroked the downy peach fuzz on his face.

Sam was right, Charlie conceded. What Charlie saw below looked positively civilized compared to the hell Brown and Forrest were creating in the north. He could see two battalions, assembling in the Texian trenchworks. One with nearly a thousand men was his own 9th. Mostly men of foreign birth, who had rallied to join the army when the East Texas rebels had stabbed the rest of the country in the back. The other was the 21st Infantry from the Rio Grande District. Most of the men were from the farms surrounding Santa Fe and Albuquerque, but one of the companies were the Negro soldiers recruited by Colonel Montoya. Charlie had no doubt those men were champing at the bit to attack the rebel fortifications.

The telegraph key began to clatter. "It's about to start, Major."

The field guns along the mile-long front began to fire, quickly obscuring the field between the two armies with black-powder smoke. Charlie had heard Andy Berry was still working on smokeless powder, but it was a long way from being ready. Even so, Charlie considered the smoke a good thing. It would mask the initial advance when it came.

Adding to the steady boom of artillery came the sound of the Gatling guns. They sounded like God rending his garments in Heaven. It would take a brave, or perhaps foolish, soldier to poke his head out of the rebel trenches.

From his vantage above the field, Charlie watched the two battalions, close to seventeen hundred men flow out of the Texian trenches. From a thousand feet overhead, the men looked no more significant than ants scurrying across the field. In his mind's eye, though, he could imagine each rifle team of four men staying close together. They'd race across the eight hundred yards of no-mans-land between the two armies, not stopping to fire until the rebels opened fire.

The rebel guns had already been firing, engaging in an ineffectual counterbattery fire. But before the men were halfway across the field, the rebel gunners shifted their targets and began firing on the advancing soldiers. Four hundred yards away was a hard shot to make for a man with a rifled musket, but possible. Hundreds of men stood up, risking being shot by the Gatling guns, and fired at the advancing men.

Charlie imagined each rifle team going to ground, seeking whatever cover they could find and firing back at the entrenched enemy. It's what they'd been trained to do. Two would race forward while the others fired and reloaded. Then those two would leapfrog ahead. It was methodical, adding aimed fire at the top of the rebel trenches while eating away at the distance. Four hundred yards, then three hundred, then two hundred.

Hundreds of yards of the rebel line were ablaze with artillery and gunfire. Charlie could see, in the distance from the middle of the rebel camp, reinforcements racing forward. There were a lot of them.

"Sam, let command know that there's a brigade, maybe three thousand men moving from the enemy's camp toward the entrenchments."

Charlie heard the clickity-clack of the telegraph key as he focused the binoculars on the attack's narrow front. At a hundred yards, the fire from the rebel rifle pits was nearly non-stop. The fire from the advancing riflemen was just as fierce, but they had stalled out, unable to advance.

At the extreme left flank of the attack, from amid the men of the 21st Infantry, dozens of riflemen climbed to their feet and screamed in defiance at the rebel line as they charged. Others leapt to their feet and followed. Charlie raised his binoculars and found the men who were leading the vanguard toward the enemy trenches. He stopped breathing as he caught sight of their ebon skin. "Oh, dear God, no!"

The Negro soldiers that Colonel Montoya had recruited, to a man, were charging across the last hundred yards, their bayonet-tipped rifles pointing toward the trenches before them. Charlie peered through the smoke and saw hundreds of men crammed into the rebel trenches. Even though to Charlie's bird's eye view, they didn't appear bigger than ants, the near constant flashes left little doubt about their ability to return fire despite the withering attack from the Texian riflemen.

He strained to watch through the binoculars as tears streamed from his eyes. The Negro soldiers slogged through the hail of bullets as dozens fell, wounded or dead. By the time they were within fifty yards of the rebel trenches, the few who remained standing looked behind them and saw the pockmarked ground littered with the bodies of their fellow soldiers.

Charlie wiped away the tears as he watched what remained of the two battalions slowly retreat.

Mid-October 1852

The bodies were bloated, buttons on their blue jackets pulling against the buttonholes. They swung from ropes slung over a branch on a tall tree, a silent message. Jimmy swallowed bile as he sat atop his horse a few feet away from Colonel Brown and the commander of the Missouri regiment, Franz Sigel.

The men closest to the hanging bodies grumbled. Jimmy Hickok overheard one soldier mutter, "We burn their plantations and kill their slavers, and they kill any of ours they capture. God in heaven, but this is getting ugly."

Jimmy turned and looked at Colonel Brown. If the commander had heard the grumbling, he ignored it. What he couldn't ignore was Colonel Sigel. "Mein Gott, Colonel," the German-born officer swore. "This killing every man who you think owns slaves has got to stop. It's madness."

Brown scowled back. "These slave masters have sown the wind; it is only fitting they reap the whirlwind."

Sigel's head shook violently. "This Forrest fellow has taken to killing those of our men he captures because of this. Those men hanging there are dead because of you."

Brown's frown deepened. "Forrest will stand before his maker and answer for his crimes against this army of liberation, Colonel, just as those men who grew fat and lazy on the whip-scarred backs of the Negro now stand before Almighty God to answer for their crimes."

Jimmy's heart sank as he listened. He'd seen some of the men Brown had ordered to their deaths. The land in Western Arkansas was hard. He'd not seen any fat or lazy men thereabouts. But the youth understood Brown's position. When the campaign had begun, the notion of sending the kind of men to hell who'd killed his father had seemed only just. But the longer the campaign lasted, the sicker he became of back and forth killing.

Sigel snapped, "Be careful, Colonel, unless your telegraph wires run directly to the Almighty, you may want to let him do the judging. This—"

Gunshots broke the silence. Jimmy involuntarily ducked as the two regimental commanders turned and looked to where the shot came from. Cries echoed among the trees as bullets found soft targets. A shrieking, keening sound rose from where the gunshots had come. Dread rose within his gut as Jimmy crouched low in the saddle, gripping his revolver in one hand and reins in the other. A gray haze settled over the ground as the men around him returned fire.

Jimmy couldn't see anything except trees and gun smoke beyond the swinging bodies, but not being able to see didn't mean death couldn't reach out and strike him down. A bullet zipped by his ear and he leaned forward, alongside his mount's neck. He fired into the unknown, once, twice and a third time before the hammer snapped down onto an empty chamber. He swore and grabbed a second cylinder. As he tried to break open the Colt revolver, the loaded cylinder slipped through his fingers, bounced off the saddle horn before disappearing into the leaves covering the ground.

"Shit," he swore as gray-clad riders emerged through the smoke. He, like most of the men in the 1st New York, was low on ammunition. Despite carrying ample supplies when the column had headed south from the railhead in St. Joseph, Missouri, the regiment had burned through most of it clashing with Forrest's cavalry the past couple of months.

He cast a glance around. Brown had moved away, his voice thundering above the crash of gunfire, "Send the heretics to Hell, boys! Reload and fire again."

After casting a final glance for the lost cylinder, Jimmy nudged his mount over to where the Colonel rallied his men, where some of them had dismounted and were firing at the advancing Southerners. He drew up a few feet away, praying no bullet would find him. If the colonel needed him, he wanted to be close at hand.

The rising din of gunfire and mounted men advancing through the swirling mist of smoke added to the confusion. A soldier, still atop his horse, lurched to one side and slid off his mount near Jimmy. *It's time to get the hell out of here.* No matter how he felt, though, he was compelled to stay by the Colonel.

Brown's horse stumbled as several bullets struck the beast. As the animal crashed to the ground, word spread quickly that the colonel was down. Morale crumbled and Jimmy watched in shock as most of the men around him ran away from the advancing Southerners.

The youth had watched the colonel's horse fall. Brown rolled away from the dying animal as his men turned to run. Finding himself alone, Jimmy wheeled his horse around and came alongside the prone colonel.

Brown blinked a few times as he struggled to sit. "Bless you, boy. Help me up. Those sons of perdition would hasten the day of our judgment I fear."

Jimmy shimmied down and grabbed Brown's arm, helped him into the saddle, and hoisted himself behind his commander as Brown dug his heels into the mount's side.

They hadn't gone far, when one of the men from the 3rd Missouri called out in German, *"Texanische Dragoner!"*

Moments later, a column of men appeared, racing through the dispirited Yankees. At the head of the column, someone carried the lone star flag. Jimmy's mouth sagged as he watched them spread out as they galloped through. Each man wore a brace of revolvers at his waist, and a bowie knife stuck in his belt. Their lack of uniforms only added to the air of menace surrounding them.

Jimmy turned, watching them spread out as they swerved around trees and jumped fallen logs. Then gunfire started anew. He could imagine the Texians emptying their pistols into the advancing Southerners. Whatever happened, happened quick. Only minutes passed before the Texians cantered back to where Brown's little army rested. One man, larger than most of the rest, guided his horse through the 1st New York's exhausted troopers until he let his reins fall on his saddle horn and stare down at Colonel Brown, where he was catching his breath.

Jimmy's eyes were drawn to the shiny silver star pinned to his brown hunting jacket. The Ranger drawled, "You'd be Colonel John Brown?"

Brown gave a curt nod. "By the grace of God, I am."

The big-boned Texian allowed a sigh to escape his lips. "I'm Colonel Bill Wallace, these boys I've brought with me are from the Frontier Battalion. And you, sir, are under arrest for murder."

# Chapter 13

25 November 1852

Horace Greeley adjusted the cloth wick on the oil lamp as he set his pen down and picked up the sheet of paper. He shook his head; writing shouldn't be this hard. But seldom before had the presidential elections been as contentious. Still, the system had worked. By the time the states had counted all their ballots and determined who won their respective electors, a victor clinched a majority of electoral votes – barely.

*Three weeks have elapsed since Columbia's men, from the sandy Florida beaches to the crowded tenements on Manhattan Island, turned out to perform their civic duty. What should have been a stately quadrennial election turned into an electoral brawl.*

*The twenty-eight states of the Union are apportioned 283 electors, from their 56 senators and 227 representatives. To win, a candidate needed to claim 142 electors. In a four-way race, even the newspaper of record feared no candidate would do so, forcing the divided House of Representatives to sequester themselves until a victor could be named. Providence favored our great nation, and we avoided that calamity.*

*As earlier reported, the Democratic Party splintered into regional factions. The northern branch rallied around Senator Stephen Douglas of Illinois while the southern faction coalesced around Senator Jefferson Davis of Alabama. The Southern Democrats captured the electors of nine states. They are Alabama, Arkansas, Florida, Georgia, Kentucky, Louisiana, Mississippi, South Carolina, and Tennessee. While they won more than two-thirds of the popular vote in Alabama, they barely mustered 42% of the vote in Kentucky. No doubt had South Carolina allowed a popular vote, Senator Davis would likely have bested his performance in Alabama. In all, the Southern Democrats won 71 electors.*

*Southern Whigs, under the tattered banner of former Congressman John Tyler, carried four states with 42 electors. They are Maryland, Missouri, North Carolina, and Virginia. Only in North Carolina was Tyler able to take more than 50%. His lowest margin of victory came in Missouri, where he carried 42% of the electorate.*

*The Northern Democrats, under Senator Stephen Douglas, convinced one in three voters across our great nation to cast their ballot for the Illinois senator. Despite collecting so many votes, the Senator only carried five states' 27 electors. He won the popular vote in Delaware, Illinois, Iowa, Rhode Island, and Vermont. He took Delaware's 3 electors with only 33% of the vote, the lowest margin of victory by any presidential candidate. The senator even failed to claim 50% of the vote in his home state of Illinois.*

*Having survived a last-minute effort by Millard Fillmore's supporters to steal the nomination, Senator William Seward of New York emerged as the candidate carrying the banner of the National Whig Party. Senator Seward won the barest plurality of the popular vote. Of more than three million votes cast, the senator collected less than 38%. He carried Connecticut, Indiana, Maine, Massachusetts, Michigan, New Hampshire, New Jersey, New York, Ohio, and Pennsylvania. Of the states he won, he carried a majority of the vote in 7 states, the strongest performance of any candidate. He clinched 143 electors and the presidency.*

*By winning the electoral college outright, President-Elect Seward thwarted Southern Democrats' attempt to deny the Whig's a majority of the electors. Had they succeeded, the election would have been decided by the House of Representatives. With 14 free and 14 slave states, each having but one vote in the House, it is likely they could have denied the Presidency to Senator Seward.*

Greeley dipped the nib into the inkwell and corrected a word as he smiled at what he wrote. The past few weeks had been nerve-wracking as the nation had waited for each state to release their results and announce their electors. South Carolina had been the first to announce. When the only votes to be counted are those in the state legislature, it's easy to know the results almost immediately. Michigan and Florida were the last to report. The telegraph lines that carried the results across most of the country barely penetrated parts of those two states. Until Michigan reported, nobody knew if Seward would get to one hundred forty-two electors.

He frowned as he continued proofing his article.

*We only learned a week ago which way Michigan would go. By a mere 9,000 vote margin in Michigan, Senator Seward became President-elect Seward. Of over three million votes cast, a mere 9,000 kept the House of Representatives from deciding the election. Southern Democrats, unhappy with those 9,000 men from the west, have determined the election was not legitimate, for reasons they alone understand.*

*These Southern Democrats will meet at Christmastime in New Orleans to discuss their response to the election. Like the South Carolinians fifteen years ago who railed against the tariff and threatened secession when President Jackson sat in the Executive Mansion, the Democrats in the South closely tied to the Southern Cross movement are now calling for secession and annexation of Texas in the same breath. The newspaper of record is hard pressed to explain to readers how these radicals demand that the federal government annex an independent nation that wants no part of annexation while calling for their own secession. It's hard to fathom that we are part and parcel of the same nation as such lunatics. If they have their way, we may not be for long.*

24 December 1852

Colonel Justin Lamont tipped his hat to the throng of women carolers singing *Joy to the World,* as he hurried by. New Orleans was decorated for Christmas, and people streamed in and out of storefronts to buy last-minute gifts.

The building he hurried toward was on the corner of Charles and St. Louis streets. The City Hotel & Exchange was the largest hotel in the historic French Quarter. Before passing through the ornate double doors, he checked his reflection in the glass windows. He ran his hand over his new gray frockcoat. The months on the Texas front had left his uniforms from South Carolina threadbare and stained. He was glad to be away from the Sabine salient, where the rebels from Texas and their Southern allies remained, waiting for the South's response to the recent presidential election.

He'd still be there, save for the fact that he was one of a dozen South Carolinians appointed by the legislature to represent the Palmetto State's interests at the convention now underway in the Exchange's large hall. At other times, the Exchange was a favorite place for public events, like slave auctions. But today, several hundred men convened there to decide the fate of the South.

When he came through the doors, he heard a familiar voice, "Merry Christmas, Colonel Lamont. I didn't expect to see you here."

When he turned, Lamont saw G.T. Beauregard coming toward him. "General, a pleasure. I am but of servant of South Carolina. When she calls, I must answer."

Beauregard returned his salute. "As must we all, Colonel. I've just returned from South Carolina where I've been working with your own Governor Means to establish schools of the soldier, to train more volunteers."

Lamont smiled at the news. "Given what may be coming, more soldiers will be necessary. I hope, though, that you'll dispense with the tactics with which my own men were trained. Massed musket fire has proved completely ineffectual in dealing with Johnston's army."

"I've reached the same conclusion. I've been in correspondence with General Hardee, and he's in agreement. We've thrown out Winfield Scott's manual and are devising our own." Beauregard paused, eying Lamont, as though taking his measure. "As a matter of fact, we're taking Travis' training manual for the army of Texas and are modifying it."

Lamont repressed the rage he felt whenever he heard William Travis' name. South Carolina's interests were a distant second to his desire to see Travis' pay for his game leg and the attack on his plantation nearly a decade earlier.

Beauregard said, "I've read that General Hardee has changed our strategy in Texas."

"You could say so," Lamont conceded, forgetting his anger at Travis, for the moment. "I had thought he was wrong to give up Beaumont to the abolitionists, but General Johnston could have flanked us as soon as more of their army was mobilized. Crossing the Neches River ain't that difficult the further north you go. You read about Johnston's failed effort a few months ago? It cost him several hundred casualties for nothing. Our position on the Texas side of the Sabine is so strong, and there's no way for him to flank us, not without invading the United States."

Beauregard shrugged, "Perhaps. But this convention will decide if it's the United States that General Johnston would be invading. Before long, things could become very different."

A few days later, Lamont stood against the outer wall of the domed Exchange as the men in the crowded hall waited to for the final vote to be taken. The debate had been rancorous and fractious. Delegates from Kentucky and Maryland left the previous day when it became clear they were not going to moderate the Convention's goals.

From a platform in the center of the hall, where auctioneers usually conducted slave auctions, the president of the Convention, Lt. Governor Joshua Ward of South Carolina leaned on a cane as he spoke, "Before we vote, I'll summarize the articles upon which we'll vote and which each delegate has received.

"The Convention of States assembled in New Orleans on December twenty-fourth, in the year of our Lord, eighteen hundred and fifty-two has been charged to determine the best way forward in the aftermath of the November election after the avowed abolitionist William Seward won the election with only the support of ten of the twenty-eight states.

"Seward campaigned on not letting any new states into the Union unless they were free. The balance of our nation has, since its very inception been a balance between slave and free. By declaring he'll countenance no new slave states, Seward has avowed the South to be an unloved and junior partner in our republic. We have been marginalized in the House of Representatives for a generation now, and under Seward, we'll be marginalized in the Senate, as well.

"Our way of life, the very fiber of our existence is found in our peculiar institution. As of the last enumeration, the total value to our nation's economy of Southern slaves is more than fifteen-hundred million dollars. That is nearly equal to that of all the northern states combined, although, in the North, it is collected most heavily among the industrialists of New York and Philadelphia."

Lamont found himself nodding in agreement. He had no notion about where industrialists in the North were congregating, but that their interests and his were at odds was indisputable, as far as he was concerned.

Ward continued, "Seward and his cohorts would doom us to penury and poverty. Despite their many protestations to the contrary, they'd as soon see the Negro our equal than to share power with us any longer. We must stand united against the depredations of the North. To that end, the convention will vote upon articles of secession, to be submitted before each Southern State's duly elected legislature. Upon ratification of the seventh state, those ratifying states will constitute a new alliance of states and shall meet again here in New Orleans to organize a new national government to secure our shared and common interests."

The speaker continued talking. Lamont thought about which states would be the first to ratify the articles. He hoped South Carolina would act first, but Louisiana was already fully committed to the war in Texas and would likely beat his native state to the punch. What bothered him were the slave states that wouldn't be ratifying the articles. Delaware failed to send any delegates. With the departure of Maryland and Kentucky's representatives, he was doubtful that their legislatures would even take up the articles.

Another speaker had risen. "Does Alabama vote to advance the articles to the various states?"

Standing on the floor of the Exchange, the delegates from Alabama shouted, "Aye!"

A roar of approval rattled the windows in the hall. "How does Arkansas vote?"

"Yes!"

"Florida?"

"Yes!"

"Georgia?"

"Yes!"

"Kentucky?"

The hall fell silent. Men who had disagreed with the direction of the convention had left, leaving Kentucky without a voice.

"Louisiana?"

"Yes!"

"Maryland?"

Silence.

"Mississippi?"

"Yes!" As though repudiating the cowardice of Maryland to not vote their conscience, the room shouted and stomped their approval.

"Missouri?"

"Yes!"

"North Carolina?"

"Yes!"

"South Carolina?"

"Yes!"

"Tennessee?"

"Yes!"

"Virginia?"

There was a long pause. "No!"

Lamont stared at Virginia's delegates. John Letcher, a Congressman, was the spokesman for the Virginia delegation. He turned around the room, glaring at those who shouted in protest at Virginia's lone voice of dissent.

The speaker took the contrarian vote in stride. Lamont couldn't help but wonder if those men on the platform already knew the results before the Alabama delegation voted aye. He figured it would be like a politician to know the direction of the wind before stepping outside.

"By a vote of ten to one, the articles shall be presented to all Southern states within the next thirty days for ratification."

Will flipped up the collar on his greatcoat and eased back on the reins, letting Juan Seguin pull up next to him. The blue norther blew in from the north, dusting a bit of frost on the trees and grass. It made him think of an old joke about the only thing between the North Pole and West Texas in winter was a barbed wire fence. It brought a smile to his chapped lips as he looked back and saw two Texas Rangers a couple of dozen yards behind. They were a constant reminder that part of the country would happily kill him as look at him.

*Of course, they're getting their due now that we've trapped most of the rebels along the Sabine River.*

Seguin broke through his thoughts, "Smart move letting some of those bastards who supported the rebels in Beaumont down easy. Shows that we're prepared to be high-minded."

Will shrugged. "These are just the folks who backed the wrong side but didn't take up arms, Juan. We've not captured very many of the rebel soldiers, but I'm keeping every one of those boys locked up until the end of the war."

Seguin said, "Even though we've got them against the Sabine, you don't sound like you expect the war to end soon."

Will swore. "It's those damned slave owners in the South that worry me. South Carolina and Louisiana have already passed the articles that came out of their Convention in New Orleans. They pick up another five states, and they'll all secede."

"I reckon it's just a matter of time before Alabama and Mississippi join them," Seguin ventured. "Who'll be next after them?"

Will let the reins fall onto the pommel as he cupped his bare hands and blew into them. "After the shitstorm John Brown and Bedford Forrest kicked up in Arkansas, it's a sure thing they'll follow. It's hard to argue that Seward will let the south keep their slaves when Brown's lining every one of them he finds up against a wall and murdering them. After Arkansas, I figure Georgia and Florida will follow. Maybe even Tennessee, Missouri, and North Carolina."

"Speaking of John Brown, what are you going to do with him now that Wallace's Rangers have brought him to Austin?"

Will grimaced as though he'd bitten into a lemon. In the years before the transference, when he'd read about the Civil War, Brown's brutality in Kansas and then his raid on Harper's Ferry, Virginia had fired up Southerners who could legitimately point to Brown's violence when Northern politicians promised compromise with the South over the issue of slavery. But this was worse. With Texas an independent nation, the South had stymied Northern efforts to bring in more free states, and with no Compromise of 1850, the Western Territory remained mostly closed to settlers.

But Seguin deserved an answer. "If the reports are true, Brown's killed more than a dozen of men between Northwest Texas and Southeast Arkansas, all civilian. Their only crime was they owned slaves. You know I believe with all my heart owning another soul is a crime against God. But, at this time, neither Texas nor Arkansas considers it a crime. I can't ignore that. Thousands of folks who still own slaves remain loyal to our government. They expect justice to be done. But Brown's very popular in the Northeastern United States, where the abolitionist movement is strongest. A trial could damage our standing with people we desperately need as allies."

Seguin whistled, low. "You, my friend, are between Scylla and Charybdis. What are you going to do?"

Will let a feral look cross his face, "I've locked him in the same cell where Lorenzo kept Santa Anna. If I can manage it, I'm going to keep him locked up until the war is over, then try him and hang him high as Haman."

They crested a hill east of San Antonio where they found the reason for their visit. Sprawled across the prairie were the men of the 26th and 28th Infantry battalions as well as an independent command, more than fifteen hundred soldiers learning their trade. As they rode down the slope and into the camp, they smelled breakfast cooking and heard Irish brogues mixed with melodic Italian and guttural German. The men who made up the two battalions arrived from across Europe. Many came because of generous land bounties, others came because things were worse in their homelands, and others, having watched the liberal revolutions beaten back across Europe, saw in Texas freedoms they'd never have in places like Prussia, Bohemia, or the Austrian empire.

Midway through camp, they came upon an officer sitting under a tarp, eating breakfast. When the officer spotted Will atop his mount, a chair clattered as it tipped over. The officer snapped a crisp salute, his palm facing outward, like in the British army.

Will's stomach growled. When he and Juan had set out from the Alamo at dawn, they had planned on inspecting the camp before dining with the fort's cadets later in the morning. He regretted the decision as the officer said, "President Travis, Vice-President Seguin, it's a pleasure to see you so early. Can I offer you breakfast?"

The officer spoke with a sophisticated Irish lilt. As the army had expanded, General Johnston had recruited men with military experience wherever he could find them. James Mahon was no exception. After losing his seat in the British parliament the previous year, Mahon had turned up in Austin with a letter of introduction to Will. As he thought back to that first meeting, Will suppressed a smile as he recalled the shock on his face when Mahon produced a letter from Merrill Taylor, a banker in London who represented powerful British interests to Will over the years.

Mahon had stood in Will's office a few months earlier, standing before his desk like he belonged there while Will read the introduction. The letter congratulated him on his election and the new direction Will was leading Texas and wished him success in suppressing the rebellion. It continued by implying if Texas needed to issue war bonds, there would be a ready foreign market for them. And lastly, it offered Mahon's services. As a former member of Parliament from County Claire, the Irishman held the respect of his fellow countrymen, many of whom were still fleeing the aftermath of the potato famine.

The letter had proven prescient. Within a month of Mahon's promotion to colonel, the number of foreigners who showed up volunteering for service exceeded the battalion's authorized strength. Before long, these trainees would complete their training, ready to join Johnston's army along the Sabine River.

"I wish we could join you, Colonel. We're due back in the Alamo shortly for breakfast with the cadets. They'd be mighty disappointed if we showed up with no appetite. General Johnston has written to me and said your boys will be ready to join him within a few weeks. Will they be ready?"

Mahon swept a hand around at the surrounding camp. "I've got the finest boys from Dublin to Kilkenny, sir. Not to mention a fair number of bonnie lads from Edenborough and some of Friedrich Wilhelm's Prussian volunteers. When General Johnston calls, we'll march forth and crush the remains of the rebellion."

It was hard to resist Mahon's optimism, as the tall, gray-haired colonel bubbled with enthusiasm. He worried, though. If all the Southern states he thought likely to secede did so and turned their combined might against Texas, it would take a miracle to stop them before President-Elect Seward could raise an army to force those Southern States back into the Union.

Seguin interrupted them, "Buck, look over there."

The Vice President pointed into the sky. Rising over the encampment were three balloons, tethered to the ground by thick, long ropes.

Will followed Seguin's gaze. One balloon was already hundreds of feet in the air. Another was a couple of hundred feet below it, and the last was but a hundred feet from the ground.

Seguin clapped and laughed as the first one reached the end of the tether, more than a thousand feet off the ground. "We've just quadrupled the amount of land we can cover with these balloons, Buck. These new aeronauts should be ready by the time we're prepared to move against the rebel salient."

Will pursed his lips. "I hope so. We'll have a half dozen crews ready by then."

Seguin slapped him on the back, "Charlie must be champing at the bit to get back to the Ninth."

Will's smile was thin, as he thought about the risk his son endured. "I'm sure he is. But life is full of disappointments. Sid's planning on putting him in charge of our little balloon corps."

# Chapter 14

29 January 1853

“Captain, the wire’s been run, and we’ve got the telegraph machine ready to transmit.” The soldier who stood before Andy Berry wore the insignia of the republic’s signal corps, a small brass pin with two crossed spyglasses on his black wide-brimmed hat.

Berry waved off the salute. He had asked for, and General Johnston had granted him, the use of a telegraph team from the front. As far as he was concerned, he was wearing the hat of inventor and industrialist and not that of reserve commander of an artillery battery.

He stepped over to the field gun. It was one of the new model breechloaders the foundry had been making for the better part of a year. He ran his hand over the cold barrel. In nearly every way this gun was identical to those entrenched on the front more than sixty miles away. The difference was the contraption fixed to the side of the gun, near the breech.

Berry propped his leg up on the carriage's wooden trail and raised his voice, "Gather round, boys. It's cold enough out here that I saw a politician with his hands in his own pockets. Let's get this over and get back to the warmth of our homes."

Most of the men standing nearby worked in his foundry. Most days found them pouring molten steel into molds, but on this Saturday, they stood, listening, hands in pockets, stomping their feet to stay warm. A few others wore the army's butternut uniforms, they were on loan for the demonstration.

"We've run a telegraph from the edge of Trinity Meadows back here to the gun. As we test the lining plane, the boys from the Signal Corps will telegraph back the results." Berry pointed to the iron and brass contraption attached to the gun and continued, "This rotatable open sight allows us to calculate the angle. For instance, if the target we want to hit is located beyond the forest here, like the plantation over yonder, we can more precisely set the gun's elevation."

Berry came over to a small camp table near the gun, picked up a pencil, and using it, pointed to a map covering the tabletop. "We need to know our position relative to that of our target. In this case, that fat bastard Owen Talmage's plantation house. It was mighty nice of him to donate it for today's experiment."

The men around Berry chuckled. Talmage fled with his slaves when Johnston's army had defeated the rebels and their Southern allies on the Trinity the previous year. Since then, the local tax assessor had ostensibly seized the property for back taxes. Berry thought it was better than Talmage deserved. But seeing as how the government in Austin wasn't seizing all the rebels' property, it didn't bother him in the least that local officials had taken matters into their own hands.

"We're going to measure the azimuth which is the number of degrees clockwise from true north, between our gun and the target. We'll use that tall live oak tree poking above the rest of the forest as our marker. We'll then get the azimuth between the gun and the marker. By subtracting the first azimuth reading from the second, we'll get the angle between the marker and the line to the target. Once that's done, we'll use the compass on the device on the rear of the gun and shift it until the gun's sight is laid on the aiming point. The gun's bore is now on target and ready to fire.

"Once we fire, our spotter at the forward telegraph box will let us know how much we need to adjust the elevation or direction once we roll the gun back into place. On the front, we'd be relying on the balloon corps to transmit where the round landed. They'll send it through the signal corps back to the gunners. Any questions?"

There were none. He and his men had practiced back at the Gunworks' testing range. But this was the first live exercise in conditions that approached what the army would face in combat.

As the men assumed their roles on the gun, Berry stayed by the map and waited as they efficiently loaded the field piece. Once they were finished, one of them shouted, "Ready!"

Berry had already calculated the geometry, but he checked his work before he came over to the metal contraption attached to the gun's bore and set the brass compass for the calculated angle. "Alright, gunnery sergeant set the elevation."

The gunnery sergeant spun the elevation screw until the bore aligned with the primitive goniometer. "Ready, sir."

"An ounce of prevention," Berry muttered as he rechecked both his calculation and the contraption's angle. Satisfied they aligned, he raised his voice, "Fire!"

The man filling the role of gunnery sergeant checked that he was clear of the recoil and pulled the lanyard. Smoke and fire spewed from the barrel and the gun rocked back. The projectile raced over the trees, and a moment later, in the distance, they heard it crash down. The telegraph machine clattered to life, and the operator called out, "Over-shot the target by eighty yards, sir."

"Reload," Berry turned back to his calculations on the table as the crew rolled the gun back into place and methodically reloaded. As reservists, they knew their roles nearly as well as the regulars under Colonel William Sherman's command and moved with an economy of motion.

Berry made another adjustment to the compass. Once the bore was lowered to match the newly measured angle, the gun fired again.

The telegraph operator shouted, "Hit! Direct hit."

Berry joined his men, laughing and patting each other on the back, before a feral grin lit up his face, "Alright, let's fire the rest of the rounds. No reason to leave that traitor's house standing."

1 February 1853

Seagulls squawked outside the window of the Galveston Customs House. Will tried to ignore them as he spoke with the two other men in the room.

"Pass on my thanks to President-Elect Seward and President Cass, Commodore. Your arrival in the Gulf is both welcome and timely."

Matthew Perry's stern countenance cracked, for a moment a smile graced his features. "It's not my place to comment on politics, President Travis, but the Southern secession finally moved Lewis Cass to act, at least enough to listen to William Seward's request to re-form our West Indies Squadron."

The third participant wore the blue jacket of the Texas Navy. He wore shoulder boards embroidered with a single gold star. Will saw no reason that an admiral shouldn't command Texas' eleven-ship navy, unlike the United States, where Matthew Perry's rank of commodore was temporary. Once command of his squadron passed on to his successor, Perry would resume his previous naval rank of captain. Edwin Moore said, "All that matters is that our hands are finally untied. Now we can act to cut the bridge between Louisiana and Texas without risking widening the war."

Will chuckled ruefully. "I trust you're not talking about our declaration of war against this new Southern alliance of states. I might construe that as lèse-majesté."

Moore returned the smile. "Of course, your Excellency. Your decision to declare war couldn't possibly have been in reaction to them calling for seventy thousand volunteers to – how did they say it? – complete the annexation of Texas."

"Touché, Admiral," Will said. "Closing that railroad bridge will give us a bit of breathing room while we see what kind of help Seward will provide once he's sworn in next month.

There was a slight hitch in Perry's voice. "William Seward will, I think, pursue an entirely different policy regarding both Texas and these wayward Southern states than President Cass. But now the gloves have come off as far as the bridge over the Sabine goes. How can the United States Navy help?"

Will had strong views about what should happen. But he'd learned over the years to trust men like Sidney Johnston and Edwin Moore when it came to tactics. He glanced over to Moore, who said, "Aside from our Pacific Squadron, we'll take our entire fleet up the Sabine Pass to the lake upriver. From there, it's just a few miles before we reach the railroad bridge."

Perry said, "Do you have current maps of the channel up the river? Our charts are old, but they show frequent sandbars up and down Sabine Pass."

Moore pointed to a map on the wall, "Yes. We've charted all our coastal rivers within the last decade. We'll have to take our ships up the Pass in single file, staying in the middle of the channel."

Will stared at the map. He knew the rebels had placed heavy artillery positions at the Pass's narrowest point. How was Moore planning on neutralizing the batteries?

Moore continued, "We've mobilized our entire Marine reserves. I've recalled Colonel West from the front with his battalion. He'll lead a light brigade of fifteen hundred Marines overland and attack the batteries at the same time as we commence our run up the Pass. Commodore, if you're able, I can provide you charts for the Pass. We need to silence the guns on the Louisiana shoreline."

Perry studied the map, apparently deep in thought long enough for Will to wonder what he was thinking. Finally, the naval officer gave a single nod. "If I can get approval, I'll lead my squadron in the steam frigate *Mississippi*. I'll dispatch my fastest steam-packet for Norfolk. Shame the telegraph network is down between Texas and Washington. Otherwise, we'd have an answer in a couple of days."

Moore leaned over the map. "We'll need time. While Colonel West is a capable officer, I'd like to give him a few weeks to train his reservists and integrate them into his command before we attack."

Will walked over to the map hanging on the wall and stared at the narrow channel separating Texas and Louisiana. He had spent the last year and a half trying to stave off total war. He'd refused Sid Johnston's requests for more mobilization because the risk of tanking the economy was real. Now, seven Southern states had seceded, and they were determined to make Texas their eighth state. They'd invested too much of their own blood over the past six months trying to prop up rebels like Robert Potter and James Collinsworth to walk away without a fight.

For the past year, he'd held off ordering an attack on the rebel batteries protecting the Sabine River and the railroad lifeline between East Texas and Louisiana because he didn't want to expand the war. Containment and suffocation had been his goal. *Hell,* he thought, *that's why that bastard John Brown is sitting in a jail cell.*

Had it been a foolish hope, that Johnston would have been able to smother the rebellion by trapping it against the Sabine River and letting it die from lack of oxygen? The secession of the southern states over Texas argued strongly he'd been mistaken. He wasn't ready to let go believing he'd been right to limit the scope of the war. Had he been able to force the rebels to surrender before the Southern secession, the conflict would have been over by now.

"Things change, gentlemen," Will said, turning away from the map and looking at Moore and Perry. His voice was heavy with emotion. "My hope for a quick war died because of that damned bridge connecting Texas to Louisiana. Take out the enemy batteries and destroy that bridge."

Clinching the newspaper in his hand, General William Hardee stepped over the railroad ties as he walked toward the thundering of heavy guns. By his side was the army's quartermaster general, Peyton Wyatt. The sound was faint but unmistakable. The sun hung low in the western sky, bathing the twilight in brilliant hues of gold, red and orange. "It appears your president has decided to attack, Payton."

The butternut uniformed Payton stared at the river, languidly flowing southward. "Not my president, Bill. I suspect he'd hang me as look at me. But you're right. I told Beauregard that if the war remained confined to East Texas, Travis wouldn't risk angering the United States by attacking the bridge over the Sabine. Now that the bridge's eastern pilings are no longer in the United States, I suspect Travis isn't worried about widening the war."

Hardee's laughter held a bitter note. "No. Our politicians in New Orleans have put paid to that. Within a couple of months, we'll muster an army of a hundred thousand."

Wyatt shook his head as he listened to the thundering down river. "Won't do us a damned bit of good, though, unless those batteries along the Pass hold the navy back."

"I've received orders from the provisional government in New Orleans to hold the salient and wait for reinforcements. If it's practical to do so, I would like to follow those orders. You've worked with Admiral Moore. What kind of man is he?"

The quartermaster scratched his chin. "Competent. While he wasn't present for the battle of Campeche back in forty-three, his leadership prepared the navy to fight. If there's a way for him to push past our defenses there, then he'll be here within a day. The artillery we have here isn't heavy enough to stop Moore's iron sheeted ships. Defeat at the Pass means defeat here. If Moore gets this far, he'll destroy the bridge."

Hardee opened the newspaper and reread the headline. It was from Galveston, only a week old. He found the article that provoked his concern.

*Orders mobilizing the following battalions have been issued by the Texas War Department*

*5th, 8th, 11th, 13th, 14th, 17th, 18th, 19th, 20th, 22nd, and 24th Infantry battalions, 6th, 7th, 8th and 9th Cavalry Battalions and the 4th and 5th artillery battalions are to be mobilized for the defense of the Republic for the duration of the conflict.*

*More than 11,000 men of the mobilized formations will join General Johnston's army or serve in other capacities as needed. Congress, which had previously authorized a field army of 15,000 has passed a funding bill, expanding the army to more than 30,000 by the summer of 1853.*

*Congress has also authorized the purchase of 4 new warships from the United States and Great Britain.*

*President Travis spoke in a joint session of Congress on January 21, "There is no way to take the mobilization of seventy-thousand soldiers in the states in rebellion against the Federal Government in Washington as anything other than an act of war, a naked and ambitious act of a desperate people to try to claim that which isn't theirs. We are not a rich land. Our people are thinly spread across the continent from the Sabine to the Pacific Ocean, but we are a proud people. We shall not yield our independence. We shall stand firm. We shall defend our borders no matter the cost. We shall fight upon our beaches, we shall fight along our eastern border, we shall fight in the forests and in the fields. We shall never surrender or retreat."*

Grudgingly, Hardee admitted, Travis had given the theatrical performance of his life when he asked his Congress for a declaration of war. But it had worked. Texas' Congress had authorized Travis to use every tool available to defend the fledgling Republic.

"A day, if they get past our batteries?"

Wyatt nodded. "Yes, sir. If they cut us off, we should be alright for a while. We've got enough food here to feed us for at least a month as well as enough small arms ammunition to sustain us through at least two pitched fights. The same with our artillery."

"But is that going to be enough?" Hardee mused. "We've got twenty-thousand men here. Johnston's got twelve or thirteen thousand opposite of us. Within a few weeks, he's likely to outnumber us."

Wyatt blanched. "I don't much fancy the boot being on the other foot, Bill. It pinches. Sid Johnston's got an entire battalion of field artillery out there. In a few weeks, he could start a contact bombardment with sixty or more guns."

Hardee turned away from the river and looked toward his army. As the last light of day silhouetted the battlements separating his army from that of the enemy, he knew he had built fortifications no army could take without massive loss of life. His problem was he would soon face an enemy ready to take those casualties to destroy his army.

"Peyton, if your Admiral Moore destroys those batteries, I believe Johnston won't give us time to receive reinforcements. Order the Third Louisiana and Tenth Texas to get ready to take the train back across the river. By the time the sun rises in the morning, I want half the army preparing a defensive line on the other side of the river."

# Chapter 15

Charlie gripped the side of the basket as a gust of wind shook it. “You know, Sam, if we crash and die, there’ll be no hallowed ground for us. The church is sure to consider it a suicide.”

Sam Williams laughed. “Strange words from the commander of the balloon corps.” He swept his hand, pointing to another balloon a couple of miles away from where they hung above the Texian line.

Swallowing bile, Charlie growled, “A little respect, soldier.”

Sam complained, “I volunteered as a civilian to man the telegraph machine. Nobody told me they’d mobilize our militia company. Still, I’d rather be floating over the line than be in it... sir.”

Charlie glanced down at the Texian line. He was almost a thousand feet in the air and rising, the men below were tiny as ants to his unaided eye. Six Texian redoubts faced the Rebel trench lines. Behind the redoubts, a long trench-line connected them together, sealing off the rebels from the rest of Texas.

To the north, another balloon floated over the line, where the last redoubt nearly touched the Sabine River. Another balloon held a similar position on the southern flank. Charlie shook his head. General Johnston had received three more balloons, made by the students and faculty at Trinity College. Like Sam, the students had found their militia company mobilized. However, for the most part, they remained behind in Trinity Park, contributing to the war effort any way they could. A few, like Sam, volunteered as telegraph operators and spotters. And Charlie was in command of the whole crazy operation.

General Johnston rebuffed his last effort at getting reassigned back to the 9th Infantry. The general had told him Colonel Garibaldi had requested two of his fellow Italian revolutionaries be promoted to the rank of major to help command the oversized battalion. And Johnston had agreed.

Charlie let out a sigh loud enough to bring a smile from his teenaged assistant. All his arguing with General Johnston had gotten him was a stern, "I'll play no favorites, Major Travis. If I want you up in that balloon until Christ's return, that's where'll you be. Dismissed."

The balloon jerked and stopped rising, as the men below secured the lines to the ground. *Time to get to work*, Charlie thought as he raised the binoculars to his eyes and scanned the enemy lines. The ubiquitous blue flag with its single star flew over the first enemy trench. From his position high over the salient, he saw a few men moving around below the lip of the entrenchment.

He shifted his view to the second line of trenches. Charlie thought, *Those West Point officers sure know how to build defenses in depth*. Three lines of trenches cut through the flood plain's soft soil.

"Today's exercise will let us know if we'll be able to use those new lining-planes for the artillery," Charlie said.

"Anything to report?"

Charlie ignored Sam's question as he noticed the second trench line was devoid of life. He scanned the third line. It was like the latter – empty. He swore and focused his view on the first one. "Son of a bitch!" he swore, "There can't be more than three or four thousand men down there."

Sam's finger tapped on the transmitter key as he sent the message to the men on the ground. A few minutes passed by until the receiver clattered to life. The youth scribbled on a piece of paper until the clattering stopped. "Major, General Johnston intends to test the new lining-planes. We're to pick a target and let them know where it's at on the map."

The army's small topography department had provided identical maps of the area to Charlie and the other spotters and to each gun battery participating in the day's demonstration. Charlie switched between looking at the enemy fortifications and the map. "Target the center of the line. Focus fire on the enemy line directly in front of redoubt number three."

Moments later, a lone shot screamed downrange, plowing into the space between the enemy trench lines. "Overshot by a hundred yards. Adjust accordingly."

Sam sent Charlie's instructions. A few minutes later another shot landed a few feet shy of the first line of trenches. "Good enough. On target."

The rest of the battery opened fire. Had the battery been firing solid shots, most of the rounds would have plowed harmlessly into the ground. But shells were detonating over the trench, showering the defenders with a deadly iron rain.

Charlie kept his eyes glued to the enemy line as some shells plowed into the ground in front of the trench while others exploded overhead. He saw several men bolt over the back of the trench and race toward the rear. After a few more shells detonated over the fortifications, the handful of men running away turned into a trickle.

"Some of their soldiers are abandoning the line."

Ignoring the clattering sound of the transmitter, Charlie saw the trickle turn into a steady stream of men. "Sam, they're breaking for the rear. I don't see evidence of anything behind them. I think we've been facing their rearguard."

Minutes ticked by as Charlie watched the stream turn into a route. Scanning the forward trench, if there were still men in there, they were keeping their heads low. In the distance, a bugle sounded, and he turned his binoculars to redoubt number three. In loose, open order deployment, the men from the 1st Infantry leapfrogged across the no-man's-land between the armies.

Like fireflies blinking in the twilight, gunfire lit up the enemy's forward trench. Ant-like soldiers scurried into craters, blasted into the loamy soil, and returned fire.

As more troops moved into the no-man's-land, those farthest forward raced toward the enemy fortifications. When they were within a couple of hundred feet, Charlie barked out, "Cease fire, they'll hit our own men."

Before the first soldier leapt into the enemy trench, the artillery fell silent. Along the entire enemy line, the last holdouts were racing toward the river. A couple of miles away Charlie could see the single span of the railroad bridge crossing the Sabine. He set his binoculars down and grabbed a long, slender leather case. He pulled a spyglass from it and set the end on the wicker basket's railing. It was long and heavy. But it was several times more powerful than the easily portable binoculars.

When he brought the bridge into focus, he watched men stepping from tie to tie as they hurried across.

"They're retreating across the bridge," Charlie said, "If we press the attack, we can bag the rebels still on this side."

The transmitter clattered as Sam sent the message. Charlie continued watching as men bunched up on the western side of the river; only so many men could start across at once. One man, already halfway across, missed a step. Charlie gasped as he watched the tiny figure plunge nearly a hundred feet into the river. Then he saw several figures climbing along the wooden trestles, below the rails.

Charlie's voice rose in excitement. "Sam, they're rigging the bridge with explosives. If we move faster, we can capture the bridge intact."

Minutes dragged by as they waited for a response. Despite the silence from the telegraph machine, a horseman raced across the field, dodging craters. He drew up before the captured trench and almost immediately, little butternut colored ant-like figures streamed after the retreating enemy.

Time seemed to stand still as Charlie watched the pursuit. The veterans from the 1st Texas were approaching the bridge when a flash of light forced Charlie to pull his eye away from the spyglass. He didn't need it to see a fireball rise into the sky above the bridge.

The siege was over.

11 March 1853

Horace Greeley looked at the yellow wallpaper adorning the oval sitting room and thought it ugly. Hardly presidential. As he wondered at the reasons President Cass or his wife had left it that way, the door opened, and President Seward entered.

Seward's smile was warm and inviting, "Horace, thanks for waiting. Things are a might unsettled still. It takes a bit of time for the boilers to build up a head of steam and so it is with me."

Greeley took the offered hand, "Quite alright, Mr. President. I'm not sure who's more pleased about this interview, my readers or me. It's quite the honor you've bestowed, allowing me the privilege of the first presidential interview of your new administration."

Seward ran a hand through his greying hair. "On days like today, I can't imagine what made my predecessor run for reelection. Forming a cabinet and transitioning things between one administration and another is worse than trying to herd cats."

Greeley said, "Can I quote you on that?"

Seward offered another smile, "I doubt you wanted to interview me about cats. You're a bit of an opinion maker among eastern Whigs, and this crisis is going to take all of our skill and resources to manage."

Greeley dipped his head in agreement. "I expected Tennessee to stay. I still find it hard to believe that Governor Trousdale allowed their legislature to vote on the secession bill those fire eaters in New Orleans put together."

"Voted and passed," Seward grimaced at the memory. "Now that Tennessee joined the other Southern states, that puts nine of the fourteen slave states in rebellion. But that also means that Virginia, Kentucky, Maryland, North Carolina, and Delaware are still loyal to the Union. At least for now."

Greeley jotted down a few notes as Seward spoke.

"That's the reason you're here Horace. Two and one-half million citizens are in those five states. If they were to join the rebellion, it would increase by half the rebels' available manpower. We can't have that."

"How do you plan on stopping them?" Pen forgotten, Greeley leaned forward.

Seward walked over to the room's windows and lifted the curtain. He pointed southward, "It tears at my heart, my friend, but I will promise George Summers and Lazarus Powell almost anything to keep Kentucky and Virginia firmly in our camp."

Hearing the names of the two governors, Greeley's stomach lurched. There was only one issue around which all others revolved. "Slavery? What do they want?"

"Guarantees, of course."

Gripping his pencil in his hand, Greeley said, "Why do they persist in defending the indefensible?"

Seward turned his back to the window, "The census office told me the other day that slaves are valued at more than one thousand million dollars. They produce tens of millions of dollars for their masters. Knowing this sickens me. But when your newspaper attacks Southerners, you're not just attacking an institution, Horace. You're attacking their livelihood."

Greeley felt his frown deepen. "They want an amendment, don't they?"

Seward nodded. "Yes. Yesterday I had the entire senatorial delegation from the five remaining slave states here. They want an amendment protecting slavery in all fourteen Southern states."

Greeley leapt to his feet, "That's extortion! You must tell them no."

The president held up his hand as though fending off a rabid animal, "Hold there, Horace. You know my heart as well as any man. You know I believe that our nation cannot exist half slave and half free. But neither am I certain we can win if the five remaining slave states join their wayward sisters. We must preserve the Union now, and if I have to give Virginia and Kentucky the keys to the kingdom to preserve their loyalty, by all that is holy, I can live with that decision."

Greeley wanted nothing more than to turn and leave. But Seward was more than just a friend, he was the successor of Washington. He owed it to the President to remain. "You didn't invite me here to interview you for my readers, you brought me here because you know how loudly abolitionists will scream you've betrayed them."

He saw the pain in the president's eyes. He'd struck home his attack. Seward's eyes cleared, and he said, "I'll have you know I refused the senator's demand. I told him no state that has seceded and remains in open rebellion can expect to have all their property respected. I told them that if they proposed an amendment to the constitution allowing slavery in perpetuity in states which remain, I would support it."

"Why?" Tears came unbidden to Greeley's eyes as he felt his heart constrict.

Seward took a letter from a table and said, "I received this from President Travis. You know he's really quite devious if you get past his rough frontier ways."

Sinking back into his chair, Greeley said, "What does he say?"

"He suggested that an amendment to the constitution allowing slavery would be bad. But it would be worse if Virginia and the other loyal states seceded. He also said that if our constitution could be amended to perpetuate slavery in our loyal states, then it could certainly be re-amended down the road to prohibit it. I like the way he said it, a constitution isn't a suicide pact. What is changed today can be changed again tomorrow."

Greeley wiped at his eyes, "How so?"

"Within the next few weeks, a vote will come up in the House to make new states from both Wisconsin and the coastal part of Jefferson Territory, forever altering the balance of power in the Senate. Given time, we'll turn Delaware into a free state, too."

Greeley folded a handkerchief he'd just used. "I'll do what I can, Mr. President to steer Whigs to support you. I don't like it, not one bit, but now I understand."

He picked up his pencil, which had fallen onto the rug. "What about one question, sir? Something I can give to my readers."

Taking Seward's silence for permission, Greeley said, "I've heard General Scott has returned to Washington from New York. What are your plans for subduing the rebellion?"

The president gestured toward a side door, "Follow me."

A large map covered several tables pushed together. It showed the United States and the eastern portion of Texas. "You see my problem? To get to the rebel states, we've got the border states in the way. If I send the army after the rebels today, I fear Virginia and North Carolina will react badly. It galls me to admit it, but to keep the upper South with us, I must let those fire eaters be the aggressors."

Greeley walked around the table, looking at the map. "Texas?"

"Texas. Every newspaper in the states in rebellion are crowing to God and his archangels that they're going to wipe the Travis administration off the face of the earth and if we try to stop them, then they'll deal with us next."

Greeley mused, "That worked so well for them the first time."

Seward pointed to the line between Louisiana and Texas, "By the time the Rebels, for that's what they are, attack Texas, Travis will have mobilized more than thirty thousand men. Additionally, I intend to open up our northern armories for volunteer regiments willing to serve in Texas. General Scott will be vetting them before we arm them. We can't have any more John Browns inflaming things. I'm convinced his murderous antics inflamed Missouri into joining the rebels."

Greeley felt his face coloring. He wished he could forget he had been responsible for introducing John Brown to the men who had funded his ill-fated expedition. "What will President Travis do with Brown?"

"The man murdered citizens of both Texas and the United States, Horace," Greeley grimaced at the President's wording. "Oh, don't worry, Texas will keep him locked up until the war is won, but after that, I expect Travis will put him on trial and then hang him."

Greeley leaned against the table, dragging in a breath full of air. He couldn't have dreamed Brown's expedition could have turned out so bad. As he worked to compose himself, he heard drums and the high-pitched shrilling of fifes. The President stood at a window, staring at Pennsylvania Avenue.

Coming up beside him, Greeley watched a long procession of infantry marching along, following behind the national flag. Seward pointed, "That's the Third Infantry Regiment. They're going to be encamping just outside of Arlington. They'll be joined by a volunteer regiment from Pennsylvania later this week. A regiment of volunteers will be arriving from New York after that."

Surprise filled Greeley's face. "I thought you had to be careful with Virginia. Putting troops on their side of the Potomac, isn't that risky?"

Seward wore a smug smile as he guided Greeley away from the window. "There'll be a regiment from the Virginia state guard joining them. But General Scott came up with an excellent suggestion. He offered command of the brigade to a native Virginian, a fellow by the name of Robert E. Lee."

17 March 1853

For three weeks the bridge once spanning the Sabine River had smoldered where it crashed into the riverbank. Now though, Jason Lamont saw it as a constant reminder of how far he was removed from his goal. On the other side of the river, he saw one of those damned balloons floating over the enemy lines.

Although the Southern coastal artillery batteries still held the eastern side of the Sabine Pass, it would only be a matter of time before the Texas Navy either destroyed the batteries or slipped by them. Even if General Hardee hadn't ordered the bridge destroyed, it was only a matter of time before the Texas Navy controlled the Sabine River. Still, he hated the sight of the bridge's charred remains, it was a constant reminder that he was a long way from taking his vengeance on William Travis.

Rocks clattered behind him, and a voice brought relief from the anger he felt. "Colonel, General Hardee's compliments, he wants to see you."

Lamont turned. His nephew, he decided, had finally turned into a reasonably competent aide. Elliott Brown's jacket was mended in several places. Supplies from South Carolina were slow in reaching his regiment, and the lieutenant was far from the only soldier wearing a threadbare uniform.

Lamont took the note from Brown, "Did the messenger say why?"

"No, he dropped it off and was gone before I could ask."

Lamont climbed out of the rifle pit, one of many crisscrossing the Louisiana side of the Sabine River, and without a backward glance, followed the lieutenant.

A bit later, Lamont found himself waiting outside the parlor of the plantation house the general used for his headquarters. When the door opened, and a well-dressed man in civilian clothes left, the officer from South Carolina was ushered into the room.

General Hardee rose from behind a desk and waved him into a seat. The general shoved a stack of papers out of the way that partially blocked his view of Lamont. "That's better. When I retired from the US Army, I thought I had left the endless requisitions behind. Now there's more than ever before. How are your boys doing?"

"Ready to tear into that damned abolitionist's army. Give us a chance, and we'll burn the capital down around Travis' ears." The ever-present anger he felt burned even brighter in Lamont's eyes at that moment.

Hardee chuckled. "That's the spirit, Colonel Lamont. We're still working on getting more men trained and ready for the offensive I'm sure will come before long. The Second Arkansas has recently arrived, and I'm pulling your men off the line, and they'll take your place, for now."

Lamont rose partway out of his seat, "But, sir, we're rested and ready for action."

Hardee gave him a crooked smile, "Who said you're not going to get a bit of action?"

Lamont sat on the edge of the chair, "Where are we going? Missouri? I hear things are tense up in Saint Louis. Lot of fools up there who didn't take kindly to the Legislature backing secession."

Hardee shook his head, "No. New Orleans. Even though our government has relocated our capital from the 'Crescent City' to Montgomery, we've been ordered to reinforce the fortifications around the city. Your regiment will be building some earthen forts on the Mississippi River below the city."

Lamont's face sagged. It wasn't what he'd joined up for. Hardee continued, "It's just for a few weeks, maybe a month or so. There'll be more regiments coming from your state, and as they arrive, you'll be brigaded together. I've heard enough men are slipping across the border from North Carolina, who don't cotton to their state's refusal to fight for our rights, to fill out another couple of regiments, too."

The news of the pending arrival of more South Carolinian soldiers perked up Lamont's spirit. Until now, his regiment was the only eastern unit to serve under Hardee. When he mentioned that, the general said,

"Our government has called for seventy thousand volunteers. Many thousands have already reported. I've heard that General Beauregard has been inundated with men passing through his schools of the soldier."

Eyes gleaming at the news, Lamont said, "How soon can we be ready? An army like that will roll over the Texian army like a tide rolling in from the ocean."

"I'll not be leading it," Hardee admitted. "It unofficial, but I've been told that President Cobb has offered command of the Army of the Trans-Mississippi, that's what they're calling us now, to Senator Jefferson Davis. He's accepted. Once Congress convenes, they'll make the appointment official, and he'll become Major General Davis."

Lamont found himself nodding at the information. He knew of Davis. The man was a West Point graduate and served on the military affairs committee in the Senate. "What'll happen to you?"

"If I have my druthers, I'll be heading to South Carolina. I'd like to work with James Longstreet to shore up our border with North Carolina. But with my luck, who knows? I might get stuck fetching coffee and filing requisition orders for General Davis, as punishment for not holding the line in Texas."

At Longstreet's name, Lamont perked up. "I've known Old Pete for a number of years, sir. He's a good man."

Hardee cocked his head, "Old Pete? How'd he get that name?"

"He had a rock-like temperament as a boy, so I've been told, and his father took to calling him Peter, like the apostle."

Hardee said, "I hope he still has that temperament, Colonel. Until Davis finishes off Texas, Longstreet may have to become that rock if President Seward decides to attack."

# Chapter 16

1 April 1853

Not much was left standing in Beaumont as Jesse Running Creek led his mount around a wagon piled with lumber. The rebels had fired the town when they retreated. Months later, the sour smell of soot lingered in the air. The Cherokee officer wrinkled his nose as the odor assaulted his olfactory senses. Despite that, constant hammering reminded him the town wasn't quite dead.

When the rebels retreated, they left a thousand civilians behind, the overwhelming majority were the town's prewar residents. While nearly all the town's public buildings had gone up in flames, a majority of the old town remained intact. The new section, around the railroad depot, had suffered the same fate as the depot when the fire spread.

He looked behind him. Men were putting up a wooden frame where the new depot would stand. They moved with a sense of urgency. The bridge over the Trinity was nearing completion, and with it, Beaumont once again would be connected to the rest of Texas' growing railroad network. Men wearing the blue uniform of a Yankee volunteer infantry regiment stood guard over the construction crew, who were a mixture of captured soldiers and known rebel sympathizers.

As the construction disappeared behind him, Jesse thought the armed guards had more to do with how fast the laborers were working rather than any desire on the part of the construction crew. Soon the army's supply situation would improve. Construction on the new bridge over the Trinity was nearing completion, and the railhead would come to within a few miles of the border with Louisiana.

He grimaced as he dug his heels into his horse's flank, cantering out of town. He knew more than he wanted of the army's shortages. He was on his way back from West Liberty and Trinity Park. On the fields where the rebel army once drilled, nine hundred men were now encamped.

In response to several Southern states ratifying the New Orleans Articles of Secession, General Johnston finally mobilized a majority of the reserves and militia. The army's near-overnight expansion fueled a need for more engineers, quartermasters, and hospital orderlies. That growth explained how he now found himself in command of a battalion wing of the newly expanded Army Rangers. After being gone for more than a week on behalf of the oversized battalion, he was glad to be back.

Row upon row of orderly tents spread across the coastal plain west of town. More than a decade of service in the Texian army gave Jesse a keen eye, and he let it rove over the encampment. Each company's tents were in a double line. Like most soldiers, each Ranger had been issued a linseed oiled canvas tent-half that when paired with another identical half, created an A-frame tent.

Twelve company streets ran perpendicular to an old wagon trail which now served as the encampment's front. Behind the soldiers' tents were the larger tents of the battalion's officers. The camp was empty at that moment, and once on the other side of it, Jesse found the entire nine-hundred-man battalion at drill. They were spread over an area of several square miles. Jesse pulled at the reins and watched one of the companies training.

Like the muddy gulf water washing up on a Texas beach, the company rushed across the flat, even ground. Jesse thought an inexperienced eye might miss the order and see only the wave of men. He saw each team of four riflemen advancing together. Every third team was commanded by a sergeant, who led a squad of three teams. Thee Squads formed a platoon under the command of a lieutenant. Two platoons formed a company under the leadership of a captain.

The exercise paused, the men gathered around the captain, who shouted, "It ain't going to be like this, boys when we go into battle. The ground will be broken and uneven, chewed to shit by artillery. When you advance under fire, the terrain is your friend. Use it to your advantage."

Jesse allowed a small smile. The young officer was doing what he'd have done. Each rifle team had to be able to work independently, and for that to happen, the men had to be able to think about why they drilled the way they did. Once a battle began, even a lowly corporal had to be able to guide the others in his team, and every man had to be able to step into the role of a corporal. The Rangers took the army's decentralized combat tactics and pushed it all the way down to the individual soldier.

Jesse listened as the officer continued, "Second platoon, you were bunched up like a gaggle of debutants at a cotillion waiting for the boys to ask you to dance. That might work there, but a single shell-burst would have decimated you. Each rifle team needs to act in concert, but the platoon needs to cover as broad a front as possible."

The captain waved back at where they had come from, "Now, let's do it again. Tomorrow we'll be wargaming against D Company, and we'll kick their asses across the field, or I'll know why."

As Jesse turned and made his way across the prairie, his memory turned back more than a decade when he had been an eighteen-year-old recruit under Major Jack Hays. The major introduced his command to nightly wargames. He'd pit one company against another. Even though Jack Hays was seeking his fortune in Jefferson Territory, the traditions he'd built remained alive and well.

After a few minutes, Jesse pulled up next to the battalion commander, Colonel Edward Brooks. The colonel sat at a field table, under a pine tree. His eyes were glued to his binoculars, watching another company at drill.

"We've got a lot of work ahead of us, Major. These boys are coming together nicely, but there's still a lot of work left to do. Did you have any luck?"

Jesse swung down from his horse and tied the beast to a bough, "No, sir. I even rode up from West Liberty to Trinity Park and talked with Mr. Berry. There's no ammunition available for drilling. Everything's being saved for the coming campaign."

Brooks swore, "Damnit, I can only run these boys through the steps so many times before it's old hat to them. But shooting, by God, is what they need the most practice on, and damned if I have enough ammunition to knock a flea off a dog's back."

Jesse offered a weak smile, "Look on the bright side, sir. Rumor is the Confederates in Louisiana will invade by the end of the month. By then, we'll get all the practice we need."

Mid-April 1853

The train clattered over an imperfectly placed rail, jostling Will out of his reverie. Since crossing the new bridge over the Trinity an hour before, the scenery reminded him of why this part of Texas was called the Piney Woods.

"Are we there yet?" a soft feminine voice beside him made him turn his head. His face lit up as he looked into his wife's sleepy eyes. It was a rare treat that she had accompanied him. When she had learned he would be touring the front lines, she had insisted she wanted to come. At first, he had refused. It was dangerous. He had told her the enemy could attack any day. It was far safer for her to stay in Austin with the children. She had countered; the newspapers from the South complained about how long it took to move an army into place. The Southern Alliance, as the seceding states had taken to calling themselves, was as hamstrung as he was when away from their own railroad network.

In the end, Becky wore him down. Will threw his hands up in defeat when she told him that Dr. Ashbel Smith would be joining them as he wanted to tour one of the hospitals at the front. The good doctor was hunched over, asleep on the wooden seat opposite their own.

Will could hardly blame Smith for wanting to come to the front. The hospital was one that the doctor had been working on with army surgeons for several years. While Will had given him the idea for a mobile unit of doctors and support staff, Smith had taken on the project with all the fervor of a convert. The unit had several wagons stocked with medicine and supplies, including tents and cots. Additionally, several more ambulance wagons were attached to the medical outfit, replete with stretchers for the hospital stewards to collect the wounded from the battlefield.

Below his breath, Will murmured, “Mobile army surgical hospital, MASH.”

“What was that, darling?”

“Nothing,” Will hadn’t realized he’d spoken aloud. “Look outside, we’re nearly there.”

The forest ended, and the coastal plain was covered with a sea of tents. Will added, “Sidney’s been using the town to drill the army away from the front.”

The train was slowing as it neared the town. New construction lined both sides of the track, and the still-under-construction depot came into view as the train slowly rolled to a stop. "Oh, Will," Becky said, "what happened to the town is horrible. The women and children hereabouts must be suffering horribly."

"The army's set up places for the civilians to collect rations," Will said defensively. "None of this would have been necessary if those hot-headed fools had accepted the election."

Becky placed her hand on Will's arm, "There, you're practically admitting if women had the right to vote, they'd have stopped their silly husbands from doing something so stupid."

Will smiled at his wife. He wasn't sure about her logic, but since he won the presidency, she seldom missed an opportunity to push him on suffrage.

"Balderdash, madam," Ashbel Smith said as he appeared to awaken. "I'd mention how women lack the temperament for the weighty responsibility of voting, but we all know that's just a fig leaf. Women control their husbands and thus his vote."

Becky harrumphed as the train came to a stop. "That's why you're still single, Doctor."

Smith laughed, "Oh, cut to the quick. Mr. President, your wife's wit is as sharp as a scalpel. I am married to my profession."

Will held his peace as soldiers in the passenger car behind them unloaded. The train stayed in the station long enough for the engine to take on fresh water and for a handful of soldiers to climb aboard.

Smith was traditionally minded. But over the years, Will learned there was a depth to the doctor. He had taken in an orphan, whose father had been killed in the opening days of the war and whose mother had died in childbirth, at his house in Trinity Park.

The train winded its way toward the Sabine River, another twenty miles before finally coming to a stop a quarter mile from the river. Will waited for Becky and Dr. Smith to head toward the carriage that would take them to the mobile hospital, then he turned and saw Sidney Johnston waiting by a stack of ammunition boxes.

"You still taking your morning constitutionals?" Johnston said as they shook hands.

Will stretched, trying to untangle the mass of muscles in his back that protested from the long travel on the train's uncomfortable wooden seats. "When I can. A walk helps to clear the head."

"Glad you feel that way, Mr. President," Johnston said with a sly grin. "Let's get to walking."

They walked away from the railhead, through stands of pine trees not yet reduced to kindling and firewood until they emerged from the woods. In front of them stretched a long earthen and wooden trench-line. Wooden stakes were placed in front of the entrenchment, the sharp, pointed end facing the river below.

The earthen trench disappeared into another stand of trees more than a mile away. "It goes on for several miles, sir," Johnston said as he led Will into the trench through a framed entry point at the back.

The front of the trench was made of logs, stacked, one on top of the other. A wooden step let men stand against the wall, where they could fire over its lip.

A few hundred yards along, Johnston stopped, waiting for Will to catch up.

"Where are the men, Sid?" Will was perplexed. They had passed by only a few dozen riflemen.

Johnston said, "This mile is held by the Sixteenth Infantry."

Will raised his eyebrows, "Only seven-hundred men along more than five thousand feet?"

"Closer to seven-fifty men and six thousand feet," Johnston said. "They're camped back behind the line. Only a third are on the line right now. Follow me, there's something I want to show you."

The army's commander turned into another trench running perpendicular to the line. Timbers were laid over the trench as Will followed Johnston up a steep climb. The overhead planking gave the narrow ditch a tunnel-like feel and left Will with a touch of claustrophobia. When they emerged, they were in a small fortified position above the line. Will looked around and whistled appreciatively.

A battery of four Gatling guns faced the river. Johnston laughed at Will's reaction. "If those secesh bastards try to cross the river here, they'll get a warm reception. Every mile we rotate these Gatling guns with field artillery."

Will ran his hand along one of the gun's brass barrels. "How many men do you have now?"

"Counting the soldiers training back at Beaumont, right at twenty-thousand men. That includes several thousand volunteers from the US."

Johnston left the battery and headed toward the army's rear. A few minutes later, Will stood in a clearing watching one of the army's reconnaissance balloon floating just above the ground, tethered with several thick ropes.

Johnston pointed, "I thought you'd like to see what the enemy is up to."

Will let slip a cry of delight as he saw Charlie walking toward them. In his mind, his son was still sometimes the eight-year-old boy he'd first met sitting on the Ayres' porch seventeen years before. The boy, now a man, stood as tall as Will now. He wore a thin mustache and neatly trimmed goatee.

As the balloon slowly ascended, Charlie pressed him for news on his own wife and child, who were living in the presidential mansion. Will handed over a daguerreotype recently taken in Austin. No matter how long he had been stranded in Travis' body, certain aspects of the nineteenth century remained a mystery to him and the stern look on Tatiana Travis' face in the picture was one of them.

When the rope played out, the basket gave a gentle tug, and Charlie said, "Normally, this is when we get to work." He pointed to the telegraph box and the chair in which Will sat, "Sam sits there, and he'll telegraph anything I see to the men below."

Will took the binoculars from his son and looked through them at the other side of the Sabine. Trench works mirroring the ones below came into view. The blue flag with a single star had been the flag adopted by the Louisiana volunteers when they first arrived the previous year. From several points along the trench lines, it still flew. But state flags from across the new Southern Alliance now flew alongside the first flag of the rebellion.

"How many men do you reckon they've got?" Will asked.

Charlie leaned against the basket, "Hard to say, we've mapped more than forty regiments so far. Mostly from the deep South."

Will turned his binoculars to the north. Eventually, the trenches ended amid the pine tree forest. "Do you think they'll try to flank the army?"

"I would if I thought I had the men, Pa. But we'll be ready if they do."

Will lowered the binoculars and turned away from the enemy lines. "How so?"

Charlie pointed to the north, "If they try getting around us, we should have enough warning to pivot the army to meet them. We've got a brigade of cavalry to the north and one of our balloons. As a matter of fact, that regiment that maniac John Brown commanded is assigned there."

In the distance, a voice called out, "Timber!"

Jimmy Hickok raised his head but couldn't see anything other than more trees. He lowered the axe handle and rubbed his raw hands against his britches. The soldier beside him slapped him on the back, "Don't you look just pretty as a peach wearing those god-awful ugly pants?"

The teenager looked down at the butternut trousers he wore. Over the past few months, Jimmy had grown several inches, and his kersey blue woolen pants no longer fit. As uniforms wore out and needed replacing, the men of the 1st Provisional New York Cavalry Regiment were issued clothing from the Texian army's supply depot.

Jimmy didn't care. They were long enough to cover his ankles. He couldn't say that about his old trousers. "Covers the dirt better, Elias. I didn't hear you complaining when they issued us new socks."

The older soldier shrugged, "We were quite the sight when we arrived here a few weeks ago. Low on ammunition and asses flapping out our trousers. Well, at least you, Duckbill."

Jimmy hated the nickname. It wasn't his fault his nose was so large. "Unless you're going to talk this tree down, it's not coming down on its own." He gripped the handle and swung at the deep gash he'd already cut in the tall pine tree.

Between swings, Elias said, "What the hell are we doing here. When those slavers decide to attack, they're going to have a go at the army, and we're miles away stuck in the woods, knocking trees down."

Jimmy pulled the blade from the tree, knocking wood chips to the ground. "Major Douglas says we're building an abatis. If the slavers try coming around the army's trenches, they'll run smack into this, once we're finished with it."

The older soldier swore and spat, "I got nothing against the major, mind you, but goddammit, why'd those Rangers have to arrest Colonel Brown? He ain't done nothing."

Jimmy swung the axe again before he said, "Not anything we all didn't want to do, that's for sure."

After they felled one tree, the two troopers moved to the next tree marked with red paint, denoting it was to be cut down, too. Elias said, "I hear the Texians are holding Brown in Austin. They're not saying anything about a trial, but I've heard some of those Texas boys say that President Travis will charge him with murder. I swear to God above, Duckbill, if these Texians hadn't forced all of the Colonel's sons out of the army, we'd be riding to free him now."

Thinking about Colonel Brown's surviving sons brought back memories when he and Watson Brown had carried messages for the dour colonel. Watson was closest to him in age, and Jimmy missed him something fierce. But John Brown's youngest son to accompany him had been dead now for months.

"Jimmy," the teenager said through clenched teeth. "My name is Jimmy, not Duckbill."

Elias shrugged, "Don't get your dander up, Hickok. It's just a nickname. You've taken a fair amount of shit, being younger than the rest of us. Why haven't you lit off for home? Not like you wouldn't be the first."

Jimmy swung the axe into the tree. The ringing numbness traveled up his arms with each stroke. It was a fair question. Since Brown's arrest, nearly one in five men had decided they'd had enough and had deserted. Of the thousand men who'd enlisted in New York the previous year, scarcely more than six hundred men remained.

"I ain't a quitter. I joined up to stop slavers from turning our neighbor into the next slave state." Jimmy said as he leaned against the tree catching his breath. "What about you, Elias. You're always talking about how unfair it was that the Texians arrested Colonel Brown. Why are you still here?"

Elias set his axe down and pulled a plug of tobacco from his pocket. He bit off a chew and offered it to Jimmy. "I might go yet. If President Seward decides to call for volunteers to put down the rebellion, I might return home and join a regiment up there. But I joined to kill slavers. For now, this is the best place to be to get that chance."

# Chapter 17

14 April 1853

Dust engulfed the coach as the horses pulling it came to a stop. Becky bit back a sigh. No sooner had she and Will returned from the front on the Sabine River than she packed her bags for a planned meeting in San Antonio for the Widows and Orphans project.

"Momma, are you alright?"

Becky's smile was worn and tired, "Yes, Liza. Just tired. When we finish here, we'll take a day or two to relax with Maria Seguin at her family's hacienda. Won't that be fun?"

Elizabeth Travis' smile lit up the coach. "Can we ride horses with the vaqueros?"

"We'll see. Come, I think we're the last to arrive."

As Becky took the hand of the driver and stepped down from the coach, she saw a long wall, more than a hundred yards long. Beyond the wall, a chapel with a dome was visible in the distance. A man wearing a black cassock hurried from the gatehouse, a crucifix around his neck swung back and forth as he hurried over.

"Madam Travis, a pleasure to see you again. Welcome to the San Jose y San Miguel de Aguayo Mission."

After exchanging pleasantries, Becky said, "Have Mr. Ayres and Reverend Bains arrived?"

Offering his arm, Bishop Odin led her into the mission's expansive plaza, "Yes. If you'd like refreshments before we start the tour, I'll ask they join us in the *convento.*"

The plaza covered a couple of acres. It was almost as large as the Alamo Plaza. Children were at play along one section of the surrounding walls.

Becky shook her head, "We are due at the Hacienda Seguin later this afternoon. If the gentlemen are ready, I don't want to be the cause of any delay." She turned to Liza, "If you'd like, you may play with the other girls."

As she watched Liza hurry across the dirt-covered plaza, Odin said, "They grow so fast. She seems to favor her mother."

Her worn smile returned, "It seems like only yesterday that I rocked her to sleep in her little crib. Now, my baby is almost a woman."

Odin gestured toward the small gatehouse built into the mission's wall. "That's why we're here, to give these children the opportunity to grow into men and women of good character."

After being greeted by Ayres and Bains, Becky joined them at the table. With three sets of eyes staring back at her, she thought about her husband, who routinely spoke before hundreds, sometimes, thousands of people, and how, on occasion, he would get nervous. She squared her shoulders and said, "A lot has happened since we first met last year to form this commission. I think we've all been humbled by the outpouring of support we've received from throughout the Republic. The Diocese of Galveston's generous donation of the property around Mission San Jose has been a godsend, and we couldn't have done this without your help, your Excellency."

Odin dipped his head in acknowledgment. "It wasn't that much. The buildings had been in disrepair, unused since before the revolution." He pointed out the window to scaffolding against the walls of the church, "We're still a long way away from having the mission repaired."

Bains added, "While I tend to think the most important work is still before us, the most urgent has already been completed. There's a dry roof over the head of every child here and plenty of food, too."

Becky knew it to be true. After the Bishop had made the abandoned mission available to the Commission, but before the first orphan arrived, they had repaired the walls and fixed up each of the dilapidated houses that lined the mission's walls.

Ayres said, "Is it true there are more than forty children housed here now?"

"Yes," Becky looked at a roster on the table, "we are providing shelter to forty-seven children. We've even started a school for them. But here's the problem, gentlemen, and the reason I asked for this meeting. Since the collapse of the rebel army around Beaumont earlier in the year, we're finding the number of orphans in the east to be greater than we first thought."

Ayres's eyes narrowed as his lips curved downward. "The get of traitors?"

Becky found her own eyes narrowing when Odin placed a gentle hand on her arm. He said, "I believe it was Saint James who said, pure religion and undefiled before God and the Father is this, to visit the fatherless and widows in their affliction, and to keep himself unspotted from the world."

Bains' eyes held a trace of mirth, "David, the bishop is right, you know. Those children are no more responsible for their fathers' actions than me or you." He waited for Ayres to relax his jaw before continuing, "The question becomes what can we do about it? We have enough money to pay the staff here through the end of the summer. Fixing up more of the buildings here isn't going to come cheap."

Becky gave a nod of appreciation at the Baptist pastor, "I want those children removed from Beaumont and the surrounding area. It's only a matter of only weeks before fighting resumes."

The bishop's chair squeaked as he leaned back, scratching gray stubble on his chin. "Gentlemen," he said, looking at Ayres and Bains, "I don't have the contacts you have among the Freemasons, but if you make an appeal for assistance, I believe they'll listen to you. I have some small influence among recent immigrants, and I'll see to it that labor is available for when you provide the material to repair the rest of the mission."

Becky beamed at the men on her committee. When they set their minds to a problem, they were good at finding solutions. There was only one other thing, they had to rescue the orphans in Beaumont before the war resumed.

26 April 1853

The springs beneath the wagon's seat squealed in protest as Charlie slammed his backside onto the wooden slats. "We've got, what? A few days at best before the Allied army attacks. Sam, we should be training the other crews and planning how we'll coordinate with the Signal Corps for what's to come."

Sam Williams grabbed a handhold and propelled himself into the seat beside Charlie. "Tell that to General Johnston, Major. This came straight from him."

"That's horse shit, Sam. This order came directly from my pa. Rather, Becky put my pa up to it." Charlie modulated his voice into a falsetto, "Send Charlie after the orphans. It's not like he's doing anything other than floating around in a balloon all day."

Sam held his sides, laughing, "Is that what the First Lady sounds like? Sounds more like one of those Indian elephants I saw one time."

The wagon rolled away from the railroad terminus. A small town nestled the side of the Sabine River. Madison's founders had aspirations of the sleepy hamlet becoming a port. Before the war, it was the last stop on the railroad out of Texas. Now, the few people who remained were those who refused to leave. Some were too pig-headed to go and others, unrepentant rebels, hoped to welcome the Southern Alliance's return.

"Take a left at that burned out building," Sam said, looking up from a hand-drawn map.

Charlie guided the mules pulling the wagon around the corner. "The orphans have been collected, right?"

"Apparently, General Johnston's had soldiers around Madison the past week, going through abandoned houses and outlying farms. We're warehousing these kids at a church."

A few minutes later, Charlie pulled on the reins, "Merciful God. Will you look at that?"

Less than a hundred paces away stood a dilapidated building. An unpainted steeple rose precariously above it and an iron cross hung by a loose bolt from the top of steeple. A soldier in butternut leaned on his rifle near the door.

As he urged the mules forward, Charlie could hear high-pitched voices coming from the building. He pulled up next to the church and set the brake. As he climbed down from the buckboard, he heard a familiar voice, "The war must be lost if they've sent you to pick up these urchins."

Charlie turned, a smile lighting up his features, "Cuffee, you son of a bitch, I haven't seen you since before the attack at Beaumont. You don't look worse for wear."

The former slave raised the brim of his hat, "We gave as good as we got. And when those bastards across the river come a-calling, we'll give 'em even more hell."

"How's Joe? Did he come through alright?"

Cuffee shrugged, "Coulda been worse. He was hit in the leg. The surgeons managed to save the leg, but he's back home with Hattie in San Antonio 'til he's able to come back."

The news was sobering, and Charlie paused at the church door. "I hadn't heard. I'll pass the news along to my pa."

The inside of the church was one large room. A podium at the front was on its side and light spilled into the room from the open windows. It smelled of unwashed bodies and waste.

Wrinkling his nose, Charlie hurriedly counted heads before raising his voice, "Listen up. We've got room for the ten of you in the back of our wagon. You're to be evacuated."

One boy rose from a stack of blankets. The way the other children looked at him told Charlie all he needed to know. The teen ran roughshod over the others.

"We ain't going anywhere with you. My pa's on the other side of the river, and soon enough, he'll be coming across the river and kicking y'all's asses."

Charlie wanted to reach across the few feet separating them and strangle the mouthy teen. Had he ever been that bad?

"No exceptions," Charlie crossed his arms and glared at the teen. "If I have to pick you up and carry you to the wagon, you'll be the sorriest boy in Madison. I'll have the private with the rifle sit on you if I have to."

Fire burning in his eyes, the boy balled his fist and took a step forward, "I ain't a-scared of—"

In the distance, thunder echoed. The ground vibrated and a moment later, they heard a crashing noise nearby.

Sam leaned in, through the door, “A shot just took out a tree. The Allies,” the name he’d taken to calling the Southern Alliance, “have opened fire.”

A flicker of fear showed in the teen’s eyes. Another thump nearby, another round tore into the ground. The boy reached over and grabbed his blankets before hurrying by Charlie.

Turning away from the window overlooking the Sabine River, General Jefferson Davis smiled appreciatively at the other men in the room, who stood around a table looking back at him, waiting.

They could wait a few more minutes. He’d been waiting for them since assuming command of the Army of the Trans-Mississippi a month earlier, he wanted to savor the moment. He commanded the largest army assembled in North America, nearly fifty-thousand men on the eastern bank of the Sabine River. He felt buoyed as he studied the faces of the men who commanded the four divisions in two army corps.

Despite replacing William Hardee as commander of the army, he’d felt the Southern Alliance’s political leadership had been unfair to the other general. Davis’ first act, once he took over, was to keep Hardee on staff. As the army had ballooned in size, he’d placed Hardee in command of the army’s I Corps.

Davis’ eye twitched as he took the measure of the II Corps’ commander. While Alexander Swift had graduated from West Point more than twenty years earlier, he had retired to Louisiana, where he eventually rose through the ranks of the state militia. He was a favorite of several influential politicians. Was he merely a political general or was there more to Swift than met the eye? Davis didn't want to find out in the heat of battle. He didn't dwell on his own short service in the army after he graduated from West Point, nor that his role as Senator from Mississippi had as much to do with his commanding the army as his military service.

Four more men crowded around the table. They were the division commanders. They were also West Pointers. Albert Blanchard commanded a division composed of Alabamans, Louisianans, and Missourians. Hugh Mercer's division was mostly from Georgia and Tennessee. Edward Deas' command came from South Carolina, Mississippi, Arkansas, and Florida. The last commander was Jones Withers, who commanded the army's nine-thousand strong cavalry division.

Running a hand down his gray double-breasted jacket, Davis joined his generals around the table, atop which lay a large map of the region. The Sabine River meandered down the center. Every regiment, all sixty, were represented by bright red pins. They formed a long line along one side of the river. Blue tipped pins representing each battalion of the Texian Army ran alongside the other bank of the river. There were far fewer blue pins than red.

"Gentlemen," Davis began, "Don't let the sea of red pins color your perception of the coming battle. The star's on Albert Sidney Johnston's shoulder have been there for a decade. And he earned them the hard way.

Before this, he commanded a brigade in Texas' war with Mexico. And since Southern loyalists rebelled against President Travis, General Johnston has commanded upwards of a division's strength."

Alexander Swift interrupted him, "We outnumber the Texans two to one."

Davis ignored the dropped *i*, as was becoming common outside of the Republic, "General Beauregard outnumbered Johnston by an equal margin, General. That didn't stop Johnston from dislodging him from fortified positions along the Trinity River last year."

Swift's brow arched and his lips turned into a frown, "Sir, Johnston's just a man, same as us. And his men are not Spartans."

"And neither are we the Persians." Davis felt his temper slipping. He tamped down on his ire as he walked over to the drawing room's wall. A rifle had been hung over the fireplace. He grabbed it off its hooks and turned back to Swift. "You're right. Johnston's men are just soldiers, not that different than the men we will lead into battle on the morrow. But his men will be armed with this."

He thrust the rifle into Swift's hands. Below the rifle's breech the trigger guard could be snapped open, dropping the breechblock, and exposing the chamber. "The average soldier can fire six to eight rounds a minute. I've been told some have even been able to fire twelve or more. This is their equalizer. With this, they can give us a tough fight tomorrow."

Back at the map, Davis pointed to a spot between the two armies on the Sabine. "We will use our numbers and the fact that Johnston has to cover a wide front against him. We've prepared a hundred barges for the attack. They'll be able to deliver three thousand men to a single point on the other side of the river."

Silent until now, Hardee said, "We've been training near Lake Charles for the past week, sir. The hard part is going to be stringing the cable between the two banks at a hundred points."

Davis cocked his head, as though thinking, "It may be difficult, but it is essential. For every cable ferry we put into operation across the river the faster we'll be able to get your division across. I want General Blanchard's division across within an hour."

"We've built in a bit of time," Hardee said, "Once they're across, I'll start sending General Mercer's division over. You know, if you can't get enough artillery focused on the enemy line where we'll attack, resistance may be very high."

A smile crossed Davis' face, "Bill, across the meadow from here, atop for what passes for hills in this flat, mosquito-infested land, I've placed ten batteries of guns. They'll soon commence firing on the enemy lines. By tomorrow morning, when your boys start across the river, they'll be joined by another fifteen batteries."

Davis turned his attention to General Swift, "I want most of General Deas' division to support the attack, along their section of the front. Those of your men with rifled muskets should be able to target the enemy's trenches."

Swift eyed the markers on the map, "I've only got two of Deas' brigades, sir. I'd like my South Carolinians back before the attack."

The next part was the riskiest; Davis had agonized over the decision, but now that he was issuing orders, he wouldn't second guess himself any longer. Still looking at Swift, he said, "You'll get them. Just not there." Davis pointed to the map where the attack was scheduled to happen. He then pointed to the map's edge. "I want you and General Withers to take his cavalry. Twenty miles north, I've assembled more barges, outside of the view of the damnable balloons the enemy have taken to using to spy on us. They're guarded by Lamont's South Carolinians. Cross over the river with Withers' Division and Lamont's brigade and turn Johnston's left flank."

A wall clock chimed the top of the hour. Davis glanced at it and said, "Gentlemen, we must wrap up this campaign against Johnston's army soon. The Yankees haven't decided how to respond to our independence. If they decide they want us to return to the fold, tails between our legs, we need to be able to shift this army north."

As the clock gave forth a final chime, the windows rattled as the field guns opened fire. Davis turned away from the map and stared out the window. "It has begun."

☆

A round plowed into the ground less than a hundred feet away as Charlie snapped a whip over the mules' heads, "Faster, damn you!"

The wagon was packed with the children from the abandoned church. Sam held a small child in his lap as he clutched the edge of his seat. "Careful, Major. Do you want me to drive?"

Charlie hazarded a look young Williams. Through gritted teeth, he said, "Want to trade seats?"

The wagon sank into a chuck hole, jostling everyone in the cart. Cries from the back erupted. "Just get us there safely, Charlie," Sam said as he held his small charge tighter.

In the back of his mind, Charlie realized the son of one of his father's oldest friends had called him by his name instead of his rank. That hadn't happened since the army mobilized the students at Trinity College. Breaking away from his reverie, Charlie focused on the animals pulling the wagon. As they approached the intersection to the road leading to the railhead, he pulled on the reins, praying they would slow down enough to make the turn.

Wood squealed against wood as he grabbed the brake bar and pulled on it. With his other hand, he gripped the reins and tugged to the left. As the wagon careened onto the intersecting road, the wheels on Charlie's side of the wagon came off the ground. From the back, Cuffee was swearing and praying while the children screamed.

The wheels slammed back onto the roadbed, and Charlie let out a sigh of relief as he realized he'd been holding his breath as they had turned the corner. In the distance, he saw a locomotive, black smoke boiling out of its chimney.

"Hurry, sir. That train ain't going to wait for long." Sam screamed, as one of the wheels found another chuckhole.

In a nearby field, dirt erupted into the sky, and a cannonball bounded into the air before plowing into a small pond.

A shell airburst over the train, raining down shrapnel on the men below. As Charlie brought the team of mules to a stop, screams tore through the air, and the iron smell of blood assaulted his senses. Toward the back of the train, a boxcar was open, and several children were being lifted by soldiers and tossed into the car.

Charlie felt a tap on his shoulder, “Them’s my boys,” Cuffee said, pointed at the ebon-skinned soldiers from the 21st Infantry, who stood guard by the open sliding door. Securing the brake, Charlie leapt down and helped Sam, Cuffee, and the other soldiers load the children.

A shell detonated on the other side of the boxcar, peppering the side with shrapnel. There were screams from inside the car. Charlie clambered into the dimly lit space, “Is anyone hurt? Check the person next to you, as well.”

A chorus of “No’s” greeted him, and he climbed down as the wheels on the boxcar began to roll. Charlie stepped back as Cuffee slammed the door to the boxcar.

A shell exploded in the middle of the Y turnabout. Charlie followed the train with his eyes as it disappeared into the west. He grabbed Cuffee by the neck and gave him a fierce hug, “Take care of yourself, my friend. There’s a storm coming.”

# Chapter 18

29 April 1853

His eyes popped open. Sleep eluded Major Jesse Running Creek. A shell exploded nearby. He had no idea how many shots and shells the enemy had thrown across the river since starting their barrage. It must have been thousands of rounds. He stretched and climbed to his feet. He could see over the rifle pit's lip. Inky darkness, punctuated by winks of light from the other side of the river, greeted his tired eyes.

From behind the lines, Texian artillery responded. The Southern Alliance's grand battery was well situated to fire on the Texian lines. The guns were shielded behind wooden and earthen walls. Staring at them the previous day had reminded Jesse, the enemy had within its ranks more than a few engineers, graduates of the United States Military Academy at West Point, the premier engineering school in North America.

Over the years since Texas formed the Cadet Corps at the Alamo, Jesse had spent a few seasons educating the cadets on the Rangers' small unit tactics and how to use those tactics to take the initiative on the battlefield. Texas' military academy focused on combined armed tactics, using infantry, cavalry, and artillery. A few officers in the army's engineering command had been trained at West Point, under an agreement between the two nations.

Another shell detonated nearby. Shrapnel rained down on another rifle pit's wooden cover. Jesse felt a presence beside him. "Major, why don't you try to get some rest. I'll keep an eye on things for you."

Jesse glanced at Sergeant Major Judah Andrade, the battalion's senior non-commissioned officer, "I've got a feeling, Sergeant. The barrage has increased over the last hour."

Andrade stared into the darkness, "Yes, sir. And if anything changes, I'll let you know."

Jesse handed the sergeant his binoculars and crouched down next to a youth who was leaning over a wooden box. "I think the line's been cut again."

A feeble light illuminated the cumbersome telegraph machine and the young face of its operator, Billy Vandergrift. Like several of his fellow students at Trinity College, the youth was a skilled telegraph operator. "I can check the wire between here and the Twentieth. See if there's a break."

Jesse eyed the copper wire running from the box out the back of the pit. The idea the army could use telegraph machines to stay connected had sounded like a grand idea when he'd first heard about it. But the practice wasn't living up to the ideal. Young Vandergrift had been forced on many occasions to repair the line, even though it only ran a couple hundred yards to the secondary line, where the 20th Infantry was stationed.

He weighed the risk against the need and eventually nodded, "Be careful. If the Allies attack, we need to know."

Once Vandergrift scampered out the back, Jesse leaned against the earthen wall and sank down until he rested on an ammunition box. His eyes closed, and he fell asleep.

Startled awake by a nudge, Jesse noticed the artillery sounded even louder. Sergeant Major Andrade leaned in, "The dance is about to start."

Jesse joined the sergeant at the edge of the pit. Pink and orange tinged the eastern sky. Andrade added, "Down on the river."

The light from the east had yet to pierce the darkness of the river, but tiny flashes of light, like a hundred fireflies punctuated the gloom. Despite the booming artillery, Jesse could hear the high-pitched sound of gunfire.

The rising noise of rifle fire came from the Rangers' left flank. Whoever was crossing the river were doing so upstream. Jesse noticed his telegraph operator had returned while he had been asleep. "Send a message, the enemy are attacking. Looks like they're hitting the Ninth's position."

From below, Vandergrift said, "The Twentieth says the line to brigade headquarters is down."

Jesse swore as he waited for the sun to rise.

"Wake up!" The voice penetrated Charlie's sleep. His eyes fluttered open. A sliver of soft light slipped through the tent's door panels. Sam Williams stood at the head of the cot, slipping an arm into his jacket. "The enemy are across the river. General Johnston's ordered the balloon corps into the sky."

Blinking until the cobwebs cleared, Charlie swung out of bed and grabbed a clean shirt from an open trunk. The fog of sleep slipped away, "Is our crew filling the bag yet?"

Sam drew back the door. Away from the unit's camp, in an open field, Charlie saw one of the balloons half full of hydrogen. A steam-powered generator rattled and clanked as a hose carried the hydrogen into the balloon.

Charlie frowned. It would take at least another thirty minutes to prepare the balloon. "Sam, go over and make sure the telegraph line is working. Once that's done, send a message to Lieutenant Jackson. I want eyes in the sky on the army's northern flank. We're most vulnerable there."

After Sam sketched a salute, Charlie finished dressing and headed over to wait for the balloon to fill.

By the time the balloon ascended into the sky, tied to the rope tethers, the sun was several degrees above the eastern horizon. Sounds of battle wafted over Charlie as he waited for the wicker basket to rise above the heavily forested area. They were a few hundred feet in the air when he was finally able to glimpse the river. He swore as he scanned the carnage. Cables ran from the east bank to the west in dozens of places along a narrow section of the front. Dozens of barges were using the cables to traverse the Sabine River. Each barge was packed with gray-jacketed soldiers.

For every barge transporting men, Charlie found another burning on the shoreline or capsized in the water. He focused his binoculars on a barge nearing the eastern shore. The men onboard were pulling on the cable as fast as they could, forcing the craft through the water. A shell burst over the boat, raining shrapnel down on the unprotected men. The barge lurched to one side as it became separated from its cable. It crashed into another vessel and tipped over, dumping into the water its entire complement of soldiers.

Several other barges slammed into the shoreline and their gray jacketed cargo spilled onto the riverbank. As the soldiers raced off the watercraft, they made no effort to reform their units but instead made a mad dash for the Texian line.

Sam said, “Message coming in. Enemy troops have breached the river line near Madison. What do you see?”

Boats were burning in the water, set afire by exploding shells, and men were struggling to get ashore. Despite the chaos, barges still traversed the river. “Sam, more than forty barges are crossing the river still. Artillery has knocked out quite a few others.”

He raised his glasses, looking at the foreign shore. Flashes of light showed where the Allies’ entrenched guns supported the assault. The earthen embankment in front of the guns had been torn apart, where Texian counterbattery fire had attempted to silence the guns. Further to the south, Charlie spied at least a battery of guns set up in a field. Every few seconds a gun fired, throwing shot or shell toward the Texian line, on either flank of where the attack was centered.

A map of the area was tacked to the wicker basket, and he looked down and found the corresponding quadrant. "Target acquired in quadrant F-twenty-four. About two hundred paces north of the railroad track and seventy-five paces east of the orchard."

Once the telegraph's clattering ended, a few minutes passed before the first explosion detonated short of the exposed enemy battery. Charlie corrected his earlier directions, "Adjust another hundred feet to the east."

Minutes passed before the next ranging shot plowed into the ground just to the right of the battery before sending up a geyser of dirt that landed on the gunners. Close enough, Charlie thought. "On target."

Another shell-burst knocked half a gun-crew down. Within a few minutes, more of the enemy battery's men raced forward with teams of horses. They'd had enough. "Sam, they're running. More explosive shells."

Before the enemy battery could escape, two of the guns were abandoned; their animals destroyed along with their gun crews.

Charlie scanned the panorama below. For the moment, the army's secondary trench line was holding. He gave Sam the next set of coordinates.

From the platform above and behind the grand battery, General Davis looked at the tranquility of the plantation house a few hundred paces away. The two-story building stood tall, with Corinthian columns rising above the wide portico. The planter and his family had heeded an earlier warning from William Hardee and fled to New Orleans. The slave cabins, beyond the house, sat empty, too. The slaves had been conscripted, serving the needs of the army, until they also were sent east, away from the coming maelstrom.

The plantation's bucolic appearance stood in stark contrast to the river, only a few hundred yards away. Bodies floated in the water, thrown from their barges when they were struck by explosive shells. While the Texian artillery had been ineffectual at wrecking Davis' grand battery, hidden behind strong earthen ramparts, the soft targets of Blanchard's division stood little chance when the Texians' murderous shells fell among the ferry-craft.

Still though, far more men made it to the other side of the Sabine than fell in its blood-tinged water. From behind, a voice reminded him he wasn't alone on the platform. "We're down to less than fifty of the barges still operational, sir."

He turned and looked at William Hardee. Soot streaked his cheek, running down to a blackened goatee. The ornate braiding on his uniform coat was torn where threads were pulled apart. Red stained the edges of the rip.

Davis felt his eyes raise involuntarily, "Are you alright, Bill?"

Hardee held up his hand, "Just a gash, Jeff." Alone, the two officers dropped the pretense of rank. He leaned against a railing, "We've captured more than half a mile of trenches along the river. The problem is that our efforts to capture the fallback line have been unsuccessful, so far."

Davis raised his binoculars and saw the blue flag with its single star flying near the river. Between the trench and the river, hospital orderlies worked their grisly trade, triaging the men who could be shipped back across the river for care and those who awaited burial. "Did the training work? You and I agreed that we needed to borrow Travis' tactics."

Hardee wiped at his face with a white handkerchief, turning it a grimy gray. "It's going to take more time to really change things, Jeff."

Davis scowled at the corps commander. Hardee took notice and added, "Some of the units managed to use the skirmish line tactics effectively. Especially our orphaned brigade from Texas. The first regiment into the enemy trenches was the Seventh Texas. The fighting was some of the fiercest of the day. Men were killing each other with knives, bayonets, and sometimes even with their hands."

"How many men have we lost?"

Hardee's shoulders sagged, "I don't know, Jeff. Blanchard's four brigades included nearly sixteen thousand men. We managed to get nearly all one hundred barges across at first. The second wave suffered the heaviest casualties. More than a thousand killed or wounded, just there. Getting into the trench line along the river didn't come cheap. The saving grace was the breechloaders of the Texas brigade let us focus overwhelming fire on a single enemy battalion. But we've tried extending our lines, but we've run into those damnable Gatling guns on our right flank. Our left flank has managed to push a few hundred yards north, but we're losing three or four men to every Texan."

Realizing the commander of I Corps was rambling, Davis cut in, “How many, Bill?”

Eyes brimming with tears, Hardee said, “At least three thousand, maybe more.”

“I wish to God they’d make up their mind,” Sergeant-Major Andrade said, “One minute, it’s solid shot plowing up the ground. The next, it’s explosive shells.”

Jesse found himself agreeing with him. The grand battery, on the opposite bank of the Sabine, made the lives of his men hell on earth. He couldn’t help thinking, *If that were all we had to deal with, that would be bad enough, but the Allied infantry only makes things worse.*

*No room for talk like that.* Instead, Jesse said, “We’ll hold them as long as it takes to break them.”

The telegraph operator, Vandergrift, winced as he tapped out a message. His arm was bandaged. A piece of shrapnel had come through the rifle slit and injured him earlier. He swore as he leaned back, “The line’s down between us and the Twentieth – again.”

Jesse bit back a sigh of exasperation. He’d send a runner if he had to, but he liked the immediacy of the telegraph. He squeezed by Vandergrift and his bulky equipment and looked back toward the reserve line. Rifle pits had been hastily thrown up perpendicularly between his line and the reserve position, using excess rail ties, lumber, and fallen trees to shelter his Rangers. Otherwise, the enemy might have succeeded in turning his flank and forcing his half of the battalion back.

Satisfied his deployment would hold, for now, Jesse sat down on an ammunition crate and pulled out a meat biscuit wrapped in wax paper and a tin of condensed milk. He used his knife to cut a hole in the tin and poured the thick, syrupy liquid into his cup. He dunked the biscuit into the milk before biting into it. The tasteless biscuit was dry and flavorless. But the sweet taste of the condensed milk turned what was an unpalatable meal into something he enjoyed.

Through a mouthful of food, Jesse wondered aloud, "Mr. Borden must be eating high on the hog what with all his contracts with the army. Both the meat biscuit and milk are his creations."

Andrade sipped his condensed milk from the tin, "Rich as Midas, I reckon. I can almost forgive him for those damned meat biscuits. I've heard tales you could trade a single tin of milk for a pound of tobacco with those Southern boys. They've taken a hankering to it, too."

Feeling the sugar rush, Jesse said, "Not that you'd know anything about illicit trading with the enemy, right?"

Andrade laughed, "No, never. Just rumors, you understand." His voice belied his words.

Gunfire, which never entirely stopped, rose in volume and a voice a few rifle pits over yelled, "They're coming again!"

Jesse and Andrade grabbed their rifles and looked through the rifle slit. The ground between them and the shoreline was empty save for a few bodies. But to their left, they heard men screaming as they rushed forward. Jesse raced to the back of the rifle pit, where the earthen lip was low. He looked around the corner and saw gray-jacketed soldiers running forward.

They made no effort to maintain their flanking firing line but instead seemed to run pell-mell at his makeshift rifle pits place perpendicularly between his line and the reserve line. He realized, as he watched, the enemy soldiers were working in small teams to cross the open terrain. Gone was the effort to use mass-volley fire. Granted, it was wasted against a heavily fortified position. As he watched the advance, the analytical part of Jesse's mind considered the challenges the army would face if, as it appeared, the enemy were trying to use their tactics against them.

A Gatling gun situated in the reserve trench opened fire when the enemy soldiers were within hundred paces of the makeshift rifle pits protecting the Ranger's flank.

Like toy soldiers being knocked aside, the advancing enemy soldiers toppled over when the machine-gun opened up on them. Another Gatling gun added its fire to its neighbor and the charge came to an abrupt halt, as the gunfire crisscrossed the enemy advance. Flashes of light and puffs of smoke confirmed the survivors hadn't retreated. They had gone to ground and opened fire.

Jesse pulled his head back inside the covered rifle pit. "It looks like we've stopped them, for now."

Andy Berry cocked his ears, he could swear he heard the rumble of artillery. Despite its reputation for showers, the last few days of April offered clear skies. A casual glance at the blue sky overhead convinced him whatever he heard wasn't thunder. More than sixty miles separated Trinity Park from the Sabine Front. It seemed unlikely the noise he heard was from the front lines. As he entered the grounds of Trinity College, he decided he'd ask Gail. If anyone would know, Andy reasoned, Gail would.

The campus had an air of abandonment about it as Andy walked along the dirt path leading to Borden's office. Most of the students were with the army, caught up in President Travis' latest round of mobilizations. It seemed as if the only folks not caught up in the newest round of mobilizations were men working in the factories, churning out the tools of war, desperately needed by the army. However, as he passed by the medical school, the sound of voices coming from a classroom reminded him not every student had been mobilized. The army needed doctors even more than it needed cannons, ammunition, and rifles.

The campus's small hospital wing, usually used by the faculty and students for training, would soon overflow with the wounded from the ongoing battle. After his taste of combat the previous year, he was glad to put his efforts into supplying the army. He knew what a bullet could do to soft human tissue.

The building housing Borden's office and lab felt as empty as the rest of the campus as Andy heard his heels echo on the polished wooden floor as he walked by empty classrooms. He found Gail Borden in his private lab where the inventor waved him over.

"Did you bring it?"

Andy gently set the heavy bag on the worktable. "Five pounds of the stuff, as you requested."

He was glad to hand the nitrogenated processed cotton off to Borden. When he mentioned how happy he was to get rid of the NPC, Borden laughed, "Putting it into a paste form seems to have helped stabilize it a bit."

Looking at the table, Andy said, "What's this contraption?"

A round, tin canister sat atop the table. It spanned almost a foot in diameter. The top was removed, revealing a smaller can, the size of a condensed milk container placed in the middle. A box containing iron ball bearings sat on the floor next to the table.

"A land torpedo. Dick Gatling and I were talking about weapons that previously were ahead of their time, but now might be possible. This was his idea. But he's busy with other projects."

Pointing to the lid, Borden continued, "That'll go on top of the torpedo. If you step on it, the top will depress and trigger this." He held up a miniaturized trigger, not unlike those used on the revolvers he manufactured, only smaller.

"The hammer will strike a percussion cap and detonate a small charge of NPC."

In Andy's analytical mind, he could follow the steps, "And that will, in turn, blow up the tin can full of ball bearings."

Gail nodded. "Exactly. During the American Revolution sea mines were deployed against the British navy."

Andy blinked in surprise. "I hadn't known."

Borden's cheeks turned red, "They weren't particularly successful. But NPC, while it isn't as stable as I'd like, is far more resistant to moisture than gunpowder, and it will still explode when detonated, even if wet. taken with the waterproof percussion caps, we're better positioned to control things our grandfathers couldn't."

Andy shook his head, "Have you tested it yet?"

"Not yet. I needed the explosives. Why don't you help me finish putting it together?"

Later, they took the assembled device over to the practice range where the foundry tested artillery. Andy helped Borden to position the device, place the lid on it, and set the trigger. They put a wooden table next to the device and tied a 6-pound cannonball to a length of twine and placed it near the table's edge.

They sheltered behind an earthen berm, and Gail handed the twine to Andy, "Why don't you do the honors?"

Wiping his sweaty palms on his trousers, Andy gently tugged on the twine. Although he couldn't see the solid shot roll off the table, he imagined the iron cannonball roll to the table's edge, balance for a moment until the tension in twine pulled it off.

Ka-boom! The ground shook beneath their feet, and Andy put his hand on the berm to steady himself. When he followed Borden back around the berm, the table was gone. The iron cannonball was nowhere to be found, and instead of the explosive device, Andy found a small crater.

He turned to Borden, a look of wonder on his face, "Merciful God, Gail, what have you made?"

Jason Lamont tugged at his mount's reins as he followed behind the line of skirmishers moving through the dense forest. Not for the first time did he curse General Davis for ordering his brigade to accompany the army's cavalry division on its flanking maneuver. Still, in a moment of charity, Lamont knew his South Carolinians were better suited to the densely wooded terrain than the men following behind his infantry, leading their mounts.

Ferrying nearly four thousand infantry and nine-thousand cavalry troopers and their mounts had taken most of the morning even with twenty flat barges assembled for that purpose. Where the army crossed the Sabine, there were no roads on the Texas side of the river, and the men were forced to make their way through the old-growth forest.

"General, according to the map, we've got another five miles or so until we hit the enemy's northern flank."

Lamont turned, his nephew, newly promoted Captain Elliott Brown followed behind him. Since taking command of the South Carolina brigade, Lamont had made sure to keep his nephew close at hand; the young man still bubbled with youthful exuberance, but if anything happened to Brown, Lamont's sister wouldn't forgive him.

Two, maybe three more hours before they'd be able to close with the enemy's flank. Not trusting the sun, hidden above the trees' foliage, he looked at his pocket watch. It would be between five and six in the afternoon before they could attack. There'd only have an hour or two of light left. He didn't like it. He'd heard old soldiers talk about night-time fights against the Seminoles. He pursed his lips and decided he wasn't going to think about it.

A few minutes later an officer came racing back, weaving through the trees, "General, up ahead, there's a balloon in the sky!"

There was nothing on the map about enemy troops being between him and the enemy fortifications on the Sabine. He swung into his saddle, "Let's take a gander, captain."

As his mount cantered after the officer, he yelled over his shoulder, "Captain Brown, relay the message to Generals Swift and Withers."

A bit later, Lamont grimaced as he stared at the observation balloon floating over the forest, through a break in the trees. His South Carolinian skirmishers waited for the order to advance, but there was no doubt the balloon wasn't alone. The question was, how many men defended the position?

"General Lamont, what's the delay?" A voice barked.

Lamont wheeled his horse around and saluted General Swift. "The Texans have eyes in the sky, sir."

Swift pulled a spyglass from a saddlebag and trained it on the balloon. He snapped the telescoping lens closed, "So much for surprise. Send your skirmishers forward, General Lamont. Maybe we can capture the balloon."

Given his orders, Lamont dug his heels into his mount's flank and drew even with his skirmishers. "Up, boys! There's abolitionist scum ahead. Let's show those bastards Southern steel and lead."

Moments later, rifle-fire echoed through the woods. The battle was joined.

# Chapter 19

Charlie gripped the frayed end of the tether and cursed. The observation balloon drifted on the wind. In the fading light, the Sabine River seemed to recede ever so slightly as he watched boats continue to ferry the Southern Alliance's soldiers across.

Sam interrupted his thoughts, "Major, we're gaining altitude. Should we open the vent?"

Charlie's companion stood next to his telegraph machine, peering over the side. The four tethering ropes slapped against the basket, free of their mooring more than a thousand feet below. Beads of sweat glistened above the youth's brow, even with the wind's chilled kiss. Despite that, his voice remained steady.

Charlie glanced at the silk ribbon, sealing the vent closed. "Not yet. We're floating away from the river. In the right direction."

"That's shit," Sam swore. "The right direction is back the other way. We had those bastards pinned in. By all rights, we should have pushed them back into the river."

Grabbing the rope connecting the basket to the balloon, Charlie couldn't help but agree. *We should have held the line*. Instead, he said, "The messages you received, before our secondary trench line fell, made me think they must have hit the northern flank with ten thousand soldiers or more. We had, what? Two thousand cavalry watching the flank."

Sam went to the other side of the basket and looked below, "I wonder if the Southern Allies had that Forrest fellow leading their flank attack. He's plum crazy."

Charlie shuddered. The Texian cavalry brigade tasked with holding back the flank included John Brown's former command. "God help those New York boys if Forrest's men were part of the flanking attack. They had a vicious grudge to settle." He considered his comment and then added, "God help our northern observation balloon, Sam. Did you see it over the cavalry?"

The young telegraph operator gazed into the twilight, "No. But the center collapsed, and we lost our signal." He turned around in a circle, scanning the sky. "At least our other two balloons are still with us."

"As long as the wind holds."

"You want to set down at the camp outside Beaumont?" Sam asked.

"Yeah. It'll be dark before then. We'll start our descent when we see the Neches," The brilliant red, gold, orange and purple sunset was fading. "If we can see the Neches," he amended.

As the sky grew dark, the ground behind them still flashed with lights, like a million fireflies. Every now and then the wind would carry the sound of cannon and gunfire. Sam leaned against the basket's edge next to Charlie, "I thought the whole army was in retreat. I guess I was wrong."

Charlie clasped his hands, helpless to do anything other than float on the wind. "From the sound of it, whoever is holding our line is giving as good as they get."

Major Jesse Running Creek eyed the heavy-laden ambulance on the road nearby. Cries from the wounded resounded through the night. Lanterns hung on the front of the wagon and the four-mule team pulling it struggled against their harnesses. *I wonder how many trips they've made today?*

Gunshots echoed in the night, and Jesse peered into the inky darkness. Indiscernible voices drifted through the forest. He groaned in exhaustion before he raised his voice, "Look alive, Rangers! We need to hold the enemy for a bit and let the ambulance get away."

Jesse scrounged around in the bottom of his cartridge box until his fingers grasped onto one of the few remaining rounds and levered it into his rifle and waited. The treetops overhead obscured the moon, reducing visibility to only a few dozen feet. Out of the gloom, two specters emerged. Against the darkness, their jackets could have been gray or butternut. The two colors were more alike than Jesse wanted to admit. *Say what you will,* he thought, *you're not going to mistake a Marine's jacket for an Allied soldier's.*

He threw the butt of his rifle to his shoulder and fired. Another rifle cracked nearby, and both men fell where they stood. Jesse couldn't tell if they were dead or simply gone to ground. But nobody returned fire.

Jesse chanced a look to either side and of the nine hundred men in the Army's Ranger battalion, all he could see were a handful. As he chambered one of his last rounds, he thought back over the past few hours. The first sign something had gone amiss came when a runner from the 20th Infantry raced over to Jesse's rifle pit out of breath. He panted that their left flank was exposed and the battalion holding that flank was in headlong retreat. Jesse hurried back to the second trench line and heard rumors that allied cavalry were behind the lines in force.

Feeling he had no choice, Jesse sent a runner to find the Ranger battalion's colonel and report that he was pulling his wing of the battalion back to the secondary line, abandoning their rifle pits. The 20th drew back a few hundred yards as the Rangers populated their trench. It was too little, too late, Jesse realized as he saw enemy soldiers working around his unit's flank.

As the Rangers retreated, the gun-crews handling the 4-gun Gatling battery fell back, too, pulling the gun carriages with ropes and backbreaking effort. Leapfrogging backward, the Rangers and the men from the 20th Infantry held the enemy at bay, allowing other units, more battered than they, to retreat.

Throughout the tumultuous evening, the closest the Rangers were to being overwhelmed came during their defense of the Republic's grand battery. They held their position in front of the battery long enough for every gun to be limbered and for teams of horses to be brought forward. Apart from a couple of field pieces too severely damaged, the gun-crews managed to extract every field piece assigned to the grand battery.

The line held for more than thirty minutes. The Rangers used every stump, tree, and gully, every imperfection in the terrain for cover, as caissons and gun carriages rolled away on the other side of the makeshift barricade that had sheltered the gun crews until moments before. But at a cost. When the allied soldiers finally flanked Jesse's defensive position, the Rangers left dozens of men behind, never to rise again.

The memory of that moment several hours earlier seared itself in Jesse's mind. And now, as he and his men waited for the ambulance to get moving, he couldn't help wondering why the enemy hadn't stopped their attack when night fell. While his men had spent hundreds of hours training for night combat, it was an unusual skill, and he was perplexed the Allied soldiers were still pushing against Jesse's rear guard. Had General Davis lost control of his men after dark or was he trying to break Johnston's rearguard to destroy the Texian army?

Minutes passed as he peered into the dark, expecting more soldiers to follow up on the attack launched by the two unfortunate souls lying a few yards away. Apart from gunfire in the distance and the sounds of voices no longer drawing closer, Jesse slung his rifle onto his shoulder and called out, as softly as he could, "The ambulance is gone, let's go."

6 May 1853

Will leaned over the injured soldier and pinned the purple ribbon to the pillow. The recipient, a Tejano who offered a weak smile at his commander-in-chief, lay on the cot.

Will returned to the end of the bed where Juan Seguin and George Fisher waited. Will came to attention and saluted the injured soldier, "A grateful nation thanks you for your sacrifice, Private Gonzales."

To Will's trained eye, the metal pinned to the pillow, called *the Order of the Alamo,* looked nearly identical to the one he recalled from his memories as the Purple Heart. In the early years after the transference, when he was still a soldier, he'd informally created the medal and issued it to every soldier, sailor or Marine injured in combat. Once he won the presidency, one of Will's first acts was to formalize the award. It was the least Texas could do for her injured warriors.

And there were so many of them. Will's back ached from bending over so many cots. Still, it was a small price to pay. He took another ribbon from Seguin and pinned it next to the head of the man on the next cot. A blue jacket was draped over the back of a camp chair next to the cot. A pair of riding boots were under the camp bed. The man lying there had a linen bandage wrapped around his head. His eyes fluttered open. He focused on Will.

"You're not Mary Lou." His voice was dry as sandpaper.

Will offered a smile, "No. I imagine she's much better looking."

The soldier's eyes dilated, and he closed them for a moment. When he opened them again, he said, "Sweet Lord above, my head is killing me."

One of the hospital's surgeons was in Will's retinue. He stepped forward and said, "Private Allen has a nasty concussion. Thank God, he's got a hard head; otherwise, that bullet might have killed him instead of bouncing off it."

"What's your unit, son?" Will had pressed a lot of flesh and kissed plenty of babies since shedding his uniform. He'd learned the art of showing interest in whomever he spoke with. He leaned in as he addressed the injured man.

"First New York Cavalry."

Will's thoughts flitted back to Austin, where in his mind, he saw John Brown sitting in a jail cell waiting for a trial that might never come. It was, Will knew, a violation of due process. Under Texian law, Brown had the right to a speedy trial and to face his accusers. But a trial would be public and could damage Texas' reputation in the United States, should a jury find him guilty. Winning the war was more important than protecting Brown's rights. *It's not like Brown protected the rights of the men he killed,* Will thought.

He patted the trooper on the lower leg, "Texas owes the people of New York a debt of gratitude, Private Allen. We're thankful y'all came to our defense. The First was with our cavalry brigade north of the front, right?"

The soldier winced as he nodded.

Will said, "What do you recall happened when the enemy attacked your position?"

After taking a sip of water offered by an orderly, Private Allen said, "We first knew something was wrong when we heard gunshots just north of our position. Our pickets ran back into camp telling us every demon of hell was behind them. Those Southern boys weren't no demons, but they were running behind our pickets fast. The first wave was almost on us when our officers ordered us to stand to, and after that, it became an ugly brawl."

The soldier closed his eyes. Will could see him fighting off the pain.

Will said, "Get some rest, trooper. Thank you for sharing."

The private's eyes opened again, "We gave as good as we got, sir. But there were just so many of them." He pointed to his bandage, "I got this after the First joined the retreat. We were ordered to hold a line along a creek, to allow another battalion time to pull back. We held until we were told to fall back, the traitors didn't force us New York boys back a second time, no sir."

The soldier's eyes closed. A moment later, his chest rose and fell in a regular pattern. He had fallen back asleep.

After touring the makeshift hospital housed in one of West Liberty's cotton warehouses, Will led Vice President Juan Seguin and George Fisher, Secretary of War back to the train depot, where they climbed aboard the presidential car.

No sooner had they sat than Seguin picked up an old argument, "Buck, give the order, and I'll tell the train's engineers to turn us around and head back to Austin."

Will scowled. “We’ve already been over this, Juan. More than a thousand men were killed, and thousands more are overwhelming our hospitals. Our defeat on the Sabine is the greatest setback our Republic has ever endured. Worse even than Woll’s invasion back in forty-two. There are upwards of fifty-thousand Southern soldiers on our side of the border.”

Secretary of War Fisher interrupted Seguin’s response, “Closer to forty thousand now, but Vice President Seguin is right, sir. In chess, you don’t needlessly risk your king.”

Will fumed. He needed them to understand, he couldn’t order thousands of men to their deaths and stay safely back in Austin. “The soldiers defending their homes, farms, and towns need to know they’re not alone and that the government has their backs. Our presence in Beaumont will bolster their morale, gentlemen.”

Seguin put the stopper back into the decanter and used the drinking glass to swirl around the amber liquid, “Unless an Allied sharpshooter gets lucky and decapitates the head of our government.”

Will grimaced at the image before sending a sharp look at his number two. “That’s why I picked you, Juan. There’s nobody better suited to take over the executive than you. Look, none of us are indispensable. If any of us died today, the government would carry on.”

He tasted the lie on his lips and decided he could live with the taste. He knew the world since the transference was entirely different than the history with which he grew up. If he died, he was uncertain Texas could survive on its own, despite the ripples to the timeline he'd introduced. As he thought of tens of thousands of enemy soldiers spilling over the border from Louisiana, he decided the ripples had turned into waves. If something happened to him, Texas likely would be swamped. Still, he couldn't help it, he had to see the front. He knew the men serving in the Texian army needed to understand their commander-in-chief would share their dangers.

He shook his head, "I appreciate your concern. Once we've inspected the defensive position at Beaumont, we'll return to Austin."

13 April 1853

Ignoring the clattering of the coach's iron-rimmed wheels over the wooden planking of the Long Bridge between the District of Columbia and Virginia, Horace Greeley focused his attention on General Winfield Scott, who sat opposite from him. The general wore a perpetual frown as he stared back at the newspaper man. Scott's brown hair had long retreated to gray and his fit figure from his time serving the nation in the War of 1812 had long ago been replaced by the girth of middle age. More to the point, Greeley couldn't help wondering how long the sixty-six-year-old general could continue serving.

Next to the general sat the officer commanding the US Regulars in Virginia. Brigadier General Robert E. Lee sat erect, his back not touching the seat back's plush cushion. Gray hair pushed the deep brown away from his temples and crept into his mustache. Despite that, at forty-six, he retained the trim physique of a man half his age. Greeley reminded himself the outer appearance was secondary to the ability of the men sitting across from him. Scott's quality was known. A hero of the War of 1812, his management of the US Army stretched more than thirty years. The younger officer was known as an able engineer. He had shown promise as superintendent at West Point. However, he'd barely assumed that role when the nine states composing the Southern Alliance seceded from the Union.

The coach shook when the wheels left the bridge's level wooden planking to the rutted road leading to Alexandria. With an abruptness that startled Greeley from his study of the officers, Scott said, "You understand, Mr. Greeley, I'm a military man, and my duty is to uphold the Constitution of our Union. I don't set policy. My job is to carry it out."

Greeley wished the road would let him make notes, but as the coach jostled over the uneven surface, the prospects of being able to read his own penmanship were nonexistent. He willed his mind to remember General Scott's every word. "General, we're going on four months since the last of the nine states seceded, yet all you've done is assemble an army. When do you expect President Seward to release you to use it?"

"In his own time, sir." Greeley sent him an antagonized look. Scott must have realized more of an answer was required. "Despite the readership of your newspaper being stalwartly Whig in their outlook, I think they understand the election of November last was not a mandate for swift action against the states in open rebellion. Five states whose livelihood depend upon Negro servitude have eschewed secession, so far."

Greeley's brow creased in frustration, "Are you saying that Virginia, Kentucky and the other remaining slave states are keeping us from putting those traitors down?"

Greeley caught a glance between the two officers, both of whom were native Virginians. The younger officer replied, "Let me ask you, sir, how would you react if the Southern and Western states allied against New England's interests? Their trade and economic interests are not the same as New England shipping magnates and industrialists. Imagine these other states threatened your livelihood. How far would you allow them to push you before you acted similarly to Louisiana, South Carolina, or the other states in rebellion?"

Greeley said, "It's not an apt comparison, those states entrap millions of Negros in bondage, General Lee."

Lee dipped his head, "I agree with you. It's an imperfect system that needs improvement. But don't ignore the beam in your eye while condemning the mote in your neighbor's. When a man is injured in the factory, he's disposed of, like a bit of rubbish. If you don't take care of the blight in your own house, don't be surprised when those workers you willfully dispose of raise the red flag in places like New York and Philadelphia."

Lee's demeanor remained impassive even as he pointed out the flaws of Northern industrialism. He offered a smile. "Your allegiance is as much to your home in New York as mine is to Virginia. Wither Virginia goes, I go."

Greeley wished he could commit every word to paper. Instead, he said, “But you’ve been entrusted with command of the US Regulars in Virginia, your duty is to the Union.”

“Of course it is,” Lee said, “However, every state, whether New York or Louisiana, Massachusetts or South Carolina, or even Maryland or Virginia is due the allegiance of their citizens. Then the Union. Were it not so, why would President Seward have asked the states to raise their armies against the insurrection? If it is as you imply, why does he not command every man in every state to attend to the Union? Each state imposes itself between her citizens and the national government.”

Against his will, Greeley found himself agreeing with the Virginian. “Why build up an army to stop the traitors?”

Scott placed his hand on the Brigadier’s arm. “I’ll take that. May I speak in confidence?”

Even more loathed than slavers, Scott’s words were anathema to a newspaperman. A source that would not let himself be quoted was at times worse than no source at all. Still, he had little choice but to agree.

Scott said, “President Seward has been in contact with the governors of Virginia, North Carolina, and Kentucky. The fire eaters in these states are vastly outnumbered by more reasonable and loyal men. Even so, they have all echoed the same sentiment. If the president were to simply order the army and the other states’ militias to invade the states in rebellion, four of the other five slave states still loyal to the union would view it," he paused, searching for the right word, "unfavorably."

Greeley connected the information with an earlier interview with President Seward and realized what he was hearing. He blurted, "The price of these slave states' allegiance is an amendment enshrining slavery in the South. That's insidious."

Scott nodded, "Oh, I agree. We'd be better off if the scourge of slavery on our nation were to die today. But that's why I'm a military man, and William Seward is the president. However, the amendment doesn't affect all of the South. Only those who remain loyal to the Union. Also, there's more. We agreed to stay any military action unless we or our allies were attacked."

Incredulous, Greeley stammered, "What about the armories the traitors have seized, the coastal forts they've captured?"

Scott offered a sad smile, "Those were deemed an acceptable loss against the risk of three and a half million more people falling into the rebel ranks. But you may have missed something in what I said."

The carriage rolled into an expansive field. Tents stretched as far as the eye could see. Elements of Lee's brigade of regulars were positioned nearest the Potomac River. Greeley spied flags from Virginia, New York, Pennsylvania, and Massachusetts. He guessed more than ten thousand soldiers were encamped along the southern bank of the Potomac River.

Ignoring the camp for the moment, Greeley replayed General Scott's words in his mind. "We have allies?"

"An ally. A month ago, Secretary of State John Wharton of Texas signed an agreement of friendship with the United States. In a closed session two weeks ago, the Senate ratified the treaty."

Greeley chewed on the news before saying, "What about Kentucky, Virginia and the other slave states that remained loyal? How will they respond?"

Lee rejoined the conversation, "As we understand it, Governors Johnson and Powell agreed that if the states in rebellion continued their attack on Texas, Virginia, and Kentucky would remain loyal. Maryland and Delaware are firmly in the Union camp, too."

Greeley felt buoyed by the news. One state remained unaccounted for. "What of North Carolina?"

Lee said, "Their legislature is in session. I don't know which direction they'll go."

Scott added, "I don't think they do, either. Governor Reid favors preserving the Union. The legislature could go either way."

A sad sigh escaped from General Lee before he added, "However they vote, the die is cast. The states in rebellion have violated our ally's sovereign territory. We will act to preserve the Union. By the end of next week, we'll be knocking on North Carolina's door. I pray they choose wisely."

# Chapter 20

17 April 1853

"Duckbill, you've gone native on us, I swear,"

Jimmy Hickok turned on the corporal, "Ain't my fault. My jacket was getting too small." But the other soldier had a point. Jimmy's kersey blue woolen trousers had been replaced several months before by the brownish trousers worn by the Texian army. Over the past few months, he'd put on several inches, and his old jacket, once too large, no longer fit. Now, except for the blue kepi the men of the 1st wore, he could have been mistaken for a trooper from one of the Texian battalions in the brigade. But of the men in the 1st New York, he was hardly alone wearing butternut brown.

Another soldier lifted a pot from the campfire and filled his tin cup with steaming coffee. He said, "What'd you think of President Travis making a to-do about visiting the camp?"

The corporal spat into the campfire. As the spittle sizzled and burned, he said, “I’d sooner he released Colonel Brown, that’s what I wish. Holding him in a jail cell on account of him ridding the world of a few slave owners don’t seem right.”

Before the nightmare in Southeast Arkansas, Jimmy would have agreed with the NCO, but seared into his sleepless nights was Bedford Forrest’s reminder that two could play that game. He’d woken during the middle of the night, blinking away the image of his companions swinging in the breeze from tree branches where they’d been hung by Forrest’s men. Had Texas’ Frontier Battalion not shown up and arrested the colonel, Jimmy wondered how far into Hell the vendetta between Forrest and Brown would have gone.

The coffee drinker wagged his mug in front of the corporal, “I miss the colonel, too. But after we were whipped, this army, this brigade, in particular, came dragging back here with its tail between its legs. Say what you will of Travis, but a’fore he talked to the other battalions, he came over here first. He didn’t have to do that.”

Jimmy found himself nodding his head. The soldier was right. Morale across the army was a lot higher now.

A bugle broke the quiet of the morning. Jimmy listened to the notes. Assembly. His stomach lurched, and the sense of wellbeing fled. He ran over to his tent and plucked his belt from the pole. Buckling it, he joined the rest of the regiment as they gathered in front of the regimental flag. Lt. Colonel Cross stood near the regimental colors waiting. He wore a stony expression. *He’s got the right of it,* Jimmy thought.

The regimental sergeant major's voice carried across the parade ground, "The First New York Provisional Cavalry is assembled, sir. All troopers are present or accounted for."

Lt. Colonel Cross stepped forward. Jimmy found his voice jarring as though every word carefully chosen for its brevity. "Effective the seventh of April, the First New York Provisional Cavalry Regiment and other regiments from the United States currently volunteering in the Republic of Texas are hereby accepted into service of the Volunteer Army of the United States, and subject to the military discipline thereof."

Everyone in the regiment knew this. Dread filled Jimmy's heart as he waited for Cross to continue, "On the tenth of April, Elijah Carter and Sean O'Malley deserted their post and were captured on a train bound for Galveston. In accordance with Article Twenty of the United States Articles of War, a court-martial was convened, and Privates Carter and O'Malley were found guilty of desertion and sentenced to death. The sentence is to be carried out now."

Drummers, borrowed from the 3rd Pennsylvania Volunteer Infantry, beat a mournful tattoo as a squad of troopers escorted the condemned across the parade ground. At one end, were two wooden coffins. When the condemned arrived next to the coffins, a chaplain stepped forward. Jimmy strained to hear his voice, but whatever the man of the cloth said, was directed only to Carter and O'Malley.

When the chaplain finished, another officer instructed the condemned to sit on the edge of their coffins and then placed a burlap bag over their heads.

Then he pinned a small red sheet of paper over their hearts.

The squad that escorted the two troopers into the parade ground now formed a line ten paces away from them. They stood at attention, their carbines in the crook of their arms, waiting.

Jimmy cringed as the young officer in command of the squad barked, “Squad, ready!”

The troopers shifted, bringing their carbines down, one hand on the stock and the other under the barrel. The metallic click of eight hammers made Jimmy flinch.

“Aim!”

In one smooth motion, the troopers raised the butts of their carbines to their right shoulders and stabilized the barrel with the other hand and waited.

A long delay tore at Jimmy’s heart. “Fire!”

Seven bullets sped across the ten paces, tearing apart the targets over the condemned men’s hearts before killing both instantly and propelling them into the caskets. As the smoke cleared, Jimmy saw the dead men’s legs hanging over the side of the coffins.

One carbine had fired a blank charge, allowing each of the executioners to believe, if they chose, that his carbine alone had been the one with the blank.

“Shoulder arms!”

With a single look from Lt. Colonel Cross, the sergeant major raised his voice over the muttering from the men, “Dismissed!”

Jimmy followed the men from his squad back toward the campfire. Conversation was subdued. Before, it was uncommon for deserters to be caught. And across the seven volunteer regiments from the North, hundreds of men had, over the past few months, decided to head for home, one way or another. Now, though, the volunteers from the United States knew there was no turning back, no going back home until the war was over.

General Jefferson Davis stepped away from the camp table, cluttered with maps and stacks of orders. He gripped the pole supporting one corner of a tarp which stretched over his headquarters. A troop of cavalry kicked up dust on the nearby road as they rode toward the Neches River. Behind the horsemen, a wagon lumbered by. It carried an overturned barge. By Davis' count, more than forty had been brought forward from the Sabine River. He pulled at his graying beard, thinking, *"Nearly enough to risk a crossing."* He cast a furtive glance at correspondence sharing the table with maps and bit his lip until he the coppery taste of blood hit his tongue.

"I need more time," he muttered.

A throat cleared behind him and Davis turned back to the table. Commander of the army's I Corps, William Hardee sauntered into the tent, laying his black service hat on the edge of the table, and leaned against it, "Time's the only resource we can't get more of."

Davis's laugh held a sharp edge to it. "That's the sad, sorry truth, Bill. Although the further away we get from the Sabine, the more inclined I am to think there are other resources we'll soon be short of than simply time."

Hardee glanced down at the maps on the table and studied it. "We're only two days away from the railhead, Jeff. What with the miracles General Wyatt seems capable of producing, supplies shouldn't be a problem."

"Until recently, we were the only army the Southern Alliance fielded. Now, there's the Army of the Tennessee near Nashville and the Army of the Carolinas to compete for resources. I'll grant you Payton Wyatt has wrangled every resource we've needed out of Louisiana, but the reports I've received tell a different story. We've got enough food for a week's campaign right now. If he doesn't come through with more, we'd better hope we can live off the countryside." Davis said, indicating to their locations on one of the maps.

Hardee gave a perfunctory nod. "I might not mind foraging a bit. Have you seen those meat biscuits Wyatt's shipped? Nasty things. Makes you hanker for a bit of spoiled sausage or hardtack. I hear tell the Texans invented them. Now, they're being manufactured in New Orleans by the wagon load."

Davis had tried a meat biscuit. Once. He figured his belly would need to be rubbing up against his backbone before he'd willingly add it to his daily diet. "I can almost forgive Gail Borden his meat biscuits, given how popular his canned milk has become. Almost."

Hardee chewed on his lip, thinking. "When we capture West Liberty and Trinity Park, we'll capture the manufacturing plant for Borden's Condensed Milk. As if we needed another reason to capture Texas." He glanced up and looked about. "But, between you and me, I wonder if we bit off more than we can chew."

Davis scanned the area. The nearest orderly was at a campfire, too far away to hear Hardee's whispered confession. "We're fighting for our rights, Bill. Without Texas, we'll be overwhelmed. Seward won the election without a single Southern state. It also destroyed the balance between our two regions. Now the North knows they don't have to compromise with us anymore and can force their policies on the nation."

Seeing the look on Hardee's face, Davis added, "Oh, I'll give you that when Beauregard failed to knock Sidney Johnston's army out, we should have tucked our tails between our legs and stayed on our side of the Sabine." A melancholy expression crossed his face, "But when Mississippi called on me, who was I to refuse?"

Hardee offered half a smile, "True. Georgia has first call on my allegiance. Where does that leave us?"

Davis took a couple of letters from next to the regional map and handed it to Hardee. "With little enough time."

Davis pointed to the regional map, adding, "We still have more than forty thousand men in the army fit for duty. I wanted more time for some of our soldiers who were lightly wounded to return to the ranks, but as you'll surmise, that's no longer an option."

He pointed to Beaumont on the map, "We'll hold Johnston's force there with your Corps. You'll have around twenty-five thousand men. I'll send Swift's corps around their flank. Both his infantry and cavalry this time to flank the Texans."

Raising his eyebrows, Hardee said, "Isn't it risky to use the same tactic twice in two fights?"

Dipping his head slightly, Davis said, “There is a risk. No doubt. We’ve sent scouts across the river, and they’ve reported back that Johnston has less than twenty-thousand men. You’ve got to hold his army on the river until the flanking movement can swing around.”

Hardee set the orders aside and came over next to Davis and looked at the map. “You’d have Swift’s corps be the hammer and mine be the anvil?”

“Exactly,” Davis said.

Hardee nodded at the orders, “You seem to be in a bit of a bind. These orders contradict each other.”

Davis grimaced. “That’s one way to look at it. President Cass has ordered me to destroy Johnston’s army. The War Department has ordered me to release your corps to return east. They want you to reinforce General Longstreet’s Army of the Carolinas. The orders from back east are as clear as the Mississippi River after a rainstorm.”

Hardee waved his hand over the map, “Can we pull this proposed attack off before my corps has to leave?”

Davis nodded toward a small writing desk near the maps table, “Given President Cass’s orders, I have asked the War Department for clarification. It’ll go out this afternoon.”

“By courier?”

Davis gave a nasty grin, “No. It’ll be bundled up with the payroll receipts. It’ll take two or three days to get to the Sabine. Another day to get to New Orleans. By then some enterprising staff officer will probably send it by telegram to Montgomery. It’ll take a couple of days to untangle the orders. And then three or four days to get them back. By the time the War Department's answer arrives, we'll have defeated Johnston's army and be halfway to Austin."

20 April 1853

"Careful, you jackass. Drop this and you'll blow us all to kingdom come!" A Ranger hissed.

Jesse Running Creek pivoted around. Several men lifted a crate out of a wagon bed. Despite the irate warning, they paid close attention to their work.

*Well they should,* Jesse thought as he waited for the container to reach the ground before he approached. He lifted a cotton tarp covering the crate and whistled in appreciation as he stared at the contents. Cushioned by thick cotton bunting were a half-dozen small iron round boxes. Next to each box was a much smaller flat piece of metal, perfectly round. Jesse retrieved one of the tiny "pressure plates" that accompanied each land torpedo, as the creators at the Trinity Gun Works called them.

He turned it over, and a thin iron spike extended an inch from the bottom of the plate.

The wagon shook a bit as the driver climbed down, "The pressure plate is harmless as a dove, Major. At least by itself."

The driver cautiously removed one of the round, iron boxes and gingerly set it on the ground. "There's enough nitrogenated processed guncotton in this little devil to blow this wagon to smithereens. But it's more or less harmless without something to trigger it."

One of the Rangers asked, "How much is 'more or less?'"

The driver offered an apologetic smile, "More to the less than to the more, if you catch my meaning. Even though the NPC is in a paste form which renders it more inert than when in a granular form, it's still too temperamental for me. Gather 'round, I'll show you how to enable this infernal contraption and how to disable it."

Jesse joined the handful of Rangers around the driver, who knelt over the torpedo. "Without a percussion cap, there's no way to detonate the NPC in the bomb." He held up a small, brass percussion cap, not unlike the ones used in a cap-and-ball revolver. "We'll hold off putting the cap on the nipple just yet."

He tipped the torpedo so that Jesse could see inside its top. "Like your revolvers, there's a small trigger that, when activated, will snap down on the percussion cap and blow up the device. So, we'll cock the hammer." He reached his fingers down the opening on top, and a moment later, Jesse heard a faint click.

"All set, except for the pressure plate." The driver gently screwed the pressure plate into the trigger mechanism. "There's not much to it. If I'd have put the percussion cap on this little piece of Hell, it'd be ready to go."

Jesse said, "What's the trigger pull?"

The driver said, "Twenty pounds. Now, watch as I disable the device."

He reversed the process, showing the Rangers how to disable the bomb before climbing to his feet. He grabbed a shovel from the back of the wagon, "Follow me, I want to show you how to place them, once the torpedoes are ready."

They were in a field on an abandoned farm, next to the northern flank of the army. The driver stopped a few paces into the tract of farmland and used the shovel to scrape away the topsoil. With a level of care that belied the inertness of the NPC, he set the bomb in the shallow hole and then pushed dirt back on top of the device, leaving only the black pressure plate exposed.

"If there aren't any questions, let's break into two-man teams and sow this field."

Jesse grabbed a notebook and waited as his men returned with the torpedoes. He sketched the field, and as each team activated their first bomb, Jesse made a note of where it was buried. The orders from General Johnston had been clear. A map of each section where the mines were planted had to be marked where each was hidden.

"Major," one of his Rangers called out, "What happens if the Allies don't come this way? The farmer will return sooner or later. He'd get one hell of a surprise if he steps on one of these things."

Jesse shuddered at the thought of a farmer's children playing in the field. He pointed to his notebook, "We'll clear these fields after we've defeated the enemy. Believe me, the last thing I want is for civilians to discover these things."

In addition to sketching the field, Jesse made notes and drew diagrams of the pressure plate and the triggering mechanism. Seeding the ground was a test run. Once torpedoes protected the northern flank, Jesse and his Rangers would repeat the process between the Neches River and Beaumont. Placing the torpedoes on the army's flank was relatively safe, as safe as anything that involved handling an unstable explosive could be. For now, they could do their work under the warmth of the midday sun. But they'd have no choice but to plant the torpedoes near the riverbank under cover of night. Every note he made today would help later.

An hour later, the driver raised his voice, "That was a single crate of forty-eight torpedoes. I've got five more just like it. We'll move over to the next field and do this again."

Jesse chanced a look into the sky. The sun was still high overhead. They had a lot more work ahead of them.

# Chapter 21

25 April 1853

Mist clung to the water's surface. General Jefferson Davis listened to the gently lapping water on the shore, although between the thick haze and the darkness of a moonless and cloudy night, he couldn't see the Neches River despite standing less than thirty paces away.

"Maybe you're right. Why spoil the surprise with an artillery barrage."

A thin smile creased his face as Davis glanced at his companion. William Hardee's face was shrouded by his hat. "We couldn't have asked for better conditions, Bill. It can't compete with the enemy balloonists, but our signal towers will let us do a better job with counterbattery fire once the fog lifts. We'll hold our fire until we can see something."

The crunching of boots on gravely ground was just loud enough for Davis to hear the soldiers hauling the barges to the water's edge. Hardee said, "The Seventh Tennessee and the Tenth Texas will go over first. Fifteen hundred men in the first wave. They'll be followed by the Forth Alabama and the Seventh Texas."

Davis placed his hand on Hardee's arm. "Putting nearly half the Orphaned Brigade into the grind so soon?"

Hardee leaned forward seeming to stare into the thick fog, "Those Texas boys are some of our best soldiers, and their breechloaders put them on an even playing field."

"Have you reconsidered going across in the third wave?" Davis' voice was pensive, "I can ill afford to risk you."

Hardee pointed into the mist, where the quiet sounds of his soldiers preparing to cross the Neches could be heard. "If something goes amiss, I'm better able to react if I'm over there."

Davis grumbled, "The days of a division commander leading from the front are over, Bill. Let alone a corps commander. I ought to order you to stay over here."

Hardee shook his head, "Jeff, the last thing I'm going to do is lead my men in some reckless attack. But we've already fought over this particular terrain. When we get a foothold in one of the trenches, we must exploit it, not get bogged down. We lost too many men on the Sabine. Had it not been for General Swift turning the enemy's flank, we might still be sitting in Louisiana."

Davis chuckled. "Had that been the case, you'd be answering to a different commander. President Cobb would have sacked me if I had squandered our largest field army in a failed assault."

An officer with a gold star on his shoulder-board emerged from the gloom, saluted, and turned to

Hardee, "Sir, it's time. If we get moving now, we should be able to get the barges over and back a few times before the sun comes up."

Davis offered his hand, and Hardee shook it. "God be with you, Bill. I'll see to it that we keep the barges moving once you've over."

Hardee offered a smile then came to attention and saluted.

A few minutes later, Davis stood on the shoreline and watched the closest barges push away from the shore and disappear into the misty gloom.

Time stretched as he leaned forward, listening. The sound of an oar splashing in the water reached his ears. The second time he found himself reaching for his pocket watch, he let his hand fall away. It was too dark to see the dials. Those minutes waiting for the barges to beach on the other side were the longest five minutes of Davis' life.

A gunshot, muffled by the heavy mist, echoed across the river. A fiery red rocket streaked into the sky and exploded over the river, where it seemed to hang in space. Davis read about their use in the Mexican War a decade earlier. He wondered about the parachute that kept the flare from falling immediately back to earth. He could see how the flare would allow the enemy to light up a battlefield at night, under better conditions. But the beacon failed to pierce the fog's heavy cloak. Despite that, the gunfire from the Beaumont side of the river grew loud as the men from Hardee's Corps attacked the enemy's fixed positions.

Teams of men pulled on ropes tied to the barges, and within just a few minutes, the watercraft slid into view as more soldiers crowded onto the shoreline, waiting to cross over. Other teams, on the western side of the river, waited a minute for the men to scramble onto the barges before they pulled on their ropes, bringing the laden watercraft back across.

Despite the gloom and the confusion of battle, Davis was gratified that all their preparation on the Sabine River over the past few days was paying off. The officers in charge of the transport hurried more troops down to the water's edge as they waited for the barges to return. Davis allowed a flicker of hope as he walked back to one of the signal towers.

As he wondered how long it would take for the enemy to open fire with their artillery, it was as if Sidney Johnston had read his mind. Guns behind the enemy lines began to fire. Men atop the tower shouted down to runners the coordinates of the enemy guns based on the dim flashes of light winking through the mist. Minutes passed before his own artillery returned fire.

Davis watched the muzzle flashes pierce the fog until he became aware that he could see the gunners racing around their guns through the gloom. The sun was rising.

*Charlie felt his fingers slip on the wicker basket's edge. He stretched his other arm and tried grabbing the slick rope between the basket and the balloon. His feet dangled as he grasped the side of the basket. Chancing a look down, the ground below spun as he felt his*

*breakfast rise. His fingers slipped, and he felt the basket bounce as a gust of wind tossed the silk balloon about.*

*He lost his grip and felt himself falling. As he plummeted toward the ground, he heard gunfire below and in the flash of a moment, wondered if he would die before he hit the ground.*

Charlie blinked his eyes open. Sweat covered his forehead as he sat up. It was just a dream, like the others before. Except the gunfire continued. He swung his legs down and stepped over to the tent flap and threw it back.

It was still dark. Tendrils of foggy mist hugged the ground. Soldiers raced through the airship's field. One of the balloons was deflated; it wouldn't fly today. Her pilot had crash-landed, damaging both the basket and the balloon's heavy silk cloth. One of the other balloons lay half inflated on the ground. The steam engine powering the hydrogen generator was broken. One airship, Charlie's, sagged in the air. The basket rested on the ground.

"Major, the Allies are on this side of the river!" Sam raced toward him, half-dressed. "A soldier from General Johnston's headquarters said they're already in the first trench."

As he bent over, catching his breath, Sam stared at their balloon. "That's not going anywhere anytime soon."

Charlie slipped a linen shirt over his head. As he buttoned it, he said, "I'll check with the crew. We've got to get up as soon as we can." Swiveling his head around, the heavy mist had to clear before he'd be able to see anything more than the palm of his hand.

A few minutes later, Charlie left his ground crew chief throwing coal into the one working steam engine. The sun would be up before the balloon would.

With nothing to do but wait, Charlie and Sam jogged across the field, hurrying by a row of makeshift tables where telegraph operators usually sat. A couple of young men were already in their seats. Charlie slowed long enough to hear one say to the other, “Grand battery is asking for confirmation of target. Tell them the balloons are down. Send a runner forward with signal flags. If we can see through this shit at all, we need someone to transmit the enemy positions.”

The operator clicked back a message as the communication hub fell behind Charlie and Sam. They stumbled through what once had been a stand of trees. Short stumps protruded from the loamy soil, the only reminder of the majestic pines once gracing the broad lowlands hugging the Neches River.

Once they passed by the stumps, Charlie paused as he glanced into the sky; a couple of flares floated above the river, the red glare reflecting off the dense fog. Despite the obscuring mist, he could see pin-prick flashes of light, the tail-tale signs of rifle or musket fire in the distance.

“The Allies might be in the trenches, Sam. We’ve got a while before the balloon will be ready. Let’s get closer.”

Charlie and Sam hadn’t gone far when they stumbled upon a fresh-turned earthen berm, behind which were several dozen field pieces. A familiar voice shouted, “Then get your ass back to the telegraph operators and tell them they had better send some observers forward. Without spotters, I can't hit what I can't goddamned see."

From the gloom, a bareheaded man emerged. His red hair looked disheveled, as though he had just been rousted from his bed. As Charlie ran his fingers through his own unkempt ginger head, he realized he must look like Colonel Sherman's younger twin. The commander of Texian artillery spotted Charlie around the same time, "Travis, I need signalmen forward. If they can point to where the enemy are congregating, I can have my guns target those positions. But there's damn all but confusion right now."

Charlie sketched a salute to the man who had commanded the Texian Cadet Corps while Charlie had attended. "Yes, sir."

He turned and pushed Sam, "Go back to where the telegraphers are and see if they can find some more folks to work the signal flags."

He turned back to Colonel William Sherman, "Sir, most of our resources have focused on telegraph operators and our observation balloons. I'm not sure how much luck the Lieutenant's going to have."

Sherman leaned against the barrel of one of his guns, "Perhaps. But if there is any way to strike the enemy before the light of day burns away this miasma, I'll find it. Why have you not yet taken to flight?"

"The balloon's hydrogen is low. Not enough lift yet. We'll be aloft as soon as we can," Charlie said.

A bit later, Sam raced back into the battery, "Colonel Sherman, the telegraph station is operational now. They've confirmed the secondary line is holding. They have your orders for coordinates."

"Bully!" Sherman nearly shouted. He turned away from Charlie and started yelling at his crews to load their guns.

"The balloon's being filled, Major. You see enough here?"

"Not a damned thing, Sam," Charlie said as he started walking back toward the airship field. "I hope by the time we're in the sky, this shitty fog clears up. How the hell can we do our job if all we see is damn all?"

Shot and shell arced over the line, flying back and forth between Allied gunners and their Texian counterparts. Major Jesse Running Creek peered over the edge of the trench and looked across the field. The first line of trenches had been overrun more than an hour before. The sun, coming up behind the Southern Allied army seemed determined to burn away the fog, tendrils of which still snaked along the ground.

Bodies in the butternut of the Texian army were mingled with the drab gray worn by the Southerners between the Rangers' trench and the river. Once the enemy had breached the line of the battalion south of the Rangers' position. Jesse had been forced to send their single reserve company to rout the enemy and plug the gap.

For now, the Allies seemed content to leave the northern flank alone. Jesse knew it wouldn't last. Barges still plied the river, shuttling men from one side to the other, although he guessed as many as half the barges were burning wrecks. Yet, every ten to fifteen minutes several hundred more Southerners reinforced their compatriots who were increasingly testing the Texian line. By now, as best as Jesse could tell, most of the buried torpedoes between the first trench and the water's edge had been detonated.

Jesse scowled. The notion the bombs had simply detonated was antiseptic. As he scanned the field in front of the trench, he knew the truth. The bombs had ripped soldiers apart. Those not killed had been maimed, most horribly. He wondered, as he saw through the haze a barge pulling back to the other side, if the injured who were being taken back to field hospitals were missing feet or legs. Despite hundreds, if not thousands of soldiers wounded by the hundreds of torpedoes, their compatriots were building for another rush at the defenders.

Jesse reached into his cartridge box. It hung heavy at his belt. At least for now, the brass cartridges his rifle depended upon were plentiful. He hoped it would remain so as the sun burned away the fog.

Jesse made his way down the line, patting a Ranger on the back, stopping long enough to take a smoke with another. Halfway down the line, facing the river, he came to two Gatling guns. The crew was filling the extended metal magazine with ammunition. As he stepped around the guns, he noticed most of the boxes were empty. Only two boxes contained ammunition.

Jesse picked up an empty magazine and handed it to the gunner, "Hold your fire until they're within fifty paces. I don't know when we'll get more ammunition. Best to save it until you can do the most damage. My boys'll do their best to keep the enemy from getting too close."

Continuing on, Jesse came to a sharp left turn. He had reached the end of the line. To his left was the army's flank. The battalion's commander, Colonel Brooks, had most of the six hundred remaining Rangers spread along a quarter mile, scattered with short trenches and deep rifle pits.

In Jesse's mind, he could see the next battalion anchoring the flank. The 21st Infantry, recruited from Santa Fe and Albuquerque, was mostly Mexicans who were still getting used to being called Tejanos. The single company of Negro soldiers anchored their flank. Beside them were the men of the 1st New York Provisional Cavalry. Dismounted and playing the role of infantry, the 1st served alongside the 3rd Pennsylvania Volunteer Infantry. Together, the Yankees covered another quarter mile. Finally, the 36th Infantry, a recently mobilized militia battalion from the Texas hill country, held the end of the line. Only two thousand men to cover more than a mile.

Rifle fire broke out behind him. Jesse turned and hurried back to the "L." He moved around the corner and raised his voice over the cacophony of gunfire. "Here they come again. Pick your target, make each shot count!"

From his perch atop one of the wooden towers, General Davis looked through his binoculars at the opposite bank of the Neches. The blue flag of the Filibusterers flew above the earthen ramparts closest to the river. Between those trenches and the river, scores of bodies still littered the ground, a painful reminder of how expensive capturing the first defensive line had been.

Worse, discovering the buried torpedoes had been a destructive lesson in Sidney Johnston's deviousness. Davis watched hospital orderlies spill out of one of the remaining barges and hurry up the slope, searching for more survivors. The reports coming in from the divisional field hospitals were ghastly. Even though less than three hours had elapsed since the attack had begun, more than a thousand broken bodies of men who might yet live had been hauled back across the river. The latest reports indicated far more men were still on the other side of the river, waiting to be transported.

The platform on which he stood shook as someone ascended the ladder. A grim face appeared, and Davis' adjutant climbed onto the platform. "We've been pushed out of their second defensive line, again sir. The Tennessee Brigade managed to hold a section of the line until they were forced back."

Davis dreaded the answer to his unspoken question. But bad news doesn't become more palatable by delaying the answer. The adjutant continued, "We'll not know the number of casualties yet, but General Mercer reports that as much as a third of the brigade have been killed or wounded."

"Merciful God," Davis swore. "We can ill afford losses like that. Where in the hell is Swift's Corps? They should have already attacked."

The officer shrugged. "Nothing yet, sir. But he had to cut upriver twenty miles before crossing. There aren't many roads cutting through this wilderness. But at least when they attack, there aren't more of those damnable balloons in the sky."

A lone balloon hung over the battlefield, no doubt telegraphing messages to operators down below, where the intelligence was sent as fast as the electrical current could travel. Davis wondered aloud, "How much time to repair the balloon we captured at the Sabine?"

"The holes in the silk were substantial, sir. But word from New Orleans is that our own signal corps will take it up soon. And, we're building another just like it."

Davis allowed a hollow chuckle to escape his lips, "Not according to my Varina. She says we've commandeered every silk dress between Mobile and Savanah to make it."

The men atop the tower laughed at the image of Southern women giving up their prized silk dresses for the good of the Alliance. Davis continued, "Still, though, the idea that we'll be able to put our own balloons over a battlefield and report on the comings and goings of our enemy has a certain appeal."

His adjutant raised a weary hand, "Perhaps, sir. But unless we're going to unstring miles and miles of copper wiring, we don't have enough wire to connect a bunch of telegraph machines together on a battlefield. My understanding is that General Johnston has been practicing with mobile telegraphy for several years. We're playing catchup."

Davis dipped his head in acknowledgment, "True. But as long as the North doesn't stab us in the back, we've got Texas outnumbered at least five to one. If, heaven forbid, we don't destroy Johnston's army today, we can still wear them down and force them to surrender."

"Yes, sir. On the other hand, with the betrayal of Kentucky, Virginia, and now apparently North Carolina we're now outnumbered four to one. If they backstab us, we'll be hard-pressed to stop them."

Davis growled, "Dismissed, Major."

In the distance, he heard several detonations, like artillery shells exploding. He peered across the river. For the moment, Hardee's I Corps was hunkered down in the captured trenches near the river. While enemy artillery continued targeting Allied barges, the explosions came from farther away. Adding to the blasts was the faint rattling of gunfire.

General Swift's II Corps had arrived.

Jimmy flinched as another torpedo exploded in the field in front of his position. He gripped his carbine and scanned the area to his front. From the direction of the river, gunfire echoed across the fields. To his sixteen-year-old ears, the explosions seemed to be rolling toward the 1st New York. He chanced a look to either side and gathered strength from the grim expressions worn by his fellow squad-mates.

Beyond the field, he saw shadows moving inside the tree-line, and a moment later, horsemen broke through the foliage, charging across the farmland. The lead horse and rider were only a few paces into the fallow field when the ground beneath the horse's hooves erupted, sending inch-round bits of shrapnel everywhere.

Riders steered their mounts around the carnage, screaming at the top of their lungs. More mounts found the buried torpedoes, turning the middle of the field into a slaughterhouse.

A hand smacked the back of Jimmy's head, "Hey, Duckbill, don't sit there with your mouth catching flies. Shoot."

The squad's corporal was already moving down the line when Jimmy turned, ready to give the NCO a mouthful. *The devil take him*, Jimmy thought as he cocked his carbine's hammer and fired into the milling mass of men and horses at the opposite end of the field.

As he grabbed a paper cartridge and tore the end off with his teeth, Jimmy envied the Texians, with their breechloading rifles. Although, as he tamped the ramrod done the barrel, seating the powder and bullet in its base, he knew that some of the militia battalions were armed with the same rifled muskets carried by the Yankee volunteers.

He braced the carbine on a fence post and watched as the horsemen retreated into the protection of the woods. Behind them, dozens of men and horses were down. Some were dead, whether from the torpedoes' explosions or from the marksmanship of the 1st New York, he couldn't say. More, though, cried out in pain. Worse were the screams from the horses. Charging a fixed position seemed like a terrible idea. A man, by himself, seemed a big enough target. Put him on a horse, and the target's more than twice as big. Given a choice, Jimmy'd just as soon shoot the rider, but in the heat of battle, he didn't like thinking about it, but he figured he'd hit a horse if it came down to him and the man on top of that horse.

Across the acreage, a couple of gunshots ended the worst of the screaming. *I don't care a damn for those bastards,* Jimmy thought, *but they've got enough grit to put those poor beasts down.*

The sun inched a bit more into the morning sky. The fog of the early morning was but a memory when Jimmy heard what sounded like steel sliding on steel. He'd barely had time to wonder what he'd heard when soldiers broke out of the tree-line on the other side of the field. The gray jacketed soldiers had socketed bayonets onto their rifles, and they were racing across ground that last year at this time was covered in cotton plants.

Jimmy sighted down the barrel of his carbine and fired. He ducked behind the fence and with practiced skill went through the steps reloading his gun. The cavalry hadn't detonated all the torpedoes, and as the Allied infantry reached halfway across the field, explosions shook the ground.

His carbine reloaded, Jimmy raised his head over the fence. Many of the soldiers were down who had started across the hundred paces of Hell between the tree line and the wooden rails behind which Jimmy sheltered. Trailing them came even more.

*Why aren't they forming a line and firing?* Jimmy puzzled, as the distance between the attacking survivors and the defenders narrowed. *That's what they're supposed to do.*

A high-pitched caterwauling rose from the men who sprinted the last fifty paces. The sound sent a chill down

Jimmy's spine even as he raised his gun, firing at a soldier less than a hundred feet away. He threw the butt of his weapon behind his feet and tore another cartridge in half. He rammed the charge down the barrel as he spat out bitter tasting black powder.

A bearded man with a long scar down the side of his face leapt over the fence, bayonet-tipped musket before him. Jimmy tumbled back, managing to hold onto his weapon even as he lost his balance. The bearded foe pivoted to his left and lunged, plunging his bayonet into the trooper who moments before had been next to Jimmy.

Unbidden, tears stung Jimmy's eyes as he fumbled for a percussion cap. As he tugged the little copper cap from its leather case, the Allied soldier used his foot to push Jimmy's companion from the gore tipped bayonet. Cocking the hammer back, Jimmy pressed the cap onto the nipple.

The gray jacketed soldier, eyes wild, swung his rifle around as he saw Jimmy, prone on the ground before him. He lowered his gun, lining up the bayonet on Jimmy. The youth cocked the hammer and fired. Gritty smoke filled the space between Jimmy and his assailant. When the smoke cleared, all the young trooper saw was a pair of feet draped over the fence's wooden railing.

Glancing around, as he crawled back to his feet, Jimmy didn't see anyone else from his squad. But, coming across the field were hundreds of more soldiers. He turned and ran.

# Chapter 22

Charlie tossed one of the ballasts over the side of the balloon, causing the airship to bounce higher. While mist still lingered over the water, the ground below was clear of fog. He shook his head as he scanned the space between the waterfront and the secondary trench line. In moments of doubt, he wondered if Heaven and Hell were real places. The carnage strewn below answered half the question. If hell had a name, it was Beaumont, Texas.

Men scoured the bank of the Neches River. When they found a survivor, they unrolled the stretcher and gently lifted the broken, injured soldier onto the canvas litter before hurrying back to one of the surviving barges.

"How do you count all of them?" Sam wondered aloud.

Charlie tried to blot out the image of the hundreds, perhaps even thousands of men broken on the riverbank. He turned toward where he could see and hear fighting. “Easier perhaps to count the enemy still on their feet.”

The army’s grand battery had been pulled back. Now more than a mile separated it from the fiery remains of Beaumont and the bloody banks of the Neches. Barges, flames still licking at consumable wood, were beached where their crews had been forced to abandon them. To Charlie’s trained eye there were more watercraft damaged, out of action, than still plying across the Neches.

“Sam, I count twenty-five barges out of action. There are still more than twenty operational. Mostly looks like they’re pulling back their wounded. If command wants coordinates, let me know.”

Charlie tuned out the noisy clattering of the key and studied the army’s flank. The fields which once flanked the army were cluttered with broken bodies. They must have paid a butcher’s bill to collapse the army’s flank. The army’s grand artillery battery now bent in an arc, covering the flanking army’s advance.

“Colonel Sherman’s compliments, Major,” Sam chimed, “Let him know if the enemy sends any reinforcements across the barges and provide coordinates for them.”

Sam leaned back, rubbing his eyes, “Let them take their dead and wounded back. I can’t imagine how many they’ve lost.”

Charlie swore and pointed at the battlefield, “Look, Sam. Our flank has failed. They’ve breached both defensive lines. The only thing holding our army here is the fact most of our battalions managed to hold their formations together when they were pushed out. But,

God have mercy, we must have lost four or five thousand men."

Sam's face was gray. In a quiet voice, he said, "Do we even know who won?"

Charlie shrugged as he lifted the binoculars. The two lines of entrenchments facing the Neches River flew the Allied flag. But most who seemed to hold those positions were among those who would never rise again. He swung his binoculars and at the army's extreme left flank, he saw a solitary lone star flag flying where the perpendicular left flank had once tied into the main line. "Wait. I see one of our flags still on the front."

He pulled a hand-drawn map from his jacket and looked at it. "Sam, send a message, do we still have a line to the Rangers?"

A few minutes passed. Sam turned away from transcribing the response. "No. It's cut."

Charlie fiddled with the focus on the glasses and strained to see the distant defensive position. He wondered how Jesse Running Creek had handled the attack. Was he still alive?

On the extreme left flank, where the defensive line created an "L," the defenders still held a narrow section. Neither the enemy attacking from the river nor those who flanked the army had broken that small section of the line.

Gray-clad bodies were scattered all the way to the edge of the trench. But over the earthworks flew the lone star flag, defiant, like Galveston Island surviving a destructive hurricane.

The telegraph machine clattered to life, and Sam's pencil scratched across a piece of paper. The pencil snapped, and Sam muttered, "Oh, shit."

Wheeling around, Charlie looked at his operator, whose gray face had grown even more ashen. Sam blinked, as though something bothered his eyes. He choked back a sob. "General Johnston. He's dead."

Dirt cascaded around his head as Major Jesse Running Creek ducked. Bullets peppered the top of the trench where his head had been an instant before.

The nearest Allied soldiers were closer than a hundred feet away. Thinking about the carpet of bodies littering the field, he amended the thought, *the nearest living Allied soldiers were closer than a hundred feet away.*

An empty box once containing ammunition was overturned. A Ranger slumped against it. As Jesse leaned in, he heard the rhythmic breathing of someone catching whatever rest he could. Another Ranger stood next to him, he had tied a shaving mirror to a bayonet and raised the mirror over the lip of the trench.

Jesse patted him on the back, "Any movement lately?"

The Ranger slid a glance away from the mirror, "Not since the last time. Any word on more ammunition, sir? I've maybe twenty rounds left.

Jesse's cartridge box still held a few rounds, and he pulled a handful of brass cartridges and handed them over. "Make every one count, Jim."

He stepped over a body as he moved down the line. It was not the first corpse he'd been forced to step over or around as he made his way down the "L" shaped perimeter. He turned the corner, continuing down the truncated line, stopping every few feet, offering a word of encouragement or leaning down to close the eyes of one of the fallen. The position which had once protected the army's flank continued for more than a mile. But most of it had fallen to the enemy hours earlier. The Rangers' line ended less than a hundred paces after the sharp turn. In the end, sandbags and broken boxes created a barricade. Behind it was a lone Gatling gun, facing the enemy-held trench. Jesse didn't want to know how his Rangers had manhandled the weapon into the trench's narrow confines.

"Sir, are there any more ammo boxes?" one of the gunners asked.

A sad look passed over Jesse's face, "No. Most of our boys are down to less than twenty rounds. How much do you have?"

The gunner held up a long, thin metal magazine, "We've got two of these left, and enough rounds to fill one up again."

Jesse did the math. A little over a hundred rounds.

He turned away from the gun and went and found Colonel Brooks. Crouching down, Jesse said, "I don't want to surrender. By God, we're Rangers, and we could hold this line until the last man. But for what? The opportunity to kill a couple hundred more of those bastards? There's less than three hundred of us still on our feet."

He looked down at Brooks, lifting the blanket covering the colonel's face. The small hole over the left eye had a rivulet of dried blood that had trickled into his hairline. Mercifully, someone had closed his eyes. Brooks was beyond answering Jesse's question. Even so, the Cherokee officer felt a sense of rightness unburdening himself to the colonel.

His knees creaked as he stood, there was no one else to talk to. Whatever decision he'd make would be on his own. The telegraph lines had been down since shortly after the flanking attack had struck. Even now, as he looked into the sky and saw a balloon floating overhead, he wondered if it was Charlie Travis' balloon.

Frustrated, he slammed his fist into the brittle earth, *If only there was a way to communicate.*

The morning sun was warm enough, even if it didn't hold a candle to the summer sun, still a couple of months away. If he decided to hold out, at least the blistering summer sun wouldn't sap the strength of his men. He blinked away the tears and turned away. The light continued to dance in his eyes as it reflected from a dead Ranger's belt buckle.

An idea sprang to life. He raised his voice, "Find the telegraph operator, now!"

A few minutes later, young Billy Vandergrift hobbled into sight. A bloody rag wrapped around his calf explained his limp. Jesse grabbed the telegraph operator by the shoulder and pointed at the balloon, "Can you use a mirror to signal that thing?"

Despite his pained expression, Vandergrift's face lit, "Hell, yes, Major. I'd get my own shaving mirror," he said, as he rubbed a hand over a downy cheek, "but I left mine at home."

Another Ranger offered the operator a mirror, and a moment later, Vandergrift flashed a signal toward the balloon.

Moments passed before a reflective light flashed back from the balloon.

Jesse said, "Tell them, we're almost out of ammunition. We need relief."

A few minutes passed before the balloon signaled a response. Vandergrift gasped, "Shitfire. General Johnston's dead, sir. Colonel Sherman holds command of the front. You're to hold. The enemy is more disorganized than we are."

Jesse's shoulders sagged. Albert Sidney Johnston had been with the army since before the Comanche War. Since William Travis had resigned to run for president, Johnston has been in command of the army. Now, who would command? He shook his head, if the Rangers didn't get relief soon, it wouldn't matter to him.

"Tell them, we need more ammunition, we're nearly out."

Minutes elapsed as the mirror flickered the sun's reflection. Vandergrift finally said, "The artillery can provide cover if the enemy attacks. The balloon can provide coordinates if we're attacked again."

The signal hadn't gone silent long before a banshee wail arose from the Southern soldiers in the secondary trenches who stood and raced toward the Rangers' much-reduced line.

"Fire!" Jesse screamed as the survivors stepped up to the trench's walls and opened fire.

Seconds passed before an artillery shell detonated over the heads of the charging soldiers, knocking more than a dozen off their feet.

A few seconds later, dozens more rained down on the charging soldiers, stopping the attack in its tracks. The survivors sheltered in holes dug by artillery or retreated to the relative safety of the trenches near the river.

General Jefferson Davis' eye twitched, and he lowered the binoculars. He ignored the constant pain from an eye disease he'd battled since a bout with malaria many years before. The last enemy position on the riverfront still remained.

Another officer standing on the wooden platform swore when the last of the explosive shells fell long after the attack failed. "Those damned guns. I thought we'd pushed them back."

Davis removed the leather cord and set the binoculars on a nearby camp table. "Not far enough, apparently. Any word from the hospital about General Hardee?"

The officer handed Davis a note, "He's lost a lot of blood, but the bullet didn't hit anything vital. If he can get some rest away from the front, the doctors say he'll recover."

Davis flinched as a wave of nausea washed over him as the pain in his eye increased. "That puts General Blanchard in command of the First Corps. I want his assessment as soon as practicable about our odds of pushing the enemy farther back."

Below, along the river, a handful of barges traversed it. Crates of ammunition flowed west, and injured soldiers flowed east, to the field hospitals that overflowed with thousands of wounded.

Davis' adjutant said, "We've received preliminary reports from Swift's flanking maneuver."

Seeing Davis' nod, he continued, "Except for a narrow section, almost all the Texans' left flank fell. General Swift thought you'd want to know that he trounced that devil, John Brown's old regiment. Even took a few captives."

Davis grimaced, recalling how depraved combat had become when Brown's regiment had tangled with Bedford Forrest's Alabama cavalry in Northeastern Texas and lower Arkansas. "Send orders that all prisoners be removed to this side of the river. I'll brook no reprisals."

The adjutant held up his hand, "There's more. We've captured a few niggers under arms. They're part of the Twenty-first Texas Infantry. Also captured some Mexicans with them."

The idea William Travis or Sidney Johnston would arm black soldiers was sure to send shockwaves through the Allied government in Montgomery when word eventually reached it. Davis recalled his plantation, Brierfield, where James Pemberton, a slave given to him many years before, had been his overseer, until Pemberton's untimely death the previous year. He'd shared a camaraderie with his slave uncommon in the South, and he recalled the two of them going hunting when Davis had been in the army. So, the notion of a black man carrying a rifle wasn't foreign.

Still, he knew many of his fellow countrymen didn't share his views. To be honest, the idea of a Negro aiming a rifle at him didn't sit well with him, either.

He returned his adjutant's gaze and said, "Did you hear me? I said, there'll be no reprisals. Prepare the order to move all the prisoners."

Once the order was signed, and on its way to the other side of the river, his adjutant continued, "General Swift's preliminary reports are that he's lost close to three thousand. But he's got five thousand men from General Deas' division ready to attack the enemy's artillery, upon your command. General Withers' cavalry division is still reorganizing. They took particularly heavy casualties when they ran into those buried torpedoes the Texans used."

Davis shook his head. The deviousness of the land torpedoes had been unexpected. And very effective. Reports from the field hospitals of men who lost a foot or a leg had been too common. There had even been reports of men blown apart, leaving only the torso intact.

Davis bit back a curse, "Airships and torpedoes. Gatling guns and breechloading rifles and cannons. These Texans are far too industrious. Every time we attack, we discover, to our horror, some new weapon of war. Should we manage to capture West Liberty and Trinity Park, we'd be fools to burn them down. Better we harness them for our own use."

A bit later, a disheveled officer climbed the tower. He saluted when he saw Davis.

Davis felt his stomach sink as he saw the commander of the I Corps standing before him. "General Blanchard, I expected a report."

Blanchard swept his battered hat from his head and ran powder-stained fingers through graying hair. "I thought it best to come in person. The First Corps has sustained upwards of five thousand casualties, sir."

Davis tried to keep a frown from his face, "That still leaves you with more than ten thousand men. Can you carry the attack forward? General Swift says he can take the enemy's grand battery."

Blanchard shook his head, "Then Albert is a fool, and would throw his men's lives away for nothing. My men are spread all over creation. I've got men from Georgia regiments mixed in with men from Missouri regiments. I need time to get my boys reorganized. Give me the rest of the day to consolidate our gains and get my boys back with their assigned units, I think we can carry the battle forward tomorrow."

Davis closed his eyes, eight thousand casualties today. How many more tomorrow?

His adjutant said, "General, if you'd like, I can lose that order from Montgomery ordering the First Corps back east, at least until we can knock Johnston's army out of the fight."

Those infernal machines that Texas kept throwing at his army had nearly wrecked it. Blanchard's disheveled look didn't give Davis the confidence he needed. He looked at the Corps commander, "Can you carry the day tomorrow, if you're given the rest of today to prepare?"

General Blanchard's response was too long coming. "Yes, sir. If you can give us enough of a barrage with the artillery, I think victory may be attainable."

Sickened by the lack of conviction in his general's voice, Davis asked, "How many men did Johnston lose today?"

His adjutant said, "Apart from a small section of the line, we've pushed Johnston's entire army back, almost a mile. I believe he had less than twenty thousand men opposing us when we attacked. We've probably destroyed a quarter of his army, maybe more. The brigade protecting his flank was so badly mauled, it's not likely even an effective force anymore. Had our victory not disorganized us so badly, we could push through the Texans now, were it not for their artillery."

"And that's the rub, gentlemen," Davis said, feeling hope slip away. "General Swift would rely upon a miracle to take those enemy guns. While I still have an army to command, I must act to preserve the army and act to follow Montgomery's orders."

He pointed to the desk, and his adjutant hastily sat as he grabbed a pencil. "General Swift is to hold and consolidate his position."

He nodded toward General Blanchard. "You'll detach your Texas Orphan Brigade. It'll stay here with the Second Corps. Tonight, under cover of darkness, the First Corps will begin the march back to the Sabine."

27 April 1853

Like a fingernail clicking on a surface, drops of rain slapped the window next to Will's desk. *April showers,* he thought. He refused to look at the sterile sheet of paper from the telegraph office as if that would soften the blow of the news.

Sidney Johnston was dead. Will felt hollow inside. The former Tennessean had been far more than just a competent general. He'd been a friend. Will leaned back in the cushioned chair and closed his eyes. He let his mind take him back to that moment when he'd first met Johnston in the months following the victory over Santa Anna at the Nueces River in 1836.

Johnston showed up in San Antonio and joined the 1st Infantry. When Will saw his name of the battalion's muster, the name clicked, and he recalled Johnston had been one of the most promising generals in the Confederate army before dying on the battlefield of Shiloh in 1862. Of course, that was in another world. As a student of history, Will knew Johnston was a graduate of West Point. He pulled Johnston from the enlisted ranks and promoted him to second-in-command.

Johnston's familiarity with early nineteenth-century military structure had melded well with Will's twenty-first-century combat experience in Iraq. Together the two had created an army Will knew could go toe-to-toe with any equal-sized force in the world.

Will felt moisture in his eyes. "Equal-sized, sure," his voice dripped with pain. The South had been able to wear his army down. The irony wasn't lost on him that the nine Southern states constituting the Southern Alliance outnumbered Texas five or six to one.

Where was the army of the United States? Seward had promised he would open a second front against the seceding states once he had secured the loyalty of the five remaining slave states.

Wiping his eyes, Will lowered his head into his hands as he prayed for his friend.

He pulled a handkerchief from a pocket and ran it over his face before he picked up more of the correspondence. Wounded from the battle were pouring into hospitals all the way back to Houston. Estimates were the army had lost at least four thousand wounded, killed, or captured. The army had been forced out of its trenches, but it had refused to retreat away from Beaumont's ruins. Colonel Bill Sherman had formed most of the army's artillery into a single grand battery and had beaten back several attacks.

Despite the heavy casualties, despite Sidney Johnston's death, the army had held. Will ran through the names of the army's general officers. The army needed a strong commander, someone who could solidify their position and stop the enemy's attack. Colonel Sherman's name kept coming to mind. Appointing him might wound the pride of several other officers more senior than the artillery colonel, but Sherman was the army's highest-ranking artillery officer. In theory, he commanded nearly two hundred batteries across the republic. In the theater of operation, practice and theory had little in common. Sherman could draw on less than one hundred field pieces, of which half were the new model breechloaders.

Will stood and walked over to the window. He looked down upon Congress Avenue. Townspeople dodged the puddles left by the earlier shower. The more he thought about Sherman, the more he liked the idea of putting him in charge of the army. A decade earlier, when he'd first asked John Wharton to recruit active duty United States Army officers in the run-up to the war with Mexico, Will had been elated to discover one of Wharton's recruits was none other than William Tecumseh Sherman.

# Chapter 23

29 April 1853

The portable writing desk thumped Horace Greeley's side as his army-issued horse followed behind General Scott's staff. How one was supposed to tell the difference between North and South Carolina was beyond him.

When he mentioned this, his companion, Lieutenant Jeremiah Jones said, "Yesterday, I'd have told you it was when the Sesesh," he used a popular name for the seceded Allied states, "started tearing up their railroads, but damned if they haven't had some help here in North Carolina."

According to the army's maps, they were near the border with South Carolina. They had just marched through the tiny hamlet of Fair Bluff. The steely stares of the women who'd watched them from their front porches told him that parts of North Carolina hadn't supported Raleigh's decision to remain in the union. The only men he saw were too old or too young to soldier, apart from the poor slaves who solemnly watched the army march by. To Greeley's practiced eye, they seemed to know the army marching through North Carolina wasn't bringing the abolitionists' promised jubilee.

When he thought of the Faustian bargain President Seward made with the Upper South, Greeley's blood boiled. Worse, his own newspaper supported Seward's efforts to mollify the state governments of Virginia, Kentucky, North Carolina, and Maryland. Already, nine of the twenty-one loyal states had passed what was sure to become the Thirteenth Amendment to the Constitution. The notion of enshrining slavery offended every fiber of his being. It was, in his opinion, too high a price for five slave states' loyalty.

Politics, he'd long ago decided, was an ugly thing. For the sake of unity and victory over the nine Southern Allied states, he had dirtied his own soul and authorized the *Tribune* to urge Whig unity and back the hateful amendment.

Lieutenant Jones interrupted his thoughts, "Sir, you wanted to know when we cross into South Carolina," he pointed to a wooden sign on the side of the dust-choked road. Stenciled on it were the words, "Welcome to South Carolina."

He added, "I don't know about you, Mr. Greeley, but I'm not feeling particularly welcome."

"At least they're not greeting us with guns a-blazing." Greeley quipped.

In the distance, gunfire erupted.

Lieutenant Jones unfastened the holster flap at his hip and cast a frown at Greeley, "You were saying?"

General Scott and his staff moved from the road into a nearby field, allowing the 2nd United States Dragoons to ride by. Greeley rode over and pulled out a notepad and pencil.

Scott barked orders, “Get the Second Dragoons forward. I want a report about what’s up ahead. I want General Lee’s brigade to deploy to the right of the road. General Buell’s brigade will deploy to the left of the road.”

Greeley noted Scott’s calm demeanor. He’d read reports of Scott’s attack at the Battle of Chippawa nearly forty years before. Despite the years and girth, Winfield Scott was still the same man. As Greeley’s pencil scratched over the page, he was forced, like Scott’s staff, to wait for news to arrive.

The sun reached its zenith before a rider raced back into the field on a winded horse. “General Scott, we’ve found Longstreet’s army, sir. They’ve fortified the other side of Lumber River, two miles ahead.”

Scott snapped, “Get this man a fresh horse.” He turned back to the rider, “Tell Colonel Harney I want to know how many men we’re facing, the fords nearby and how far the enemy’s line stretches.”

After the rider galloped away, Greeley finished his notes and listened to the officers. Most, like Lieutenant Jones, were eager to attack. Scott, on the other hand, seemed indifferent.

Artillery joined the smattering of gunfire as the noon-hour faded into the afternoon. Jones said, “Like as not, that’s the Sesech guns firing on our scouts.”

When the rider didn’t return after an hour, Scott left most of his staff to set up the army’s headquarters and rode ahead. Greeley nudged his mount forward, following the army's commander toward the sound of the guns.

They passed by several gun batteries set up in a field. Green cotton stalks were trampled under hundreds of feet as the gunners wheeled their field pieces into place.

Farther along the road, they came upon a unit of infantry, deployed in line. In the distance, Greeley saw puffs of smoke. Seconds elapsed before he heard the boom of the guns.

An officer ran up, bareheaded, and grabbed at General Scott's bridle. "Sir, they've got snipers over there. They're targeting officers."

Greeley felt naked as he realized the officer holding Scott's mount was the Virginian, General Lee. Blood ran down his face, dying his mustache red.

Scott glared at the brigadier and then scanned the enemy position on the other side of the languid river. "I sent a rider forward for information on the enemy position. He hasn't returned."

Lee released the bridle and gestured across the river. "The Second Dragoons are still skirmishing along the banks. They've taken some casualties. If we're to offer battle here, might I suggest we set up one of our mobile hospital units behind our lines?"

Scott swung down from his mount and gruffly nodded, "Of course. What have you found out?"

Lee dabbed at an injury on his scalp as he led Scott to shelter under the boughs of a tree. "I believe we're facing General Longstreet's Army of the Carolinas. I've seen the South Carolina banner as well as those from

Georgia. Most of their regiments seem to fly the old West Florida flag."

Scott pulled a pair of binoculars from his saddlebag and scanned the enemy line, "They've taken to calling it their bonnie blue flag. It's what you'd expect from a passel of Scotch-Irish hillbillies."

Greeley thought nothing of the term. He traced his own roots in America to the earliest days of the Massachusetts Bay colony, more than two hundred years earlier. The descendants of the Ulster Scots who settled South Carolina and Georgia were a backward lot, as far as he was concerned, deserving General Scott's contempt.

As Scott scanned the enemy line, Lee said, "We've identified four regiments opposite my brigade. General Buell's confirmed another five regiments are opposing his brigade."

Scott grunted, "I doubt a division is all we'll face. Before I order an attack, I want to know. The newspapers from Columbia and Charleston brag Longstreet has more than thirty regiments."

Lee pointed toward a rider, "We'll know soon enough."

The rider slipped from his mount and sketched a salute, "The Allied position extends for another two miles south from here. All the ferries have been pulled to the other side of the river. There are no good fords hereabout."

"We'll need to bring up pontoon bridges from Raleigh," Scott said.

Lee raised his hand, "What about flanking the enemy? If we split the army, Buell and most of the volunteers could stay here while pontoon boats arrive. I could take a division and swing wide, striking their flank."

Scott swung into the saddle, "I'll consider—"

His head snapped back. His substantial bulk tumbled off the back of his horse. The back of the general's head was gone, where a sniper's bullet had exited.

Greeley knelt next to Scott's body as two of his staff rushed over. Lee grabbed the general's skittish horse, and as the beast pawed the ground, Greeley heard the Virginian's soft drawl as he calmed the animal.

One of Scott's aides, shock etched on his face, took a handkerchief, and lay it over the general's face. The young officer turned to General Lee, "Sir, what do we do?"

Lee used his bloody handkerchief and wiped gray matter from his jacket. "Send a rider back to the nearest telegraph office. Order the pontoon boats forward."

He pointed at another staff officer, "Find General Buell, tell him to report to me. We have a battle to plan."

2 May 1853

Horace Greeley grimaced as both knees popped as he sat down on the stump of a tree. *Only two score and two years, but heaven help me, I feel as though I've reached my three score and ten.*

If he'd gotten more than ten hours' sleep over the past four days, he'd have eaten his hat. It was no wonder he felt so old. The Federal Army was deep inside South Carolina, and precious little time remained for him to pen an article before the day's courier headed north. He had no doubt news of General Winfield Scott's death had made the front pages of every newspaper in the North that was within a day's ride of a telegraph station. But since then things had happened at such a pace, he mused as he pulled his notebook from his saddlebag, which rested against the stump.

Licking the graphite, he started to write.

*The Battle of Lumber River began as light skirmishing between the troopers of the 2nd Dragoons and the General Longstreet's secessionist Allied Army on the afternoon of the 29th. General Lee, taking command of the Federal Army, after Scott's heroic sacrifice, held the balance of the enemy's army in place, strategically using General Don Buell's brigade, staging them in front of the enemy. All the while, General Lee took the volunteer divisions from New York, Pennsylvania, and Virginia on a wide flanking maneuver.*

*Having audaciously divided his army, Lee commanded the flanking maneuver with nearly 15,000 soldiers. He traveled up the river more than twenty miles before securing his crossing back in North Carolina. Once on the same side of the river as Longstreet, General Lee forged forth in the same revolutionary spirit of his father, Lighthorse Harry Lee, striking Longstreet's flank yesterday. Were Lee alone in attacking the well-fortified enemy position, this writer cannot but speculate the attack may have failed. But while Lee led the flanking attack, the pontoon bridges arrived, and General Buell put them to good use and was, at the moment of Lee's onslaught, ferrying men across the Lumber River to engage the enemy.*

Greeley lifted the pencil up and weighed his words. He had remained with General Buell and had watched Buell's forces flounder in the river, unable to get a single pontoon boat to the other side. All the general had managed to do was to lose several hundred men. No, Greeley reconsidered, he had squandered the better part of a brigade's worth of men but had held Longstreet's army's attention long enough for General Lee to smash the Allied army's flank. Even so, Greeley thought Buell's performance was underwhelming. Sometimes, though, the truth needed to be sacrificed for the greater good.

*General Don Buell's brigade covered themselves with glory, holding more than 20,000 enemy soldiers against the river. However, General Buell was not the only one to cover himself and his nation in glory. General Robert E. Lee's attack was almost a total surprise. The Virginia Division under the command of a young officer, Brigadier General Thomas Jackson, routed a larger brigade of South Carolina and Georgia infantry. Before the sun had set, General Longstreet had been forced to retreat.*

*Even now, as the writer hastens to prepare this note for the courier to Raleigh, General Lee is in pursuit of the rebel Allied Army. With the blessings of benevolent Providence, we shall be at the gates of Columbia within a fortnight.*

Greeley folded the note and rose to his feet. Again, his knees popped, and he winced in pain. He hobbled over to the mail sack and dropped the article in the canvas bag.

# Chapter 24

4 May 1853

General Jefferson Davis crinkled his nose as he walked through the ruins of Beaumont. There was more to the odor than just soggy burned wood. Something sickeningly sweet hung in the air, masking the smell of burned wood. How many times had Beaumont's railroad depot burned since the rebel Texans revolted against the Travis government in Austin? Twice? Three times? He wasn't sure.

Now a few soldiers sifted through the debris, looking for wood that could be used to fuel the army's cooking fires. Davis had no intention to rebuild the depot. There was no bridge across the Neches anymore and no prospects that it would happen any time soon. The railroad from West Liberty to Beaumont that General Johnston had painstakingly rebuilt was no more, at least the last few miles of it. Colonel Sherman had destroyed them as he slowly retreated. Davis adjusted the thought, if the rumors were true, it was General Sherman now. Sherman had torn up the tracks and burned the railroad ties and then twisted them, rendering them completely unusable. Davis smirked as he thought the nickname his soldiers had given the twisted metal; they called the twisted iron beams "Sherman's neckties."

He turned away from the ruins and let his thoughts turn to Sidney Johnston. The Texan had graduated two years before Davis. In a student body of fewer than two hundred men at West Point, there had been a camaraderie among the cadets that the officers carried forward into their military careers. He'd admired Johnston as a student, and later as an officer. Davis had been far from the only graduate of the military academy who secretly envied Johnston's meteoric rise in the Army of the Republic of Texas, at least before the present unpleasantness.

Johnston had proved an able commander, pressing his attacks, and mounting simple but effective defenses. He was gone. William Sherman was an unknown. Only twenty-nine years old, and yet President Travis had apparently promoted him over the brigade and division commanders. Davis shook his head. What did Travis know that he didn't?

His walk had brought him back to his command tent outside of town. As he sat and looked at the correspondence and reports awaiting his attention, he regretted the time he'd spent looking at the damage in Beaumont. The first report was in his hands when a shout arose from a tent housing the headquarters' telegraph office. As an operator sprinted from the tent, Davis left the report unread and came to his feet.

The lad, barely eighteen if Davis was any judge, hastily saluted, "Sir, the fort north of Lake Sabine reports enemy ships approaching."

Davis followed the young soldier back to the tent from which he'd raced only moments before. Tall poles ringed the canvas shelter, and copper wiring ran from below the tent flaps to the top of the posts. A line of posts led back to the river, carrying the strand of wire. One of the ropes which had been used as a guideline for a barge now had copper wiring wrapped around it. On the other side of the river, a line ran east, back toward Louisiana. Another ran south, skirting the Neches River, ending at a large river battery, where Davis has placed several dozen heavy guns, behind solid earthen embankments.

The Southern Allied government had yet to get serious about producing any artillery, let alone heavy coastal guns. But thanks to several coastal forts along the Gulf Coast, Davis had been able to assemble a formidable battery and place them north of Sabine Lake, where the Neches emptied into the salty body of water feeding into the Gulf of Mexico.

Within the tent, several telegraph machines had been set up, each connecting to one of the wires running into the tent. For the briefest of moments, Davis marveled at how technology was changing warfare.

As the operator leaned over the telegraph key, Davis said, "How many ships are coming up the lake?"

The clattering of the transmitter key, with its rapid clicks, sent the message along an electric current to a receiver seventeen miles away. Despite the worry he felt at the thought the Texas Navy might try forcing their way past the gun emplacements, Davis was amazed the message took so little time to send.

Less than a minute elapsed before a response arrived. The operator's pencil sped across the page as he transcribed the dashes and dots into letters and words. “Sir, there are seven ships. They’re approaching slow.”

Davis patted the operator’s shoulder, “The enemy’s navy must not be allowed to pass.”

The general turned as the operator tapped out the order. If the ships were coming in slowly, they were no doubt using sounding lines. The lake was shallow; it made sense the ships’ captains would take time to avoid the lake’s treacherous submerged sandbars.

Davis turned and looked toward the Neches. The ruins of Beaumont stood between him and the river, but he had planned the recent battle with meticulous care, and it was easy to envision every curve of the river. Although they had been burned to the waterline, piers had once lined the west bank, and ships brave enough to risk the shallows of Sabine Lake had once offloaded goods from New Orleans or farther afield and taken aboard cotton and other produce. That meant if the heavy coastal guns failed to stop the Texas Navy, those ships would only need a couple of hours to cut off his army from the east.

Returning to his headquarters pavilion, Davis examined a map of the area. “Maybe three hours. The Neches twists and turns a lot between here and the lake,” he muttered.

As he puzzled over the map, Davis heard someone arrive. He looked up and saw Major General Swift. “What’s this I hear about the enemy’s navy showing up on our doorstep?”

After explaining about the ships, Davis gestured at the map, “If the enemy forces the river, we run the risk of being cut off. More than sixteen thousand men would be stranded if that happened.”

Swift glanced at the map before turning when a faint sound of cannon fire echoed from the south. "Damn them," he swore. "If we still had General Buchner's corps, we could have already pushed the enemy back to West Liberty or even Houston. Instead, Sherman's sitting square on the way to the west, and we likely don't have enough men to push him back."

No matter how true the words, Davis didn't like them. He bit back a sigh, unwilling to let Swift see the dig had hit home. Instead, he said, "Tell General Deas to break camp. I want his men back on the barges within the hour. Then pass the word to the rest of the army, we're breaking camp and heading back the way we came."

With orders issued, the army came alive. As a tent city disappeared, replaced by a cloud of dust, infantry, cavalry, and artillery waited in line as the thunder of heavy artillery echoed in the distance.

Long before his army had finished transiting the Neches, the booming sound of battle from the South stopped. Davis and his staff stood next to the charred remains of a warehouse near where Beaumont's wharves had once stood. The telegraph operator who had first delivered news of the enemy ships shouted down from where he was perched near the top of a telegraph pole, "Sir, the enemy's got two ironclads past the fort. Most of our guns are out of commission."

The operator leaned toward the tapped wire for a moment. "The line's dead, sir."

The next two hours were the longest in Jeff Davis' life, as he watched each barge glide across the water, as its handlers hauled on the overhead ropes. Every few minutes, he'd glance downriver, expecting to see the telltale signs of enemy ships, black smudges of smoke rising over the river.

The northern flank of the army had not yet arrived when an orderly tugged at Davis' arm, "Sir, the enemy ships ain't more than a mile away. You've got to get across now, sir."

Rather than risk the humiliation of being hustled onto the last barge, Davis cast a backward glance before stepping onto the floating wooden platform. Even though he'd dislodged General Johnston from Beaumont, he'd failed to do more than push the enemy back a few miles. Now that the Texas Navy had threatened to cut him off, there was no choice but to retreat.

Withdrawal should have been humiliation enough. But worse than that, several thousand men who held the northern end of the Allied position had not yet arrived and were now cut off from retreat.

Jason Lamont braced himself against a tree, steadying the binoculars as he stared through the magnifying lenses. Despite the thicket, he saw several soldiers in their butternut-brown jackets sitting on a log in front of a cooking fire. He cursed the similar color of the Texans' uniforms to the Southern Alliance's gray. *No surprise,* he thought, *we've been using gray for our militia units since the beginning of the century.*

Still, an untrained eye could mistake the two countries' uniforms. However, Lamont's were not untrained. Over the past couple of days, the right flank, well to the north of the main army, had pushed the Texans back several miles. As he studied the enemy soldiers, they looked tired and worn. Dare he think it? Maybe even beaten?

He turned and looked at his old 3rd South Carolina Infantry. They'd come a long way since he first began training them in the fields in front of his plantation. Now, they were veterans. They'd come west a thousand strong. After several major fights, in which the 3rd had been in the thick of it, now only four hundred men were still in the ranks. Hundreds of his men crowded hospitals from the Red River all the way back to New Orleans. Those who recovered enough to rejoin the army might swell the regiment again to six hundred, maybe.

He nodded to the regiment's colonel, "Let's see if we can push them back. Get them on the run here, and maybe General Davis can roll up the whole damned line."

The 3rd swept through the trees in open order. Long gone was any pretense at forming a rifle line as his soldiers advanced. Like the Texans, rifle teams and squads worked together to cover each other as they raced to close the distance with the enemy riflemen.

Gunfire crackled and the fight was on. Lamont swung onto his mount and rode north until he found the 7th South Carolina Infantry. Still numbering more than five hundred men, they seemed eager to join in the attack. Lamont leaned over to talk to the regiment's commander when a bareheaded horseman pulled up next to him. The horse looked winded, as sweat glistened on its chestnut flanks, which heaved in and out. The empty shoulder straps revealed the officer was a second lieutenant. He saluted, "General Davis' compliments, General Lamont, but General Dea's Division has been ordered back to the river. The damned Texas Navy has forced the mouth of the Neches."

The officer wheeled on his horse and urged his mount into a gallop as he raced farther north to where the 3rd Cavalry Brigade anchored his own flank.

The colonel commanding the 7th looked at him, an air of resignation on his face. "If they'd just give us enough time, we'll put the enemy to rout, sir."

Privately, Lamont agreed. And inside, he raged at the news. Every step forward only seemed to end with the army taking two back. It wasn't fair. Instead, he gave the officer a curt nod, "We certainly would, but orders, Colonel, are orders. If the Texas Navy pushes past our guns, they can cut our supply lines, and that would complicate things."

The officer laughed at Lamont's understatement, as he continued, "Hold here. You'll support the 3rd as they disengage."

He found his nephew close at hand and sent his sister's son forward with orders for the attacking regiment to fall back. Minutes stretched by as the gunfire continued. After what Lamont considered too long, his nephew rode back, "General, the 3rd's trying to pull back, but the enemy ain't staying put. They're advancing."

"Shit," Lamont swore. If his brigade couldn't make a clean break from the enemy, their retreat would be slowed. He waved the colonel from the 7th back over, "Deploy your men to support the 3rd. Let them through. Put up a fight if the Texans keep coming. Hold them back for a few minutes, then fall back. I'll get the 5th in place. They'll relieve you once you fall back."

The morning dragged by as Lamont rode back and forth along his brigade's line of retreat toward the river.

Every attempt to disengage the enemy riflemen failed, as they clung to his rearguard like a dog working on a bone.

After nearly two hours of this, Lamont dismounted and grabbed his cane as he set off toward his rear guard. The 3rd currently held the line. He found them firing from behind trees, using fallen logs as shelter and using a dry creek-bed as a makeshift trench. His bad knee gave way as he attempted to navigate his way into the creek-bed, and he slid on his backside most of the way.

An officer scurried over, "General, sir. They're just sitting there firing on us. As soon as we start to move back, they're back on us like fleas on a dog."

Frustrated by how long it was taking for his command to retreat to the river, Lamont swore and pulled his sword, "That dog don't hunt no more, Captain. Pass the word, we advance on my command."

Lamont raised his voice, "Fix bayonets, boys! We'll teach those bastards to respect Southern steel."

Steel grated on steel as his old regiment slotted their bayonets onto their rifles. Holding his sword high, Lamont shouted, "Up, men, up!"

With help from the men surrounding him, Lamont crested the shallow creek and scampered across the forest floor, dodging between trees. The men of the 3rd South Carolina screamed like banshees, racing across through the trees toward their foes.

Bullets clipped branches overhead, and leaves rained down on Lamont as he drove after his men. The constant rattling of gunfire rose to a fever pitch as his men collided with the Texans who had hounded them for so long. He cursed Will Travis for shooting him in the knee all those years before. Otherwise, he would be leading his men from the front, where a proper brigade commander should be.

When he arrived where his men had stopped, the gunfire had fallen off. Some of his men were helping their wounded while others stood guard over a few prisoners.

He pointed back toward the rest of the brigade, “Get the wounded moving.” Looking at the enemy prisoners. All five of them were injured.

Part of him wanted to pull out his pistol and give them what they deserved, but he’d listened to Colonel Forrest, who had described the savagery into which his cavalry had sunk as they fought the abolitionist, John Brown’s 1st New York. He left his pistol in its holster and said, “What unit y’all with?”

One with sergeant stripes eyed him with suspicion before he replied with a strong accent, “Ninth Texas Infantry.” His eyes flitted to Lamont’s shoulder boards, and he added a belated, “Sir.”

The alien accent grated on his ears. It was nothing like the typical drawl of most Texans. “Where ‘bouts you from?”

The sergeant shrugged, his wary expression softened, “Naples. Kingdom of the Two Sicilies.”

“All of you?”

The soldier shook his head and pointed to one of his companions, who was leaning against a tree, tying a bandage around a leg wound. “Shamus is from Dublin.”

While nearly all of Lamont’s 3rd South Carolina ware native sons of the South, some of the other regiments, drawing recruits from Charleston, had more foreign-born soldiers in their ranks. Regardless of where they hailed from, he didn’t have time to keep them as prisoners. And despite the burning hatred he felt for

William Travis, killing them out of hand would be opening Pandora's box. He pointed to the west, "Get out of here before I change my mind."

With that, he turned and started back toward the rest of his brigade.

The 3rd's attack worked. The enemy finally stopped hounding his men, and they made good time racing back toward the river. But when Lamont stepped out from dense tree line, Beaumont's ruins were down-river. Several dozen barges burned where they'd been beached on the other side of the Neches.

Worse though, in the middle of the river were two warships flying the lone star banner from their masts.

8 May 1853

Brevet Lt. Colonel Jesse Running Creek brushed a speck of coal dust from his uniform as he stepped off the station platform's wooden planking. A crack of a whip over a team of mules alerted him to a heavy wagon laden with supplies rumbling by. Apart from a few soldiers hurrying about on the army's business, the streets were empty. He peered through plate glass windows as he passed by several stores. The signs on their doors informed passersby they were closed, despite the goods and produce available within.

His destination was a large hacienda style building in town. Don Garza, president of the Gulfco Farming Corporation, had left town after the Texian rebels nearly captured West Liberty the previous year. General Sherman now used it for the army's headquarters.

The hacienda's red-tiled roof came into view as Jesse turned a corner. Soldiers stood guard outside its entrance. His feet landed on the mansion's slate walkway as a church bell pealed under the warm noon-day sun. Down the street, the local Methodist church's doors swung open, and townsfolk streamed down the steps and into the street. Jesse felt abashed, forgetting the day was Sunday. Of course, the stores were closed.

The guards snapped to attention at Jesse's approach. He felt their eyes on him, as one seemed to stare at the newly sewn shoulder straps embroidered with a golden oakleaf. "Colonel, is General Sherman expecting you?"

Jesse waited for the guard to read his summons before being escorted into the house's foyer. While he waited, he browsed the paintings on the wall as well as ivory figurines displayed on expensive marble-topped tables.

Examining Señor Garza's many baubles, Jesse lost track of time and nearly jumped when a voice from behind said, "General Sherman'll see you, sir."

Sherman sat at the end of a long table which was covered by a vast map, in a room more suited for a chairman of the board instead of an army general. Sherman waved away Jesse's salute, "Glad you were able to make it back here so fast given we can't seem to keep the railroad running much on the other side of the Trinity."

Jesse relaxed as he studied Sherman. The former Ohioan, only a year older than his own twenty-eight years, appeared eager despite the heavy weight that came with command of the army.

Jesse offered a smile, "Word has it that you're getting ready to re-cross the Neches. My men are ready to lead the charge, sir."

A lopsided grin creased Sherman's feature. "An army leaks secrets like an old boat leaks water. Still," he said, gesturing toward the window behind him, "all those supplies we're collecting tell the tale better than a gossiping old hen."

Jesse accepted the invitation to sit as Sherman continued, "I've already sent the orders out. McCulloch's Division has been ordered to cross back over the Neches."

Jesse liked Henry McCulloch, the younger brother of Ben McCulloch, but he didn't like feeling sidelined. It should be his Rangers leading the way.

When he mentioned that to Sherman, the army's commander threw back his head and laughed. "As God is my witness, Colonel, I admire your audacity. With officers like you and soldiers like your Rangers, we'd already be in New Orleans."

Jesse's ears perked up as he heard the name of the largest city in the Southern Alliance. "Is that where we're going?"

Sherman cocked his head to one side, as though deep in thought. "Not 'we,' Colonel. I have a project for your men that requires that you remain here."

Aware of the frown on his face, Jesse crossed his arms and leaned back in the chair until it creaked in protest. Sherman pointed at the map. "When Davis retreated, not all of his men were able to escape across the Neches. I fear what they could do behind our lines if we don't capture them."

Jesse's arms remained crossed, but he leaned forward a bit. "How many of the enemy were left behind?"

Sherman's eyes traveled to a map pinned to the wall. "We don't know. If we're lucky, maybe a couple hundred. But it could be more than a thousand. Our balloon corps has spotted them a few times. We've conducted un-tethered flights over the area the north of Beaumont, but I fear they could become a thorn in our side."

Jesse started to rise from the seat when Sherman snapped, "If I didn't make myself clear, Colonel, this is an order."

As Jesse settled back in his seat, his face flushed with anger, Sherman added, "President Travis has a way with words, sometimes. He's afraid of something he called asymmetrical warfare."

Jesse forgot to be angry as he digested the words. Sherman continued, "I know, it's enough to choke a mule. Basically, he means that the enemy can attack our farms, towns, and outposts that are hard to support or reinforce."

"Sounds to me like what the Comanche were doing before we put them in their place."

Sherman dipped his head, "That's as good a way of explaining it as I've managed. If the choice were my own, I'd take your Rangers with me, but the fact is, President Travis asked for your command by name to stay and hunt down any enemy soldiers."

There was a note of finality in Sherman's words. Jesse surrendered himself to the inevitable. As he was dismissed, he was already making a list of what he'd need to track down the secessionist soldiers left behind.

# Chapter 25

18 May 1853

The drums rolled as Horace Greeley committed the scene to memory. A color guard paraded down the street in front of the men of the 3rd United States Infantry Regiment, who stood at attention, presenting arms. The star-spangled banner fluttered in the warm, gentle breeze, held aloft by the color sergeant. Their destination, the old capitol building in Columbia.

The ease by which the capital of South Carolina had fallen had caught Greeley by surprise. Since pushing Longstreet out of his first defensive position on the border with the loyal state of North Carolina, Lee had driven toward the state capital as fast as he could. The Southern army had attempted several times to interject itself between Lee and his target. Each time, the wily Virginian had used one part of his army to hold Longstreet's attention while another swung around one flank or another. It didn't hurt that as Lee moved southward, his army continued to receive a trickle of regiments released by their various states for Federal service.

Greeley had expected Longstreet to put up a strong defense of the state's capital, but the enemy army had swept through the town the previous day. Along with the army, the civil government fled, too. Now Lee's Federal army held the city.

The color guard reached the wooden steps leading into the Capitol building and pivoted on the color sergeant, turning to face the 3rd Infantry's long blue line. Their regimental band burst into music, playing *Columbia, Gem of the Ocean*. The popular song personified America as the goddess of liberty, Columbia. That a military band was playing it, in the state capital of South Carolina with the same name, was an irony Greeley appreciated.

On a flagpole atop the state house rose the Stars-and-Stripes. It was now official; Columbia was a town under occupation. Greeley looked at the civilian populace who watched the ceremony. Made up mostly of women, children, and old men, the white population wore stony expressions. Slaves made up close to half the town's population, and those on the street looked pensive, uncertain.

Greeley thought about the dreadful Thirteenth Amendment that the loyal slave states had strong-armed upon the rest of the Union. Slavery in perpetuity in the states not under rebellion, their price of allegiance. Fifteen of the twenty-one loyal states had already ratified it. He was still heartbroken that New York had provided the fifteenth vote, and now only one more state needed to ratify the abominable amendment for it to become the law of the land. Even with President Seward's assurance that another amendment to the constitution could be added, revoking the hateful amendment, he worried that it would be easier said than done.

The ceremony now over, most of the soldiers from the 3rd marched away, back to the army's camp outside of town. Those that stayed guarded the state house or patrolled the streets. Seeing General Lee and several other officers head inside the capitol building, Greeley hurried after them. His next report needed to be sent north by courier before the end of the day. His readers would devour a quote from the victorious general. Despite being a slave owner, Lee would be the toast of New York once word of Columbia's fall reached Gotham.

Greeley found Generals Lee, Buell, and several others arranging chairs around a table in one of the capitol's many rooms. When Lee spotted him standing at the door, the general waved him into the room. "Mr. Greeley, I trust the *Tribune's* readers will celebrate the rebels' defeat."

Thinking of the deep South lying prostrate before the rest of the Union, Greeley couldn't keep a smile from his face. "Indeed, sir. My readers would like to know your thoughts on the matter."

Was that a note of distaste passing over the general's face? Greeley wasn't sure. Lee had a reputation for treating kindly everyone with whom he interacted. Lee pointed at the table, which was covered with map rolls and stacks of paper. "Tell your readers that war is an evil and cruel thing. It separates and destroys families and friends and mars the purest joys and happiness God has granted. It fills our hearts with hatred instead of love for our neighbors and devastates the fair face of this beautiful world. On that table are the names of several thousand who will lie in the soil of the land we invaded to preserve our national union. Make sure your readers understand the cost of this war."

Greeley knew he should have felt something, a sadness perhaps for the great loss of life. But the war was the fault of the slaveholding Southern aristocracy. Were it not for their rebellion, those men would still be alive. Lee's somber expression gave him pause. Instead, he said, "You've liberated nearly half of South Carolina. As the enemy has fled before you, more than ten thousand slaves have been freed from their bondage. What will you do with them?"

As Lee returned his stare, he seemed to weigh the question. Greeley grew uncomfortable with the silence before the general finally said, "I have long felt that in this enlightened age, there are few that will fail to acknowledge, that slavery as an institution is a moral and political evil in our country."

Greeley found himself nodding at the general's words, "Indeed. But those few are determined to rip the heart of our nation apart."

A look of sadness flitted across Lee's face, "Indeed, Mr. Greeley. As the Scriptures admonish us, those who sow the wind, shall themselves reap the whirlwind."

Lee stepped over to the table and found a sheet of paper. "The need for secrecy now past, I am at liberty to share this with you."

As Greeley scanned the document, Lee continued, "Once word of Columbia's fall reaches Washington, President Seward will release the document in your hand. It will free any slave within any state that remains in rebellion beyond the end of next month."

Greeley struggled to grasp the meaning of the words. Was this the beginning of the end of slavery? He tried to stammer out a question as his mind grappled with this new development, Lee said, "My hope is that our rebellious brothers will see President Seward's proclamation as an olive branch and surrender before the deadline."

"Do you really think South Carolina or Mississippi will surrender before they're defeated on the battlefield?"

With a sad shake of his head, Lee said, "No."

1 June 1853

"Let me get this straight, since the beginning of this cluster..." Will stopped in mid-speech. The look of confusion on George Fisher's face was enough to silence him. The corpulent Hungarian immigrant deserved better than his temper. Even Juan Seguin, who sat next to the Secretary of War, across the desk from Will looked surprised. Taking a deep breath, Will stepped over to the window of the Executive Office. The corner office in the Capitol building overlooked Congress Avenue. It had been a few weeks since it had last rained and dust billowed behind wagons as they rolled through the street.

Will pinched the bridge of his nose and drew in another ragged breath as he tried to bring his emotions under control. With a heavy sigh, he turned around and said, "My apologies, George, please continue."

"While it's true that General Sherman's army crossed the Sabine River the day before last with fourteen thousand men, that's not the sum total of our army, sir."

Gesturing him to continue, Will leaned against his desk.

"While it's true that we've mobilized thirty-five battalions, totaling twenty-six thousand men, let's not forget that we've also received support from seven regiments of volunteers from the United States. That's an extra five thousand men who've joined in defending our liberty." Fisher sagged in his chair. Dark circles under his eyes showed a man nearing exhaustion.

Will grimaced, despite Fisher's optimistic tone. "It doesn't change the fact that we've lost half the army, George, in only one year."

Seguin leaned forward, "Buck, while it's not good, it's not as bad as that. We've got four battalions, three thousand men that have been stationed elsewhere. Also, the Yankee volunteers have taken heavier casualties, too."

Will shook his head, "I regret that as much as either of you. They were thrown into battle without the training our own soldiers have gone through." He rummaged through a folder next to him and handed it to Fisher, "I know you want more soldiers, but we can't afford to mobilize more of our militia. If we do, we'll be taking men out of the factories. Can General Sherman manage with what he's got?"

Fisher's eyebrows narrowed as he thought. "Perhaps. They're joining Colonel West's light brigade of Marines as well as United States Marines and Infantry. If the information Commodore Perry provided me is correct, they'd swell our combined land force to about twenty-two thousand. The question is, between Sherman's land army and Perry's naval forces, will it be enough to capture New Orleans?"

Fisher inclined his head, "I pray to God it is, sir. In truth, between Admiral Moore's squadron and Commodore Perry's, there should be enough of a fleet to blast any fortification protecting the Mississippi River to Hell and gone. I understand that General Davis has taken over the defenses of the city. He escaped into Louisiana with no more men than we have. Most of the enemy's forces have shifted to the east. The Yankees have consolidated their gains in the western part of South Carolina. They've launched another army from Kentucky into Tennessee."

Will let a rare smile cross his face at that news. "Which brings us to Missouri. Is it true the Federals have arrested Governor Price?"

"Indeed," Seguin said. "It's funny what a bit of news will do. When President Seward released his Emancipation Order, he was hung in effigy across the deep South. But the smart among them didn't miss that any state that rejoins the union voluntarily before the first of July will be covered under the Thirteenth Amendment. Moderates among the Missouri secessionists decided they'd not risk the loss of their property. They made common cause with the German unionists in Springfield and Saint Louis. And now, Governor Price is in prison and the Missouri legislature has repudiated their earlier vote for secession."

He scratched as his clean-shaven chin, "It makes you wonder; will this move preserve slavery in Missouri?"

Will returned to his chair and leaned back until it squeaked in protest. "Unfortunately, for a little while. Despite Seward's strong abolitionist sentiment, he's playing a long game. The nine Southern states that voted to secede, their seats in Congress weren't even cold before Wisconsin and Jefferson were admitted as free states. The Southern states that don't rejoin in the next thirty days, I do believe that Seward will free their slaves. Then what?"

Seguin said, "The remaining slave states will be outnumbered."

Will nodded. "Exactly. Five or six slave states surrounded by twenty-five or more free states. I wouldn't be surprised if the Whigs make a concerted effort to turn Delaware into a free state."

Fisher chimed in, "Easier to do in Delaware than anywhere else. Less than two thousand slaves in a state with nearly a hundred thousand souls."

"The question is what happens next," Will said. "Will the remaining slave states let the vile institution die out? Will they opt for compensated emancipation or will they watch it all stripped away when some enterprising Yankee congressman introduces an amendment to abolish the newly passed Thirteenth Amendment?"

Seguin chuckled. Will noted the skepticism in his vice president's voice. "It takes three-fourths of the states to pass an amendment. Do you really think the Whigs can pick off one of those states to abolish the amendment?"

It was Will's turn to laugh. "Juan, how long do you think it will be before Iowa, or the Oregon Territory are admitted as states? Within twenty years, there'll be a dozen new states, all of them free. When that happens, whatever remains of slavery in the US will die."

1 June 1853

Wagons were lined up in front of the two-story log cabin. Soldiers laden with bags of grain and corn came from around back and heaved the burlap bags into the wagon-beds. A civilian, wearing a brown jacket and a matching pair of trousers stood on the porch wearing a deep scowl. A woman stood behind him in a calico print dress. A young girl stood behind the woman, wearing a matching dress.

As General Jason Lamont rode up the winding narrow wagon path toward the house, he took in their rustic appearance. Despite the house's size, it still looked crude and poor compared to Saluda Groves. Behind the house, were a half-dozen small log cabins inhabited by the planter's slaves. Lamont was surprised a planter with twenty slaves, and a sizable cotton crop in the ground couldn't afford a house more fitting with his station.

Lamont's nephew, Captain Elliott Brown stood between the planter and the head wagon, his hand resting on his sword's hilt. As he pulled up next to his nephew, Lamont tipped his hat toward the planter and his family. “Mighty nice of you folks to contribute to the Southern cause.”

The planter crossed his arms, “If by donate, you mean your men riding off with anything that’s not nailed down? Where I come from that’s called theft.”

Over the past couple of weeks as the small army he commanded had made their way northwest, following the Neches River, he’d become inured to such comments. He reached into his pocket and found a few crumpled bank notes. They were Texas cotton-backs. Lamont had picked up a small amount of currency as he’d plundered the farms along his path. He leaned over and offered them to the planter. “We’re not stealing. We’ll pay. I’ve got a bit of local money, but the rest will have to be in an Alliance promissory note.”

The planter pocketed the cotton-backs and glared at Lamont, “Keep your damned promissory note. It ain’t worth the paper you’d write it on.”

Lamont felt his cheeks grow flush and he snapped, “We might have had a setback or two in Texas, but we’ll rout anybody who tries to take our liberty from us.”

The planter said, “Ain’t you heard? General Scott and Lee invaded a few weeks back. I got a newspaper in the house says they’ve captured Columbia.”

Lamont felt a vise squeeze at his heart at the news. With a note of reluctance in his voice, he said, “Mind fetching that paper of yours? I’d like to see it.”

The Planter escorted his family back into the house and reappeared a moment later holding the newspaper, “Might as well, y’all took everything else.”

As he handed the folded newspaper over, he added, "And Missouri has abandoned you, too."

Lamont felt his jaw sag as he saw in a giant 3-inch headline, "Missouri Rejoins the Union!"

In smaller type over the headline, was the name of the newspaper, *The Telegraph & Texas Register*. Lamont scanned the article.

*Rebel governor Sterling Price was moved by rail from Jefferson City to St. Louis under the guard of loyal state militia forces, as provisional governor Hamilton Gamble assumed control of the state capital with the aid of Missouri and Iowa volunteers. These loyal soldiers were mustered into service immediately following President Seward's Emancipation Order.*

*This was made possible when legislators who previously supported the secession resolution recanted their earlier vote and sustained efforts by Unionists, whom they had previously run out of Jefferson City, to depose Governor Price.*

*In the North, many view their actions as self-serving, given that President Seward has stated the states still in rebellion on 1 July will forfeit their slaves as punishment for their rebellion. Slaveholders in Missouri own more than 70,000 slaves, and the threat of losing more than 30 million dollars in property scared them back into the Federal Union.*

Stunned at the news, Lamont fell into a dark mood, waiting for the wagons to pull away with enough food to feed his small army. As he turned, he tossed the newspaper on the ground and dug his heels into the side of his mount.

A few minutes later, he slowed down. Getting angry was no reason to take it out on his mount. It took his nephew a bit to catch up, and when he did, his voice sounded even more morose than Lamont felt. "General, what're we going to do? If the newspaper is telling the truth, our homes have already fallen to the Yankees. Lord help us, I hope my ma is safe."

Lamont kept his horse moving at a slow walk. "If the Yankees were under the command of a bunch of codfish aristocrats from the North, I'd worry more, Elliott. But even though they've betrayed the South, Winfield Scott and Robert E. Lee won't let their army come down hard on womenfolk. Unfortunately, I expect they'll burn Saluda Groves to the ground and run off with my niggers."

In a soft, worn voice, much older than his twenty years, his nephew said, "What now? There's a ferry a few miles up the way. We can cross it and head back toward Louisiana. Maybe hook up with General Davis?"

The thought had crossed his mind. He still had the five regiments of the South Carolina Brigade in addition to three cavalry regiments that had been even further north on the army's right flank in the last battle of Beaumont. Over thirty-five hundred men. But if the war was truly lost, why throw their lives away on another battle under General Davis?

In a whisper that Lamont had to lean over to hear, his nephew said, "What'll there be to return to, Uncle? Nothing?"

The boy had a point, Lamont conceded. The way of life for millions of Southerners would soon be over. That Yankee president had threatened the South with his

Emancipation Order. Aside from Missouri, Lamont was sure the rest of the Alliance would go down swinging, and in the end, lose everything.

When he voiced his fears, once again, Elliott reminded him the boy had a brain between his ears, "Damn Texas for starting this. If they hadn't revolted, we'd still be back home."

With a note of reproach, Lamont said, "They'd not have rebelled except that damn-fool Travis had to go off and pass that free-birth bill."

Thinking of Travis made his bad knee twinge in pain. He'd never forgive Travis for shooting him when he was down. If only he'd been able to strike that insufferable abolitionist down, everything would have been worth it.

*If only,* he thought. Something else crept into his mind, and he turned to his nephew, "How many miles to the Sabine from here?"

After rummaging through his saddlebag, Brown said, "About one-hundred-twenty miles to Charlestown, Louisiana."

"What about to Austin?"

Young Brown jerked his head up, his eyes looked like a startled deer. Slowly, a grin settled on his face as he eyed the map. "A bit less than two hundred."

For the first time since seeing the newspaper, Lamont felt a sense of purpose. He may have lost everything, and his men would become paupers in their own country, but there was one thing he could do.

"Pass the word, Captain Brown, we march to the southwest, to Austin!"

# Chapter 26

Horace Greeley clamped a hand over his hat as he slid into the trench. Blue-jacketed soldiers who sat on the firing steps scarcely glanced at him as he landed at their feet. His escort, on loan from General Lee's headquarters, slid down next to him. The riflemen barely gave the officer a second look.

As he hurried to catch up to the young officer, Lieutenant Terrell, he said, "Why didn't they salute you?"

Without turning, Terrell said, "They just came off the primary trench line this morning. Instead of moving them away from the front, General Lee's ordered them into our secondary trenches to rest. With the arrival of General Blanchard's Corps from out west, Longstreet's army is close to parity with us."

Greeley gave a sage nod, as though a month earlier he'd have understood the importance of Longstreet's decision to defend the city of Augusta, Georgia against the Federal onslaught. In truth, Longstreet's decision to mount a determined defense had caught him off guard. The speed with which the enemy general had stayed one step ahead of Lee's army across the western half of South Carolina had led Greeley to think the rapid retreat signaled the collapse of the Southern Alliance.

Several miles of earthen and wooden fortifications ringed Augusta, proving his earlier view too optimistic.

His escort turned a sharp corner leading into a narrow trench that zig-zagged toward the forward trench works. "Keep your head down, Mr. Greeley. The Allies have snipers that can shoot a tick off a dog's nose at four hundred yards. We're considerably closer than that."

Feeling an itch on his nose, the newspaper man hunched even lower as he picked up his pace to keep up with Terrell. The zig-zagging communication trench intersected with the main fortified trench-line. Greeley followed close on the officer's heels as they passed by several regiments. When they arrived at their destination, the trench sloped down sharply.

Wooden roofing reached over the trench, and as they entered the gloom, Greeley felt himself growing claustrophobic as the walls seemed to close in around him. Lanterns clung to the walls, casting a weak light the further away from sunlight the men traveled.

They turned another corner, and still heading downward, even Greeley's poor sense of direction couldn't be fooled, "Lieutenant, why are we heading toward the enemy line?"

Terrell held up a hand, "We're nearly there, sir."

True to the officer's word, from the narrow walkway they entered a small room barely larger than an outhouse. The walls and ceiling were made of heavy wooden planks. Opposite the entrance was a small open door, not quite three feet wide and tall that led deeper underground. An older officer bent over a table, pen in hand as he wrote on a sheet of paper.

Greeley's guide would have stood straighter, save the ceiling was low and had he rose to his full height, he'd have concussed his head. "Colonel Hancock, sir. Mr. Greeley to see you."

Greeley stretched out his hand, "Colonel, a singular honor. I'd heard rumors about this in General Lee's headquarters, but were I not standing here, I'd not believe it."

The colonel's smile was tired, and his face was lined with lack of sleep as he said, "That'll be all, Lieutenant. I think I can manage one newspaper editor."

Once alone with Greeley, the colonel offered a chair, and as the two sat across from each other, he said, "I heard you wanted to see what a bunch of Pennsylvanian coal miners are up to."

Greeley's eyes darted to the cavernous hole on the far wall. "It's true then. You're mining under the enemy's fortification."

Hancock nodded. "Tell me, Mr. Greeley, does General Lee truly support our endeavors, or to him, is this just a diversion, to keep my men busy?"

Blinking in surprise at the direct question, Greeley stammered, "I'm not privy to the general's private thoughts. He keeps his own counsel for the most part, but I don't believe Robert E. Lee is one to issue orders just to keep men busy."

Greeley hadn't come all the way to the forwardmost trench to have Colonel Hancock ask the questions. He pulled out his worn notepad and licked the tip of the pencil, ready to dig into the mine tunneled by Colonel Winfield Scott Hancock's Sixth Pennsylvania Volunteer Infantry.

The door to the small room burst inward, and another officer from General Lee's headquarters stood in the frame, "It's on! General Lee's ordered the mine to be readied with explosives. How soon until the mine's done?"

Hancock came to his feet, a feral smile on his lips. "We finished a couple of days ago."

It took two days to prepare the mine, and on the twenty-first of June, Greeley found himself standing on an elevated platform far enough away that he was forced to borrow Lt. Terrell's binoculars to see the forward trenches. Beyond, he could see the Southern Alliance's unofficial battle flag flying over the enemy ramparts. The single white star rippled on the blue field as gusts of wind snapped at the banner.

Raising the field glasses, Greeley saw the steeple of the First Presbyterian Church of Augusta in the distance, rising above the town.

In the middle of the elevated platform, General Lee lowered his own binoculars, "Send the telegraph message when the mine blows. I want General Jackson's Virginia Brigade to support Buell's Division when they attack."

Below the platform, the faint clattering of a telegraph machine confirmed the order's transmission. Greeley resisted the urge to look at his pocket watch as the minutes ticked by. Finally, when his hand was reaching to his waistcoat, the earth shook beneath his feet and the platform's wooden supports swayed. An explosion ripped the ground open in the middle of the rebel fortifications, throwing fire, smoke, earth, wood, and men into the sky.

Despite the distance, the throaty screams of Buell's division reached the platform, and like a blue carpet being unrolled on a field, the federal troops charged across the distance between the two armies. More than a hundred field pieces and heavier siege guns added to the explosion's confusion.

Greeley committed everything he saw to memory as the blue wave crashed into the enemy trenches. The binoculars brought into focus that enough of the enemy had recovered from the thunderous explosion to hurt Buell's attack, as he saw scores of men falling to the ground in the last hundred paces before the Alliance's fortifications. But it was too little, as the Federal troops surged into the enemy trenches.

Greeley felt a rush of righteous fury, watching the gray-uniformed ant-like figures streaming away from the trenches. Blue-jacketed soldiers chased them, stopping only to fire.

He lowered the field glasses as moisture gathered at the corners of his eyes. "Is this the beginning of the end?" he whispered, he closed his eyes and added, "Lord, smite your enemy and destroy them."

General Lee turned and said, "Amen. Don't forget, Mr. Greeley, when you write your reports, that war is cruel. I wonder if they would still clamor for their neighbor's blood if they could pick up your newspaper and see daguerreotypes of the battlefield littered with the broken bodies of their sons and fathers."

29 June 1853

Major Charlie Travis willed his stomach to settle down as the balloon shifted. A brief glance below showed what he feared. A few of his ground crew raced after one of the four ropes tethering the balloon.

Standing beside the telegraph machine, Sam Williams swore as one of the ground crew leapt into the air and grabbed hold of the thick rope. The soldier came off the ground as the wind whipped the tether higher into the air. "Damned if I'd rather be free-floating, Major. At least then we'd be able to see them enemy forts better."

Charlie gripped the wicker basket until his knuckles turned white. "Not me, I'd rather be on solid ground, Sam. If this thing comes loose, we'd likely crash somewhere in Mississippi. I doubt they'd leave the latch string out for us."

Several more soldiers managed to grab hold of the wayward tether, and the balloon stopped twisting in the breeze. Charlie loathed taking the fragile airship into the sky under windy conditions, but the continuous thunder of heavy guns to the south forced his hand. Even so, the other two balloons remained grounded. He'd not risk anyone else.

"Look, sir," Sam pointed toward the expansive Mississippi River. Black smudges revealed the location of the Yankee and Texian ships, whether from their coal burning engines, their heavy guns or from damage taken from the steady artillery barrage from the earthen forts alongside the mighty river, Charlie couldn't tell. There was but a single fort firing on the combined fleet. A second fort, on the river's western bank, sat empty; its guns transferred to the eastern fort in the days immediately following General Davis' retreat into Louisiana.

A large square-masted ship led the procession of vessels, an iron-plated box sat on the side of the ship, protecting the side paddlewheel from shot and shell. As Charlie stared through his binoculars, Sam said, "That's the *Powhatan.* She's a Yankee frigate powered by a side-paddlewheel."

The ship shuddered, as Charlie focused his glasses on the *Powhatan,* whether from taking a hit or the recoil of her guns, he couldn't tell. The balloon was simply too far away even with the binocular's magnification.

"I count thirty-six gun emplacements at Fort Jackson, sir. Some of those guns have got to be firing one-hundred-pound rounds. They'll pulverize a wooden ship," Sam said as he sent the information down the attached telegraph line.

Charlie nodded and kept his eyes glued to the river. The water around the *Powhatan* churned where shots slammed into the water. Heavy solid shot clanged into the armored wheelhouse casing, bending the iron plating, and turning severed rivet-heads into deadly projectiles.

A flash of light filled the binocular's lenses, and Charlie blinked in pain as he pulled the glasses away from his face. In the distance, where the *Powhatan* once sailed, flames burned along the waterline.

"Dear God, there had to have been three hundred men on that ship," he muttered as he watched another ship, the *Zavala,* one of Texas' seven ships in the attacking squadron, seem to leap forward as black clouds billowed from her smokestack. She appeared to have made it through the barrage of guns as Charlie turned his focus to a trio of squat ships lagging behind the rest of the squadron. They were still nearly a mile away from the fort when the first one's bow dipped. A heavy mortar fired a shell from the ship's deck. Charlie followed the shell's trajectory, watching it as it fell short, landing in the river just a few dozen paces from the earthen fort.

The next ship fired a few minutes later. The shell disappeared within the walls of Fort Jackson before it exploded, sending smoldering debris into the air. Every few minutes one of the ships fired and dropped their shells in and around the fort. Despite the steady barrage, the fort's guns continued to fire on the ships racing by.

"Major, we're losing the daylight. Should I send the signal to bring us down?"

Where had the day gone? Sam had sent dozens of Charlie's updates about the river-borne battle throughout the day, and to Charlie, it seemed as though only a couple of hours had passed, but a quick glance behind him, showed the sun sinking.

"One moment, Sam," he said as he watched Fort Jackson burn. Most of the combined fleet had passed through Hell to get beyond the fort's guns. Two Yankee ships still burned where they had been beached on the opposite shoreline. Another, the *Nueces* had been run aground earlier in the day and was abandoned, when a lucky shot had destroyed the ship's helm and disabled the *Nueces'* ability to steer. But the other ships had made it past the fort.

The flagpole over which the rebels flew their blue banner, was afire. The flames licked at the flag and burned through the rope that had secured the ensign over the fort. Charlie felt grim satisfaction as he watched the enemy flag flutter to the ground, as flames consumed it.

The chair legs scraped the wooden floor as Lt. Colonel Jesse Running Creek stood and stretched. The office he shared with West Liberty's telegraph operator was small, but he liked being close whenever news arrived. A shrill blast from the railroad depot announced the arrival of another train pulling into the station.

Through the window, he saw stevedores rushing toward a boxcar and slide the door open. The foreman shouted orders, as the freed slaves began hauling boxes from the car. Some of the freight was destined for wagons that traveled the ten-mile route between the railhead and the factories at Trinity Park. Jesse had a strong feeling that if the army's engineers hadn't been kept busy rebuilding the single line of track on the other side of the Trinity River that another line would have been pushed north, connecting the manufacturing facilities at Trinity Park with the Republic's rail network.

Jesse stepped outside the stifling telegraph room. Watching the ex-slaves working on the platform sent his mind back to his father's warehouse. Even before the

Cherokee diaspora, his father had been a man of substance among the Cherokee. Despite their copper skin, the Cherokee of Georgia and South Carolina had been Southerners in all but name. The wealthy among them owned plantations and slaves.

More than a year had gone by since he'd seen or heard from his father and he wondered how Simon Running Creek fared. The Cherokee of Texas had fractured as bad as the rest of the Republic. Men like Stand Waite had declared for the Rebels in Beaumont, while others like Sam Houston, had backed President Travis. His father's trade with the South as well as the slaves he owned led him to support Waite.

Jesse wondered if any of the ex-slaves working in the hot summer sun had been liberated from those among the Cherokee who had joined the rebellion. He was uncertain how he felt about President Travis taking a page from the Yankee president, William Seward, and releasing an emancipation order, freeing the slaves of anyone who was still actively supporting the rebellion. On the one hand, it resulted in many immigrants from the American South, who had been tepid in their support of the uprising, disavowing it. He had no idea how President Travis would untangle the mess the rebels had created.

"Colonel, there's a message coming through you need to read," the voice of the telegraph operator broke Jesse's musing, and he stepped back into the office.

Leaning over the operator's shoulder, Jesse read as he transcribed the code. "Large body of enemy troops spotted near Boonville in Brazos County."

Swearing, Jesse grabbed the note and turned to look at the map pinned to the wall over his desk. This message was the second of its type received, although the first was now a week old. He scanned the map, searching for Brazos County. It seemed like every time the Republic's cartographers released a new map, Congress was forming another county, making the map's boundaries unreliable. "There's Boonville," he muttered as he grabbed a pencil stub and marked it on the map.

He found the mark from the previous week, in Angelina County. Tracing between the two, the enemy force wasn't moving very fast, but given the dense forests and unpredictable river crossings, it was no surprise.

Scanning the map, Jesse mused aloud, "Where are you bastards going?"

He grabbed a newspaper from his desk and used its edge to line up the two points on the map, and he drew a line between them. He moved the paper along an imaginary line from Boonville, and then he extended the penciled line and swore again.

"Oh, shit. Send a telegram to Austin. An enemy force of unknown size is headed in their direction."

After the transmitter clattered to a stop once the operator sent the message, Jesse said, "Send another up and down the line. I want the army's Ranger battalion to assemble in Houston by any means necessary."

He grabbed his black, battered hat and headed out the door at a run, racing over to the station master.

"Turn this thing around, I want the train headed back to Houston within the hour."

# Chapter 27

"Get your asses onto the barge, boys!" Jimmy Hickok pulled on his horse's rein as they navigated the muddy riverbank's steep slope. They followed in the deep footprints of the engineers who slid the long flat-bottomed boat into the Mississippi River's fast-flowing brown water. The sound of several dozen horses' shoes clopping on the boat's wooden planks nearly drowned out the sound of heavy guns firing downriver.

"Grab a paddle and get to it," another voice shouted as the boat slipped away from the bank, filled with horses and their troopers. A wooden oar was thrust into Jimmy's hands, and he found himself propelled toward the barge's side, where he joined several others, who were paddling with all their strength. The strong current swept the boat toward the middle of the river, traveling downstream at several miles an hour.

With each stroke, the barge pulled closer to the eastern shoreline, which was half a mile from the western bank. Jimmy's arms started to burn as he dug his oar into the murky water and as he chanced a look down the river, in the distance he saw several tall stone pylons rising out of the water. Atop the pylons, he could see blackened wood where the enemy had torched the half-completed railroad trestles. The bridge would have been the first permanent structure to cross the mighty river.

The Texian engineers, whose boats the 1st New York Cavalry used, had planned the crossing well. No matter how hard the men paddled, the current was going to carry them downstream. Their target was nearly a mile downriver from where they started.

Jimmy looked down as a splinter grazed his hand. A bullet sent slivers of wood everywhere as it struck the boat. Ignoring the red streak on the back of his hand, the youth saw soldiers kneeling on the shoreline firing at them.

"It's simple, they said," he muttered. "You'll take your horses down to the boats, they said."

"You'll cross upriver of the main assault, they said." He flinched as bits of wood showered him as a bullet gouged the planking near his feet. "You'll be unopposed, they said."

A loud crash echoed across the river. Smoke billowed from atop the eastern bank, and a boat next to his own tipped over as solid iron shot pulverized the stern. The screams from the soldiers were bad enough, but they paled in comparison to the terrified horses dumped into the river.

"Hickok," A voice yelled in his ear, "Paddle or I'll throw you in and let you swim. A duckbill like yours shouldn't have any problems with a little water."

Jimmy wanted to turn around and drive his fist into the mushy face of his sergeant, but that thought was cut short by a wet splat. He turned and watched his squad's sergeant claw at his throat before toppling over the side of the boat.

The barge lurched as it dug into the river's eastern bank. Jimmy threw the oar into the water and turned to fetch his horse. Several of the beasts were down, struck by bullets. His own bay gelding was still standing, and Jimmy grabbed the reins and followed several other soldiers off the boat. With the reins in one hand, he yanked his revolver from its holster and fired at a gray-clad soldier who was reloading his rifle. Several bullets struck their target, and a rammer went flying into the river as the soldier crumpled to the ground.

Confusion ruled as Jimmy joined several other troopers as they battled their way up the riverbank. He became aware of a group of soldiers wearing butternut brown next to his own band. One of those men, when he scrambled to the top of the riverbank waved forward, "Come on, Fourth Texas, we've got them on the run!"

As he climbed into the saddle, a bullet struck the trooper, and he tumbled off the back of his mount and slid down the steep riverbank. Jimmy scrambled behind his horse and scanned the nearby field. A few rebels were showing their backsides as they disappeared over a low stone fence in the distance. Closer in to the river, Jimmy saw several gray jacketed soldiers running toward a field gun, pulling a pair of horses. A half-dozen men were grabbing equipment and hooking up the gun carriage to the caisson. Jimmy dug his heels into his mount and screamed at the top of his lungs and charged.

His mount closed the distance and Jimmy raised his revolver and fired as he raced by one of the gunners. When he pulled up on the reins and turned around, he saw the gunner on the ground. Closing fast with the enemy gun crew were a couple of his fellow troopers from the 1st New York and the three remaining Texians who had crested the embankment with Jimmy.

The youth pointed his pistol at another gunner and pulled the trigger. The hammer fell on an empty chamber. He swore and threw himself from the saddle, landing on a gunner who was fumbling with a fastened holster. Knocking the rebel off his feet, Jimmy realized he still held the gun in his hand, and he raised it over his head and brought it down with all the force he could muster on the fellow's head.

The gunner's hand fell away from his weapon, and he collapsed next to the now immobile field gun. Filled with rage, Jimmy leapt on him, swinging the gun against the other man's head.

"Damnit to hell, Hickok," Jimmy recognized the voice as hands pulled him away from the obviously dead artillerist. "You done killed the bastard."

Jimmy stared at the dead man. Blood and gore covered his head. A glance at his pistol showed the barrel was slimy with gray matter. He dropped it, and the gun landed with a dull thud in the dirt. One of the men from his squad pulled him away from the body, which was one of several gunners who had been killed in their attempt to escape. "Damned if I'm ever going to call you Duckbill again. After that, you're a pistol, a real wild Bill."

Jimmy swallowed hard, the feeling of nausea nearly overwhelming before he forced a smile onto his pale face, "Call me Wild Bill Hickok, Corporal. If I hear anyone else call me duckbill again, I'll kill him where he stands."

An officer rode up to the abandoned field cannon and waved at the men, "Get going, men. We're only a mile away from the railroad. We cut that, and New Orleans is cut off from the rest of the South!"

*Strange,* Charlie thought as the balloon floated over the city of New Orleans, *you don't really feel the wind.* The peculiar sensation he got whenever he went up in the balloon never went away, no matter how many times he went up in the flimsy contraption. For the most part, he'd gotten used to it. But his worst fear was free flying. The notion of leaving behind the tethering rope and ground crew filled him with a sense of dread that he couldn't explain.

He'd have rather been with the 9th Infantry the previous day when they stormed across the Mississippi River in their fragile wooden barges than floating over the largest city in the American South without a single tether. Without the copper wire connecting the bulky telegraph machine to the ground, his operator, Sam, leaned against one of the ropes connecting the basket to the hydrogen-filled balloon and looked at the city below.

"Major, did you know almost a hundred and twenty thousand folks live down there?"

The idea of that many people in one place was hard to grasp. The thought that nearly one person was living in New Orleans for every five Texians was hard to wrap his mind around. Galveston had just edged San Antonio out as the largest city in Texas in the last census, and neither had managed to break ten thousand souls.

"You don't say," Charlie said. What he meant was, *tell me something useful*.

As though reading his mind, his eighteen-year-old telegraph operator said, "Let me see the binoculars. It looks like there's a parade down there."

Instead of handing the glasses over, Charlie scanned the area where Sam was pointing. Sure enough, a long line of blue-jacketed soldiers was marching down the center of a wide boulevard more than a thousand feet below. "Yankee Marines from the look of them. Parading through the center of town like they own the place."

Sam finally captured the glasses and peered at the parading Marines. "How can you tell? Who thought it was a good idea to give surplus US Marine uniforms to our own Marines?"

Charlie turned away, hiding a smile. He'd wondered the same question when growing up in his pa's house. His father's response had been short, "I like the way they look."

From where he stood, they looked like ants to the unaided eye. And it seemed like they were marching through hell. Charlie's map of New Orleans showed the US Marines were parading through the Eleventh Ward. That section of town had been bombarded, and buildings set afire the previous day. Charlie was impressed that all that remained of the fires were a few smoldering buildings. The rebels in Beaumont hadn't cared one way or another about the town when they abandoned it. But most New Orleans' residents, amid a coordinated attack from the Federal and Texas armies, stayed and fought the fires before they spread from the Eleventh Ward.

With the glasses firmly pressed against his eyes, Sam said, "I can see one of our warships alongside one of the wharves. A couple of Yankee frigates, too."

Charlie flinched at the memory of the Yankee frigate blowing up a few days earlier when the US and Texas navies had joined together to destroy Fort Jackson and push past it to New Orleans. "Did you see the casualty reports? Three ships sunk and more than six hundred casualties, most of them died when that frigate blew up."

With the resilience of youth, Sam quipped, "And we still beat the hell out of the Secesh, Major."

The young operator pointed north, toward Lake Pontchartrain, where the balloon slowly drifted. Charlie's eyes locked onto a scene just outside of town. Fields of white, like a canvas carpet, stretched out for the better part of a mile. There were thousands of tents hugging the estuary's shoreline. There the Allied army of the Trans-Mississippi was encamped, ordered there following General Davis's surrender of the city following a fierce fight throughout the previous day.

Within Charlie, something stirred as he gazed at the massive camp, housing twenty thousand surrendered soldiers, including the remnants of the rebel Texian battalions that had sided with traitors like Robert Potter nearly two years before. With the defeat and capture of Davis' command, the only army capable of threatening the Republic was removed.

"This is nearly the end, Sam. If the newspapers Admiral Perry brought with him are true, General Longstreet's army is not long for this world. Why, the publisher of the New York Tribune, Mr. Greeley, has been sending reports to his newspaper almost daily."

The younger man leaned in and in a sly voice said, "I bet you can hardly wait to see your wife. How long has it been?"

Turning away from the encampment, Charlie's thoughts drifted to his wife, whom he hadn't seen since taking command of the balloon corps. *It has been too long*. While he carried a daguerreotype of his wife and infant son next to his heart, it was too little. For years he'd wondered why his father had complained when work took him away from home, but as the balloon passed over the sea of tents, he understood what his father had missed when duty had called.

2 July 1853

Horace Greeley sat on the open windowsill, enjoying the cool of the morning. All the windows in the courtroom of the DeKalb county courthouse were open, letting in the light breeze. Despite a temperature below seventy degrees at that moment, he knew the day would still be a scorcher by the afternoon. When he mentioned this to the commander of the Virginia Brigade, General Jackson chuckled. "Sir, if you think a southern July afternoon is hot, accept my invitation to visit Lexington in August. While I can assure you, hell's gates are hotter, you'd be forgiven for questioning the veracity of the statement."

Greeley found himself smiling at Jackson's quip. Throughout his time with the Federal army, he'd found the devout Virginian to be awkward company. But the newspaper publisher couldn't deny Jackson's success as one of Lee's brigade commanders. The speed with which he'd moved his men around the enemy's flank at the Battle of Lumber River would be the stuff military academies would study for generations. Now, though, Jackson seemed downright lighthearted. Not so much that Greeley had any interest in accepting his offer once summer's oppressive heat had settled over the land.

"Send me a telegram, General Jackson, I'd enjoy reading about it more than experiencing it." Greeley joked.

An officer stepped into the room, interrupting Jackson's retort. "Longstreet's here. He's come alone!"

Jackson recovered, "I dare say, Old Pete would rather not experience today any more than you'd enjoy August in Virginia."

Any thought of response died on Greeley's lips as General James Longstreet entered the room. His gray coat came down to his knees. Golden braiding ringed his sleeves. The Southern Alliance had adopted the European practice of ornate piping on their officers' jackets to denote their rank. The Southern General looked dignified as he accepted General Lee's hand.

Greeley wished for the newfangled picture boxes that were all the rage in cities. What he would have done to capture the image. Instead, only artists' drawings would provide a visual detail of the meeting.

Longstreet opened, "Thank you for your forbearance, General Lee. Absent your offer of a ceasefire yesterday, I fear today would have been the bloodiest day of this terribly cruel war."

Greeley studied the Federal commander's expression. Behind the salt and pepper beard, Lee's eyes were opaque, hard for the publisher to read. "I could do no less, sir. We are all Americans, and the sooner the bloodshed stops, the sooner we can heal this terrible divide."

Longstreet glanced out the window, beyond Greeley's perch, "I warned my fellow South Carolinians that without Virginia and Kentucky, we'd be hard-pressed to prevail."

Folding his hands and placing them on the table, Lee said, "I could no more be disloyal to Virginia than you against South Carolina or," he nodded toward General Buell, "General Buell raise his sword against Ohio. Virginia remained in the Union and I with her."

Longstreet leaned back in the chair and ran his fingers through his hair. He said, "I suspect history will be kinder to you than to me. However, you've surrounded my army, sir. I cannot go west nor to the south. You've cut us off by rail from Montgomery. No doubt, as you have guessed, I have come to seek terms."

Greeley leaned in to hear the Federal officer's response. "You must surrender your arms, artillery, and public property except for your officer's side arms. Instruct your officers to provide rolls for all of your men.

Your officers will provide their parole and promise to not take up arms against the government of the United States. They will also take it upon themselves to sign the same parole for the men under their command. If they do these things, they will be allowed to return to their homes to wait until they are properly exchanged. If they honor their parole and the laws of the federal government, they will not be disturbed by Washington."

Longstreet bowed his head as Lee finished laying out the terms. The silence seemed to stretch on as Greeley watched the Southern general weigh Lee's words. When he finally looked up, moisture clouded his eyes as he extended his hand and said, "Your terms are generous, sir. On behalf of all of the officers and men of the Army of the Carolinas, I accept your terms."

Greeley repressed the sense of joy that threatened to spill onto his face. Seeing General Longstreet's crestfallen face, he knew not everyone in the room rejoiced as he did. Instead, he gripped his pencil and wrote, *"With a firm handshake between victor and vanquished, the war in the east, like that west of the Mississippi, came to an end."*

# Chapter 28

July 10 1853

General Jason Lamont jerked his head up as he heard feet splashing through the nearby creek. It was only Elliott. A smile lit the young man's features as he knelt beside him. "Uncle, scouts from the Third Tennessee just rode back in. We're only ten miles away from Austin."

Neither the young man's dirty, torn uniform nor his gaunt frame dimmed his enthusiasm as he knelt by Lamont. He continued, "It's still early, folks won't be at work yet if we strike soon."

Lamont set the chunk of buffalo meat he'd been eating on a worn handkerchief and wiped his hands on the grass, "Church. It's Sunday. They'll not yet be at church. Pass the word, I want to meet with the regimental commanders before we ride. Best to hit them while the good folks of Austin are sitting in their pews."

As his excited aide raced back across the creek, Lamont thought about the last few weeks since turning away from the Neches River. They had raided some farms and traded Alliance script for supplies at several plantations as they made their way toward the Republic's capital. Once they crossed the Brazos River though, towns were few and far between. Farms were spread out, too. In one way, that worked to his little army's advantage, as they raided their way across the central Texas prairie. When they hit a farm, they could round up the farmer and his family and keep word from getting out. But it also worked against his force. Given how gaunt many of his men now appeared, the produce from one of the small farms might feed a family for a year, but it was a drop in the bucket for what his army required. Even now, several dozen prisoners accompanied Lamont's small army after the soldiers raided their farms. Lamont disliked bringing the farmers and their families along under guard, but he'd not risk word of his advance reaching Austin before him.

He was pleasantly surprised his advance upon Austin hadn't resulted in some element of the Texas Army falling upon his men yet. Once his force had learned he was planning on attacking Austin rather than returning to Arkansas or Louisiana, men had slipped away under cover of darkness, in ones and twos until now he commanded only twenty-five hundred men.

As his regimental commanders arrived, he said, "We'll move out within the next thirty minutes. The infantry will quick march. I want to be in Austin within the next two hours. When we strike, I want to catch William Travis sitting in his pew in church."

One of the cavalry officers said, "We could ride ahead, be there within the hour and secure the town, General. We've still got the better part of seven hundred cavalry."

Lamont laughed and patted the officer on the shoulder, "I like how you think, Bill. Even so, I'd rather you and your boys not get too far ahead of the infantry. God help us if Travis knows about us and is just sitting in Austin with a couple of thousand men. You'd be riding right into a trap. I want our infantry able to support you when it comes to a fight."

He pushed the idea that Travis might be prepared out of his mind. He hadn't come so far to come up empty-handed. He would bag the man who humiliated and crippled him. He felt his face flush as he leaned forward and said, "Now, when we get to Austin, this is what we're going to do—"

From the top of the Capitol Building's stairs Lt. Colonel Jesse Running Creek could see the iron trestles crossing the Colorado River. Less than a mile separated the building from the river, and although houses and businesses filled the city between the two points, they were mostly single-story buildings, with a smattering of taller structures sprinkled amidst them.

The town had yet to come alive, and the streets were mostly empty. Here and there, he saw a few people heading toward one of the dozen churches in town. Jesse enjoyed moments like this the most, when the sounds of freight wagons, carts, and buggies had yet to turn the city into the hustling frontier city it was.

As he started down the steps, the jingling of keys caught his attention, and he turned as the portly Secretary of War, George Fisher opened one of the double doors and slipped from the building. He jumped when he saw Jesse standing atop the stairs. "Good morning, Colonel. I see I'm not the only early bird."

His curiosity piqued, Jesse said, "I like the view from here, sir. I thought I'd have capitol hill to myself this morning."

Fisher locked the door back and said, "Even with the Southern Alliance crumbling, there's still much to do. I was meeting with one of the other cabinet secretaries. Tomorrow, the Senate's budget committee is holding a hearing. Now that the war is as good as over, the first thing they want to do is slash spending."

Jesse frowned, "I hope the war is over. We're still trying to find that band of rebels who didn't retreat with Jeff Davis back across the Sabine."

"What's the latest?"

Jesse shook his head in frustration, "Nothing since they were spotted near Boonville on the Brazos River."

As the two men came down the stairs, Fisher said, "Do you really think they're coming to Austin?"

Shrugging, Jesse said, "Given that I've pulled the garrison from the Alamo, I'd hate to be wrong."

"How many men have you collected here?"

Reaching the bottom of the steps, the Colorado River disappeared from view. Jesse said, "I've mustered what's left of the Army's Ranger battalion, about three hundred men. Austin has a company from the Frontier Battalion, that's another forty. There's also the corps of cadets training at the Alamo, that's another fifty. Lastly, there's the Alamo garrison, which is mostly men who are still recovering from their wounds who haven't been released back to their units. In all, less than seven hundred men."

Jesse and Secretary Fisher parted company when they reached the bottom of the hill at Congress Avenue. Church bells clanged, calling the citizens of Austin to worship and Jesse headed north, toward the encampment on the edge of town.

"You look like a thousand dollars, Will."

Will Travers turned and smiled at Becky. She wore a green dress and her hair flowed down her back, kept out of her eyes with a simple emerald ribbon. The color of the dress reminded Will of her gown the evening they met so many years earlier. He remembered her standing in the reception line at the Christmas party between her parents. To Will, she was even more beautiful now.

"Would that be a thousand pre-war dollars or a thousand now?"

Becky stuck out her tongue, "If my love is subject to inflation, then you look like a million dollars, Mr. President."

Will laughed. "I'm a poor sight compared to you, Mrs. Travis."

His wife gave him a fierce hug and whispered, "If we weren't already late for church, I'd show you what your flattery would get you."

Will gave an exaggerated sigh. "There's simply not enough time in the day, my love."

Becky turned, offering her back, “Button me up.” As Will complied, she continued, “I’m counting down the months until the next election. I’m ready to leave Austin and return to our home, where I’ll be better able to compete for your time. Do you think Juan will run for president?”

“I hope so,” Will said. “I was talking with him about this just the other day. While he’s threatened on more than one occasion to resign and return to his family’s ranch, I think it’s because the office of vice president is a bit like the fifth wheel on a wagon. It’s kind of useless unless one of the others breaks. Still, I told him that I think he’s a shoo-in to win if he runs. Winning the war against our rebels and their allies means that for now, there’s no organized opposition to Juan.”

Becky stepped back, “How do I look?”

“Like a hundred million dollars. Plus, if Juan doesn’t run, I fear that Sam Houston, like Don Quixote charging at windmills, will try one more time for the office. Say what you will of him, Sam has been unfailingly supportive of the government among the Cherokees and the other civilized tribes.”

Becky laughed. “Sometimes I think you’ve been telling Davy that Sam Houston is like the monster hiding under his bed. That’s the first nice thing I’ve heard you say about him in a long time.”

Will smiled ruefully, “I’ve never quite forgiven him for more than a decade of preaching annexation. Men like him failed to see how if they had tied us to the South that we’d be facing the Federals, too.”

A confused look crossed Becky's face, "I don't understand. President Seward didn't attack the South until they attacked us."

Will brushed a loose strand of hair out of her face. "Seward is a strident abolitionist. Most of the Whigs in the North share his views. They're becoming stronger, and if the sectional conflict hadn't happened over the South attacking us, it would have been something else in a few years. That's what men like Sam Houston—"

A shriek from one of the children's rooms interrupted Will, and a shrill voice screamed, "Davy, I'm going to hit you if you touch my braids one more time!"

A moment later Will heard a slap and then a howl from ten-year-old David Stern Travis.

Will found his two younger children in twelve-year-old Liza's room. Davy leaned against the door frame cradling his hand. His daughter stood in the middle of the room, holding a brush in her hand like it was a knife.

"Pa, she hit me with her brush!" Davy's voice was indignant.

"Daddy, make him stop it. Davy won't leave me alone." Liza's lower lip protruded like a catfish on a hook.

Will found his lips twitching as he stifled a smile. He seldom thought about how much he had lost when his mind and soul had been transferred, but in a moment like this, he didn't miss it at all. The love of a good woman and children who still looked up to him as their hero outweighed the things he missed from his life before.

Instead of smiling, Will forced a stormy look onto his face as he gripped his son's shoulder. "Son, if you think your sister's brush hurt, wait until I help you remember to leave her alone."

As Will corralled his son toward his room, he was nearly certain he saw Liza stick her tongue out at her little brother. With a soft prod, he pushed Davy into his room, where the boy zigzagged around tin soldiers and a wooden train.

"I'm not going to tell you this is going to hurt me more than it's going to hurt you, because that's not going to be the case—" Will started.

He paused as he heard a pop in the distance. He stepped around his son, sending toy soldiers hurtling in several directions and opened the lone window in the boy's bedroom. The sound of gunfire was more distinct.

Will slammed the window shut, rattling the glass panes. "Becky," he shouted, "the town's under attack!"

He grabbed Davy's hand as he raced back toward the master bedroom, where Becky was running a brush through Liza's hair. "Take the children and hurry to the church."

Startled, Becky said, "Won't it be safer here?"

"What if this is their target? Go, now," Will hustled his family toward the street. On his way to the front door, he found his mother-in-law already in the foyer along with Charlie's wife and young son.

After watching his family hurry toward the Methodist Church, Will ran back into the house and returned a moment later. His rifle slung over one shoulder, he buckled his belt and felt the comforting weight of the revolver at his hip as he headed toward the sound of the guns.

When he heard the crackling of gunfire Jason Lamont nudged his horse into a gallop as he raced alongside the wagon trail down which his infantry marched. The dust of nearly four thousand feet reduced visibility to a couple of hundred paces. Had his cavalry disregarded his order and ranged too far ahead? If they had, heads would roll, he thought as he ground his teeth, willing his horse to gallop faster.

Once he reached the front of the infantry column, he saw the 2nd South Carolina Cavalry Regiment, who had been with his little army since falling in with his brigade after the final battle at Beaumont. They were deployed in a long single line as they rode forward, screening Lamont's infantry. Here and there, along the line, he saw troopers topple from their mounts, struck by an enemy Lamont couldn't see.

He felt the blood rush to his face as he resisted the overwhelming urge to charge and come to grips with the enemy. Whoever battled his cavalry stood between him and a decade-long thirst for revenge. Instead, he wheeled around and found the regimental commander for the lead infantry regiment, "Colonel Evans, deploy your men into line of battle, send half of them forward in open order. Don't let your men bunch up!" As an afterthought, he added, "Pass the word for the third infantry and the fifth infantry to deploy on your flanks. The rest will act as a reserve."

Satisfied his riflemen wouldn't remain straggled out along the poorly maintained road, Lamont galloped toward his cavalry. *Who the hell is stopping us?*

Arriving among the troopers of the 2nd Cavalry, Lamont saw a dismounted skirmish line heading southward, toward Austin. Finding the regiment's colonel, Lamont said, "Why have you stopped? Where's the enemy?"

The officer wiped blood from a gash on his cheek, "We was ambushed, sir. A bunch of horsemen hit us hard when we came around a copse of trees. I deployed my boys, and we're in pursuit," he said, pointing to the troopers who were spread out and sweeping forward across the open prairie.

Lamont scanned the plain beyond the skirmishers. He knew his men were being observed, but wherever the enemy were, they were, for the moment, out of sight. Frustrated, he said, "You've got to close with the enemy, no matter the cost."

Seeing a look of frustration in his subordinate's eyes, Lamont changed his mind, "Bring up the rest of the cavalry. I'll lead the Second myself."

Before the colonel could protest, Lamont bolted forward and drew his sword, "Forward men, we're not leaving our skirmishers hanging in the wind."

Reaching the cavalry skirmishers' thin line, Lamont saw puffs of smoke and felt a tug at his sleeve. He glanced down and saw the material was cut where a bullet had clipped the jacket.

Pointing the tip of his sword towards the gunfire, he dug his heels into his mount and let loose a feral scream, channeling a decade's worth of hate.

One good thing about Congress Avenue, Jesse thought, it's straight as an arrow, except when it circled the Capitol building. He and the forty-man company following hard on his heels made good time as they raced northward. The sound of hard-soled boots crunching gravel filled his ears as adrenaline coursed through him.

Gunfire told him the Texas Rangers from the Frontier Battalion had run into something during their morning patrol. From the sound of it, they may have found more than they'd bargained for. Once they had passed by the last street on which homes and businesses were constructed, there were still a few blocks of undeveloped land crisscrossed with streets. Austin's council proactively managed the town's growth, and until the war, Texas' capital city had been one of the fastest growing cities in the Republic. Now, all of that was endangered. As Jesse had feared since the first sighting of the enemy force a few weeks before, they had made their way to Austin. If he and his men, nearly seven hundred strong couldn't stop them, the capital of the Republic could go up in flames.

When he reached the edge of town, several more companies from the Army Ranger Battalion were overturning wagons on Magnolia Street, the last road between the town and the prairie. A block over was one of the companies he had ordered north from the Alamo. The men carried themselves with the air of veterans. But many still wore visible scars of terrible wounds, rendering them unsuited for frontline combat. The irony of the situation weighed on Jesse's conscience, but what choice did he have? Without the

Alamo garrison, he'd have mustered less than four hundred.

An officer in a clean and pressed uniform jogged over to him. After saluting, he said, "Colonel, my cadets are ready and eager for action. Where do you want us?"

As the veteran soldiers from the Alamo garrison were taking up positions on either side Jesse's Rangers, the Cherokee officer pointed back the way he had come earlier. "I want your cadets to take up a position along Chestnut Street."

The officer wore an offended look. "But, sir, these cadets are well trained. Once they graduate, they'll be assigned as officers throughout the army."

"I know," Jesse snapped. "And I want them one block back. If those bastards out yonder force us off our line, there aren't many things worse than a fighting retreat. What I want is some of our best soldiers back there, to form the backbone of such a retreat."

After the officer left, Jesse climbed on top of the overturned wagon's tongue for a better view of the milling melee north of town. The Rangers from the Frontier Battalion were mixed in with the gray jacketed troopers, and although heavily outnumbered, they were armed to the teeth and gave better than they received. However, despite their superior firepower, the Texas Rangers were pushed back. Watching them wheel away, trying to break free, he recalled something General Johnston had said about quantity having a quality all its own. No doubt the Southern cavalry would have swept the Rangers aside had it not been for the number of revolvers each Ranger carried into the fight.

In twos and threes, the Texians veered away from the enemy troopers; they'd had enough. To Jesse's trained eye, too many Ranger saddles were empty as the survivors galloped back toward the makeshift position at the edge of town. Riders who had vanquished the Texians from the field chased after them, staying hard on their heels.

Jesse leapt from the wagon tongue, "Get ready, boys. Aim true."

Rifles cracked, and Jesse watched gray jacketed riders tumble from saddles even as the men from the Frontier battalion streamed through the defenders on their way to the rear. The entire battalion of the army's Rangers stood behind the makeshift barricade or knelt or lay in the knee-high grass along the roadside. Hundreds of rifles lashed out sheets of lead, knocking gray uniformed horsemen from the mounts by the dozens.

In just a few minutes, a thick haze of smoke covered the field in front of the Texians' position, masking the Southern horsemen's retreat. Climbing back on top of the wagon tongue, Jesse strained to see through the fog of war. The smoke eddied and drifted along, carried by a light, morning breeze that was too warm to be cool but held not a hint of the blazing heat the early summer afternoon promised.

The haze dissipated, moment by moment and Jesse felt his stomach lurch as he saw, advancing toward Austin, a long line of gray-jacketed infantry.

He stepped down and told a sergeant who was filling his pockets with ammunition from a wooden box, "Pass the word, fill your cartridge boxes, haversacks, and pockets with cartridges. We're going to need them."

Once his family had disappeared down the street toward the Methodist Church, Will turned and headed in the opposite direction, toward the sound of the gunfire. The holster slapped against his thigh each time his right foot pounded the dirt street. Despite his regular walks, he found himself gasping for air before he'd gone more than a couple of blocks and he was forced to slow to a jog.

*When did I get to be forty-four years old?* He thought as he gasped for air. As little as four years earlier, he would have been able to run the entire length of Congress Avenue from one end of town to the other. Now, as he sucked in a lungful of air, a few blocks were too much. He cursed the desk that he'd been tied to since being elected President.

The rifle felt good in his hands. It was a gift from Andy Berry, an experimental weapon Berry had gifted to him only a few months earlier. A tubular magazine below the barrel held sixteen cartridge rounds. Instead of using the falling breechblock, Berry chose a lever action to chamber a round from the magazine. The same lever action that chambered a fresh round ejected the spent.

In all likelihood, Berry would give the rifle some name tied to the Trinity Gun Works, but to Will, it looked remarkably like the Model 1860 Henry rifle, a gun he'd been familiar with as a student of history before the transference.

Beyond the last building, Will saw men and horses well back from a makeshift defensive position on Magnolia Avenue. The men, Rangers from the Frontier Battalion, by their dress, were huddled around their wounded. Will came upon them as one of them was wrapping a leg wound with an undyed cotton bandage. The Ranger, lying on the ground swore at his companion and said, "A plague on you, Wendell, you're more a threat to me than those bastards over yonder."

The Ranger named Wendell tied the bandage off. "That'll hold you 'til we can get you to see a doctor, Frank. I'm a mite gentler than those Allied soldiers."

As he stood, wiping his hands on his trousers, he left a streak of red. Stepping back, he admired his handiwork and, in the process, bumped into Will. When the Ranger turned and saw who he bumped into his mouth fell open, "Mister President, what in the blazes are you doing here?"

Only four hundred feet away, riflemen from behind overturned wagons, or crouching in the tall grass were firing at an enemy not visible from where he stood. The first gunshot he'd heard less than ten minutes earlier had crystallized in Will's mind that this attack wasn't merely about destroying the Republic's capital. What kind of men would travel deeper into Texas after General Davis had chosen to save his army by retreating? Any man whose primary goal was the wellbeing of his soldiers would have fallen back into Louisiana, saving his men to defend their homes and states. The list of men who Will's policies had impacted was long. Growing within him was a certainty that whoever led the Southern soldiers was someone who had taken Will's political views on slavery personal. What would a man like that do if he captured Will's family? Would Southern notions of honor prevail? That was a thin reed he'd not trust. No, whoever sought revenge against him needed to be stopped here and now, not in the heart of town where so much more than just his family would be at risk.

Blue eyes flashed with anger as Will stared down the Texas Ranger. "Like you, I'm here to defend my home."

The Ranger sergeant stepped between Will and the battle. "I can't let you do that, sir. You're the goddamned president. What if something happens to you?"

Will gripped the rifle in his hands and stared daggers at the Ranger. In the back of his mind, he knew the man was right. His duty, at least until the next election, was the lead the Republic. But his heart led him to say, "What good is a life lived behind security's wall? Liberty, to be of any value, can't be kept hidden. If you try to protect me for the sake of my security, you deprive me of my liberty."

The Ranger took a step back, a look of uncertainty on his face, as Will continued, "This war, thrust upon us by men who draw their wealth and the very notion of who they are from their ability to enslave others, for me has always been about freedom and liberty. We fight so that no child will ever again be born a slave in Texas. Who will join me?"

Will took a step forward, and the Sergeant moved aside and said, "If you've gotta stay, then the least I'll do is fight by your side, Mr. President."

Without looking behind to see how many of the Texas Rangers followed, Will sprinted the remainder of the way, arriving at the makeshift barricade in time to see a wall of men in gray charging the last hundred paces. The smooth lever action chambered the first round as he raised the rifle to his shoulder. There were plenty of targets at which to shoot. He drew down on someone carrying the blue and white flag with a palmetto tree in the center and fired. The flag dipped as the man dropped it as he pitched backward.

Will levered the action and fired again as a fierce grin crossed his features. He still had thirteen more rounds in the magazine.

The rattle of musketry surrounded Jason Lamont as he guided his mount between two regiments of advancing soldiers. The regiments were ghosts of their former glory. A year before they'd marched to war with nearly a thousand men per regiment. Now, only one of the five infantry regiments contained close to four hundred men. The others barely mustered three hundred. But they were all veterans. Even so, their attack seemed to be stalling as soldiers in ones and twos stopped and fired their rifled muskets at the enemy.

Gripping his mount with his legs, he nudged his way forward. A makeshift barricade covered less than a hundred yards. The rest of the enemy fired from whatever cover they could find, be it a fallen log or a drainage ditch alongside the road. Moreover, there weren't that many men. *By God, I've got the advantage, but we're stalled out.*

"Up, men, up!" he screamed until his voice was hoarse as he rode his mount between the two regiments. "Fix bayonets!"

Lamont dug his heels into his mount's flanks, and the beast reared up on his hind legs. He held on with one hand gripping the saddle horn and the other gripping his sword and reins together. With less force, he urged his horse forward, ahead of his command. "At the bastards. At them!"

He cantered forward, pointing his sword toward the enemy. It was working, he thought, as his men charged forward with the tips of their bayonets leading.

Lamont knew this attack was the last bit of devotion his men retained. They were tired, hungry, and too far away from home, fighting not for their homes nor for their Southern Alliance, but to destroy the government center of the little Republic that had started this war when their President had signed slavery's death warrant. Their hopes, their aspirations, even their very future, were at death's door. Destroying Austin and William Barret Travis was a final act of defiance.

As though thinking of him would make the hated President of Texas appear, Lamont caught a glimpse of a face he'd never forget, standing at the barricade. Every other thought fell away as Lamont focused on his old enemy. He pushed his mount to a gallop and ignored the zip of bullets that missed him by mere inches. Had he looked behind him, he would have seen nearly his entire brigade break into a reckless charge. But his focus was dead ahead.

Until he found himself somersaulting over his mount's head as the horse screamed in pain and stumbled. With no time to think about it, Lamont tucked his head into his chest as he slammed into the ground and rolled to a stop. His sword spun out of his hand as his breath was forced from his lungs at the point of impact. A quick look behind showed his mount was down, its legs still feebly kicking.

Climbing to his feet as he sucked in air, Lamont pulled his revolver from its holster and searched the enemy barricade for Travis. He was so close, scarcely thirty paces away. Unaware his men were only steps behind him, Lamont screamed in primal rage and charged toward Travis, his pistol at the ready.

CRACK! Will felt something both soothing and exhilarating each time the repeating rifle punched his shoulder. As he sent leaden death at the soldiers racing across the battlefield, he had never felt more alive. Somewhere inside, he knew he should be worried about being shot. The only time, he'd felt anywhere close to how he felt at that moment was when he and David Crockett had been firing into a milling mass of Mexican infantry following the Battle of the Rio Grande. Nothing in his time before the transference compared.

The Southern soldiers were closing fast, and Will wasn't blind to the bayonet-tipped rifled muskets the enemy carried. In close quarters, the advantage in firepower his men held over the enemy fell off fast. He looked around. On either side were Rangers from the Frontier Battalion interspersed with the Army Rangers in their mottled butternut uniforms. Surrounding him was a *lot* of firepower.

In front of the barricade, men were falling by the scores, but they were led by their officers, pulling them forward across the last few yards. One officer, on horseback, waved a sword toward the barricade and Will felt as though the man was pointing straight at him.

As he levered another round into the chamber, Will aimed at the man and was about to pull the trigger when the man's horse was struck by gunfire and tumbled to the ground, throwing him overhead.

As the enemy officer sailed through the air, Will realized he'd seen him somewhere before. As he wracked his mind trying to decide who the officer was, the attacking enemy soldiers swept up to him and propelled him along the last few yards to the barricade.

Will felt himself propelled away from the overturned wagon. He twisted away from grasping arms and found himself facing the Ranger sergeant from earlier. "Sir, the line's not going to hold, we've got to get you back."

Will bushed past him and fired at a gray jacketed soldier tangled between two wagons' interlocked tongues. "Go if you want, but I'm staying."

The Ranger stepped up next to him and shot someone crawling over the barricade before he crumpled to the ground, hit in the stomach. Will fired again as the body on top of the barricade was pushed over, where it fell in a heap at the wagon's base. As the officer, who had taken the tumble from his horse, scampered across the overturned wagon, Will recognized him.

Will swore and aimed. He hadn't given a single thought to Jason Lamont in nearly a decade and yet the way the South Carolinian gave him a murderous stare told him the rebel officer hadn't forgotten.

*CLICK.*

The rifle was empty. Will had failed to count the rounds as he fired and at the moment he needed the gun most, it was empty.

A pistol was in Lamont's hand, and he raised and pointed it at Will.

The rifle might have been empty, but Will stepped forward, trying to close the distance with Lamont as he grabbed his gun by the still-warm barrel and swung it back like it was a baseball bat.

Lamont fired. *CRACK.*

Will felt the heat as the bullet passed next to his ear. He started swinging forward with the rifle-turned-bat as Lamont fired a second time.

He flinched as he felt a searing pain in his side. But the rifle stock connected with the side of Lamont's head and the man who had given safe haven to his son's kidnappers so many years earlier fell like he'd been hit by a ton of bricks.

Will dropped the gun, the stock connected to the rest of the firearm by nothing more than a screw. He reached to his side, and his hand came away sticky and red.

He fell to his knees beside Lamont. One glance at the Southern officer told Will what he needed to know. Lamont's head was at an impossible angle to his body, and his eyes blankly stared back at Will.

From the direction of town came a piercing battle cry. As Will knelt beside a man, who for a decade had wanted him dead, the Alamo cadets attacked and struck the barricade, throwing back the Southern soldiers, who, without their leader, retreated, exhausted, and demoralized.

"Sir, are you alright?"

Flinching from pain as he raised his head, Will saw the young Cherokee-born Ranger colonel standing over him. "You're Running Creek, right?" he gasped as he accepted a hand and was helped to his feet.

When the colonel saw Will stagger and saw blood spreading across his white shirt, he yelled, "Get a doctor, the president's been hit."

Someone had found a box that hadn't been turned to kindling in the battle, and Will found himself forced to sit down as a medical orderly knelt beside him and lifted the shirt to see. A moment later the man whistled, "Another inch and we'd be hoping for a miracle, sir. The bullet gouged you pretty good and may have bruised or broke a rib or two. Let me get a bandage on you, and we'll get back into town where a doctor can look you over."

Behind the makeshift barricade on the edge of town, hundreds of men were down. To Will, it seemed as though as many wore the butternut brown of the Texian army as wore Southern gray. The bravery of the defenders had saved Austin, but at a terrible price. The South was done for, Will thought, Longstreet's army was paroled, and it was merely a matter of time for the federals to take control of the rest of the rebellious states. Lamont's quest had been bloody and pointless.

With a steadying arm from the orderly, Will climbed to his feet. In the distance, hundreds of civilians congregated just beyond the last house on the north side of town. Most were dressed in their Sunday best, and all looked somberly on as the defenders started separating the wounded from the dead. Letting the orderly lead, Will stepped around the dead Ranger who had tried to get him away to safety. Then they were beyond the carnage.

A single shout rose above the murmuring, "Will!"

A woman in a green dress was running down Congress Avenue toward him. Not even when he'd seen her the first time so many years earlier had she looked so beautiful. She stopped when she was but a few feet away, her eyes fixed on the bandage around his chest. "Lord please, are you alright?"

Will nodded, "Yes. Everything is going to be alright." He closed the last few feet and swept Becky into an embrace, kissing her.

# Chapter 29

With a faint click, the door closed as the blue-uniformed soldier stepped outside, leaving the men in the room to their meeting. It was, to Horace Greeley's assessment, an august assortment of men. On one side of an ornate desk sat Secretary of State Fletcher Webster. Flanking him were Generals Robert E. Lee and Don Carlos Buell. Next to Lee was a third general, the young Texan who had captured New Orleans in a joint operation between the Republic and the United States, William Sherman. On the other side of the desk sat James Longstreet and Jefferson Davis, formerly of the now defunct Southern Alliance.

"Mr. Secretary, we're grateful for your forbearance in agreeing to meet with us,"

Sitting in the corner of the room with his notepad open, Horace Greeley leaned forward. He didn't want to miss a word from Longstreet, who, three months after his surrender in Georgia, still wore the gray dress uniform of the Southern Alliance's now non-existent army.

Webster chewed on an unlit cigar as he nodded back at the former general. "The sooner we can put your states back on the path to readmittance, the sooner things will improve for the citizens hereabouts. I agreed to this meeting to hear your grievances, General."

Greeley thought the young Secretary was showing too much forbearance acknowledging Longstreet's former rank. The ex-Southern commander should have been sitting in a holding cell next to the Southern Alliance's former president, Howell Cobb, as far as Greeley was concerned.

Longstreet gestured to his companion, and Davis offered a wan smile, as though he were in pain. Forgoing the uniform he'd worn over the past year, the one-time Senator from Mississippi looked as though he used the same tailor as Secretary Webster. His somber black frockcoat was in stark contrast to the gold braiding on Longstreet's uniform.

Davis said, "We've come at the request of several prominent men to ask for the release of Howell Cobb. He's been your prisoner for more than two months in a damp prison cell."

Greeley was incensed the former rebels dared to ask for the man who had presided over the failed rebellion to be released. He leapt to his feet, "Mr. Davis, you forget yourself. Like Cobb, you should be imprisoned for your treason instead of taking up Secretary Webster's time."

Instead of being cowed by the Newspaper editor's outburst, Davis returned his heated glare. General Lee pointed to the door and snapped, "Mr. Greeley, please be mindful your presence is a courtesy. If you wish to remain and record this meeting, you'll remember that. Down the hall are several other reporters who would happily give their eye teeth to trade places with you."

General Buell leaned against the desk, "I don't know, General, thousands of good Yankee boys were buried in poor Southern soil putting down this insurrection. Howell Cobb is exactly where he needs to be, to remind the rest of this lot that we've been more than fair. The army will stay here as long as it takes for you to understand you've been whipped."

Webster tapped his finger on the desk, impatiently, "Enough of this. When you gentlemen surrendered your armies, we accepted your paroles. We're not going to put anyone else into prison unless they disturb the peace or persist in rebellion." Greeley saw the look Webster sent his way and doubted his relationship with President Seward would help him if he made a second outburst. Lee was right; several other newspapermen would happily take his place.

The Secretary continued, "While President Seward continues to consult with the attorney general about Mr. Cobb's legal status, we are prepared to provide each of the seven states which remained in rebellion as of the first of July of this year a pathway to readmittance into the federal union."

The two Southerners traded looks of apprehension as they waited for Webster to continue. Since the end of the conflict, the US Congress had adopted several constitutional amendments that were making their way through the ratification process.

"The thirteenth amendment was ratified by fifteen of the twenty-one loyal states. Missouri's legislature has recently ratified it, too. Ironic, if you ask me, that a former state in rebellion provided the final ratification that makes the amendment the law of the land," Webster said.

Greeley gripped his pencil, frustrated. The Thirteenth Amendment was being called the Bitter-Pill amendment in Whig newspapers. It stipulated slavery would remain legal in all slave states not in rebellion as of July 1, 1853. Of the seceding Southern states, only Missouri repudiated their secession. Virginia, Kentucky, North Carolina, Maryland, and Delaware had remained loyal. The amendment also stipulated states in rebellion against the federal government would be subject to whatever requirements for readmission the government chose to impose.

"Before your states will be allowed back into the Union, your legislatures will be required to ratify the Thirteenth Amendment."

Davis' face twisted into a frown, "That's as good as giving every Negro his manumission papers, given President Seward's emancipation order."

Webster shrugged, "Perhaps. But just in case there's any question. The Fourteenth Amendment will clarify that. It will require that anyone in your eight states who aided or abetted the rebellion forfeit all chattel property. Said property shall be manumitted."

Davis sagged against his chair, "So, it's true, then. I had hoped the rumor was false. This will ruin us."

General Lee shook his head, "Only for a season, sir. I am convinced that slavery as an institution is a moral and political evil. By forswearing this evil now, your states will lay the foundation for the remainder to surrender it peaceably. By Providence's blessing, this sectional war was short, and despite the thousands of deaths from disease and battle, very few of your young men died in this folly. The deep South shall rebuild quickly if you but accede to Secretary Webster's requirements."

Davis muttered, "All we wanted was to be left alone."

The lone man wearing the butternut-brown of the Army of the Republic of Texas, William Sherman's laughter was tinged with bitterness, "You folks picked a peculiar way to demonstrate your desire to be left alone when you aided our rebels and then invaded us with a view of annexation. I'll not deny the damage done in places like South Carolina and Georgia, but the worst battles of this sad war were fought across East Texas. A country with scarcely a half million souls lost more than ten thousand men resisting your desire to be left alone."

Webster stood and gestured toward the doorway, "Go, tell your friends that readmission will only come by ratifying the thirteenth and fourteenth amendments. Rest assured, if the current state legislatures won't do it, they'll be replaced by ones that will."

Late December 1853

"What are you going to do with your bounty, Wild Bill?"

Jimmy Hickok turned, a smile on his face. He liked his new nickname. The circumstances under which he'd acquired it still gave him nightmares, but all the same, Wild Bill was, he thought, a hell of a lot better than Duck Bill. He said, "How many acres is it?"

His squad's sergeant said, "Six hundred forty acres. Here I was hoping Texas would give us some money for helping them, but now that we've been mustered out, I think I've a mind to redeem the bounty. I hear some folks this side of Jefferson have discovered gold, too. I understand the Texas land bank will redeem the bounty anywhere west of the Brazos.

Looking at the printed bounty from the government of Texas in his hand, it was hard to think it represented a whole square mile of land. It was harder still to imagine him doing anything with it. He had no interest in farming or ranching. The last couple of years had been the most exciting in his young life, and he wasn't quite ready to trade that in for a pickaxe or a plow.

"I'll figure it out later, Sarge." With that, Jimmy grabbed his hat and strolled out of the New Orleans Barracks. He liked walking on the sidewalks of the old French Quarter. Decorations for Christmas were in most windows. Signs of the June battle were gone, although over in the American quarter, homes destroyed in the battle's aftermath were still being rebuilt. The stores he passed by were full of goods. Once the city had fallen, the blockade of navy ships had been lifted.

He stopped at a newspaper stand, along the plank, held up by two barrels were several newspapers. The local, the *New Orleans Picayune* sat prominently on display. Next to it was the Galveston Daily News. It was only a few days old. On the banner of the foreign newspaper was written, "John Brown Guilty!"

Eying the stand's proprietor, who was busy with another customer, Jimmy scanned the article. He hadn't made it more than a couple of paragraphs into it, when a voice behind the stand said, "Either buy it or move along."

The idea of laying down a couple of pennies for a newspaper was more than the youth was willing to do, so he continued walking. He was troubled about the news out of Texas. John Brown had been larger than life to an impressionable teenager. Sure, he wasn't perfect, but Jimmy wasn't quite willing to admit that the people they'd killed didn't deserve to die.

He turned a corner and saw a dozen flags, all of them variations of the United States' flag. Below the flags, several men wearing dragoon uniforms stood in the street. One voice carried over the din of the road, "Get your citizenship back, men. The Second Dragoons are recruiting, and if you've got experience, we've got a place for you!"

Jimmy stopped and watched the recruiter deftly talk a man who was wearing the tattered remains of a rebel jacket into signing his name to a sheet pinned to the top of a barrel. The recruiter spied the youth, and before Jimmy could turn, the man was in his face, "First New York, lad?"

Jimmy nodded, "Yeah. Just mustered out."

The recruiter said, "We could use a strapping lad like yourself. Were you part of the attack on New Orleans?"

Jimmy nodded, "Uh, huh. Why're you all recruiting. The war's over."

"This one is. Congress has just opened up the Western Territory. The Second Dragoons have been ordered to pay a visit to the Comanche. Let them know these raids have got to stop. Can't have settlers getting a haircut from an Indian barber."

Jimmy stared at the recruiter with a confused expression. The recruiter pulled his own hair up into a bunch and then used his other hand to mimic getting scalped.

The notion of seeing the Great Plains sounded fun. Fighting Comanche sounded exciting, too. "Where do I sign up?"

June 1854

Lt. Colonel Jesse Running Creek opened the heavy, wooden door to the Alamo's chapel and slipped inside. As additional buildings had been added to the Alamo complex, the chapel once again reverted to its sacred purpose. Gas lamps cast a soft glow on the unpainted ceiling. Pews flanked both sides of the central aisle through the nave and an altar sat in the middle of the transept. The one concession to the chapel's recent history was the heavy artillery battery placed over the Apse on a reinforced platform.

The chapel was empty, and Jesse slid into a pew and leaned his head back. He'd needed to get away from the small office reserved for his use, as commander of the army's Ranger battalion. He amended the thought, soon-to-be-former commander. With a sigh heard only by the spirits, he pulled the crumpled letter from his trouser pocket and looked at his father's precise script.

Simon Running Creek, a wealthy Cherokee merchant, had supported the men like James Collinsworth in the opening days of the rebellion. He'd owned several slaves and had bitterly opposed the Free Birth law when it was enacted a few years before and told Jesse it was a dagger posed at the heart of his business. Jesse had written his father several times over the course of the war's first year, but after no response, his letters had grown infrequent, and since the last Battle of Beaumont, he'd not written his father at all.

He set the letter down on the pew next to him. He wasn't ready to see what the old man had to say, not yet. He closed his eyes, amazed how much time had passed since defeating Lamont's lost brigade, as the rebel unit had come to be known. Almost a year gone since then. Although a couple of regiments were still strategically placed across East Texas, keeping an eye on the people who had rebelled, the army was once again reduced to its peacetime size. During the height of the war, the army's Ranger battalion had briefly reached twelve companies and nine hundred men. By the end of the Battle of Austin, less than two-hundred-fifty men remained. Even now, the five companies he was authorized to command were understrength; the battalion mustered barely three hundred.

Soon, though, the duty would fall to another. He had put off the moment for as long as possible. He broke the glue seal on the envelope and unfolded the monogrammed paper, with an embossed R and C in the corner. A smile slipped onto Jesse's face as he saw the letters' indention. He could practically hear his father saying, "What good's a little wealth if others don't know you've got it?"

*My dearest son,*

*I received all of your letters. They have been read and reread until the paper cracked with age. I don't know if I can apologize for favoring our family's interests above that of your chosen calling, but you should know my desire was always to hand you a grand inheritance. I used the tools available to me, and for that, I can't apologize, either. I bought the slaves because I needed labor to load and drive our freight wagons. But for my silence and my anger to you I will apologize, for despite my flaws, I raised you to follow your conscience and how can I blame you when your conscience dictated that you honor the oath you took to the republic that took us in when the United States branded us as little more than our own slaves. Know, my son, that I love you and miss you. I thank God you have come through the crucible of the war alive when so many have not.*

*When the war was lost, I feared I would lose your inheritance, having backed the losing side. Those of us in Uweya Township watched in fear as those who had served with the rebels had their property taken from them. But I should have known that Sam Houston would protect those of us who merely voiced support for the rebellion. He vouched for me and several others when the army came through.*

*In the end, it was for naught. All the slaves except Jackson have run off, and the government has said that I can put in a request for compensation, although I expect I'll be called to account for my life on this earth long before the government makes good on the claim.*

*I've read about your new assignment in the newspaper. Sam has said being Texas' official military observer is a singular honor. He even had to show me on a map where Russia and the Ottoman Empire are located. But the idea that you will be observing a war in some place on the other side of the world worries me, and I'll be asking the folks at church to pray for your safety each week.*

*If you are able, come and see me before you leave.*

*Your loving Father,*

*Simon Running Creek*

Jesse wiped a tear from his eye. It had taken more than two years, but he'd finally received the letter he'd longed to receive. Folding the letter, he tucked it in his waistcoat and stood. He had packing to do before leaving.

28 July 1854

"Are you sure this is going to work?" Charlie said as he studied the contraption in the middle of the large room's floor.

Andy Berry nodded toward a man kneeling beside the contraption with pipes and tubing running one way or another, as far as Charlie could tell. "Ask Dick. He's the one who proposed it and built it."

Richard Gatling adjusted a bolt with a wrench before he gave Berry a baleful stare, "Oh, ye of little faith. Just because we've not yet found the ideal solution for harvesting cotton, doesn't mean we're devoid of talent."

He wiped the grease from his hands onto a dirty towel and stood up, "I'd like to tell you the idea for this little beauty is all my own, but back when I ran the patent office, I received a publication from the English about a fellow who built something similar. Basically, it's a gas vacuum engine. According to the math, it should produce the same horsepower as a steam engine four or five times heavier."

Charlie's eyebrows shot up. Since the end of the war, the nascent balloon corps had experimented with putting a small steam engine into a balloon with a rigid frame. But the weight to power ratio simply didn't work, not well enough to risk the lives of his pilots.

"Step back, I'm going to start it." With that, Gatling attached a lanyard to a friction primer. "With the artillery switching to breechloading guns, there are a lot of these laying around. The spark from the primer will ignite the engine – I hope."

With his back against the wall, watching the inventor, Charlie wondered if this was what the ancients felt like when confronted with the mysterious unknown. His lips twitched as he thought of this as industrial magic. He supposed that made Gatling a modern-day Merlin.

Gatling offered a smile to the other men as he pulled the lanyard. There was a snap and a bang. A long thin copper rod rose into the air before a clanking noise caused Charlie to cover his ears. Black, billowy smoke seeped from a round cylinder. Charlie beat a hasty retreat from the room as Gatling opened the windows before joining the other men outside, where they watched tendrils of smoke eddy through the openings.

Berry slapped Gatling on the back, "Works better than the last model, Dick." He turned to Charlie, "This ain't exactly easy, Major. We'll study what went wrong and try again in a couple of months. Give us time, and your boys will be flying over future battlefields like birds."

Charlie didn't share the inventors' optimism, nor was he sure he wanted to ride in a basket with a smelly, smoky contraption. But now the demonstration was over, he headed home. Since the war's end, he had moved with his wife and son into his parents' house. A couple of months remained before the election and even then, a couple of more months until the new president would be sworn in. His parents would return then. He stopped on a street corner and looked at the framing going up on a new house. It was hardly the only building going up in town, but unlike the others, this one would be his when it was finished.

According to the carpenters working on it, the house would be finished by the end of the summer, long before President Travis would become ex-President Travis. Until then, he was happy to live comfortably in his parent's house.

The last hundred paces brought him to the house with a wide covered patio, he'd lived in for a couple of years before joining the army. A red brick path led from the dirt street to the steps leading to the patio. His feet had scarcely touched the brick when he heard a shriek. He looked up and saw his nearly three-year-old son scampering down the stairs, racing toward him.

Charlie swooped down and snatched the toddler into the air as the boy squealed with delight. As he hugged the child, he saw his wife standing on the patio, beaming. Charlie flashed a grin at her as he climbed the stairs.

Tanya Travis said, "I've seen that look before, Major Travis. Every time you give me that look, I get pregnant." To underscore her words, her hands rested atop a distended belly.

Charlie's laughter could have been heard by the next-door neighbors, had there been any. "Mrs. Travis, you're more beautiful every day." He leaned over her pregnancy and kissed his wife.

11 December 1854

Will glanced to his side, smiling at Becky as they stood to one side under the lofty portico over the Capitol Building's porch. He gripped her hand as she slid it into his own. Had it been six years since he'd stood in the middle of porch to take the oath of office? It didn't seem that long.

Now, Juan Seguin stood where Will had six years previous, with his wife, Maria beside him. His hand lay on an open Bible as the Chief Justice of the Republic's Supreme Court, John Birdsall stood on the other side of the holy book. "Mr. President, repeat after me," he said, **"I, Juan Seguin, President of the Republic of Texas, do solemnly and sincerely swear, that I will faithfully execute the duties of my office, and to the best of my ability, preserve, protect, and defend the Constitution of the Republic of Texas, so help me God."**

Will felt a heavy burden lifting as he listened to his oldest friend repeat the words transitioning the responsibilities and duties onto his shoulders. Of all the eighteen years since the transference, Will felt the last six had been the hardest.

Looking back, a year and a half after the end of the war, he could see that without the aid of the Southern states, the rebellion in Texas would have collapsed within a few months. He found it ironic that the Southern army had retreated into the South's heartland, having failed to advance more than a hundred miles into the Republic, and yet the Republic's capital had come so close to falling because of a rogue general with a personal vendetta.

Will's attention was drawn to the newly minted President Seguin, who stepped up to the edge of the steps. There was a clear view down Congress Avenue to the Colorado River. But today, despite the crisp air, the terraced hillside was crowded with people who had turned out to see the inauguration.

Seguin chanced a look behind and flashed his irrepressible smile at Will and then turned to face the crowd, "I have been informed that Yankee newspaper editors, who obliterate the written word with the scalpel of their pens, having decided we are wasteful, have exiled the letter *i* from our very name. So, without further ado, my fellow Texans, I wish to thank you for your support. While I could never have won the race without the broad support of so many people, before I could even run, I first needed to win over my beloved Maria, for, without her consent, I would be relaxing in retirement on my ranch near San Antonio."

Will admired Seguin's words, although as the Tejano spoke, Will's mind wandered. The memories from before the transference were still rattling around inside his head, but around their edges, they were fuzzy. Events once crystal clear now bled together. Sometimes he woke up trying to remember his parents' features, even though his memories of his family remained the strongest from before. Those memories kept him grounded between two existences, reminding him everything before 1836 was more than just a dream. For the first time in several years, Will let his mind play through the cosmic mystery stranding his mind and soul in the nineteenth century. He'd considered some advanced science, but why had it only switched the essence of who he was with William Barret Travis? Why not just take him back in time? If this was even the same universe he'd come from.

Perhaps God had done this to him. As someone who had found his way back to the Methodist roots of his childhood this side of the transference, the idea that the creator of the universe, or was that universes? Had done this to him was easier to accept than the notion he inhabited Travis' body as the result of a metaphysical accident.

A pounding from behind his eyes reminded him why he tried to not think about life before or what caused the transference. He winced and felt Becky's hand grip his. It was a little thing, just a reminder she was by his side. She was the single most important reason he had stopped trying to reason out the transference. Other reasons were sitting on chairs below the Capitol steps. From his perch, he could see the back of his younger children's heads. Liza seemed to be ignoring her younger brother, who sat beside her. She was thirteen, and he was eleven. For once, Davy seemed to be behaving himself.

Despite everything that happened to him over the past eighteen years, from defeating Santa Anna at the beginning, to forcing a peace treaty on the Comanche bands, to defending Texas against Mexico and overseeing the beginning of the end of legal slavery at the cost of a civil war, his wife and children were more important than everything else.

But for the first time since the transference, he was at a loss. What would he do next? He was only forty-five years old. The idea he was unemployed brought a smile to his face, and when he leaned over and whispered this to his wife, her eyes widened, and she gave him a scandalized look.

Leaning over, she whispered, "You're going to take me and our children back to Trinity Park. Then you can go through the stack of ideas you've received from Sam Williams. If you don't find something to do with him or Trinity College, rest assured, my love, I've got a list of things for you."

Will glanced over at his wife and saw her lips twitching as she tried to repress a smile. Becky was right. On his desk were stacks of projects and proposals from the college and his business partner. With men like Sam Williams, Gail Borden, and Dick Gatling as partners, the world lay at Will's feet. Before long, the oil trapped under Texas' soil would be tapped, available to fuel the expanding industrial revolution Texas was only now joining in earnest. Borden's factories were turning out products like condensed milk and canned foods in high demand throughout the world.

Will smiled at Becky. Yes, there were many things waiting on him when they returned home to Trinity Park. She nudged him and inclined her head to Juan Seguin, who was wrapping up his speech.

"And finally, my fellow countrymen, over my term of office, I will continue my predecessor's policies that bring more and more freedom and opportunity to every Texan. God Bless Texas!"

# Epilogue

Sharon Travers cut off the ignition as she stared at the seven-story building. Over the past few years, she'd lost track of the number of times she sat in her car in this very parking lot, often even in the same spot. She grabbed her purse and made sure she had her ID and book before getting out.

Brooke Army Medical Center stretched out before her, a sprawling campus treating thousands of military personnel, veterans, and their families in San Antonio. In the building, she showed her license and registered before getting onto the elevator. She knew the way by heart; she could have walked it blindfolded.

She slipped into the smallish room, leaving the corridor's antiseptic smell, and made sure the door closed behind her before standing at the foot of the bed. Laying in the same comatose position she had left him in a couple of weeks before on her last visit was her son, Will.

Habit took over as she set her purse in the chair next to the bed and leaned over and kissed Will's forehead. His face was as pallid as ever, the result of nearly four years with little sunlight. She stepped over to the window and pulled the heavy curtain aside and raised the shade, letting sunlight spill into the room.

Taking out her book, Sharon settled into the padded chair. Glancing at Will, she blinked back a tear. *Really,* she thought, *it's been four years, old girl. What would Ellis, let alone Will, think to see me tearing up?*

Even though four years had passed since the accident in Iraq had left her son in a coma, she still made time to make the five-hundred-mile round-trip trip twice a month. Ellis joined her every couple of months, but her husband's schedule wasn't as predictable as her own. At least that's what she told herself. Despite the doctors expressing hope Will would one day awaken, her husband's faith in their opinions had faded with time, and Sharon understood her husband well enough to know that when he came he did so only to support her.

Reclining the chair, Sharon opened her book and found her place. As she read, her hand found Will's and she gripped it without giving it much thought. It was simply part of her routine. The heart monitor beeped regularly in the background, something she'd learned to tune out a long time ago.

Sharon lost track of time as she turned page after page. Closing out the noise from the ticking wall clock, she lost herself in the romance of the Scottish Highlands. Something changed in the room, and Sharon glanced up and looked around.

The clock continued to tick as the second hand made its way around the dial. The heart monitor beeped. Sharon closed the book. Something was different, but she couldn't see anything out of place. She'd have noticed it. She knew this room almost as well as any in her house.

Then she noticed the difference. Will's hand gripped hers. A thousand times, her hand had clasped his and never once had he responded. She came to her feet, still holding his hand and saw his eyelids, although closed, were twitching.

The hand she held flexed and Will's eyes began to flicker. She saw his irises as Will blinked. He was waking up! After four years and what seemed like hundreds of visits, her son was coming to. As quickly as the thought came into her head to go fetch a nurse, she dismissed it. This was her moment.

Will's eyes fluttered open and stayed open. Sharon realized she was holding her breath as for the first time in four years Will stared back at her.

"Sweet Lord above!" she gasped, "Will, can you hear me?"

Will nodded as his eyes closed, his mouth twisting in pain. He croaked, "Where am I?"

Hearing her son's voice brought tears to Sharon's eyes. "You're at Brooke Army Medical Center in San Antonio. Oh, Will, you've been unconscious since you were injured."

He licked his dry lips, "Ma'am, I'm grateful to you for being here, but who are you?"

A tear slid down her cheek. The doctors had told her many times, they had no idea if he had sustained any brain damage. His words had been one of her many fears. What had happened that he didn't remember her?

Her voice trembled and she began to worry something was terribly wrong, "Will Travers, I'm your mother. Your father would have been here, but he had to work."

Will's eyebrows raised in surprise, and he slowly shook his head. "I'm sorry Mrs. Travers. My name is William Barret Travis."

Thank you for reading In Against All Odds

If you enjoyed reading Against All Odds please help support the author by leaving a review on Amazon. For announcements, promotions, special offers, you can sign up for updates from Drew McGunn at:

https://drewmcgunn.wixsite.com/website

# About the Author

A sixth generation Texan, Drew McGunn enjoyed vacations to the Alamo as a kid. Stories rattled around in his head throughout school, but as with most folks, after college the nine-to-five grind intruded for many years.

His passionate interest in history drove him back to his roots and he decided to write about the founding of the Republic of Texas. There are many great books about early Texas, but few explored the what-ifs of the many possible ways things could have gone differently. With that in mind, he wrote his debut novel Forget the Alamo! as a reimagining of the first days of the Republic.

Drew's muse is his supportive wife, who encourages his creative writing.

Made in the USA
Middletown, DE
19 September 2019